SELF-
DEFENSE

JONATHAN KELLERMAN

SELF-DEFENSE

BANTAM BOOKS
NEW YORK   TORONTO   LONDON   SYDNEY   AUCKLAND

A special thanks to Dr. Jerry Dash

This is a work of fiction. Names, characters, places, and incidents are either the product of the author's imagination or are used fictitiously. Any resemblance to actual persons, living or dead, or locales is entirely coincidental.

SELF-DEFENSE
A Bantam Book / February 1995

All rights reserved.
Copyright © 1995 by Jonathan Kellerman
Book design by Mierre
No part of this book may be reproduced or transmitted
in any form or by any means, electronic or mechanical,
including photocopying, recording, or by any information
storage and retrieval system, without permission in
writing from the publisher.
For information address: Bantam Books.

Library of Congress Cataloging-in-Publication Data

Kellerman, Jonathan.
    Self-defense / Jonathan Kellerman.
        p.   cm.
    ISBN 0-553-08920-X
    1. Delaware, Alex (Fictitious character)—Fiction.
2. Psychologists—California—Los Angeles—Fiction. 3. Los
Angeles (Calif.)—Fiction.   I. Title.
PS3561.E3865S45   1995
813'.54—dc20   94-26175
                                                    CIP

Published simultaneously in the United States and Canada

Bantam Books are published by Bantam Books, a division of Bantam
Doubleday Dell Publishing Group, Inc. Its trademark, consisting of
the words "Bantam Books" and the portrayal of a rooster, is
Registered in U.S. Patent and Trademark Office and in other
countries. Marca Registrada. Bantam Books, 1540 Broadway, New
York, New York 10036.

PRINTED IN THE UNITED STATES OF AMERICA

0 9 8 7 6 5 4 3 2 1

*To my daughter Ilana,
a fine and magical mind, a sweet soul,
and, always, music*

SELF-
DEFENSE

1

She smiled, as usual.

From her chair she had a fine view of the ocean. This morning it was a wrinkled teal sheet gilded with sunrise. A triangle of pelicans reconnoitered overhead. I doubted she'd notice any of it.

She moved around a bit, trying to get comfortable.

"Good morning, Lucy."

"Good morning, Dr. Delaware."

Her purse was at her feet, a huge macramé bag with leather straps. She had on a light blue cotton sweater and a pleated pink skirt. Her hair was fawn-colored, sleek, shoulder length with feather bangs. Her slender face was lightly freckled, with great cheekbones and fine features ruled by huge brown eyes. She looked younger than twenty-five.

"So," she said, shrugging and still smiling.

"So."

The smile died. "Today I want to talk about *him*."

"Okay."

She covered her mouth, then removed her fingers. "The things he did."

I nodded.

"No," she said. "I don't mean what we've already been over. I'm talking about things I haven't told you."

"The details."

She squeezed her lips together. One hand was in her lap, and her fingers began to drum. "You have no idea."

"I read the trial transcript, Lucy."

"All of it?"

"All the crime-scene details. Detective Sturgis's testimony."
Private testimony, too.

"Oh . . . then I guess you do know." She glanced at the
ocean. "I thought I'd dealt with it, but all of a sudden I can't get it
out of my head."

"The dreams?"

"No, these are waking thoughts. Images float into my head.
When I'm at my desk, watching TV, whatever."

"Images from the trial?"

"The worst things from the trial—those photo blowups. Or
I'll flash on facial expressions. Carrie Fielding's parents. Anna
Lopez's husband." Looking away. "*His* face. I feel like I'm going
through it all over again."

"It hasn't been that long, Lucy."

"Two months isn't long?"

"Not for what you went through."

"I suppose," she said. "The whole time I sat there in that jury
box, I felt as if I was living in a toxic waste dump. The grosser the
testimony got, the more he enjoyed it. His staring games—those
stupid satanic drawings on his hands. As if he was *daring* us to
see how bad he was. Daring us to punish him."

She gave a sour smile. "We took the dare, all right, didn't
we? I suppose it was an honor to put him away. So why don't I
feel honored?"

"The end result may have been honorable, but getting
there—"

She shook her head, as if I'd missed the point. "He *defecated*
on them! *In* them! After he—the *holes* he made in them!" Tears
filled her eyes.

"Why?" she said.

"I couldn't even begin to explain someone like him, Lucy."

She was silent for a long time. "Everything was a big *game*
for him. In some ways he was just like an overgrown kid, wasn't
he? Turning people into dolls so he could play with them. . . .
Some kids play like that, don't they?"

"Not normal kids."

"Do you think he was abused the way he claimed?"

"There's no evidence he was."

"Yes," she said, "but still. How could someone . . . could
he really have been in some kind of altered state, a multiple personality like that psychiatrist claimed?"

"There's no evidence of that either, Lucy."

"I know, but what do you *think*?"

"My guess is that his crazy behavior at the trial was faked for the insanity plea."

"So you think he was totally rational?"

"I don't know if rational's the right word, but he certainly wasn't psychotic or the prisoner of uncontrollable urges. He *chose* to do what he did. He *liked* hurting people."

She touched a wet cheek. "You don't think he was sick."

"Not in the sense of benefiting from a pill or surgery or even psychotherapy." I handed her a tissue.

"So death's what's called for."

"What's called for is keeping him away from the rest of us."

"Well, we did that, all right. The DA said if anyone's going to get gassed, it's him." She gave an angry laugh.

"Does that trouble you?" I said.

"No . . . maybe. I don't know. I mean, if he ever makes it to the gas chamber I'm not going to be standing around watching him asphyxiate. He deserves it, but . . . I guess it's the calculated aspect that gets to me. Knowing that on such and such a day, at such and such a time . . . but would I do anything different? What would be the alternative? Giving him a chance of getting out and doing those things again?"

"Even correct choices can be agonizing."

"Do you believe in the death penalty?"

I thought for a while, composing my answer. Normally, I avoided injecting my opinions into therapy, but this time evasion would be a mistake. "I'm where you are, Lucy. The idea of someone being calculatedly put to death bothers me, and I'd have trouble pulling the switch. But I can see cases where it might be the best choice."

"So what does that make us, Dr. Delaware? Hypocrites?"

"No," I said. "It makes us human."

"I didn't jump at gassing him, you know. I was the holdout. The others were really on me to finish up."

"Was it rough for you?"

"No, they weren't nasty or anything. Just persistent. Repeating their reasons and staring at me, like I was a stupid kid who'd eventually come around. So I guess I have to wonder if part of it was good old peer pressure."

"As you said, what would have been the alternative?"

"Guess so."

"You're in conflict because you're a moral person," I said. "Maybe that's why the images have started returning."

She looked confused. "What do you mean?"

"Maybe at this point in time you *need* to remember exactly what Shwandt did."

"To convince myself what *I* did was right?"

"Yes."

That seemed to calm her, but she cried some more. The tissue in her hand was wadded tight, and I handed her another one.

"It all boiled down to sex, didn't it?" she said, with sudden anger. "He got off on other people's pain. All that defense testimony about uncontrollable impulses was bull—those poor, poor women, what he made them—God, why am I starting my day *talking* about this?"

She looked at her watch. "Better be going."

The clock on the mantel said fifteen minutes to go.

"We've got time left."

"I know, but would you mind if I left a little early? Stuff's been piling up; my desk is a—" She grimaced and looked away.

"It's what, Lucy?"

"I was going to say a bloody mess." Laughter. "The whole experience has warped me, Dr. Delaware."

I reached over and touched her shoulder. "Give it time."

"I'm sure you're right. . . . Time. I wish there were *thirty-four* hours in the day."

"Are you backlogged because of jury duty?"

"No, I cleared the backlog the first week. But my workload seems heavier. They keep shoving stuff at me, as if they're punishing me."

"Why would they be punishing you?"

"For taking three months off. The firm was legally obligated to grant me leave, but they weren't happy about it. When I showed my boss the notice, he told me to get out of it. I didn't. I thought it was important. I didn't know what trial I'd be assigned to."

"Had you known, would you have tried to get out of it?"

She thought. "I don't know. . . . Anyway, I've got eight new major corporate accounts to clear paper on. Used to be only tax season was like this."

She shrugged and stood. Behind her, the pelicans began a dive in formation.

When we reached the door, she said, "Have you seen Detective Sturgis lately?"

"I saw him a couple of days ago."

"How's he doing?"

"Fine."

"What a nice guy. How does he deal with this kind of stuff constantly?"

"Not every case is like Shwandt."

"Thank God for that." Her skirt was in place but she tugged at it, smoothing the thin fabric over hard, narrow hips.

"Are you sure you want to leave early, Lucy? We've gotten into some pretty disturbing stuff."

"I know, but I'll be fine. Talking about it's made me feel better."

We left the house and walked across the footbridge to the front gate. I turned the bolt and we stepped out to Pacific Coast Highway. This far north of the Malibu Colony, coastal traffic was thin—a few commuters from Ventura and produce trucks rattling down from Oxnard. But the vehicles that did pass were speeding and deafening, and I could barely hear her when she thanked me, again.

I watched her get into her little blue Colt. The car fired up and she gave the wheel a quick turn, peeling out, burning rubber.

I went back inside and charted the session.

Fourth session. Once again, talking about Shwandt's crimes, the trial, the victims, but not the dreams that had brought her to me in the first place.

I'd mentioned them the first time, but she changed the subject abruptly and I backed off. So maybe the dreams had ceased as she got some of the horror out of her system.

I started some coffee, went out to the deck, and watched the pelicans while thinking about her sitting in the jury box for three months.

Ninety days in a toxic dump. All because she didn't eat meat.

"*Pure* vegetarian," Milo had told me, over his glass of scotch. "*Save The Whales* sticker on her car, donates to Greenpeace. Naturally the defense had the hots for her."

"Compassion for all living things," I said.

He grunted. "Defense thought she'd be too knee-jerk to send that piece of shit to the apple-green room."

He gave an ugly laugh, drank his Chivas, and ran his hand over his face as if washing without water. "Bad guess. Not that he's likely to eat cyanide soon, what with all the paper his lawyers are churning out."

He was pretty much drunk, but maintaining. It was 1 A.M. and we were in a half-empty cocktail lounge in a half-vacant high-rise office building downtown, a few blocks from the Hall of Justice where Jobe Rowland Shwandt had held court for one-quarter of a year, leering, giggling, picking his nose, squeezing blackheads, rattling his chains.

The press turned every twitch into news and Shwandt luxuriated in the attention, loving it almost as much as the pain he'd caused. The trial was a rich dessert for him after a ten-month banquet of blood.

The Bogeyman.

The more repulsive the testimony got, the more he smirked. When the death penalty verdict was read, he yanked his crotch and tried to expose himself to the victims' families.

"No fish," said Milo, putting his glass down on the bar. "No eggs or dairy products either. Just fruits and vegetables. What's that called, a *vegan*?"

I nodded.

The bartender was Japanese, as were most of the patrons. The bar food was soy-flavored trail mix, cucumber and rice wrapped in seaweed, and tiny pinkish dried shrimp. Conversation was low and polite, and even though Milo was talking softly, he sounded loud.

"Lots of do-gooders are full of shit, but with her you get the feeling it's real. Real soft-spoken, gentle voice; pretty but she doesn't make a thing out of it. I knew a girl like that in high school. Became a nun."

"Does Lucy seem nunnish?"

"Who'm I to say?"

"You're a pretty good judge of character."

"Think so, huh? Well, I don't know anything about her love life. Don't know much about her, period, other than that she's having bad dreams."

"Is she single?"

"That's what she said at the voir dire."

"What about a boyfriend?"

"She didn't mention any. Why?"

"I'm wondering about her support system."

"She said her mother's dead and she doesn't see her father. In terms of social life, she comes across a little like Miss Lonelyhearts. Defense guys probably loved that, too."

"How come the prosecutors didn't eliminate her?"

"I asked George Birdwell about that. He said they were running out of disqualifications and figured her for a fooler. Inner toughness that would make her do the right thing."

"Do you sense that, too?"

"Yeah, I do. There's a . . . solid core there. You know the old joke about a conservative being a liberal who's been mugged? She impresses me as someone who's been through rough times."

"What does she do for a living?"

"Crunches numbers for one of those big accounting firms in Century City."

"CPA?"

"Bookkeeper."

"Did she mention any problems other than the dreams?"

"Nope. And the only reason the dreams came up is I told her she looked tired and she said she wasn't sleeping well. So I took her out for a piece of pie and she told me about having them. Then she changed the subject fast, so I figured it was something personal and didn't push. Next time she called, she still sounded wiped out so I suggested she see you. She said she'd think about it; then she said okay, she would."

He took a cigar out of his pocket, held it up to the light, put it back.

"Are any of the other jurors having problems?" I said.

"She's the only one I had any contact with."

"How'd she hook up with you in the first place?"

"I was studying the jury the way I always do, and we happened to make eye contact. I'd noticed her before because she always seemed to be working real *hard*. Then, when I went up to testify, I saw her staring at me. Intense. After that, we kept making eye contact. The day the trial ended, the jury was being escorted out back and I was parked there, too. She waved at me. *Really* intense look. I felt she was asking me for something, so I gave her my card. Three weeks later she calls the station."

He pressed one hand down on the bar and inspected his knuckles. "Now I've done my good deed for the year. I don't know how much she can afford—"

"I don't imagine bookkeepers are investing in bullion," I said. "We'll work something out."

One hand pulled at his heavy jowls, knockwurst fingers tugging heavy flesh down toward his bull neck. In the ice-blue light of the lounge, his face was a pockmarked plaster cast and his black hair hung over his forehead, creating a hat-brim shadow.

"So," he said. "Is a day at the beach really a day at the beach?"

"Bitchin', dude. Wanna come by and catch some waves?"

He grunted. "You ever saw me in a bathing suit, you wouldn't offer. How's the house coming along?"

"Slowly. *Very* slowly."

"More problems?"

"Each trade seems to have a sacred obligation to ruin the work of the previous one. This week, the drywallers covered over some electrical conduit and the plumbers damaged the flooring."

"Sorry Binkle didn't work out."

"He was competent enough, just not available. We needed more than a moonlighter."

"He's not that good of a cop, either," he said. "But other guys he did construction work for said it came out fine."

"As far as he got, it was fine. With Robin taking over, it's even better."

"How's she handling that?"

"Now that the workers are taking her seriously, she's actually enjoying it. They've finally learned they can't snow her—she gets up on the scaffold, takes their tools, and shows them how."

He smiled. "So when do you think you'll be finished?"

"Six months, minimum. Meanwhile, we'll just have to suffer along in Malibu."

"Tsk, tsk. How's Mr. Dog?"

"He doesn't like the water but he's developed a taste for sand—literally. He eats it."

"Charming. Maybe you can teach him to shit adobe bricks, cut your masonry costs."

"Always the practical one, Milo."

2

It had been a nomad year.

Thirteen months ago, just before Jobe Shwandt had started climbing through bedroom windows and ripping people to shreds, a psychopath high on vengeance had burned my house down, reducing ten years of memories to charcoal. When Robin and I finally mustered the strength to think positively, we began plans to rebuild and looked for a place to rent.

The one we found was on a beach on Malibu's far west end. Old rural-route Malibu, nudging up against the Ventura County line, light-years from the glitz. The recession made it affordable.

Had I been smarter or more motivated, I might have owned the place. During my hyperactive youth, working full-time at Western Pediatric Hospital and seeing private patients at night, I'd earned enough to invest in Malibu real estate, buying and selling a couple of land-side apartment buildings and turning enough profit to build a stocks-and-bonds portfolio that cushioned me during hard times. But I'd never lived at the beach, thinking it too remote, too cut off from the urban pulse.

Now I welcomed the isolation—just Robin, Spike, and me, and patients willing to make the drive.

I hadn't done long-term therapy for years, limiting my practice to forensic consultations. Most of it boiled down to evaluating and treating children scarred emotionally and physically by accidents and crimes and trying to untangle the horror of child-custody disputes. Once in a while something else came along, like Lucy Lowell.

The house was small: a thousand-square-foot gray wood

saltbox on the sand, fronted on the highway by a high wooden fence and a double garage where Robin, after deciding to sublet her storefront in Venice, had set up her luthier's shop. Between the house and the gate was a sunken garden planted with succulents and an old wooden hot tub that hadn't been serviceable for years. A planked footbridge was suspended over the greenery.

A rear gate opened on ten warped steps that led down to the beach, a rocky spit tucked into a forgotten cove. On the land side were wildflower-blanketed mountains. The sunsets were blindingly beautiful and sometimes sea lions and dolphins came by, playing just a few feet from shore. Fifty yards out were kelp beds, and fishing boats settled there from time to time, competing with the cormorants and the pelicans and the gulls. I'd tried swimming, but only once. The water was icy, pebble-strewn, and seamed by riptides.

A nice quiet place, except for the occasional fighter jet roaring down from Edwards Air Force Base. Lore had it that a famous actress had once lived there with two teenage lovers before making the Big Movie and building a Moorish castle on Broad Beach. It was documented fact that an immortal jazz musician had spent a winter shooting heroin nightly in a rundown cottage on the east end of the beach, playing his trumpet to the rhythm of the tide as he sank into morphiate peace.

No celebrities, now. Almost all the houses were bungalows owned by weekenders too busy to recreate, and even on holiday weekends, when central Malibu jammed up like a freeway, we had the beach to ourselves: tide pools, driftwood, and enough sand to keep Spike licking his chops.

He's a French Bulldog, a strange-looking animal. Twenty-eight pounds of black-brindled muscle packed into a carry-on body, bat ears, wrinkled face with a profile flat enough to write on. More frog than wolf, the courage of a lion.

A Boston terrier on steroids is the best way to describe him, but his temperament is all bulldog—calm, loyal, loving. Stubborn.

He'd wandered into my life, nearly collapsed from heat and thirst, a runaway after his mistress died. A pet was the last thing I was looking for at the time, but he snuffled his way into our hearts.

He'd been trained as a pup to avoid water and hated the

ocean, keeping his distance from the breakers and growing enraged at high tide. Sometimes a stray retriever or setter showed
up and he romped with them, ending up winded and drooling.
But his new appetite for silica more than made up for those indig-
nities, as did a lust for barking at shorebirds in a strangulated
gargling tone that evoked an old man choking.

Mostly he stayed by Robin's side, riding shotgun in her
truck, accompanying her to the jobsite. This morning, they'd left
at six and the house was dead quiet. I slid open a glass door and
let in some heat and ocean noise. The coffee was ready. I took it
out to the deck and thought some more about Lucy.

After getting my number from Milo, she'd taken ten days to
call. Not unusual. Seeing a psychologist is a big step for most
people, even in California. Somewhat timidly, she asked for a
7:30 A.M. appointment that would get her to Century City by 9:00.
She was surprised when I agreed.

She arrived five minutes late and apologizing. Smiling.

A pretty but pained smile, rich with self-defense, that stayed
on her face almost the entire session.

She was bright and articulate and full of facts—the small
points of the attorney's legal wranglings, the judge's mannerisms,
the compositions of the victims' families, Shwandt's vulgarities,
the yammerings of the press. When the time came for her to
leave, she seemed disappointed.

When I opened the gate to let her in for the second session, a
young man was with her. Late twenties, tall, slender, with a high
brow, thinning blond hair, Lucy's pale skin and brown eyes, and
an even more painful version of her smile.

She introduced him as her brother, Peter, and he said, "Nice
to meet you," in a low, sleepy voice. We shook. His hand was
bony and cold, yet soft.

"You're welcome to come in, take a walk on the beach."

"No, thanks, I'll just stay in the car." He opened the passenger door and looked at Lucy. She watched him get in. It was a
warm day but he wore a heavy brown sweater over a white shirt,
old jeans, and sneakers.

At the gate Lucy turned to look back, again. He was slumped
in the front seat, examining something in his lap.

For the next forty-five minutes, her smile wasn't as durable.
This time, she concentrated on Shwandt, intellectualizing about
what could have led him to sink to such depths.

Her questions were rhetorical; she wanted no answers. When she began to look beaten down, she switched the topic to Milo and that cheered her up.

The third session, she came alone and spent most of the time on Milo. She saw him as the Master Sleuth, and the facts of the Bogeyman case didn't argue with that.

Shwandt had been an equal-opportunity butcher, choosing his victims from all over L.A. County. When it became apparent that the crimes were connected, a task force involving detectives from Devonshire Division to the Sheriffs substation in Lynwood had been assembled. But it was Milo's work on the Carrie Fielding murder that closed all the cases.

The Fielding case had brought the city's panic to a boil. A beautiful ten-year-old child from Brentwood, snatched from her bedroom in her sleep, taken somewhere, raped, strangled, mutilated, and degraded, her remains tossed on the median strip that bisected San Vicente Boulevard, discovered by joggers at dawn.

As usual, the killer had left the crime scene impeccable. Except for one possible error: a partial fingerprint on Carrie's bedpost.

The print didn't match the little girl's parents' or those of her nanny, and neither was it a mate for any swirls and ridges catalogued by the FBI. The police team couldn't conceive of the Bogeyman as a virgin and went looking through local files, concentrating on newly arrested felons whose data hadn't yet been entered. No leads emerged.

Then Milo returned to the Fielding house and noticed planter's mix in the dirt beneath Carrie's window. Just a few grains, virtually invisible, but the ground beneath the window was bricked.

Though he doubted the importance of the find, he asked Carrie's parents about it. They said no new planting had been done in their yard since summer, and their gardener confirmed it.

The street, however, had been planted extensively—magnolia saplings put in by a city crew to replace some blighted old carrotwoods—in a rare show of municipal pride stemming from the fact that one of the Fieldings' neighbors was a politician. Identical planter's mix had been used around the new trees.

Milo set up fingerprinting sessions for the landscaping crew. One laborer, a new hire named Rowland Joseph Sand, didn't show up, and Milo went to his apartment in Venice to see why. No sign of the man or his registered vehicle, a five-year-old black Mazda van.

The landlord said Sand was paid up for another two months but had packed some bags and driven off yesterday. Milo got permission to search and found the apartment scrubbed neat as a surgical tray, reeking of pine cleaner. A little more searching revealed a disconnected hot water heater and the seams of a trapdoor barely visible underneath.

An old cellar, said the landlord. No one had used it in years.

Milo removed the heater and climbed down.

Straight down to hell, Alex.

Spatter and shreds and gobbets in formalin. Needles and blades and beakers and flasks.

In one corner of the cellar stood sacks of peat moss, sphagnum moss, planter's mix, human excrement. A shelf of pots planted with things that would never grow.

A background check showed Sand had given the city a false name and ID. Further investigation showed him to be Jobe Rowland Shwandt, alumnus of several prisons and mental hospitals, with convictions for auto theft, exhibitionism, child molestation, and manslaughter. He'd been in prison most of his life but had never served more than three years at a time. The city had given him a chain saw.

He was picked up a week later, just outside of Tempe, Arizona, by a highway patrolman who spotted him trying to change a tire on the black van. In his glove compartment was a mummified human hand—a child's, not Carrie's, and never identified.

The fingerprint on the bedpost turned out to be a false lead, belonging to the Fieldings' maid, who'd been in Mexico during the week of Carrie's murder and hadn't been available for comparison printing.

I sat silently through Lucy's recitation, recalling all those meetings with Milo for late-night drinks, listening to him go over it.

Sometimes *my* head still filled with bad pictures.

Carrie Fielding's fifth-grade photo.

Shwandt's methedrine eyes and drooping mustache and salesman's smile, the oily black braid twisting between his long white fingers.

How much restoration of innocence could Lucy hope for?

Knowing more about her background might educate my guess.

So far, she'd kept that door closed.

I did some paperwork, drove to the market at Trancas to buy groceries, and returned at two to catch Robin's call telling me she'd be home in a couple of hours.

"How're things at the money pit?" I said.

"Deeper. We need a new main for the sewer."

"That's metal. How could fire burn through that?"

"Actually it was clay, Alex. Apparently that's how they used to build them. And it didn't burn. It was demolished by someone's heavy equipment."

"*Someone?*"

"No one's 'fessed up. Could have been a tractor, a Bobcat, one of the hauling trucks, even a pickax."

I exhaled. Inhaled. Reminded myself I'd helped thousands of patients relax. "How much?"

"Don't know yet. We have to get the city out here to take a meeting with our plumbers—I'm sorry, honey, hopefully this is the last of the major damage. How'd your day go?"

"Fine. And yours?"

"Let's just say I'm learning new things every day."

"Thanks for handling all the crap, babe."

She laughed. "A girl needs a hobby."

"How's Spike?"

"Being a very good boy."

"Relatively or absolutely?"

"Absolutely! One of the roofers had a pit bull bitch chained up in his truck, and she and Spike got along just fine."

"That's not good behavior. That's self-preservation."

"Actually she's a sweet dog, Alex. Spike charmed her—she ended up grooming him."

"Another conquest for the Frog Prince," I said. "Want me to fix dinner?"

"How about we go out?"

"Name the place and time."

"Um—how about Beauvilla around eight?"

"You got it."

"Love you, Alex."

"Love you, too."

*   *   *

The beach house had cable hookup, which meant foolishness on sixty channels instead of seven. I found an alleged hard news broadcast on one of the local stations and endured five minutes of happy talk between the anchors. Then the male half of the team said, "And now for an update on that demonstration downtown."

The screen filled with the limestone facade of the main court building, then switched to a ring of chanting marchers waving placards.

Anti–capital punishment protestors bearing preprinted posters. Behind them, another crowd.

Twenty or so young women, dressed in black, waving crudely lettered signs.

The Bogettes.

At the trial, they'd favored ghost-white face makeup and satanic jewelry.

They were chanting too, and the admixture of voices created a cloud of noise.

The camera pulled in close on the preprinted placards:

LOCK THE GAS CHAMBER, GOVERNOR! ALL KILLING IS WRONG!

NO DEATH PENALTY!

THE BIBLE SAYS: THOU SHALL NOT KILL!

Then, one of the hand-scrawled squares: pentagrams and skulls, gothic writing, hard to make out:

FREE JOBE! JOBE IS GOD!

The marchers came up to the court building. Helmeted police officers in riot gear blocked their entry.

Shouts of protest. Jeers.

Another group, across the street. Construction workers, pointing and laughing derisively.

One of the Bogettes screamed at them. Snarls on both sides of the street and stiffened middle fingers. Suddenly, one of the hard hats charged forward, waving his fists. His companions followed and, before the police could intervene, the workers knifed into the crowd with the force and efficiency of a football offense.

A jumble of arms, legs, heads, flying signs.

The police got in the middle of it, swinging batons.

Back to the newsroom.

"That was—uh, live from downtown," said the woman anchor to her deskmate, "where there's apparently been some sort of disturbance in connection with a demonstration on behalf of Jobe Shwandt, the Bogeyman killer, responsible for at least . . . and—uh, we seem to have regained our . . . no, we haven't, folks. As soon as our linkup is restored, we'll go right back to that scene."

Her partner said, "I think we can see that passions are still running pretty high, Trish."

"Yes, they are, Chuck. No surprise, given the fact that it's serial murder we're dealing with, and—uh, controversial issues like the death penalty."

Grave nod. Shuffle of papers. Chuck fidgeted, checked the teleprompter. "Yes . . . and we'll have something a little later on the situation regarding capital punishment from our legal correspondent, Barry Bernstein, and some face-to-face interviews with prisoners on Death Row and their families. In the meantime, here's Biff with the weather."

I turned off the set.

The death penalty opponents were easy enough to understand: an issue of values. But the young women in black had no credo other than a glassy-eyed fascination with Shwandt.

They'd started as strangers, standing in line outside the courtroom door, sitting through the first few days of trial, sullenly, silently.

The gore level rose, and soon there were six. Then twelve.

Some press wit dubbed them the Bogettes and the morning paper ran an interview with one of them, a former teen hooker who'd found salvation through devil worship. Personality-cult magazines and tabloid TV picked them as freaks-of-the-week, and that attracted a dozen more. Soon the group was huddling together before and after each court session, a uniformed cadre in black jeans and T-shirts, ghostly makeup, iron jewelry.

When Shwandt entered the courtroom, they swooned and grinned. When victims' families, cops, or prosecutors stepped up to the stand, they put forth a battery of silent scowls, prompting protest from the DA and warnings from the judge.

Eventually, some of them earned jail time for contempt: exposing breasts to Shwandt; shouting "Bullshit!" at a coroner's sworn statement; flipping off Carrie Fielding's mother as she got off the stand, sobbing uncontrollably.

While locked up, they granted interviews full of sad autobiography—all claimed abuse; most had lived on the streets and worked as child prostitutes.

Low self-esteem, said the talk-show therapists. But that was like trying to explain Hitler in terms of artistic frustration.

Restricted from the courtroom during the last weeks of the trial, they assembled on the steps and howled for justice. The day of the verdict, they promised to liberate Shwandt at all costs and to seek their own "personal justice."

Milo had seen them up close, and I asked him if he thought they might act on the threat.

"I doubt it. They're publicity whores. When the talk-show morons stop calling, they'll crawl back into their holes. But you're the shrink, what do you think?"

"You're probably right."

The person who'd stalked me had warned me first. Other victims had died without warning.

Sometimes I thought about the others and thanked God that Robin and I had been lucky.

Once in a while I thought about the night the house had gone up in flames and found my hands clenching so hard they hurt.

Maybe I wasn't the right therapist for Lucy.

On the other hand, perhaps I was eminently qualified.

3

Robin and Spike came home at 4:15. Robin's green sweatshirt was smudged with dirt. The green played off the auburn in her hair.

She kissed me and and I put my hands under the shirt.

"I'm filthy," she said.

"Love a dirty woman."

She laughed, kissed me harder, then pushed me away and went off to bathe.

Spike had tolerated the display of affection, but now he looked put-upon. A visit to the water bowl perked him up. I fed him his favorite dinner of kibble and meat loaf, then took him for a waddle on the beach and watched him ingest silica. The tide was low, so he stayed mostly on track, pausing from time to time to lift his leg at the pilings of other houses. Neutered, but the spirit remained.

Robin spent some time soaking and reading and I polished a report to a family court judge, a custody case where a happy ending was too much to hope for. I just hoped my recommendations could save three kids from some of the pain.

At 7:30, I checked in with my service; then we left Spike with a Milk-Bone and a rap-music fest on MTV and took my old '79 Seville past Pepperdine University and the Malibu pier to Beauvilla.

It's a French place on the land side, ancient by L.A. restaurant standards, which means post-Reagan. Monterey colonial architecture, a bit of water view past a public parking lot, beautifully cooked Provençal cuisine, genuinely friendly service, and a slouching, smoking pianist who used to play soap-opera sound tracks and manages to turn a Steinway grand into a Hammond organ.

We had a quiet dinner and listened to a weird musical medley: "Begin the Beguine," something from Shostakovich, a slew of Carpenters' songs, the sound track from *Oklahoma*. As we were having coffee, the maître d' came over and said, "Dr. Delaware? You have a call, sir."

I picked up the phone behind the bar.

"Hi, Dr. Delaware, this is Sarah from your service. I don't know if I did the right thing, but you got a call a few minutes ago from a patient named Lucy Lowell. She said it wasn't an emergency, but she sounded pretty upset. Like she was trying not to cry."

"Did she leave a message?"

"No. I told her you were out of the office but I could reach you if it was an emergency. She said it wasn't important; she'd call you tomorrow. I wouldn't have bothered you, but she seemed *really* nervous. When I deal with the psych patients I like to be careful."

"I appreciate it, Sarah. Did she leave a number?"

She read off an 818 exchange that I recognized as Lucy's home number, in Woodland Hills.

Peter's sleepy voice answered my call. "We're unable to come to the phone right now, so leave a message."

As I began to speak, Lucy broke in: "I told them there was no reason to bother you, Dr. Delaware. I'm sorry."

"It's no bother. What can I do for you?"

"Really, it's okay."

"Long as I'm on the phone, you might as well tell me what's up."

"Nothing, it's just the dream—the one I was having when I first started seeing you. It went away right after the first session, and I thought it was gone for good. But tonight it came back—very vivid."

"One dream?" I said. "A recurrent one."

"Yes. The other thing is I must have sleepwalked, too. Because I dozed off on the couch watching TV, the way I usually do, and woke up on the kitchen floor."

"Are you hurt?"

"No, no, I'm fine, I don't want to make a bigger deal out of it than it is—it was just a little weird, finding myself that way."

"Is the dream about Shwandt?"

"No, that's the thing; it's got nothing to do with him. That's why I didn't want to get into it. And then, when it went away, I figured . . ."

I looked over at Robin, alone at the table, powdering her nose. "Would you like to tell me about it?"

"Um, this is going to sound terribly rude, but I'd really rather not get into it over the phone."

"Is someone there with you?"

"No, why?"

"Just wondering if it was an awkward time."

"No. No, I'm alone."

"Peter doesn't live with you?"

"Peter? Oh, the machine." Soft laugh. "No, he's got his own place. He made the tape for me—for safety. So people wouldn't know I was a woman living by myself."

"Because of the trial?"

"No, before. He tries to look out for me—really, Dr. Delaware, I'm okay. I'm sorry they called you. We can talk about it next session."

"Next session isn't for a week. Would you like to come in sooner?"

"Sooner. . . . Okay, thanks."

"How about tomorrow morning?"

"Could I impose on you to meet early again? If it's a problem, just tell me, but work's still piling up and the drive from the Valley—"

"Same time. I'm an early riser."

"Thank you very much, Dr. Delaware. Good night."

I returned to Robin as she was putting away her compact.

"Emergency?"

"No."

"You're free?"

"Nah, but I'm cheap."

"Good," she said, touching my cheek. "I was thinking of a walk on the sand and who-knows-what later."

"I don't know, you're a little clean for my taste."

"We'll roll in mud, first."

*   *   *

When we got back, MTV was broadcasting the Headbangers Ball and Spike had lost interest. We changed into sweats and took him with us down to the beach.

The sand was frosty, the breakers rising, with just enough space for a stroll up to the tide pools and back. Lights from some of the other houses cast gray stripes across the dunes; the rest was black.

"Pretty cinematic," said Robin. "I feel like I'm in one of those dreadful Movies of the Week."

"Me, too. Let's talk earnestly about our relationship."

"I'd rather talk about what I'm going to do to you when we get back."

She leaned in and did.

I laughed.

"What, it's funny?" she said.

"No, it's great."

The next morning, she was late leaving and Lucy met her coming through the gate.

"Your wife's really *gorgeous*," she told me, when we were alone. "And your dog is adorable—what is he, a pug?"

"French Bulldog."

"Like a miniature bulldog?"

"Exactly."

"I've never seen one before."

"They're pretty rare."

"Adorable." She turned toward the water and smiled.

I waited for a few moments to pass, then said, "Do you want to talk about the dream?"

"Guess I'd better."

"It's not an assignment, Lucy."

She chuckled and shook her head.

"What is it?" I said.

"This is a pretty good deal, Dr. Delaware. You cut your fee in half for me, and I still get to call the shots. Did you know there are quack hotlines on TV—dial-a-psychic-pal—that cost more than this?"

"Sure, but I don't claim to tell the future."

"Only the past, right?"

"If I'm lucky."

She turned serious. "Well, maybe the dream is *coming* from

my past, because it has nothing to do with what's going on with me now. And in it I'm a little kid."

"How little?"

"Three or four, I guess."

Her fingers moved nervously.

I waited.

"Okay," she said. "Better start from the beginning: I'm somewhere out in the woods—in a cabin. Your basic log cabin."

More fidgeting.

"Is the cabin somewhere you've been before?"

"Not that I know of."

She shrugged and put her hands in her lap.

"A log cabin," I said.

"Yes. . . . It must be at night, because it's dark inside. Then all of a sudden I'm outside . . . walking. And it's even darker. I can hear people. Shouting—or maybe they're laughing. It's hard to tell."

Closing her eyes, she tucked her legs under her. Her head began to sway; then she was still.

"People shouting or laughing," I said.

She kept her eyes closed. "Yes . . . and lights. Like fireflies —like stars on the ground—but in colors. And then . . ."

She bit her lip. Her eyelids were clenched.

"Men," she said.

Quickening her breath.

She dropped her head, as if discouraged.

"Men you know, Lucy?"

Nod.

"Who?"

No answer.

Several quick, shallow breaths.

Her shoulders bunched.

"Who are they, Lucy?" I said softly.

She winced.

More silence.

Then: "My father . . . and others, and . . ."

"And who?"

Almost inaudibly: "A girl."

"A little girl like you?"

Headshake. "No, a woman. He's carrying her—over his shoulder."

Eyes moving beneath the lids. Experiencing the dream?

"Your father's carrying the woman?"

"No . . . one of the others."

"Do you recognize him?"

"No," she said, tensing, as if challenged. "All I can see is their backs." She began talking rapidly. "She's over one of their shoulders and he's carrying her—like a sack of potatoes—with her hair hanging down."

She opened her eyes suddenly, looking disoriented.

"This is weird. It's almost as if I'm . . . back in it."

"That's okay," I said. "Just relax and experience what you need to."

Her eyes closed again. Her chest heaved.

"What do you see now?"

"Dark," she said. "Hard to see. But . . . the moon. . . . There's a big moon . . . and . . ."

"What, Lucy?"

"They're still carrying her."

"Where?"

"Don't know. . . ." She grimaced. Her forehead was moist.

"I'm following them."

"Do they know that?"

"No. I'm behind them. . . . The trees are so big . . . they keep going and going . . . lots of trees, everywhere—a forest. Huge trees . . . branches hanging down . . . more trees . . . lacy . . . pretty . . ." Deep inhalation. "They're stopping . . . putting her on the ground."

Her lips were white.

"Then what, Lucy?"

"They start talking, looking around. I'm scared they've seen me. But then they turn their backs on me and start moving—I can't see them anymore, too dark . . . lost . . . then the sound —rubbing or grinding. More like grinding. Over and over."

She opened her eyes. Sweat had trickled to her nose. I gave her a tissue.

She managed a weak smile. "That's basically it, the same scene over and over."

"How many times have you had the dream?"

"Quite a few—maybe thirty or forty times. I never counted."

"Every night?"

"Sometimes. Sometimes it's just two or three times a week."

"Over how long a period?"

"Since the middle of the trial—so what's that, four, five

months? But like I said, after I started seeing you, it stopped till last night, so I figured it was just tension."

"Does the girl in the dream look like any of Shwandt's victims?"

"No," she said. "I don't—maybe this is wrong, but I get the feeling it has nothing to do directly with him. I can't tell you why, it's just something I feel."

"Any idea what it does have to do with?"

"No. I'm probably not making much sense."

"You never had the dream before the trial?"

"Never."

"Did anything happen in the middle of the trial to make you especially tense?"

"Well," she said, "actually, it started right after Milo Sturgis testified. About Carrie. What she went through."

She stared at me.

"So maybe I'm wrong. Maybe hearing about Carrie evoked something in me—I identified with her and became a little girl myself. Do you think that's possible?"

I nodded.

Her eyes drifted out toward the ocean. "The thing is, the dream feels *familiar*. Like déjà vu. But also new and strange. And now, the sleepwalking—I guess I'm worried about losing control."

"Have you ever sleepwalked before?"

"Not that I'm aware of."

"Did you wet the bed as a child?"

She blushed. "What does that have to do with it?"

"Sometimes sleepwalking and bedwetting are related biologically. Some people have a genetic tendency for both."

"Oh. . . . Well, yes, I did do that. A little, when I was very young."

She shifted in her chair.

"Do the dreams wake you up?" I said.

"I wake up thinking about them."

"Any particular time of night?"

"Early in the morning, but it's still dark."

"How do you feel physically when you wake up?"

"A little sick—sweating and clammy, my heart's pounding. Sometimes my stomach starts to hurt. Like an ulcer." Poking her finger just below her sternum.

"Have you had an ulcer?"

"Just a small one, for a few weeks—the summer before I started college. The dreams make me feel the same sort of way, but not as bad. Usually the pain goes away if I just lie there and try to relax. If it doesn't, I take an antacid."

"Do you tend to get stomachaches?"

"Once in a while, but nothing serious. I'm healthy as a horse."

Another glance at the water.

"The grinding sound," she said. "Do you have any theories about that?"

"Does it mean anything to you?"

Long pause. "Something . . . sexual. I guess. The rhythm?"

"You think the men may be having having sex with her?"

"Maybe—but what's the difference? It's just a dream. Maybe we should forget the whole thing."

"Recurrent unpleasant dreams usually mean something's on your mind, Lucy. I think you're wise to deal with it."

"What could be on my mind?"

"That's what we're here to find out."

"Yes." She smiled. "Guess so."

"Is there anything else you want to tell me about the dream?"

She thought. "Sometimes it changes focus—right in the middle."

"The picture gets clearer? Or fuzzier?"

"Both. The focus goes back and forth. As if someone inside my brain is adjusting a lens—some kind of homunculus—an *incubus*. Do you know what that is?"

"An evil spirit that visits sleeping women." And rapes them.

"An evil spirit," she repeated. "Now I'm lapsing into mythology. This is starting to feel a little silly."

"Does the girl in the dream resemble anyone you know?"

"Her back's to me. I can't see her face."

"Can you describe her at all?"

She closed her eyes and, once again, her head swayed. "Let's see . . . she's wearing a short white dress—*very* short. It rides up her legs . . . long legs. Trim thighs, like from aerobics . . . and long dark hair. Hanging down in a sheet."

"How old would you say she is?"

"Um . . . she has a young body." Opening her eyes.

"What's weird is that she never moves, even when the man carrying her jostles her. Like someone . . . with no control. That's all I remember."

"Nothing about the men?"

"Nothing." Eyeing her purse.

"But one of them is definitely your father."

Her hands flew together and laced tightly. "Yes."

"You see his face."

"For a second he turns and I see him."

She'd gone pale and her face was sweaty again.

I said, "What's bothering you right now, Lucy?"

"Talking about it . . . when I talk, I start to feel—to feel it. As if I'm dropping back into it."

"Loss of control."

"Yes. The dream's scary. I don't want to be there."

"What's the scary part?"

"That they're going to find me. I'm not supposed to be there."

"Where are you supposed to be?"

"Back inside."

"In the log cabin."

Nod.

"Did someone tell you to stay inside?"

"I don't *know*. I just know I'm not supposed to be *there*."

She rubbed her face, not unlike the way Milo does when he's nervous or distracted. It raised blemishlike patches on her skin.

"So what does it *mean*?" she said.

"I don't know yet. We need to find out more about you."

She brought her legs out from under her. Her fingers remained laced, the knuckles ice-white. "I'm probably making much too big a deal out of this. Why should I whine about a stupid dream? I've got my health, a good job—there are people out there, homeless, getting shot on the street, dying of AIDS."

"Just because others have it worse doesn't mean you have to suffer in silence."

"Others have it a *lot* worse. I've had it good, Dr. Delaware, believe me."

"Why don't you tell me about it."

"About what?"

"Your background, your family."

"My background," she said absently. "You asked me about that the first time I came in, but I avoided it, didn't I? And you didn't push. I thought that was very gentlemanly. Then I thought, Maybe he's just backing off as a strategy; he probably has other ways of getting into my head. Pretty paranoid, huh? But being in therapy was unnerving. I'd never done it before."

I nodded.

She smiled. "Guess I'm waffling, right now. Okay. My background: I was born in New York City twenty-five years ago, on April 14. Lenox Hill Hospital, to be precise. I grew up in New York and Connecticut, went to fine upstanding girls' schools, and graduated from Belding College three years ago—it's a small women's college just outside of Boston. I got my degree in history but couldn't do much with that, so I took a job as a bookkeeper at Belding, keeping the accounts straight for the Faculty Club and the Student Union. Last thing I thought I'd be doing, never had a head for math. But it turned out I liked it. The orderliness. Then I spotted a job card from Bowlby and Sheldon on the campus employment bulletin board and went for an interview. They're a national firm, had no opening except in L.A. On a whim, I applied and got it. And came West, young woman. That's it. Not very illuminating, is it?"

"What about your family?" I said.

"My family is basically Peter, whom you met. He's one year older than me and we're close. His nickname's Puck—someone gave it to him when he was a little boy because he was such an imp."

"Is he your only sib?"

"My only full sib. There's a half brother who lives up in San Francisco, but I have no contact with him. He had a sister who died several years ago." Pause. "All my grandparents and uncles and aunts are deceased. My mother passed away right after I was born."

Young, I thought, to be so surrounded by death. "What about your dad?"

She looked down quickly, as if searching for a lost contact lens. Her legs were flat on the floor, her torso twisting away from me, so that the fabric of her blouse tightened around her narrow waist.

"I was hoping we could avoid this," she said softly. "And not because of the dream."

Wheeling around. The intense stare Milo'd seen in the courtroom.

"If you don't want to talk about him, you don't have to."

"It's not a matter of that. Bringing him into it always changes things."

"Why's that?"

"Because of who he is."

She gazed up at the ceiling and smiled.

"Your line," she said, extending one hand theatrically.

"Who is he?"

She gave a small laugh.

"Morris Bayard Lowell." Enunciating.

Another laugh, totally cheerless.

"Buck Lowell."

I'd heard of M. Bayard Lowell the way I'd heard of Heming-
way and Jackson Pollock and Dylan Thomas.

When I was in high school, some of his early prose and verse
were in the textbooks. I'd never thought much of his paint-
splotched abstract canvases, but I knew they hung in museums.

Published in his teens, exhibited in his twenties, the postwar
enfant terrible turned Grand Old Man of Letters.

But it had been years since I'd heard anything about him.

"Shocked?" said Lucy, looking grim but satisfied.

"I see what you mean about things changing. But the only
relevance he has to me is his role as your father."

She laughed. "His role? Roll in the hay is about it, Dr. Delaware. The grand moment of conception. Old Buck's a love-'em-
and-leave-'em kind of guy. He cut out on Mother when I was a
few weeks old and never returned."

She smoothed her bangs and sat up straighter.

"So how come I'm dreaming about him, right?"

"It's not that unusual. An absent parent can be a strong presence."

"What do you mean?"

"Anger, curiosity. Sometimes fantasies develop."

"Fantasies about *him*? Like going to the Pulitzer ceremony on
his arm? No, I don't think so. He wasn't around enough to be
relevant."

"But when he comes into the picture, things change."

"Who he *is* changes things. It's like being the President's kid.
Or Frank Sinatra's. People stop perceiving you as who you are

and start seeing you in relationship to him. And they get shocked
—just like you did—to find out the Great Man spawned someone
so crashingly ordinary."

"I—"

"No, it's okay," she said, waving a hand. "I *love* being ordinary: my ordinary job, my ordinary car, my ordinary apartment
and bills and tax returns and washing dishes and taking out the
garbage. Ordinary is *heaven* for me, Dr. Delaware, because when I
was growing up *nothing* was routine."

"Your mother died right after you were born?"

"I was a couple of months old."

"Who raised you?"

"Her older sister, my Aunt Kate. She was just a kid herself,
new Barnard grad, living in Greenwich Village. I don't remember
too much about it other than her taking Puck and me to lots of
restaurants. Then *she* got married to Walter Lazar—the author?
He was a reporter back then. Kate divorced him after a year and
went back to school. Anthropology—she studied with Margaret
Mead and started going on expeditions to New Guinea. That
meant boarding school for Puck and me, and that's where we
stayed all through high school."

"Together?"

"No, he was sent to prep academies, and I went to girls'
schools."

"It must have been tough, being separated."

"We were used to being shifted around."

"What about the half siblings you mentioned?"

"Ken and Jo? They lived with *their* mother, in San Francisco.
Like I said, there's no contact at all."

"Where was your father all this time?"

"Being famous."

"Did he support you financially?"

"Oh, sure, the checks kept coming, but for him that was no
big deal, he's rich from his mother's side. The bills were paid
through his bank, and my living expenses were sent to the school
and doled out by the headmistress—very organized for an *artiste*,
wouldn't you say?"

"He never came to visit?"

She shook her head. "Not once. Two or three times a year
he'd call, on the way to some conference or art show."

She pulled something out of her eyelashes.

"I'd get a message to come to the school office and some

secretary would hand me the phone, awestruck. I'd brace myself, say hello, and this thunderous voice would come booming through. 'Hello, girl. Eating freshly blooded moose meat for breakfast? Getting your corpuscles moving?' Witty, huh? Like one of his stupid macho hunting stories. A summary of what he was doing, then good-bye. I don't think I spoke twenty words in all those years.''

She turned to me.

"When I was fourteen, I finally decided I'd had enough and got my roommate to tell him I was out of the dorm. He never called again. All you get with a Great Man is one chance."

She tried to smile, lips working at it, struggling to form the shape. Finally, she managed to force the corners upward.

"It's no big deal, Dr. Delaware. Mother died when I was so young I never really knew what it was like to lose her. And *he* was . . . nothing. Like I said, lots of people have it worse."

"This issue of being ordinary—"

"I really *do* like it. Not a shred of talent, same with Puck. That's probably why *he* has nothing to do with us. Living reminders that he's produced mediocrity. He probably wishes we'd all disappear. Poor Jo obliged."

"How did she die?"

"Climbed a mountain in Nepal and never came down. His wives oblige him, too. Three out of four are dead."

"Your mother must have been very young when she died."

"Twenty-one. She got the flu and went into some sort of toxic shock."

"So she was only twenty when she married him?"

"Just barely. *He* was forty-six. She was a Barnard girl, too, a sophomore. They met because she was in charge of bringing speakers to campus, and she invited him. Three months later she dropped out, he took her to Paris, and they got married. Puck was born there."

"When did they get divorced?"

"They didn't. Right after I was born, he went back to France. It wasn't long after when she died. The doctors called him, but he never came to the phone. Two weeks after the funeral, a postcard arrived at Aunt Kate's, along with a check."

"Who told you this?"

"Puck. He heard it from Aunt Kate—he went out to visit her in New Zealand after he finished college."

"Ken and Jo are older than you and Puck?"

"Yes. Their mother was his second wife, Mother was his third. The first was Thérèse Vainquer—the French poet?"

I shook my head.

"Apparently she was pretty hot in postwar Paris, hanging around with Gertrude Stein and that bunch. She left him for a Spanish bullfighter and was killed in a car crash soon after. Next came Emma, Ken and Jo's mom. She was an artist, not very successful. She died around fifteen or sixteen years ago—breast cancer, I think. He left *her* for my mom, Isabelle Frehling. His fourth wife was Jane something or other, an assistant curator at the Museum of Modern Art in New York. *They* met because the museum had a bunch of his paintings stored in their basement and he wanted them exhibited in order to revive his painting career—it's pretty dead, you know. So is his writing career. Anyway, he dumped *her* after about a year and hasn't married since. But it wouldn't surprise me if he's got another sweet young thing right now. Illusion of immortality."

She crossed her legs and held one knee with both hands.

Tossing out details about a man who supposedly had no role in her life.

She read my mind. "I know, I know, it sounds as if I cared enough to find all this out, but I got it from Puck. A few years ago, he was into this discover-your-roots thing. I didn't have the heart to tell him I couldn't care less."

Folding her arms across her chest.

"So," I said, "at least we know the log cabin wasn't somewhere you've actually been. At least not with your father."

"Call him Buck, please. Mr. Macho, the Great Man, whatever, anything but that."

Touching her stomach.

Remembering the ulcer she'd had before college, I said, "Where did you live the summer after you graduated from high school?"

She hesitated for a second. "I volunteered at a Head Start center in Boston."

"Was it difficult?"

"No. I loved teaching. This was in Roxbury, little ghetto kids who really responded. You could see the effects after one summer."

"Did you ever consider a teaching career?"

"I tossed it around, but after all those years in school—growing *up* in schools—I just wasn't ready for another classroom. I guess I might have eventually done it, but the bookkeeping thing came up and I just rolled with the flow."

I thought of the isolation that had been her childhood. Milo had talked about tough times strengthening her—a mugging of sorts. But maybe it was nothing specific, just an accumulation of loneliness.

"That's it," she said. "Now do you understand my dream?"

"Not in the least."

She looked at me and laughed. "Well, that's straight out."

"Better no answer than a wrong one."

"True, true." Laughing some more, but her hands were tense and restless and she tapped her feet.

"I guess I'm ticked off," she said.

"About what?"

"Him in my dreams. It's an . . . invasion. Why now?"

"Maybe you're ready, now, to deal with your anger toward him."

"Maybe," she said doubtfully.

"That doesn't feel right?"

"I don't know. I really don't think I'm angry at him. He's too *irrelevant* to get angry at."

Anger had stiffened her voice. I said, "The girl in the dream, how old is she?"

"Nineteen or twenty, I guess."

"About your mother's age when she married him."

Her eyes widened. "So you think I'm dreaming about his violation of *Mother*? But Mother was blond and this girl has dark hair."

"Dreams aren't bound by reality."

She thought for a while. "I suppose it could be that. Or something else symbolic—the young chicks he always chased— but I *really* don't think I'd dream about his girlfriends. Sorry."

"For what?"

"I push you for interpretations and then keep shooting them down."

"That's okay," I said. "It's your dream."

"Yes—only I wish it wasn't. Any idea when I'll get rid of it?"

"I don't know, Lucy. The more I know about you, the better answer I can give you."

"Does that mean I have to keep talking about my past?"

"It would help, but don't make yourself uncomfortable."

"Do I need to talk about *him*?"

"Not until you're ready."

"What if I'm never ready?"

"That's up to you."

"But *you* think it would be useful."

"He was in the dream, Lucy."

She started to crack a knuckle and stopped herself.

"This is getting tough," she said. "Maybe I *should* call the psychic buddies."

5

After she was gone, I thought about the dream.

Somnambulism. Bedwetting.

Fragmented sleep patterns were often displayed as multiple symptoms—persistent nightmares, insomnia, even narcolepsy. But the sudden onset of her symptoms implied a reaction to some kind of stress: the trial material or something the trial had evoked.

Her allusion to an incubus was interesting.

Sexual intrusion.

Daddy abducting a maiden. Grinding noises.

A Freudian would have loved it: unresolved erotic feelings toward the abandoning parent coming back to haunt her.

Feelings awakened because the trial had battered her defenses.

She was right about one thing: This father *was* different.

And relevant.

I drove down toward the city, taking the coast highway to Sunset and heading east to the University campus.

At the Research Library, I looked up M. Bayard Lowell in the computer index. Page after page of citations beginning in 1939—the year he'd published his landmark first novel, *The Morning Cry* —and encompassing his other novels, collections of poems, and art exhibitions.

Covering all of it would take a semester. I decided to start with the time period that corresponded to Lucy's dream, roughly twenty-two years ago.

*   *   *

The first reference was a book of poems entitled *Command: Shed the Light*, published on New Year's Day. The rest were reviews. I climbed up to the stacks and began my refresher course in American Lit.

In the poetry shelves, I found the book, a thin gray-jacketed volume published by one of the prestige New York houses. The circulation slip showed it hadn't been checked out in three years. I went to the periodicals section and lugged volume after volume of bound magazines to an empty carrel. When my arms grew sore, I sat down to read.

Command: Shed the Light turned out to be Lowell's first book in ten years, its predecessor an anthology of previously published short stories. The New Year's release date was also Lowell's fiftieth birthday. The book had attracted a lot of attention: six-figure advance, main selection by one of the book clubs, foreign rights sold in twenty-three countries, even a film option by an independent production company in Hollywood, which seemed odd for poetry.

Then came the critics. One major newspaper called the work "self-consciously gloomy and stunningly amateurish and, this writer suspects, a calculated effort on the part of Mr. Lowell to snare the youth market." Another, describing Lowell's career as "glorious, lusty, and historically indelible," gave him credit for taking risks but labeled his verse "only very occasionally pungent, more frequently vapid and sickening, morose and incoherent. Glory has yielded to vainglory."

Lots more in that key, with one exception: A Columbia University doctoral student named Denton Mellors, writing in the *Manhattan Book Review*, rhapsodized "darkly enchanting, rich with lyric texture."

From what I could tell, Lowell hadn't reacted to the debacle publicly. A bottom-of-the-page paragraph in the January twenty-fourth *Publishers Journal* noted that sales of the book were "significantly below expectations." Similar articles appeared in other magazines, ruminating on the death of contemporary poetry and speculating as to where M. Bayard Lowell had gone wrong.

In March, the *Manhattan Book Review* noted that Lowell was rumored to have left the country, destination unknown. In June, a cheeky British glossy reported his presence in a small village in the Cotswolds.

Having confirmed that the sweatered-and-capped
personage meandering among the sheep was indeed the
once-touted American, we tried to approach but were
accosted by two rather formidable mastiffs who showed
no interest in our bangers-and-chips and convinced us
by dint of grease-and-growl to beat a hasty retreat. What
has happened, we wonder, to Mr. Lowell's once insatia-
ble Yankish appetite for attention? Ah, fleeting fame!

Other foreign sightings followed throughout that summer:
Italy, Greece, Morocco, Japan. Then, in September, the *Los Angeles
Times Book Review* announced that "Pulitzer prize-winning author
M. Bayard Lowell" would be relocating to Southern California
and contributing occasional essays to the supplement. In Decem-
ber, the Hot Property column in the *Times* Real Estate section
reported that Lowell had just closed escrow on fifty acres in
Topanga Canyon.

Sources say it is a heavily wooded, rustic campsite
in need of repair. Last utilized as a nudist colony, it is off
the beaten track and seems perfect for Lowell's new Sal-
ingeresque identity. Or maybe the author-cum-artist is
simply traveling West for the weather.

May: Lowell attended a PEN benefit for political prisoners, a
"star-studded gala" at the Malibu home of Curtis App, a film
producer. Two more westside parties in April, one in Beverly
Hills, one in Pacific Palisades. Lowell, newly bearded and wearing a blue denim suit, was spotted talking to the current Playmate
of the Month. When approached by a reporter, he walked away.

In June, he delivered a keynote speech at a literacy fund-
raiser where he announced the creation of an artists' and writers'
retreat on his Topanga land.

"It will be a sanctum," he said, "and it will be called Sanctum. A blank palette upon which the gifted human will be free to
struggle, squiggle, squirt, splotch, deviate, divert, digress, dig in
the dirt, and howsoever indulge the Great Id. Art pushes through
the hymen of banality only when the nerves are allowed to twang
unfettered. Those in the know, know that the true luxuries are
those of synapse and spark."

A September piece in the *L.A. Times* entertainment section
reported that a grant from film producer App was financing con-

struction of new lodgings at Sanctum. The architect: a twenty-four-year-old Japanese-American prodigy named Claude Hiroshima, whose last project had been the refurbishment of all the lavatories in a Madrid hotel.

"At Sanctum," he said, "my goal is to be true to the essential consciousness of the locus, selecting materials that provide a synthesis with the prevailing mental and physical geometry. There are several log structures already on the property, and I want the new buildings to be indistinguishable from them."

Log structures.

Either Lucy had read about the retreat or her brother had told her about it.

December, another *Publishers Journal* squib: Paperback publication of *Command: Shed the Light* was canceled and sales of Lowell's backlist—his previously published books—had bottomed, as had prices for his canvases.

March: *The Village Voice* ran a highly unfavorable retrospective of Lowell's body of work, suggesting that his place in history be reassessed. Three weeks later, a letter from someone named Terrence Trafficant of Rahway, New Jersey, attacked the article, labeling the author a "bloodsucking, motherfucking nematode" and hailing M. Bayard Lowell as "the dark Jesus of twentieth-century American thought—all of you are just too fucking blocked and preternaturally dense to realize it, you asshole-fucking New York Jew revisionist Pharisees."

July: Completion of construction at Sanctum was announced by Lowell in the *L.A. Times Book Review*. The first crop of Sanctum fellows was introduced:

Christopher Graydon-Jones, 27, sculptor in iron and "found objects," Newcastle, England.

Denton Mellors, 28, former doctoral candidate in American Literature at Columbia University and critic for the *Manhattan Book Review*; "Mr. Mellors will complete work on his first novel, *The Bride*."

Joachim Sprentzel, 25, electronic music composer from Munich.

Terrence Gary Trafficant, 41, essayist and former inmate at the New Jersey State Prison at Rahway, where he had been serving a thirteen-year sentence for manslaughter.

Next day's paper cared only about Trafficant, describing how acceptance as a Sanctum Fellow had hastened the ex-con's parole and detailing Trafficant's criminal history: robbery, assault, narcotics use, attempted rape.

Jailed almost continuously since the age of seventeen, Lowell's protégé had earned a reputation as a combative prisoner. With the exception of a prison diary, he'd never produced anything remotely artistic. A photo showed him in his cell, tattooed hands gripping the bars: skinny and fair, with long, limp hair, bad teeth, sunken cheeks, a devilish goatee.

Questioned about the appropriateness of Trafficant's selection, Lowell said, "Terry is excruciatingly authentic on smooth-muscle issues of freedom and will. He's also an anarchist, and that will be an exhilarating influence."

Mid-August: Sanctum's opening was celebrated by an all-night party at the former nudist colony. Catering by Chef Sandor Nunez of Scones Restaurant, music by four rock bands and a contingent from the L.A. Philharmonic, ambience by M. Bayard Lowell "in a long white caftan, drinking and delivering monologues, surrounded by admirers."

Among the sighted guests: a psychology professor turned LSD high priest, an Arab arms dealer, a cosmetics tycoon, actors, directors, agents, producers, and a buzzing swarm of journalists.

Terry Trafficant was spotted holding forth to his own group of fans. His prison diary, *From Hunger to Rage,* had just been bought by Lowell's publisher. His editor called it "an intravenous shot of poison and beauty. One of the most important books to emerge this century."

The New York police lieutenant who'd arrested Trafficant on the manslaughter charge was quoted, too: "This guy is serious bad news. They might as well light a stick of dynamite and wait for it to blow."

The next few citations on Lowell turned out to be cross-referenced interviews with Trafficant. Describing himself as "Scum made good, an urban aborigine exploring a new world," the ex-con quoted from the classics, Marxist theory, and postwar avant-garde literature. When asked about his crimes, he said, "That's all dead and I'm not an undertaker." Crediting Buck Lowell for his freedom, he called his mentor "one of the four greatest men who ever lived, the other three being Jesus Christ, Krishnamurti, and Peter Kurten." When asked who Peter Kurten was, he said, "Look it up, Jack," and ended the interview.

The article went on to identify Kurten as a German mass

murderer, nicknamed the Düsseldorf Monster, who'd sadistically raped and butchered dozens of men, women, and children between 1915 and 1930. Kurten had other quirks, too, enjoying coitus with a variety of farm animals and going to his execution hoping he could hear his own blood bubble at the precise moment of death.

When recontacted and asked how he could term that kind of thing "greatness," Trafficant replied, "It's all a matter of context, friend," and hung up.

A storm of outraged letters ensued. Several religious leaders condemned Lowell in their Sunday sermons. Lowell and Trafficant refused further interviews, and after a week or so the fuss died down. In May, *From Hunger to Rage* was published to uniformly strong reviews, went into a second printing, and made it to Number 10 on *The New York Times* best-seller list. A scheduled book tour for Trafficant was canceled, however, when the author didn't show up for an interview on a national morning talk show.

When questioned about Trafficant's whereabouts, Buck Lowell said, "Terry walked out on us a couple of weeks ago. Right after all the *sturmdrang* idiocy about Kurten. Words mean different things to a man like that. He was wounded deeply."

A sensitive soul? asked the reporter.

"It's all a matter of context," said Lowell.

Over the next two decades, coverage of Lowell diminished steadily, and by the end of the period nothing was left but a few doctoral theses, inflicting upon him that peculiar gleeful viciousness that passes for wit in the academic world. *Command: Shed the Light* went out of print, and no further books or paintings materialized. No mention at all of Terry Trafficant, though *his* book did go into paperback.

Checking out the gray volume, I drove home. When I passed Topanga Canyon, I wondered if the great man was still living there.

6

At Las Flores Canyon, static wiped out the music on my radio. I fooled with the tuner and caught the word *Shwandt* at the tail end of a news broadcast. Then the disk jockey said, "And now back to more music."

I couldn't find a newscast and switched to AM. Both all-news stations were doing the sports scores, and everything else was chatter and music and people trying to sell things.

I gave up and concentrated on the beauty of the highway, open and clean as it ribboned past true-blue water. Even the commercial strip near the Malibu pier didn't look half bad in the afternoon sun. Bikini shops, diving schools, clam stands, real estate companies pretending they still had something to do during the slump.

Once home, I took a beer and Lowell's poetry onto the deck. It soon became clear this wouldn't be reading for fun.

Nasty stuff. Nothing like the luxuriant verse and lust-for-life stories Lowell had put out during the forties and fifties. Nearly all the poems dealt explicitly with violence, and many seemed to glorify it.

The first, entitled "Home-icide," was almost a haiku:

> He walks in the door
> briefcase-appendaged. And
> Finds
> She's shot the kids.
> But the dog's still alive.
> Time to feed it.

Another proclaimed:

> Over the meadows and through the woods to:
> Clarity
> Chastity
> Priapisty
> Buggery
> Butchery

> Prepared perfectly for truncation:
> Hone the bone. Toss the I Ching,
> then toss the rules out the window.

The title poem was an empty black page. Several other pieces seemed no more than random collections of words, and a six-page poem entitled *Shaht-up* consisted of four four-line verses in a language that a footnote explained was "Finnish, stupid."

The final piece was printed in letters so tiny I had to strain to read them:

> Slung and arrowed, she begs for it.
> Shitsmear idiocy—who does she think she is?

Snap.

> To give up!

Snap.

> Just like that—
> LIKE THAT

Easy to see why the book hadn't worked—and why it had enchanted Trafficant.

I pictured him poring over it in his cell, then rushing to Lowell's defense.

His motive would have been more than shared literary taste. With a few supportive words, he'd bought himself early parole.

I reread the final poem.

A woman begging for it, then scorned for giving up.

Classic male rape fantasy?

Lucy's incubus . . .

The abduction imagery in the dream.

Had she come across this dreadful little book, perhaps as part of her brother's "roots" research?

Reading it and identifying with the victim?

Or what if the dream represented something more personal
—being molested herself?

At the voir dire, she'd denied ever having been a crime victim. But if it had happened long ago and she'd repressed it, she
wouldn't have remembered.

The dream had started right after she'd listened to Milo testify about Carrie.

Identifying with a child victim.

Abused in childhood, not by her father—he hadn't been
around to do it—but by a father surrogate? A teacher or some
other trusted adult?

Other men in the dream—melding with her father because
he had hurt her in another way?

I thought of her waking up on the kitchen floor.

The helplessness of the position.

Victimization.

Or maybe none of the above.

I wrestled with it a while longer, got no further, and went
back inside. Remembering the radio broadcast I'd heard in the
car, I flipped TV channels till I found a news show. Something
about Eastern Europe; then Shwandt's face appeared, leering,
over the anchor's left shoulder.

"Police in Santa Ana are investigating the mutilation slaying
of a young woman, still unidentified, whose body was found,
stuffed in a trash bag, by the side of the Santa Ana Freeway early
this morning near the Main Street exit. Sources close to the investigation say the slaying bears striking similarities to the serial
murders for which the Bogeyman, Jobe Shwandt, was recently
sentenced to death, and the possibility of a copycat killer operating out of Orange County is being considered. More on this
breaking story as details emerge."

Too much bad stuff, time to sweat it out of my system. Pretending my knees were eighteen years old, I took a hard jog on
the beach. When I got back, the phone was ringing. My service
with Lucy, again.

"Dr. Delaware? I'm . . . calling from work. I had a . . . bit
of a problem." Her voice dropped so low I could barely hear it.
Noise in the background didn't help.

"What happened, Lucy?"

"The dream. I . . . had it again."

"Since this morning's session?"

"Yes." Her voice shook. "Here. At work, at my desk. . . .

God, this is so—I have to talk softly; I'm at a pay phone in the lobby and people are staring. Can you hear me?"

"I hear you fine."

She caught her breath. "I feel so *stupid*! Falling asleep at my *desk*!"

"When did this happen?"

"Lunch hour. I was brown-bagging, trying to catch up. I guess I nodded off, I don't know, I really don't remember."

"Had you taken any sort of medication?"

"Just Tylenol for a headache."

"No antihistamines or anything else that would make you drowsy?"

"Nothing. I just . . . fell asleep." She whispered: "It must have woken me up—I found myself on the floor, my legs . . . the dream was still in my head, reverberating. Right in the middle of the *office*! *God*!"

"Are you hurt?"

"Not physically. But the humiliation—everyone thinks I'm crazy!"

"Were there a lot of people around when you fell?"

"Not when I fell, but right after. It was lunchtime; a whole crowd was coming back and saw me on the floor! I ran to the ladies' room to straighten up. When I got back, my *boss* was there. He *never* comes into the staff area. The look on his face—like what kind of *nutcase* do I have working for me!"

"If he's worried about anything, Lucy, it's probably that you'll file a worker's comp suit."

"No, no, I'm sure he thinks I'm some kind of bizarro. Falling asleep in the middle of the day—I excused myself to the bathroom again, went down to the lobby, and called you."

"Come over, let's talk."

"I—I guess I'd better. I'm sure not in any shape to go back up there."

I called a neurologist in Santa Monica named Phil Austerlitz and told him I had a possible referral. When I recounted what had happened, he said, "You're thinking narcolepsy?"

"She's got a troubled sleep pattern. Some childhood enuresis."

"But nothing chronic in adulthood."

"It just started five months ago. While she was a juror on the Bogeyman trial."

"Sounds more like stress."

"That's what I think, but I want to cover all bases."

"Sure, I'll see her. Thanks for the referral. Sounds like a fun one. I've been dealing with brain tumors all week. People our age or younger. Must be something in the air."

She rang the gate bell just after five. Her hair was tied back in a ponytail and her face was drawn. When I took her hand it was limp and damp.

I gave her a glass of water and sat her down. She took a sip and put her face in her hands.

"What's happening to me, Dr. Delaware?"

I touched her hand. "We'll find out, Lucy."

She tightened her mouth. "It was different this time. This time I *saw* more."

Taking a deep breath. And another. Sliding her hand out from under mine. I sat back.

It took a few more minutes for her to compose herself. "Remember the grating noise I told you about? What I thought might be sex? It had nothing to *do* with sex."

She leaned forward. "I saw it. They were digging a grave— burying her. The grating was their shovels hitting the rocks. This time, I was closer. Everything was clearer. It's never felt this *real* before. It was . . ."

She put a hand over her eyes and shook her head.

"I was close enough to touch them—right behind them. It felt so *real*."

"The same men."

"Yes. Three of them."

"Including your—including Lowell."

She bared her eyes and licked her lips and stared at the floor. "He was one of the diggers. Working hard—huffing and puffing. They all were. And cursing. I could hear their breathing—harsh, like runners. Then they put her in, and . . ."

Her shoulders started to shake.

"I started to feel myself *transforming*—my soul leaving my body. I actually saw it, fluttering like this thin white feather. Then it entered *her* body."

She stood suddenly.

"I need to walk around."

Pacing the room, she covered the width of the glass doors, then retraced her steps. Repeated it twice more before returning to her seat.

She remained standing, both hands on the chair back. "I could taste the dirt, Dr. Delaware. It felt as if I was in that grave. . . . I tried to shake the dirt off of me but I couldn't move. It kept coming *down* on me—*stuffing* me. I thought: *This* is what death is like, this is *terrible;* what did I do to *deserve* this, why are they *doing* this to me?"

Her eyes closed and she swayed so low I jumped up and caught her shoulder. Her body tightened but she didn't seem to notice me.

The sound of the tide rose up from the beach, like a swell of applause. Suddenly, her breathing quickened.

"Lucy," I said.

As if her name were a posthypnotic suggestion, she opened her eyes and blinked hard.

"What happened then, Lucy?"

"I woke up. Found myself on the floor . . . again. My legs . . ." Wincing.

"What about your legs?"

"They were . . ." Spots of color appeared on her cheeks. "Spread—spread wide, in front of everybody. It made me feel so sluttish."

"People understand accidents, Lucy."

She looked at my hand on her shoulder. I removed it and she sat down.

"God," she said. "This is crazy—am I going off the deep end?"

"No," I said firmly. "You're obviously reacting to some kind of stress, and we're going to find out what it is. I also want you to see a neurologist to rule out anything organic."

She caught her breath and looked at me, terrified. "Like what? A brain tumor?"

"No, nothing like that, I didn't mean to alarm you. We just need to rule out a sleep disorder that responds to medication. It's unlikely, but I want to be careful, so our road's clear."

"Our *road*. Sounds like some kind of journey."

"In a way it is, Lucy."

She turned away from me. "I don't know any neurologists."

I gave her Phil's name and number. "It won't be intrusive or painful."

"I hope so. I hate to be pawed. I'll call him tomorrow, okay? I'd better get home now."

"Why don't you stay here and relax before you set out?"

"I appreciate the offer, but no, thanks. I'm *really* tired, just want to crawl into bed."

"Want some coffee?"

"No, I'll be fine—it's more emotional fatigue than sleepiness."

"You're sure you want to go right now?"

"Yes, please. Sorry for the hassle."

"It's no hassle at all, Lucy."

"Thanks for your time—we'll figure it out." Looking to me for confirmation.

I nodded and walked her to the door. She opened it and thanked me again.

"I don't want to add to your load," I said, "but you're going to see it on the evening news. A body was found today that matches the Bogeyman victims. There may be a copycat out there."

"Oh, no," she said, leaning against the doorpost. "Where?"

"Santa Ana."

"That's Orange County—so Milo won't be in on it. Too bad. He could solve it."

7

Phil Austerlitz called me the following day at five.

"Clean bill," he said. "Healthiest person I've seen in a long time, except for her anxiety. Even with that, her blood pressure was great. Wish mine was as good."

"What kind of anxiety did you notice?"

"Jumpy. Nervous about being touched—wanting to know exactly what I was going to do to her, how, when, why. Want to know my guess? Extreme sexual inhibition. Is that what she originally came to you for?"

"I'm not dealing with her sex life right now, Phil."

"No? What kind of shrink are you?"

She didn't call for an appointment that day, or the next. The murder down in Santa Ana was a page-ten story, the victim a twenty-one-year-old prostitute named Shannon Dykstra who'd grown up a couple of blocks from Disneyland and had gotten addicted to heroin while still in junior high. The media had fun with that—lots of ironic comments about the Magic Kingdom gone wrong.

That night I cooked a couple of steaks and made a salad, and at seven Robin and I sat down to dinner, with Spike begging for sirloin. When we were through, Robin said, "If you've got no big plans, I thought I might do a little work. The time I'm spending at the house is crimping me."

"Want me to take a shift?"

"No, honey, but if I could catch up, it would help."

Spike watched her depart with longing, but he decided to

stay and finish his table scraps. He hung around as I washed the dishes and followed me to the couch when I played guitar, settling next to me, loose lips blowing out B-flat snores that missed harmony by a mile.

Shortly after nine, Milo called and I asked him if he was involved in the Dykstra case.

"Involved but not committed—know the difference? In a ham-and-egg breakfast, the chicken's involved, the pig's committed. Santa Ana called me to compare notes, and they're driving down tomorrow to look at the Shwandt file."

"Is it that similar?"

"Damn near identical. Body position, wound pattern, decapitation with the head put back in place, shit smeared all over the body and stuffed in the wounds. But all that came out at the trial; anyone could have copied it."

"Another monster," I said.

"The press made such a goddamn celebrity out of Shwandt, they pump this one up as Bogeyman Two, we'll really have fun. Anyway, glad I'm not on it. Keeping busy with some nice old-fashioned drive-bys. . . . So how's Miss Lucy?"

I cleared my throat.

"I know, I know," he said. "You can't get into clinical details. Just tell me she's basically okay. 'Cause she left four messages at my desk today. Called her back but got some lazy-sounding guy on a machine."

"That's her brother. I haven't heard from her for a couple of days. When'd she call you?"

"This morning. I was just wondering if some problem had come up—you *are* still seeing her—no, scratch that, you can't even tell me that, right?"

"Let's put it this way," I said. "If a patient's in imminent danger of self-injury, it's my ethical duty to call the police and/or appropriate medical personnel. I haven't called you or anyone else."

"Okay, good. So I'll try her tomorrow. How's everything by you?"

"Rolling along. How's Rick?"

"Cutting and suturing. With our schedules, there ain't much quality time. We keep talking vacation, but neither of us is willing to make plans."

"Commitment," I said. "Men have such a problem with it."

"Bullshit," he said. "I'm totally committed. I'm a pig, right?"

*   *   *

She called on Friday morning. "If you have time today, I could come in."

"After work?"

"Any time. I'm home."

"Sick?"

"No, I haven't gone back since the . . . fall. Dr. Austerlitz *was* very nice, by the way. He says I'm fine."

"I know. I spoke with him. How've you been sleeping the last couple of nights?"

"Pretty well, actually, since I spoke to you. No dream, and I wake up in my bed, so maybe it was just a short-term thing and I needed to get things off my chest."

I recalled the last session. Lots of questions, no answers. "Did you ever reach Detective Sturgis?"

"He told you I phoned?"

"He called me last night wanting to know if some sort of emergency had come up. Said he hadn't been able to reach you."

"The two of you are close friends, aren't you?"

"Yes, we are."

"He talks about you as if you're some kind of genius. Did you tell him I was okay?"

"I didn't tell him anything. Confidentiality."

"Oh. That's okay; you can talk to him any time. I give you permission."

"There'd be no reason to, Lucy."

"Oh. Okay. All I'm saying is I trust him, and after what I've been through, I'm a good judge of men. Anyway, I reached him. The reason I wanted to talk to him is just, I've been getting some phone calls over the last few weeks."

"What kind of phone calls?"

"Hang-ups. I'm sure it's no big thing."

"How many?"

"Couple a week, maybe four or five in all, mostly when I'm cooking dinner or watching TV. For all I know it's some screwup with the phone lines. Milo didn't seem that concerned. Said I should hang up right away, and if it didn't stop there was a machine I could get from the phone company that would record the caller's number."

"Sounds like a good plan," I said, keeping my voice calm.

The killer who'd burned down my house had worked up to it with harassment. "Would you like to come in at noon?"

"Oh," she said, as if she'd forgotten she'd called to make an appointment. "Sure. Noon would be perfect."

She was five minutes late and breezed in wearing a snug white cotton turtleneck and red bandanna over jeans, white socks, and moccasins. Tiny ruby studs in her ears and her hair was loose. First time I'd seen it that way. It flattered her.

She said, "Everything's really pretty fine."

"Glad you're feeling better," I said.

"I really am. Maybe it's taking a break from work. I always thought my job was so important to me, but after being away from it for a couple of days I don't miss it."

"Are you thinking of quitting permanently?"

"I'm not much of a spender, so I've got enough saved up to last awhile." She gave an embarrassed smile.

"What is it?"

"I've also got a trust fund—not enough to live rich, but it *is* a thousand a month, so that's a pretty good cushion. That's what I meant by others having things a lot worse."

"Are you uncomfortable having a cushion?"

"Well," she said, "I didn't do anything to earn it. And it comes from *his* side of the family—his mother. A generation-skipping thing, they call it. To save taxes. I generally give a big chunk of it away to charity, but if it can help me mellow out a little now, why not take advantage of it?"

"I agree."

"I mean, I've got nothing to prove. In three years I've never taken a sick day—do you think it's irresponsible? Quitting, just like that?"

"Not at all."

"Really?"

"Really."

"So . . . like I said, everything's fine. . . . I also talked to Milo about the new murder. The Santa Ana police are consulting with him, which is smart. I remember how impressed I was when he testified. All those details at his fingertips, he never let the defense lawyer intimidate him—I guess his size helps; what is he, six-four?"

"Six-three."

Her color was high and her fingers were knitting an invisible sweater.

"There's something I want to tell you," she said. "I'm highly attracted to him."

Keeping my face neutral, I held eye contact.

She crossed her legs and touched an earring. "It's been a long time since I've felt this way about a guy." Looking away. "Except for a few mistakes, I'm basically a virgin."

I nodded.

"Big mistakes," she said, "I grant you. But I've put them behind me."

"Is that what you meant this morning when you said after what you'd been through you were a good judge of men?"

She muttered something I couldn't make out.

"Lucy?"

Another mumble that sounded like "Take a look."

I leaned closer.

Her mouth continued to work. She closed her eyes.

"I *hooked*. Okay?"

I didn't answer.

"Just for a summer," she said.

Remembering the ulcer, I said, "The summer you taught in Boston?"

"I was a bona fide virgin. Then I met someone at Head Start, the uncle of one of my students. Gorgeous, very charming, bright black guy. He used to come and pick the little boy up, and we started talking. One thing led to another. I thought I was in love. After we were together for a while, he asked me to be with a friend of his. I didn't like the idea but I agreed. It ended up not being as bad as I'd thought—the friend was okay and he gave me a gift, some shampoo. L'Oréal. I still remember that."

Her eyes opened. Tears filled them.

"I was able to put myself in another place and get through it. And Raymond was so proud of me. Telling me he loved me, I was showing real love for him. Next week he brought another friend over."

She threw up her hands.

"It was bad, but it could have been a lot worse. His other girls were all working on the street. He let me work out of a room. Clean, warm, color TV. He made sure I didn't get any violent ones. The men came to *me*. It was almost like being popular."

She let out a dead laugh.

"That's it. My sordid past. Ten weeks of white slavery and mortal sin, and then I went on to Belding and Raymond found some other gullible idiot."

Pushing hair away from her face, she forced herself to look at me. "I haven't been with a man since then. Do you think I'm still too sullied for your best friend?"

"It took courage to tell me," I said.

"Don't worry about my having evil designs on him or being some freak-case co-dependent. When I say I'm attracted to him, I mean *psychologically*. His kindness, his solidity. I'm working up my courage to let him know how I feel. Is that okay with you?"

"You don't need my permission, Lucy." Thinking of the complications that were sure to come.

She stared at me.

"You *don't* approve, do you?" Snapping her head down, she studied the floor. "Big mistake to tell you."

"Lucy, it's not—"

"I should have known," she said softly. "You're entitled to your feelings. I tell you I was a whore, it's only natural you wouldn't want me near your friend."

"It's not that at all."

"Then *what*? Why does your face change when I talk about liking him?"

"There's nothing terrible about that, or you. What goes on between you and Milo or anyone else isn't any of my business."

She studied me.

"Forgive me, Dr. Delaware, but that just doesn't ring true. You're a lovely man and I really appreciate all you've tried to do for me, but there's something going on here, some kind of resistance. I've got a feel for things like that." Another joyless laugh. "Maybe it comes from screwing ten strangers a day. You get good at gauging people quickly."

She got up and walked across the room.

"Lucy flunks therapy. . . . Seeing Milo's friend was a mistake—how can I expose myself to you and expect you to be impartial? How can I expect you to take any sort of *voyage* with a whore?"

"You're not a whore."

"No? How can you be sure? Have you had other patients who were whores?"

"Lucy—"

"For seven years," she said, between clenched jaws, "I haven't *touched* a guy. For seven years I've been double-tithing my income to the poor, not eating meat, doing every good deed I can find to cleanse myself. *That's* why I wanted to be on that jury. To accomplish some greater good. And now I finally find a man I like, and I'm feeling dirty—judged by you just like I judged Shwandt. I *should* have gotten out of it. Who am I to judge *anyone*?"

"Shwandt is a monster," I said. "You got caught up in something."

She turned her back on me. "He's a monster and I'm sleazy—we're all defendants in one way or another, aren't we? Is that the only reason you don't want me near Milo, or is he involved with someone else?"

"It's not appropriate for me to discuss his personal life."

"Why not? Is he your patient, too?"

"We're here to talk about you, Lucy."

"But I like *him*, so doesn't that make it relevant? If he wasn't your friend, we'd be talking about him."

"And I wouldn't know anything about his personal life."

She stopped. Licked her lips. Smiled. "Okay, he's committed. Though I know he's not married—I asked him if he was and he said no." She turned sharply and faced me. "Did he lie to me?"

"No."

"So he's going with someone—maybe living with someone—is she beautiful? Like *your* wife? Do the four of you double-date?"

"Lucy," I said, "stop tormenting yourself." Knowing my reticence was feeding her fantasies. Knowing I couldn't warn Milo—strangled by confidentiality.

Turning her back on me, she pressed her hands up against the glass doors, saw the fingerprints she'd made, and tried to wipe them off with a corner of her sweater.

"*Sorry.*"

Nearly sobbing the word.

"There's nothing to be—"

"I can't believe I just said all those things. How could I be so—"

"Come on." I guided her back to her chair. She started to sit, then walked past it, snatching up her bag and racing for the door.

I reached her just as she opened it. A marine breeze ruffled her hair. Her eyes were watering.

"Please come back, Lucy."

She shook her head violently. "Let me go. I just can't take any more humiliation."

"Let's talk it ou—"

"I *can't*. Not right now. Please—I'll come back. I promise. Soon."

"Lucy—"

"Please let me go. I really need to be alone. I really need that."

I backed off.

She stepped out onto the footbridge.

8

Had I screwed up or was it something that couldn't have been avoided?

Seeing a friend of his was a mistake.

Who knew trauma counseling would turn into this?

Damn, what a *mess*!

I tried to call her an hour later. No answer. One more try, an hour after that, and I decided to give her time to think.

That evening, Robin and I cooked sand dabs and home fries and lingered over the meal. I was preoccupied and tried to hide it by being extra affectionate. She knew something was going on but said nothing as we watched the sunset.

Then she went to do some carving, Spike fell asleep, and I got in the Seville and drove aimlessly up the coast, getting off the highway at Ventura, for no particular reason, and gliding through dark, empty streets. Lots of boarded-up storefronts and FOR LEASE signs. The recession had hit the town hard, and seeing it did nothing for my mood.

When I got back, Robin was in bed reading *Command: Shed the Light*.

She closed it and dropped it on the covers. "Why did you check this out?"

"Research."

"Into what?"

"The dark side."

"Such garbage. I can't believe this is the same guy we had to read in English."

"The critics couldn't believe it either. It killed his career."

"He used to write totally differently," she said. "*Dark Horses*. That long poem about Paris: 'The Market.' I remember *Dark Horses* especially because we had to analyze it in freshman English. I hated the assignment but I thought the book was fascinating, the way he turned the racetrack into a miniature world, all those quirky characters. This stuff is dreadful. What happened?"

"Maybe he used up his ration of talent."

"What a woman-hater! Seriously, what kind of research are you doing?"

"It has to to with a patient, Rob. Someone he's influenced."

"Oh. Sounds creepy."

I shrugged and got out of my clothes.

"Nice of you to empathize with your patient to that degree," she said.

"That's what they sent me to school for." I put the book on my nightstand and slipped under the covers. She rolled toward me.

"You sound upset."

"No, just bushed."

She didn't say anything. Her huge dark eyes snared mine and held them captive. Her curls fell over bare shoulders like a shadow on the moon. I wrapped her in my arms.

"Okay," she said. "Do you have enough energy to empathize with me? I've got *all* sorts of feelings."

I was still in my bathrobe when the phone rang at 7:10 the next morning.

"Dr. Delaware? This is your service. I have a Dr. Shaper for you."

The name was unfamiliar. "I'll take it."

A man's voice said, "Who do I have?"

"This is Dr. Delaware."

"This is Dr. Shapoor over at Woodbridge Hospital. We've got a suicide attempt came in last night. Lucretia . . . Lowell. She's finally awake and claiming she's your patient."

My heart rocked and rolled. "How is she?"

"Stabilized. She'll survive."

"When did she come in?"

"Sometime last night. She's been going in and out of consciousness. Claims she's never done this before. Has she?"

"Not to my knowledge, but I've only seen her a few times."

"Well, we're putting her on a seventy-two-hour hold—*One second!*" Then: "You know how those seventy-twos go?"

"Yes."

"She'll be seeing one of our staff psychiatrists. You can probably get some kind of temporary privileges—you're an M.D., right?"

"Ph.D."

"Oh. Then I don't know. Anyway—"

"What method did she use?"

"Gas. Turned on the stove and stuck her head in."

"Who found her?"

"Some guy brought her in. I just came on shift and saw the message in the chart to call you."

"Did she take any drugs or alcohol?"

"According to the chart, she denies any drug use, but we'll see when the blood work gets back. Does she have a drug history?"

"Not that I know of, but she *has* been through some rough times recently."

"Uh-huh—hold on. *What? Tell them just to wait!* . . . Anyway, I have to go now."

"I'd like to come over and see her now."

"Sure," he said. "She's not going anywhere."

After I hung up, I realized I had no idea where Woodbridge Hospital was. Obtaining the number from Information, I connected with a bored receptionist, who said, "They call it Woodland Hills, but it's really Canoga Park. Topanga just north of Victory."

I got dressed and drove south on PCH, taking Kanan Dume Road to the 101 Freeway, where I got stuck in a jam. Squeezing out at the next exit, I drove north till I found Victory and followed it ten miles to Topanga Boulevard. The hospital was a three-story brown-brick column that resembled a giant chocolate bar. Small smoked windows, small brass letters, and an illuminated emergency entrance sign bright enough to pierce the morning light.

Parking was free, in a giant lot. The guard at the door barely glanced up as I passed. I gave the clerk my name and she buzzed me in.

The place was brimming over with misery, injured and sick people propped up in plastic chairs. Periodic moans soloed above efficient medical chatter. A colostomy reek hung in the air.

As I passed, someone said, "Doctor?" in a weak, hopeful voice.

Shapoor was outside a room marked Observation 2, reading a chart. A tall, elegant Indian around thirty, he had wavy black hair, humid eyes, and nicotine breath. His badge said he was a second-year resident. His necktie was hand-painted, and the disks of his stethoscope were gold-plated. I introduced myself. He kept reading.

"Lucy Lowell," I said.

"Yes, yes, I know." Pointing to the door.

"How's she doing?" I said.

"We patched her up."

"There were wounds?"

"I was speaking figuratively." He snapped the chart shut. "She's fine. We saved her. For the time being."

"Has her blood work come back yet?"

"No narcotics that we pick up."

"What are the side effects of the gas?"

"A very unpleasant headache for the next few days, some general weakness, maybe disorientation, congestion, shortness of breath—it all depends on how much she actually took in. We cleaned her out thoroughly."

"Was she conscious when she came in?"

"Semi. But she keeps going in and out. Typical."

"Is the person who brought her in still here?"

"Don't know. The psychiatrist on call can fill you in. She won't be in till later today, but she feels an involuntary hold is definitely called for."

"What's her name?"

"Dr. Embrey. You can leave your card with the front desk or the triage nurse and ask them to give it to her." Pulling his stethoscope off, he walked to the next door. I pushed Lucy's open.

She was in bed, eyes closed, breathing through her mouth, hands flat on her thighs. Her hair had been topknotted with a rubber band. A plastic bag of something clear dripped into her veins; oxygen hissed into her nose from a thin tube that ran from a pressurized tank. A bank of monitors behind the bed beeped and flashed and gurgled, trying to quantify the quality of her life.

Her vital signs looked good, the blood pressure a little low. Her face was sweaty but her lips were dry.

I stared down at her, replaying our sessions, wondering if there had been warning signs.

Of course there'd been, genius. All that shame and rage.

Confession gone very sour.

Nothing to indicate she'd go this far, but what the hell did I know about her?

Out of my hands now. She was in the system, locked up for three days. More, if the psychiatrist convinced a judge she remained a danger to herself.

A woman psychiatrist. Maybe it was what she needed. God knows I wasn't her savior.

She made a deep snoring sound, and her eyes moved under swollen lids.

More fragile than I'd thought.

Was her summer as a prostitute the cause or, more likely, a symptom?

I wondered if everything she'd told me was true.

For all I knew, her father was really a truck driver from Bell Gardens, no closer to fame than a subscription to *People.*

Who'd brought her to the hospital?

Who'd pulled her head out of the oven?

Her eyes opened partially. She tried blinking but couldn't. I moved into her field of vision; at first she didn't focus. Then I saw her pupils dilate. One hand moved, the fingers stretching toward me. Suddenly, they dropped.

I took hold of them. Her mouth shifted, struggling for an expression, finally settling on weariness.

I smiled down at her. She gave a feeble nod. The oxygen tube fell out of her nose, the hiss growing louder as precious gas leaked.

I replaced it. She licked her lips, and her eyes opened completely.

Trying to talk, but all that came out were wordless croaks. Tears in her eyes.

"It's okay, Lucy."

She fell back. Her fingers grew cold and loose.

For the next twenty minutes, she slept as I held her hand. A nurse came in, checked her, and left, closing the door hard. Lucy woke up with a start, systolic pressure jumping.

Panic in her eyes.

"You're okay, Lucy. You're in the emergency room at Woodbridge Hospital, and you're doing fine."

She started coughing and couldn't stop. The oxygen line flew out again. Each spasm lifted her from the mattress, an involuntary calisthenic that tightened her face with pain. She coughed harder and spit up vile-looking gray mucus that I wiped away.

When the coughing stopped, I put the line back.

It took a long time for her to catch her breath.

"*What*," she said, very softly and hoarsely, "*happen?*"

"You're in the emergency room. Woodbridge Hospital."

Confusion.

"What's the last thing you remember, Lucy?"

She gave a mystified stare. "Sleeping."

Her face screwed up and her eyes closed. More pain—or shame? Or both?

The eyes opened. "Hurts."

"What does?"

"Head."

She moaned and wept.

I checked the contents of her IV bag: glucose and electrolytes, no analgesic. I pressed the nurse call button. A bark came through a wall speaker. "Yes?"

"Miss Lowell's in pain. Is there anything she can have?"

"Hold on."

Lucy had another coughing fit and spit up. She stared at me as I wiped her lips.

"What . . . happened?" She started to shiver and her teeth chattered.

I put another blanket over her. She said something I couldn't make out and I bent down to hear her.

"Sick?"

"You've had a rough experience."

"What?"

Tears trickled down her cheeks, flowing under the oxygen line and into her mouth. Fear was twisting her face like taffy.

"Sick?" she repeated.

I took her hand again. "Lucy, they say you tried to commit suicide."

Shock widened her eyes.

"No!" A whisper, more lip movement than sound. *"No!"*

I gave her fingers a soft squeeze and nodded.

"How?"

"Gas."

"No!"

Behind her, the monitors jumped. Heart rate up, systolic blood pressure rising. The hand in mine was a sodden claw.

"No!"

"It's okay, Lucy."

"No!"

"I believe you," I lied. "Try to relax."

"Didn't!"

"Okay, Lucy."

"No!"

"Okay, just calm down."

She shook her head. The oxygen line shot out of her nose like a slingshotted stone. When I tried to replace it, she turned her head away from me, chest heaving, breathing harshly.

The door opened and the same nurse came in. Young and heavy-faced with chopped hair. "What's going on?"

"She's upset."

"What happened to her line?"

"It came loose. I was just putting it back."

"Well, we'd better get it *right* back." She took the line from me and tried to insert the nosepiece into Lucy's nostrils.

Lucy turned away from her, too.

The nurse put one hand on her hip and twirled the tube with the other.

"Now you listen to me," she said. "We're busy and we don't have time for fooling around. Do you want us to run tape all the way around your head to keep the line in? It'll have to be really tight, and believe me, your headache will get a lot worse. Do you *want* that?"

Lucy bit her lip and shook her head.

"So be still, it's for your good. We're just trying to take care of you and fix you all up."

Nod.

The line went back in. "Good girl." The nurse checked the monitors. "Your pulse is up to ninety-eight. Better relax."

No response.

"Okay?"

Nod.

The nurse turned to me. "Are you family?"

"Her therapist."

Quizzical look. "Well, that's good. Maybe you can get her calm." She headed for the door.

"About her pain," I said.

"She can't have anything. Not until we really make sure she's been cleaned out."

Lucy croaked.

"Sorry, hon, it's for your own good." The nurse swung the door open, letting in fluorescence and noise. "Just try to think of something pleasant. And don't get upset again, it'll only make your head feel worse."

The door closed. I picked up Lucy's hand again. Lifeless as a glove.

She said, "I didn't."

I nodded.

"Really!"

"I believe you, Lucy."

"G'home?"

"They want to watch you for a while."

Her back arched.

"Please?"

"It's not up to me, Lucy."

She tried to push herself up from the bed. The line flew out, hissing and coiling on the bedcovers like an angry snake. The monitors were dancing.

"Listen to me," I said, putting my hands on her shoulders and easing her down without resistance.

Again, I replaced the line. She pushed up against me.

"Take m'home!"

"I can't, Lucy. That nurse was no diplomat, but she was right about one thing: You need to relax right now. And to cooperate."

Terrified looks, roller-coaster eyes.

More coughing.

"Why," she said, nearly breathless, "can't . . . home?"

"Because they think you're a suicide attempt. They've got you on something called a seventy-two-hour hold. That means legally they can keep you here for three days and offer you psychiatric treatment. After that, if you're no danger to yourself or anyone else, you'll be free to go."

"*No!*" She moaned and rolled her head from side to side.

"It's the law, Lucy. It's for your own protection."

"*No!*"

"I'm really sorry you have to go through this, and I want to see you up and around as soon as possible. That's why you need to cooperate."

"You . . . treat?"

"I'm sorry, Lucy. I'm not on the staff here. A psychiatrist named Dr. Embrey will be treating you, a woman. I'll talk to her first—"

"No!"

"I know it's frightening, Lucy, but please ride it out."

"Three *days?*"

"I'll stick by you. I promise."

More moans. She flinched and managed to raise a hand to her temple.

"*Ohh!*"

"Settle down," I said. "I know it's hard."

"*Ow!*"

Her hand left her head and settled at her side. She poked her rib cage with one finger.

"What is it?" I said.

"Broken."

"You think you broke a rib?"

Headshake. "Me. Broken."

"No, you're not," I said, stroking her face. "Just a little bruised."

"No . . . broken."

"You'll be fine, Lucy. Try to get some rest."

"Milo."

"You want me to tell Milo you're here?"

"Tell him . . . someone—"

"Someone?"

"Someone—" Struggling for breath, she took a deep, wheezing inhalation.

Her heart rate had climbed over a hundred. A hundred and ten . . .

"Someone—" she repeated. Poking her ribs. Terror in her eyes. *"Someone . . ."*

"Someone what?" I said, leaning in closer.

"Killing me!"

9

She sank back and fell asleep. It took the monitors another minute to slow down.

I waited a while, then left to find some coffee. A man down the hall said, "Excuse me, are you her doctor?"

He looked to be around thirty. Five-ten, broad-shouldered, stocky, and round-faced, with light brown hair, a golf-course tan, and wide brown eyes. His blue blazer had some cashmere in it, his burgundy shirt was broadcloth. Beige linen trousers broke perfectly over oxblood tassel loafers.

"I'm Dr. Delaware, her psychologist."

"Oh, good." He extended his hand. "Ken Lowell. Her brother."

Movement down the hall distracted both of us. An old man, waxy white and skeletal, was being eased by an orderly into a wheelchair. Blood dripped from under his hospital gown, painting a winding, crimson trail on the gray linoleum floor. His eyes were blank and his mouth was open. Only his tremoring limbs said he was alive.

Ken Lowell stared as the chair was wheeled away. No one rushed in to clean up the blood.

He turned back to me, looking queasy. The good clothes made him seem a tourist who'd wandered into a slum.

"Dr. Delaware," he said. "She was asking for you. I thought she was delirious and wanted to go to Delaware for some reason." Shaking his head. "How's she doing?"

"She's recovering, physically. Did you bring her in?"

He nodded. "Has she done this before?"

"Not as far as I know."

Pulling a burgundy silk handkerchief out of his breast pocket, he mopped his forehead. "So what happens to her now?"

"She'll be here involuntarily for at least three days, and then a psychiatrist from the hospital will determine a treatment plan."

"She could be committed against her will?"

"If the psychiatrist—Dr. Embrey—believes she's still in danger, she can go to court and ask for an extension. That's unusual, though, unless the patient makes another suicide attempt in the hospital or experiences some sort of massive breakdown."

"What led up to this, doctor? Was she very depressed?"

"I'm sorry, but I can't discuss details with you—confidentiality."

"Oh, sure. Sorry. It's just that I don't know much about her. For all practical purposes, we're total strangers. I haven't seen her in twenty years."

"How'd you come to bring her in?"

"Pure chance. It's pretty scary. I was looking for Puck—my half brother, Peter—Lucy's brother. We had a dinner appointment at my hotel at seven, and he didn't show. It bothered me; I didn't think it was something he'd miss. So I waited for a while, then drove out to his apartment in Studio City. No one was home. He'd told me how close he and Lucy were, so, on a long shot, I decided to look for him at her place. It was after ten by the time I got there, and I wouldn't have gone up but her lights were on and the drapes were partially open. When I got to the door, I thought I smelled gas. I knocked, got no answer, looked through the window, and saw her kneeling on the kitchen floor. I tapped the glass hard and she didn't move, so I broke the door down and pulled her head out of the stove. She had a pulse and she was breathing, but she didn't look too good. I called 911. It took a really long time to get through. While waiting for the paramedics to arrive, I looked up hospitals in the phone book and found this place. When they still hadn't shown up, I said, Screw this, and brought her in myself."

He stuffed the handkerchief back in his pocket and shook his head.

"You're from San Francisco?" I said.

"How'd you know that?"

"Lucy told me."

"She was talking about me?"

"I took a family history."

"Oh. Actually, I'm from Palo Alto, but I'm down in L.A. quite a lot on business—real estate, mostly buyouts and bankruptcies. What with the economy, I've been down here more than usual, and I started thinking about connecting with Puck and Lucy—it seemed wrong that we never even tried to get together. Lucy wasn't listed but Puck was, so a few weeks ago I called him. He was shocked to hear from me; it was awkward. But we talked a few more times, finally agreed to try dinner."

"Was Lucy going to be there, too?"

"No, he didn't want her to be—protecting her, I guess. It was a trial balloon. The deal was that if it worked out, we'd get her involved . . . he was pretty nervous about the whole thing. Still, I was surprised when he stood me up."

"Have you heard from him since?"

"No. I tried him a couple times from here, no answer." He looked at his watch. "Maybe I should try again."

There was a pay phone up the hall. He called, waited, and came back shaking his head.

"Poor kid," he said, looking at the door to Lucy's room. "Puck said she'd been through some kind of rough jury duty and was pretty freaked out, but I had no idea she was this . . . vulnerable."

He buttoned his jacket. Tight around the waist. "Too many business dinners," he said, smiling ruefully. "Not that I imagine she's had it easy. Did she tell you who our father is?"

I nodded.

He said, "I don't know if she's had any contact with him, but if she has, I'd be willing to bet that's at least part of her stress."

"Why's that?"

"The man's a total and complete sonofabitch."

"Have you had contact with him?"

"No way. He lives here—up in Topanga Canyon, big spread. But that's a call I'll never make." Unbuttoning his jacket. "When I first started in the business, I used to have fantasies of his going bankrupt and me buying his land up cheap." Smile. "I've been in counseling myself—got divorced last year."

"What happened twenty years ago?"

"Pardon?"

"You said the last time you saw Lucy was twenty years ago."

"Oh. Yeah, twenty, twenty-one, something like that." He squinted and scratched the side of his nose. "I was nine, so it was twenty-one. It was the summer my mother decided to go to Europe to take painting lessons—she was an artist. She drove us —my sister Jo and me—down to L.A. and dropped us off at Sanctum. That's the name of his place in Topanga."

"I've heard of it—a writer's retreat."

"Yeah. Anyway, here she is, dumping us on him, no advance notice. He was about as happy as getting a boil lanced, but what could he do, kick us out?"

"And Lucy was there too?"

"Lucy and Puck. They came up a couple of weeks after we did. Tiny little kids, we didn't know who they were; our mother had never told us they even existed, only that he'd left her for another woman. As it turned out, *their* mom had died a few years before, and the aunt who had taken care of them had gotten married and dumped *them*."

"How old were they?"

"Let's see, if I was nine, Puck would have had to be . . . five. So Lucy was four. We looked at them as babies, had nothing to do with them. Tell the truth, we resented them—our mother was always bad-mouthing their mother for stealing him away."

"Who took care of them?"

"A nanny or some kind of baby-sitter. I remember that because they got to sleep with her in the main house while Jo and I had to stay in a little cabin and basically fend for ourselves. But that was okay. We ran around, did whatever we wanted."

"Twenty-one years ago," I said. "That must have been right after Sanctum opened."

"It had just opened," he said. "I remember they had this big party for the opening, and we were forced to stay in our cabin. Along with plates of food. Tons more spread out on these long white banquet tables, leftovers for weeks. I used to sneak into the kitchen and swipe pastries. I gained ten pounds—that was the beginning of my weight problem."

People shouting or maybe they're laughing . . . and lights like fireflies.

Another glance at his watch. "Well," he said, "good to meet you. If there's anything I can do—"

He turned to leave.

"How long will you be in L.A.?"

"I was supposed to fly back tonight. Do you think—is there a chance Lucy would want to meet me?"

"Hard to say, right now. She's pretty out of it."

"Yeah, I understand," he said sadly. "I wonder where Puck is, why he didn't show. Here."

Pulling out a crocodile billfold, he removed a business card and gave it to me.

THE ALPHA GROUP

Kenyon T. Lowell
Senior Vice President,
Acquisitions
(415) 547-7766

"I've got meetings all day, but I probably can stick around till tomorrow morning. If she does want to meet me, or if you hear from Puck, I'm staying at the Westwood Marquis."

"Do you have Puck's number handy?"

"Right here." An identical card came out of the wallet. On the back was a Valley exchange, written in blue ballpoint.

"Let me get some paper and copy it down," I said.

"Take it," he said. "I know it by heart."

10

He left and I returned to Lucy's room. She was still sleeping, and I gave my name to the ward clerk along with a message for Dr. Embrey. Then I phoned West L.A. Detectives and got Milo at his desk.

"What's up, Alex?"

"Lucy tried to kill herself last night. She's out of danger, physically, but still pretty knocked out. I'm at Woodbridge Hospital, out in the Valley. They'll be keeping her here."

"*Fuck.* What'd she do, cut her wrists?"

"Stuck her head in the oven."

"You find her?"

"No, her half brother did. Lucky for her he stopped by looking for the other brother and saw her through the window, on her knees in the kitchen. Talk about Providence."

"Her drapes were open and she's got her head in the oven? What was it, a cry for help?"

"Who knows? She never dropped any hints to me. Still, I'm trying hard not to feel like an idiot."

"Jesus, Alex, what the hell *happened*?"

"It's complicated. More than you could ever imagine."

"And you can't tell me."

"No, in fact, I need to. But not over the phone. When can we get together?"

"Coming back into the city?"

"Yup."

"Gino's in forty-five."

*   *   *

Gino's Trattoria is on Pico, not far from the West L.A. station: checkered tablecloths, hanging Chianti bottles, rough wines.

Even during the day, the place is murky, lit by table candles in amber globes that are never washed. The one at Milo's rear corner table illuminated him from the bottom, accentuating every crater and lump, giving him the look of a gargoyle with chronic back pain.

He was wearing a dark suit, white shirt, and dark tie. Even at that distance I could tell his hair was freshly cut—military clip at the sides, long and shaggy on top, to-the-lobe sideburns that were hip, now, and against department regulations.

Two beers sat in front of him. He pushed one over to me. In the dirty glare his green eyes were gray-brown.

"How come all of a sudden you can talk to me?"

"Because Lucy asked me to. She said someone was trying to kill her, and she wants you to protect her. I'm sure it's some sort of gas-induced delusion—or massive denial because she just can't face the fact that she tried to kill herself. But I'm taking it as a formal instruction."

"How does she figure someone tried to kill her with gas? Dragged her to the stove and jammed her *head* in?"

"She's nowhere near coherent enough to discuss details."

"Remember those four calls she put in? Seems she's been getting some hang-ups."

"She told me. Said you didn't think it was serious."

"I didn't because *she* didn't. She told me it might be some technical problem with her phone; the line goes out all the time. Kind of casual about the whole thing, made me wonder if she just wanted to talk."

"I'm sure she did. That's part of what I have to tell you. She's got a major crush on you. Admitted it to me during yesterday's session."

He was silent and still.

"She wanted approval from me, Milo. I couldn't tell her you were gay because I didn't want to violate your privacy. And I couldn't warn *you* about the way she felt because of confidentiality. She got really upset and left. Now this. I feel like I've really screwed up, but I don't know what I could've done differently."

"You coulda told her about me, Alex. I'm not your patient."

"I didn't think it was appropriate to get into your personal life. She was the patient; I was trying to keep the focus on her."

"Jesus." His cheeks turned to bellows and he blew out beery air.

"Has she ever shown any romantic feelings?"

"I don't know," he said furiously. "I guess looking back . . . I mean, she hung around, phoned, but I figured it was a cop-victim thing. Looking for big brother." Rubbing one eye. "Pretty fucking dense, huh? *Goddammit!* I'm an asshole to let it get this far. All these years I've been careful not to get personal with victims or their families. So why her?"

"You didn't do anything wrong," I said. "You gave her support, and when it became clear she needed something more, you referred her to me."

"Yeah, but there *was* more. In *my* head. She probably picked up on it."

"More what?"

"Involvement. I'd find myself thinking about her. Worrying. Couple of times I called *her,* just to see how she was doing."

He slammed a big hand down on the table. "How else could she take it? What am I, brain dead?"

He shook his head. "For chrissake, she was only a *juror.* I've dealt with thousands of *victims* who had it a helluva lot worse. I must be losing it."

"You didn't put her head in the oven."

"Neither did you, but you still feel like shit."

Both of us drank.

"If I hadn't tried to help her," he said, "I wouldn't *know* about her head being in the oven, would I? And you and I would be sitting here talking about something else."

His glass was empty and he called for a refill, looking at me. "No, thanks."

He said, "Ignorance is bliss, right? All the talk about insight and self-understanding, but far as I can tell, being a good *ostrich* is the key to psychological adjustment. Christ, now I have her sitting on my *shoulder.* . . . So what do I do, tell her, Gee, honeybunch, if I went for women you'd be at the top of my list? Might as well shove her head back in the oven."

"There's no need to do anything right now," I said. "Let's see how she handles the seventy-two hours. If the psychiatrist at Woodbridge is good, she'll know how to deal with it."

"Seventy-two hours . . . praise the law."

"There's more you need to know about." I told him about Lucy's summer as a prostitute.

"Oh, man, it keeps getting better. Just a summer fling, huh?"

"So she says. She confessed right after she told me how she felt about you. Asked me if I thought she wasn't good enough for you. As if she was giving me a reason to reject her."

"Not good enough for me." He gave a scary laugh. "Remember I told you she reminded me of a girl in high school who became a nun? Someone else who convinced herself I was wonderful."

This time he rubbed his face. Hard.

"Prom night back in Hoosierville. All the little virgins and would-be virgins from Our Lady on the arms of us pimpled lads from St. Thomas. I was eighteen and knew I was gay for a couple of years, no one to tell it to. Her name was Nancy Squires, and when she asked me to be her date I said yes because I didn't want to hurt her feelings. Orchid corsage, tux, Dad's car washed and waxed. Doing the Twist in the gym. Mashed Potatoes and the fucking Hully Gully. Drinking the fucking spiked *punch*."

He looked into his beer glass.

"She was pretty, if you liked skinny and pale and tortured. Wrote poetry, collected these little porcelain doohickeys, didn't know how to dress, tutored the boys in math. Of course the other girls treated her like a leper."

He turned and faced me.

"She was nice to talk to, a little lady. Then when I drove her home, she put her hands all over me, and when I parked in front of her house she told me she loved me. It was like being sucker-punched. Genius that I was, I told her I liked her as a friend but couldn't love her. Then I explained why."

He gave another frightful laugh. In the bad light he looked homicidal.

"She didn't say a thing for a while. Just let her hands drop and stared at me as if I was the biggest goddamn disappointment in her eighteen-year life. She didn't have it easy. Her whole family was a bunch of assholes, brothers in jail, father a drunken shit who slapped her around from time to time, maybe worse. And here I was, the last straw."

He rubbed his eyelids. "She kept staring at me. Finally shook her head and said, 'Oh, Milo, you're going to end up in Hell.' No anger. Sympathetic. Then she patted her brand-new Tonette and got out of the car and that's the last I saw her. Next week she shipped off to a convent in Indianapolis. Five years ago my mother wrote me she was murdered, over in El Salvador. She and a bunch of other nuns washing clothes in a stream." He threw up his hands. "Let's do a screenplay."

"Lucy reminds you of her that strongly."

"They could be *sisters,* Alex. The way she carries herself—the vulnerability."

"The vulnerability's definitely there," I said. "Given what I've learned of her childhood, it's no surprise. Her mom died right after she was born; her father deserted the family. She's functionally an orphan."

"Yeah, I know. She was talking to me about Shwandt, once. Said he had two parents, nice home, father who was a lawyer, so what was his excuse? Said her own father was a lowlife."

"Did she tell you who her father is?"

He looked up. "Who?"

"M. Bayard Lowell."

Staring, he put his hands around his beer glass. "What *is* this, Big Fucking *Surprise* Day? The goddamn moon in Pisces with Herpes or something? Lowell as in Mr. Belles *Lettruh?*"

"None other."

"Unbelievable. He still alive?"

"Living in Topanga Canyon. His career died and he moved to L.A."

"I read him in school."

"Everyone did."

"She's his daughter? Unreal."

"You can see why he'd have impact, even being absent."

"Sure," he said. "He's just there, like the goddamn Ten Foot Gorilla."

"Lucy compared it to being the President's kid. I can understand her looking for a benevolent authority figure. Maybe your thoughts about a big brother weren't all that far from the truth."

"Great. And now I disappoint her, too. . . . So how do I handle this? Visit or keep my distance?"

"Let's see how she does during the next few days."

"Sure. Head in the oven. . . . No idea what could have led her to it?"

I shook my head. "She was upset, but nothing that pointed to suicide."

"Upset about me."

"That, but we'd also started to get into other things—the prostitution, feelings toward her father. And the dream she mentioned to you. That's something else I want to talk to you about."

I described the buried girl story.

He said, "I'm no shrink, but I hear, 'Daddy scares the shit out of me.' "

"She started having it midway through the trial, right after you testified about Carrie. I figured all that horror raised her anxiety level and released long-buried feelings toward Lowell—seeing herself as some kind of victim. His last poems are viciously anti-woman; she may have read them and had a strong reaction. And the last time we discussed the dream she said she'd felt her soul entering the dark-haired girl's body—as if she were being buried too. Explicitly identifying with the victim. But something the half brother told me in the hospital makes me wonder if there's even more. She claims she's had no contact with Lowell her entire life, but the brother said twenty-one years ago she spent the summer with him in Topanga. All four of his kids did. Lucy was four years old at the time—the age she feels in the dream. And Lowell's place has log buildings, exactly what she describes. Now, the newspapers did cover the opening of the retreat, down to the architecture; I found the clippings so she could've also. Or she could have heard about it from her brother Peter. He did some family research and filled her in. If that's the case, she's flat out denying being there. But the alternative is that she really *doesn't* remember. Maybe because something traumatic happened that summer."

His jaw flexed. "Daddy did something to her?"

"Like I said, his last poems are grossly misogynistic. If he abused her, I can see why the trial might kick in the memories—sex and violence thrown together. One thing's for sure, she's struggling with something major. The recurrent nature of the dream and its intensity—when she talks about it she actually seems to experience it—she's trancelike. Almost as if she's going into hypnosis by herself. That tells me her ego boundaries are weakening; this is something potent. So maybe I should've been more careful. But there was no profound depression, no hint she'd do this."

"What about the other two guys in the dream?"

"Could be that part's fantasy, or maybe what happened to her wasn't a solo act. And I've got another possible participant.

That summer, Lowell had a protégé living with him named Terry Trafficant. Career criminal, history of attempted rape, assault, manslaughter. Locked up long-term till Lowell helped him get parole and publish his jail diary. It became a best-seller."

"Yeah, yeah, I wasn't a cop yet, still in college, but I remember thinking how asinine."

"So did a lot of other people. The last cop who arrested him called him a stick of dynamite waiting to go off. There was a stink about Lowell's patronage, then Trafficant disappeared. A guy like that, all those years in confinement, stick him in Topanga Canyon with a cute little girl running around, who knows."

He grimaced. "Trafficant's record include pedophilia?"

"I don't remember reading that, but a guy like him might very well not be repulsed by sex with a little girl."

"Yeah. The other possibility, Alex, is that nothing happened directly to her but she saw something. And not even criminal violence— maybe wild sex, some kind of orgy. A girl and three guys—that would freak out a four-year-old, right? What if the grinding was exactly what she first thought it was and her mind ran away with it? Like you said, sex and violence are all mixed up in her head."

I thought about that. "It's sure possible. The half brother said the kids were at the retreat for the opening. A big party took place. The papers described it as a pretty wild scene. And in the dream, Lucy talks about noise and lights the night she leaves the cabin. She could've seen something X-rated."

"Involving Daddy. He and a couple of buddies having their way with a girl," he said. "Not the kind of thing a little kid could handle easily."

"And the trial reawakens it. . . . On the other hand, what if she did witness violence and *that's* why hearing about Shwandt evoked memories of a crime? Maybe—unconsciously—she was motivated to be a juror in order to right some kind of wrong. Maybe that's the toughness the prosecutors sensed."

"Possible," he said.

"Trafficant *was* an attempted rapist, Milo. And he dropped out of sight right after the party."

"On the lam?"

"Why else would he disappear at the height of his celebrity? All those years behind bars, then he's a best-seller; it wouldn't have made sense to quit unless he had something to hide. He *and*

Lowell—the publicity would have been devastating. So maybe he took the money and ran. For all we know, he's on some tropical island living off his royalties."

He rubbed his face and contemplated the table light. "For that to make sense, there would have to be no witnesses, meaning violence taken all the way."

"Maybe Lucy actually did witness a burial. Lowell and Trafficant and someone else getting rid of the body."

He thought a long time. "It's a helluva leap based on a dream. For all we know, Trafficant disappeared because he died. Blew all his dough on dope and OD'd. He was a psychopath loser. Don't they always end up doing something self-destructive?"

"Usually. But still, the idea of him and Lucy, up there at the same time, her blocking out that summer, and now she's dreaming about a dead girl. . . . I could call Trafficant's publisher and see if they know where he is. If you feel up to it, you could run a background check."

"Sure, why not. . . . Best-seller." Shaking his head. "What is it with these intellectuals anyway? All those fools marching for Caryl Chessman as if he was a saint. Norman Mailer with *his* pet creep, William Buckley rooting for that asshole Edgar Smith— beat a fifteen-year-old girl to death with a baseball bat."

I thought about that. "I suppose artists and writers can lead a pretty insulated life," I said. "No freeway jams or time cards. Getting paid to make things up, you could start to confuse your fantasies with reality."

"I think there's more to it, Alex. I think the so-called creative bunch believe they're *better* than everyone else, don't have to play by the same rules. I remember once, when I was first on the force, I pulled jail duty down at the Hall of Justice, and some sociology professor was leading a tour—earnest students, pens and notebooks. They walked past one asshole's cell and it was full of drawings—bloody stuff but very well done; the guy had real talent. Not that it stopped him from robbing liquor stores and pistol-whipping the owners. Prof and the kids were totally blown away. How could someone that talented be in there. Such injustice! They started talking to the guy. He's a stone psychopath, so he immediately smells an opening and plays them like guitars: Mr. Misunderstood Artist, poor baby robbed 'cause he couldn't afford paints and canvas."

He shook his head. "Goddamn professor actually came up to

me and *demanded* to know who the guy's parole officer was. Letting me know it was *criminal* for such a gifted fellow to be *shackled. That's* the equation they make, Alex: If you're talented, you're entitled to privileges. Every few years you see another bullshit article, some idealistic fool setting up a program teaching inmates to paint or sculpt or play piano or write fucking short stories. Like that's going to make a damn bit of difference. Truth is, there's always been plenty of talent in jail. Visit any penitentiary, you'll hear great music, see lots of nifty artwork. If you ask me, psychopaths are *more* talented than the rest of us. But they're still fucking psychopaths."

"There's actually a theory to that effect," I said. "Psychopathy as a form of creativity. And you're right, there's no shortage of artistically brilliant people who had low moral IQ's: Degas, Wagner, Ezra Pound, Philip Larkin. From what I hear Picasso was pretty hard to live with."

"So why are people so goddamn stupid?"

"Naïveté, wanting to believe the best about others—who knows? And it's not just the creative bunch who buys into it. Years ago, social psychologists discovered something called the halo effect. Most people have no trouble believing that if you're good at one thing it transfers to unrelated areas. It's why athletes get rich endorsing products."

"Yeah," he said. "Trafficant shoulda stuck around. Somebody would have paid him to endorse cutlery."

"Lowell set him loose on society. Dropped him in a totally unstructured situation full of booze, dope, groupies. And cute little kids."

He laughed wearily. "Get us together, feeling like failures, and we do build a nice house of cards. I'll grant you it's interesting—scumbag on the loose almost always spells some kind of trouble. But like you said, Lucy could have read about him or heard about him from her brother. Maybe the goddamn dream is pure fiction."

"Could be," I admitted. "He got plenty of media coverage."

"Much as I like her, she's got problems, right? The head in the oven, this paranoid talk about someone trying to kill her. And those hang-up calls. I feel like a bum saying this, but now that I know she's been wanting to get close to me, I'd be an idiot not to wonder if she made them up to get attention. Even the way she tried to kill herself has a touch of that, doesn't it? Gas, with the drapes open?"

He gulped down the rest of his beer and looked at me.

"Yes, there is a hysterical quality to it," I said. "But let's be charitable and assume that even if she is making things up it's out of neediness rather than manipulation. That still doesn't eliminate the possibility that something traumatized her that summer. Don't forget, she's not trumpeting herself as a victim or trying to make anything out of the dream. On the contrary, she tends to minimize things, just as she did with the hang-ups. She's an ostrich, Milo, blocking out that entire summer. My gut tells me *something* happened when she was four and it's stuck down in her unconscious. Something that relates—directly or indirectly— to Lowell. She's not the only one with strong feelings about him. The half brother called him a total sonofabitch. *He's* in the real estate business and his big fantasy's foreclosing on Dad's land. Maybe that summer was bad for all the Lowell kids."

"Okay," he said. "Let's say we do somehow get to the bottom of it, find out Daddy *did* do something terrible twenty-one years ago. And let's assume Lucy gets herself to a point where she can deal with it. Then what? Bring the bastard to the bar of justice? You know what uncorroborated memories are worth in court. And the fact that it came out in therapy makes it even weaker. Nowadays prosecutors assume anything retrieved in a shrink's office is bullshit till proven otherwise. Too many cases thrown out of court, too much pop-psych crap, satanic bullshit— if you *feel* you've been abused, you *have* been."

"Baby-with-the-bathwater," I said, "just like when the courts tossed out hypnotic evidence. But you know as well as I do hypnosis *does* help some witnesses remember facts. And plenty of patients do retrieve valid memories during therapy. I've seen dozens of corroborations. The key is never to plant anything in a patient's head and never to lead. Stay skeptical as hell but keep it to yourself, and if you end up with something, check it out to the max."

"I know, I know, I'm just saying it's an uphill battle."

"Look, even if it never goes anywhere legally, I think, at some point, knowing what really happened—or didn't—will help her."

"What if we learn Daddy did something, can't touch him legally, and the bastard gets away with it? What does *that* do to her psyche?"

"So what do you suggest, drop it?"

"I'm not suggesting anything, just creating problems to keep your mind active."

"What a pal," I said. "Anyway, it's probably theoretical. After the way the last session went, I doubt Lucy'll want to see me. Maybe she'll hook up with Embrey—maybe seeing a woman will make it easier. Whoever her therapist turns out to be, they'll need to know what's going on."

"Think they'll keep her in past the seventy-two?"

"Not unless she really falls apart. It's what'll happen when she gets out that worries me."

Neither of us spoke for a while. I thought of all the possibilities we'd just raised. Wondered if Lucy would connect with Embrey. I found myself hoping so.

"What?" he said.

"That summer," I said. "At least we could try to narrow things down by finding out if any dark-haired girls were reported raped or murdered or missing in Topanga that summer. If they were, we've got possible corroboration. If not, that will also define the focus of Lucy's therapy. Either way, she doesn't need to be told until the time's right."

"Narrow things, huh?"

"I can't see it hurting."

He scraped a tooth with a fingernail. "Guess I could make a call to Malibu Sheriffs. It's a low-crime neighborhood, there shouldn't be too much paper to wade through, assuming they keep their old files. I can also look into any public records on Mr. Trafficant. When exactly was this party?"

"August—mid-August."

He took out his notepad and wrote it down. His beer glass was empty and he reached for a breadstick.

"Hope she heals," he said softly.

"Amen."

Twirling the breadstick, he put it down. "Haven't had lunch yet. You in any mood to eat?"

"Not really."

"Me neither."

11

He'd left his unmarked around the corner from the restaurant, in a loading zone, and a meter maid was approaching it with a predatory look in her eyes.

Milo flashed his badge, wagged his finger, and grinned. The meter maid snorted, returned to her buggy, and putt-putted away.

"Power!" he said. "Intoxicating as fine cognac and it won't damage your liver."

As he got in the car, I said, "Anything new on the Santa Ana murder?"

"Shwandt's lawyers are going to use it as grounds for a mistrial."

"You're kidding."

"In lawyer logic, the similarity between this one and the Bogeyman murders casts doubt on Jobe's guilt for all of them. We only had physical evidence on Carrie, Marie Rosenhut, and Berna Mendoza. All the others were circumstantial."

"So what? He still did *those* three."

"Three versus fifteen. The victim load—their phrase—prejudiced the jury against him and was responsible for the death penalty. They want a retrial on Carrie and the other two physicals, too—fruit of the poisoned tree or some shit like that."

"Absurd," I said. "Like you said, anyone who'd been at the trial or read the transcripts would have had enough information to copycat."

He put his hand on my shoulder.

"Logic has nothing to do with it. It's a *game*. There's a whole subspecies of sharpies makes a living filing death penalty appeals. They've got it down to a science, and we pay for it with our taxes."

He shook his head and laughed.

"What does that say about our society, Alex? A piece of shit like Shwandt can cut up women and kids, gouge their eyes out, shit on them, and get himself a supporting case of legal beagles, access to a law library, three squares, TV, magazines, nutritious snacks. I mean, let's cut through all the theology and ideology and tell me what reason can there possibly be to let someone like that *live*?"

"No argument from me."

"Does that mean you've finally converted?"

"To what?"

"The Church of Abject Hostility."

"Depends on what day you catch me."

He laughed and started his engine.

I said, "Do you think there's really any chance of a new trial?"

"Who the hell knows? The goddamn press corps loves the slimy fuck. He feeds them like trained seals."

I wondered how Lucy would react to the legal circus. Would she see it as diminishing what she'd done in that jury box?

Right now that seemed the least of her problems.

I called Woodbridge Hospital and used my title to cadge information from a nurse.

The patient was still sleeping. Dr. Embrey had not come in yet.

I tried to reach Peter Lowell. No answer.

Phoning my service, I discovered Dr. Wendy Embrey had left a message. My callback got her voice mail. I said I'd be happy to speak to her and returned to the Seville.

I couldn't rid myself of the thought that something had happened to Lucy that summer. Couldn't erase the idea of a little girl and a paroled killer thrown together. Heading north on Westwood Boulevard, I drove to Vagabond Books, parked in the back, and entered the store.

The owner was playing his sax. He looked up as I approached, not missing a note. Then he recognized me and said, "Hey."

The glass case of first editions fronting the register had something new in it, along with the books. Big silver automatic.

He saw me looking at it. "There's a guy running around robbing used bookstores. Comes in just before closing time, pulls a gun, beats and sodomizes the clerk, and takes the cash. Kid over at Pepys Books is getting tested for AIDS."

"God."

He fingered his ponytail. "So what can I do for you?"

"Terrence Trafficant. *From Hunger to Rage.*"

He took the gun out, put it in his waistband, and stepped out from behind the counter. Ambling over to the rear of the store, he came back with a worn-looking paperback. Bright red cover, black title letters that resembled knife slashes.

Two cover blurbs:

"It stirs and jolts with all the cruel authority of the electric chair!"—Time

"Twisted, heroic, visionary, touched with genius, Trafficant holds us by the scruff and forces us to stare into our own nightmare. This may be one of the most important books of our century."—Denton Mellors, The Manhattan Book Review

"Doing some kind of psychology research?" he said, ringing up the sale. "You couldn't be reading for pleasure. It's really a piece of crap."

I opened the book. More raves from *Newsweek, Vogue, The Washington Post,* the *Times* on both coasts.

"The critics didn't think so."

"The critics are brainless sheep. Trust me, it's crap."

"Well," I said, paying him, "you've got the gun."

I got home at three, feeling antsy, yet tired. The ocean was green and silky. Putting the book on the coffee table, I went out, lay down on a lounge chair, caught a face full of ultraviolet, and fell asleep.

Robin kissed me awake.

"Someone on the phone for you."

"What time is it?"

"Five-fifteen."

"Must have dozed off."

She wiped my forehead. "You're really hot. Better watch that sun, honey."

I took the call in the kitchen, rubbing my eyes and clearing my throat. "Dr. Delaware."

"Doctor, this is Audrey from Dr. Wendy Embrey's office. Dr. Embrey said to tell you she'd like to meet with you concerning Lucretia Lowell, if you've got the time. Would sometime tomorrow be okay?"

"Tonight would be okay, too."

"Dr. Embrey's all over the place tonight—she attends at a bunch of different hospitals. How about tomorrow around lunchtime?"

"Sure. Where?"

"She'll be over at the university all morning. If it's convenient, she could meet you in the med school dining room at twelve-thirty."

"That would be fine."

"Good, I'll tell her."

"How's Ms. Lowell doing?"

"I'm sure she's doing as well as can be expected."

I read *From Hunger to Rage* over breakfast. The bookseller had been right.

Trafficant's style was crude and uncontrolled, boiling with junior-high revolutionary rhetoric and obscenities. His editor had left his faulty spelling and grammar intact, aiming, I suppose, for gritty authenticity.

In the first half, he worked two themes to the death: "Society screwed me" and "I'm getting even." The next fifty pages were letters he'd written to various celebrities and officials. Only two had answered, the congressman from Trafficant's home district in Oklahoma—who responded with a Dear Constituent form letter —and M. Bayard Lowell, who praised Trafficant's "bloody poetry."

The two men began to correspond, Trafficant ranting and Lowell commiserating. The final page was a photocopy of Trafficant's approved parole application.

A biography and picture were on the inside back cover, the mug shot the papers had run.

> *Terrence Gary Trafficant, of uncertain parentage and hot blood, was born April 13, 1931, in Walahachee, Oklahoma. Beaten often and suckled by wolves, he spent his formative years in various institutions and hells-on-earth. His first major punitive adventure came at the age of ten, when he was locked up at The Oklahoma Institute for Children for stealing cigarettes. He proved an uncooperative prisoner and alternated for the next thirty years between steadily escalating violence and incarceration, much of it in solitary confinement. He brings a unique perspective to our perception of right and wrong.* From Hunger to Rage *has been purchased for adaptation as a major motion picture.*

A psychopath making it in Hollywood—not a huge stretch. Yet Trafficant had turned his back on it.

A best-seller who admired the Düsseldorf Monster.

Steadily escalating violence. . . . The more I thought about it, the harder it was to ignore his presence that summer.

Call his publisher . . . too late to phone New York.

I let my own imagination run on: Trafficant seducing the long-haired girl. Things getting out of hand . . . or maybe she'd resisted and he'd raped, again, then killed her. And told Lowell. Lowell panicking, rushing to bury the evidence, unaware that a little girl was watching.

A little girl who wet the bed—maybe dank sheets had aroused her.

Waking and walking and witnessing.

And paying for it now.

The med school cafeteria was a mass of flatware clatter, white coats everywhere. Soon after I walked in, a pretty Asian woman in a plum-colored silk suit came up to me.

"Dr. Delaware? Wendy Embrey."

She was young and petite with long, straight, blue-black hair and onyx eyes. A faculty picture badge clipped to her lapel showed her hair permed. W. TAKAHASHI-EMBREY, M.D., PSYCHIATRY.

"I've got a table over there," she said. "Would you like to get some lunch?"

"No, I'm fine."

She smiled. "Have you eaten here before?"

"Occasionally."

"Are you on staff?" she said, as we walked to her table.

"Crosstown."

"I interned crosstown. Are you in Psychiatry?"

"Pediatrics. I'm a child psychologist."

She gave me a curious look and we sat down. On her tray were a tuna sandwich, coleslaw, red Jell-O, and milk. She unwrapped her utensils and spread her napkin on her lap. "But Lucretia *was* your patient?"

"Yes. Once in a while I see adults—short-term consults, usually stress-related. She was referred by the police."

Another curious look. She couldn't have been more than a year or two out of residency, but she'd learned her therapeutic nuances.

"I consult to the police occasionally," I said.

"What kind of stress had she been through?"

"She was a juror on the Bogeyman trial."

She picked up her fork. "Well, that could certainly be difficult. How long did you treat her?"

"Only a few sessions. She came to me because of sleep problems. A recurrent nightmare and, later, some somnambulism."

"Walking in her sleep?"

"At least once, before the suicide attempt. She woke up in her kitchen. I guess, looking back, it can be seen as a rehearsal for the attempt. She also had an episode of something that looked like narcolepsy—falling asleep at her desk at work and waking up on the floor."

"Yes, she told me about that. Said you'd sent her to a neurologist and he pronounced her healthy."

"Phil Austerlitz. He's on staff here."

"Did he come up negative, the way she claims?"

"Yes. He thought it was stress."

The fork dipped into the coleslaw. "That's what the neurologist at Woodbridge said, too. Interesting, though, the somnambulism. Do you think the suicide attempt could have occurred during some sort of sleepwalking trance? I've read case histories of self-destruction during arousal from deep sleep. Have you ever seen anything that extreme?"

"No suicide attempts, but I have treated children with night terrors who hurt themselves thrashing and walking around. I even had a family where the children *and* the father had terrors. The father used to try to strangle the mother in his sleep. And there are cases of people committing murder and claiming somnambulism.''

''Claiming? You don't believe it's possible?''

''It's possible, but it's rare.''

She ate some slaw, looked at her sandwich, then at me.

''It's a strange case. Her denial's so absolute. Usually, with attempters, you see just the opposite: guilt, confessions, promises never to do it again, because they feel physically lousy and want to get out of hold. The really severe ones—the ones who're *sorry* they failed—either get really mad or go mute. But Lucretia's cooperative and articulate; she understands why she has to be observed. Yet she remains *adamant* that she never tried to kill herself. Which would be a dumb approach to take if you were trying to convince your psychiatrist to let you go, right? In the wrong hands you could be tagged as delusional.''

''You don't see her as delusional?''

''I'm not sure how I see her yet, but she sure doesn't look crazy. Maybe I'm missing something, but I think she truly believes, on a *conscious* level, that she didn't make an attempt.''

''Did she give you an explanation for what happened?''

''She says she fell asleep and woke up in the hospital and that her first thought when you told her why she was there was someone had tried to kill her. Now that she's fully awake, she realizes it makes no sense. All in all, she's pretty confused. I could be missing the boat completely, but I don't see any schizophrenic output. Just depression—but not the crushing depression you'd associate with an attempt. I had our psychologist test her for a bipolar disorder. She seems to have such a big stake in keeping busy, I thought maybe there was some mania going on and the daytime sleep was crashing after an episode. He found her MMPI somewhat elevated on depression and anxiety but no hint of anything manic. And her Lie Scale was normal, so she seemed to be telling the truth. He said unless she's been tested a lot and knows how to fool the instruments, there's no serious personality disturbance.''

''She'd have other reasons to be anxious,'' I said. ''Just before the attempt, we got into some areas that upset her. She had a very isolated childhood—a mother who died when she was an infant, a highly troubled relationship with an absentee father. But she was always coherent, and if she was really disturbed I doubt she could have lasted three months on that jury."

"What areas upset her?"

I described the dream.

"Interesting," she said. "Any indication he molested her?"

"She denies ever being with him, but her brother told me she spent a summer up at his place when she was four. So she's either denying *that* or she's repressed it completely. As to what happened up there, I don't know."

I told her about Trafficant, emphasizing how speculative everything was.

"Well," she said, "at the very least it sounds like lots of garbage coming to the surface. Going to take a long time to sift through. This is one where we'll have to tread carefully."

"Adding to the garbage, she had a brief episode of working as a prostitute when she was eighteen. She denies any guilt, but there's probably lots. And she developed a crush on one of the detectives who worked on the Bogeyman case, the one who referred her to me. He's gay."

She put the sandwich down. "Just a few sessions and all *that* came out?"

"Most of it during the last one," I said. "Too much, too soon, but I couldn't stop her. That night she put her head in the oven."

"Lovely."

"Are you planning to let her go after the seventy-two's up?"

"She's not psychotic or violent, I can't see a judge giving me any more time. But she sure needs careful outpatient follow-up. . . . A prostitute—she seems so prim. How long is brief?"

"Part of a summer. She claims she's been celibate since. And Phil Austerlitz said she had a real aversion to being touched."

She put her hands together. "I can see what you mean about that summer with her father. . . . Despite all that, she relates well to a male therapist—talks very fondly about you. Are you planning to follow her?"

"The last thing I want is for her to be abandoned again," I said, "but I may not be right for her. The policeman she likes is a close friend."

I recounted Lucy's request for permission to love Milo. My silence. The reaction.

"So she doesn't know he's gay."

"Not yet."

She opened the milk carton. "I don't want to get personal, but is he your lover?"

"No, just a friend," I said. Adding, "I'm straight," and wondering why it sounded so defensive.

"I can see what you mean by complications."

"It might be in her best interests to transfer her care, if it can be done without traumatizing her. When I heard she was going to be seen by a woman, I was glad."

"We seem to have a good rapport," she said. "She cooperates, appears to be relating. Then I review my notes and realize she hasn't told me much."

"I felt the same way about her in the beginning," I said. "Like I said, most of the substantive material came out in the last session."

"Maybe it's her family style. I spoke to her brother, and he didn't tell me much of anything either. Given the situation, you'd think he'd want me to know as much as possible."

"He doesn't know much about her himself. He's a half brother, hasn't seen her in over twenty years."

"No, I'm not talking about the one who brought her in. This was the other one, Peter. He phoned me this morning from Taos. Said he'd heard about Lucretia from Ken. Very upset about not being able to be with her, but he couldn't fly back. And when I tried to ask questions, he backed away, like he was in a big hurry to get off the phone."

"Why can't he be with her?"

"Business obligations. I called Ken—he's gone back to Palo Alto. He knew nothing, like you said. Pretty nice of him to pay for her care."

"I got the sense he wants to make contact."

"Me, too. He offered to handle everything—he seems to have money. Lucretia has no insurance because she quit her job, so that's lucky. The hospital looks askance at doctors who treat nonpaying patients. Nowadays, we have to be bookkeepers, too, right?"

I nodded.

"Anyway," she said, "sounds like a complicated family. Are there any other relatives in town for support?"

"In town," I said. "But not for support."

12

I told her who Lucy's father was, and she reached for her Jell-O without registering much reaction.

"I was a math major, never much for fiction," she said. "Then you get into med school and your whole world really narrows. . . . So the pain of abandonment would be that much worse. He's available to the whole world but not to her . . . and now that dream, that's pretty darn Freudian. This is starting to sound like old-fashioned psychiatry. I don't get much of that."

"What do you do mostly? Medication?"

"Almost totally. I attend at six different ER's and I rarely get to do any follow-up. So yes, if Lucretia's willing to see me, I'd be very interested. She's an interesting woman."

"Where's your office?"

"Tarzana. I rent space from another psychiatrist." She gave me her card. "Where are you?"

"Malibu."

"Not too shabby. I would like you to stay closely in touch. We need to make sure she doesn't see you as yet another man who's walked out on her."

"I was planning to visit her while she's in. When would you like me to start?"

"Any time you're ready. I'll leave your name with the charge nurse."

She ate some more Jell-O and finished her milk, wiping away the white mustache. "While you're there, though, I'd keep it casual. Especially in terms of your gay friend. I'd just as soon hold off on any more surprises until I have a better feel for what's going on with her. Make sense?"

"Yes, but once she's out, she's likely to seek him out. She views him as a protector."

I described how Lucy and Milo had connected at the trial.

"Well," she said, "for now I'd tell him to keep a low profile. What she needs is protection from her own impulses."

I drove home thinking Wendy Embrey might be very good for Lucy. But I wondered how Lucy would react to a change in therapists.

I had conflicts of my own about the transition: relieved at the chance to get out of a mess, but more than a bit guilty at how good that freedom sounded. And I still wanted to know what had happened that summer. For her sake or mine? The answers weren't comforting.

I put on some music and drove like a robot. When I got home, surfers' vans were parked all along the turnoff to the public beach.

When I opened the door, the phone was ringing.

My service with a long-distance call from Ken Lowell.

"Hi, doctor. Anything new on Lucy?"

"She seems to be holding her own."

"I spoke to Dr. Embrey and she sounded pretty sharp, but I'm a little confused. Who's going to be Lucy's doctor?"

"As long as Lucy's in the hospital, Dr. Embrey's in charge."

"Unfortunately, I can't seem to reach Dr. Embrey now. Are you going to be speaking to her? If you are, I'd like to pass something along. I think she should know."

"Sure."

"I got a call from my brother early this morning, explaining why he hadn't shown up for dinner. Some sort of business emergency. In Taos, New Mexico, of all places. I told him what had happened to Lucy and he really went ballistic. But then he said he couldn't come back because he was tied up."

"He said the same thing to Dr. Embrey. Must have called her right after he spoke to you."

"But it doesn't make any sense. Because when we met last week he wasn't involved in any business—told me he'd been unemployed for a long time. So what was so urgent?"

"I really don't know, Ken."

"No, no reason for you to. . . . I have to tell you, doctor, he sounded very edgy. I can't help thinking he's in some kind of trouble. I was just wondering if Lucy said anything to you that you could divulge without breaking confidentiality."

"She really didn't, Ken."

"All right. Thanks. I'll be back and forth to L.A. for the next few weeks. Would visiting Lucy be appropriate?"

"I'd talk to Dr. Embrey about that."

"Yes, of course. I have to tell you, doctor, this is strange."

"What is?"

"Instant family."

At 4:10 Robin called to let me know she'd been invited to attend a showcase that night at the Whiskey, a band of thrash-metal heroes brandishing guitars she'd built.

"Would you mind if I passed?" I said.

"If I had a good excuse, I'd pass too. Zero showed up at the site and invited me personally."

"What time do you think it'll be over?"

"Late."

"How about if I come by before and we grab some dinner "

"What about Spike?"

"I can bring takeout."

"That would be great."

"When should I get there?"

"Soon as possible."

I picked up earplugs at a pharmacy in Point Dume and sand-wiches and drinks at a deli nearby. It took forty minutes to get to the jobsite. Several trucks were pulling away, and Robin was con-ferring with a bare-chested man with a tobacco-stained walrus mustache. Nearly bald except for some yellow back fringe and a ponytail, he was concentrating hard as she spoke.

She saw me and waved and continued to talk to him, waving a roll of blueprints. Spike was on the rear bed of her truck, and he stuck his frog face above the tailgate and barked. I went over and lifted him out. He licked my face and waved his forelegs in the air, and when I put him down, he stood up, hugged my knees, and rubbed his head against my leg.

"What a *handsome* guy you are," I said. "Handsome" was his

favorite word, after "meat loaf." He started panting; then his nose went after the bag in my hand.

Robin said, "Okay, Larry?" in a tone of voice that meant she was working at patience.

"Yes, ma'am."

"So let's try for inspection by next Monday. If there are any other problems, let me know *right* away." She shifted the blueprints to the other hand.

"Yes, ma'am. For sure." Larry looked at me.

"This is Dr. Delaware. He pays the bills."

"Sir," said Larry, "we're fixing up a nice new place for you, you bet."

"Great," I said.

He scratched his head, walked up toward the house, and began talking to another worker. The pond was empty and half filled with dirt. What had once been a garden was a muddy pit. The new house's roof points sliced the sky at sharp angles. The sun that showed through was platinum-white.

"What do you think?" she said.

"Very nice."

"Soon." She kissed my cheek.

I kept looking at the construction. The framing was complete and the walls had been papered and partially mudded. The mud was ridged with trowel marks and still wet in spots. The original house had been redwood walls and a cedar roof. "Kindling on a foundation," the fire marshal had called it. The new building would be stucco and tile. I'd get used to it.

Robin put her arm around me and we walked to the truck. "Sorry about tonight."

"Hey, everyone has their emergencies. Here's something for your sanity."

I gave her the earplugs and she laughed. Pulling down the tailgate, she spread an army blanket and we set out the food. We ate listening to the sounds of hammer guns and saws, feeding Spike bits of sandwich and watching birds circle overhead. Soon, I felt pretty good.

I brought Spike home, fed him dinner, took him for a jog on the beach, and settled him in front of the tube. Then I showered, changed into fresh clothes, and headed for Woodbridge Hospital, making it to the parking lot by seven.

The Psychiatric Unit was on the third floor, behind swinging doors labeled LOCKED. I pressed a buzzer, gave my name, and heard the tumblers click. Pushing, I entered a long well-lit hallway.

The chocolate carpet was freshly vacuumed, the walls a pleasant brownish-white. Ten closed doors on each side, the nursing station at the end. One nurse sat there. Soft conversation came from somewhere, along with television dialogue, radio music, and an occasional ringing phone.

When I got to the station, the nurse said, "Dr. Delaware . . . yes, here it is. Lucretia's in 14, that's back there on the left side." She was very young and had yellow cornrowed hair studded with tiny blue ribbons, and beautiful teeth.

I retraced my steps. Before I got to 14, the door to 18 opened and a small, sweet-faced woman around fifty looked out at me. She wore a pink dress, pearls, and pink pumps. The back wall of her room was covered with family photos, and the aroma of chocolate chip cookies poured out.

"Have a nice day," she said, smiling.

I smiled back, trying not to look at the bandages around her wrists.

Her door closed and I knocked on Lucy's.

"Come in."

The room was eight by eight, painted that same brownish-white, with a bed, a fake-wood nightstand, a tiny doorless closet, and a desk and chair that looked child-sized. The TV was mounted high on the wall, the remote control bolted to the nightstand. Next to it was a stack of paperbacks. The top one was entitled *Grievous Sin*.

No bathroom. A single immovable window, embedded with metal mesh, offered a view of the parking lot and the supermarket that was the hospital's neighbor.

Lucy sat on the bed, on top of the covers, dressed in jeans and a white button-down shirt. Her sleeves were rolled to the elbow, her hair was pinned up, and her feet were bare. An open magazine rested in her lap. She could have been a college girl relaxing in a dorm room.

"Hi." She put the magazine aside. *Good Homemaking*. The cover promised "Holiday Snacks Your Family Will Love You For."

"How's it going?" I said, sitting in the chair.

"I'll be glad to get out of here."

"They treating you okay?"

"Fine, but it's still prison."

"I spoke to Dr. Embrey. She seems nice."

"Nice enough." Flat voice.

I waited.

"Nothing against her," she said, "but I'm not going to have anything to do with her when I get out."

"Why's that?"

"Because she's too young. How much experience could she have?"

"Did she do or say something to weaken your confidence?"

"No, she's smart enough. It's just her age. And the fact that she's the one who's keeping me in—a jailor's a jailor. Once I'm out, I'm finished with this place and anyone associated with it. Do you think that's foolish?"

"I think you need someone to talk to."

"What about you?"

I smiled and touched the gray at my temple. "So I'm old enough for you."

"You're *experienced*, Dr. Delaware. And we've already got a relationship, why start from scratch?"

I nodded.

"You don't agree," she said.

"I'll never abandon you, Lucy."

"But you think I should see Embrey." Her voice had tightened.

"I think ultimately you make the choice. I don't want you to feel abandoned, but I also don't want to sabotage Dr. Embrey. She seems very capable, and she's interested in you."

"She's a kid."

I said nothing.

She scooted to the edge of the bed and sat there, legs dangling, toes brushing the carpet. "So that's it for my therapy with you."

"I'll always be here for you and I'll help you any way I can, Lucy. I just want you to do what's best for you."

She looked away.

"Who knows, maybe I don't even need a therapist." She turned back to me sharply. "Do you really think I tried to kill myself?"

"It looks that way, Lucy."

A painful smile flickered. "Well, at least you're honest. And at least you call me Lucy. *They* call me *Lucretia. He* gave me that name. After Lucretia *Borgia*—he *hates* women. Jo's full name was *Jocasta.* How's that for *Oedipal?*"

"What about your brothers?"

"No, the *boys'* names are okay. He let the *boys* be named by their *mothers.* He was only out to ruin the girls."

"Ruin, how?"

"Rotten names, for one. How can I have confidence in this place when they don't even respect me enough to call me what I want? I keep telling them Lucy, but each time a new nurse comes on shift, all they do is read the chart. Lucretia this, Lucretia that. 'How are *you,* Lucretia?' "

She got up and looked out the window.

"I *didn't* put my head in that oven," she said. "I have no idea how I ended up there, but I didn't *do* it. Not sleepwalking or any other way."

"How can you be sure?"

"Because I just *know.* Not that I'd ever tell Embrey that. She'd think I'm crazy."

"She doesn't," I said. "And neither do I. But I do think you might have done it while sleepwalking. It's unusual but not impossible."

"Maybe for someone else, but not me."

She turned around. She'd cried, and moisture streaked her cheeks.

"I know it sounds bizarre and paranoid, but someone's trying to kill me. I told Embrey I changed my mind about that because I didn't want her to lock me up forever. But there's something you should know about. Can I tell you in confidence, without your telling her?"

"That puts me in a bind, Lucy."

"Okay," she said. "I understand. I don't want to do that to you. But either way, she won't know. Not until I get out of here."

We didn't speak. She dried her eyes and smiled.

"Thanks for coming. Thanks for doing what you think is right. . . . I didn't put my head in that oven. Why would I do that? I want to live."

She dried her cheeks. "Those phone calls. I thought they were nothing—maybe they were nothing. But I *am* . . . going to tell you, even though you'll probably think I'm nuts and I'll get locked up till who-knows-when."

She began to cry.

I put my hand on her shoulder and it made her cry harder. When she stopped, she said, "I so don't want to be locked up. I cherish my independence."

"I won't do anything to lock you up, if you promise not to hurt yourself."

"That's easy. I don't want to hurt myself. I promise, Dr. Delaware—I *swear*."

She sat quietly for several moments. "One time—right after I started seeing you—I came home and found some of my stuff moved."

"What kind of stuff?"

"Clothes . . . underwear. I'm no neat freak, but I do have places for everything. And my panties and bras had been moved —reversed in the drawer—as if someone had taken them out and put them back, folded a way I never fold them. And one pair of panties was missing."

"Why didn't you tell anyone about this?"

"I don't know. It only happened once, and I thought maybe I was imagining it. I'd just done a load of laundry the day before; I figured it was possible I'd left the panties in the machine and maybe I *had* put my stuff back differently—absentminded. I mean, I'm not the kind of person to imagine the worst. But now I realize someone must have been in my place."

She grabbed my arm. "Maybe that's why I started having the dream again. Because I felt threatened. I don't know; sometimes I think I *am* imagining everything. But I'm not crazy."

I patted her shoulder and she let go of my arm.

"Did Ken really save me?"

"Yes."

"What's he like?"

"He seems nice."

"Another thing I'm worried about is, where's Puck? Embrey's giving me some story about his calling her from New Mexico, but that makes no sense."

"He called Ken from there, too."

She took hold of my arm again, harder. "Then why hasn't he called *me*?"

I was silent.

"It doesn't make sense," she said.

"He told both Dr. Embrey and Ken that he was on some kind of business trip. He had a dinner date with Ken a couple of nights ago but didn't show up. That's how Ken came to save you. He was looking for Puck at your place because Puck told him you were close."

"We are. . . . Puck never told me about any dinner date."

"It was a trial balloon the two of them had worked out, to see how they'd get along. If they did, they were going to get you involved."

"Protecting me? Typical." She stood up and yanked her hair loose. "Puck's always trying to protect me, even though—so why hasn't he called?"

"Even though what?"

Hesitation. "Even though he's not the toughest guy in the world himself."

"What does he do for a living?"

Another pause. "Different things, over the years."

She turned around, brown eyes hot. "Right now, he's not doing anything. He has three years of college with a major in history. Try to find something decent with that. Well, I'm sure he'll be back soon and we'll straighten it out. I've got lots of things to straighten out. Thank God I'm getting out soon."

13

I left the hospital parking lot and got onto the freeway. I agreed with Embrey: Lucy really believed she hadn't tried to kill herself.

Had the walk to the oven occurred during sleepwalking?

Not impossible, I supposed. For some people, slumber could be a shadow life. Some sleepwalkers denied walking; lots of snorers claimed they were silent. I'd seen patients experience shrieking night terrors only to wake up the next morning claiming they'd had sweet dreams. The man who'd tried to strangle his wife in his sleep refused to believe it until confronted by videotape.

And Lucy did have a history of fractured sleep.

So maybe it all boiled down to a physiological quirk.

But what of her newly expressed belief that someone had stolen her underwear?

The hang-up calls . . . delusional thinking?

Embrey had found no psychosis or major personality disorder, and neither had I.

Both of us wanting to believe the best?

Even Milo had put aside his cop cynicism and gotten more involved with her than anyone he'd met on the job before.

I remembered his guilt as he aired his doubts about her credibility.

My quick response that she was needy, rather than manipulative.

I thought about the way she'd just gotten me to promise not to collude in locking her up.

My *gut* was telling me she was sincere, but was that worth as much as I wanted to believe?

Should I have tried to convince her to stick with Embrey?

Maybe Embrey could handle that on her own.

"Who knows, maybe I don't even need a therapist."

Had I let that go by too easily?

Should haves, could haves. . . .

Tomorrow night she'd sleep in her own bed.

I hoped I hadn't made a terrible call.

I hoped freedom wouldn't kill her.

Milo phoned the next day, just after noon, and I recounted my visit to Woodbridge and Lucy's feelings about Wendy Embrey.

"What's Embrey like?"

"Personable, bright, motivated."

"But she ain't you."

"I'm not sure Lucy'll want me either. Last night she made noises about dropping out of therapy completely. A moment later, she's telling me she's scared someone's out to get her."

I told him about the underwear.

"All of a sudden, she *remembers* this?"

"She passed it off as absentmindedness, same way she dismissed the phone calls as technical problems. Like I said, she's not one to play victim. Has a hard time being dependent. She talks about her brother, Peter, as being her sole protector, but he's not exactly coming through. Out of town on urgent business, even though he hasn't worked for years. And he took the time to phone Ken and Embrey but not Lucy."

"Avoiding her?"

"Looks like it. Lucy insists they're close, but he's an odd one. I met him once when he came with her to a session. Refused to come in and sat in the car the whole time. Kind of withdrawn."

"Withdrawn as in schizo?"

"It was only a brief encounter and I didn't pick up anything bizarre—more like intensely shy. He was protective enough to shield her from meeting Ken right away, but when I asked Lucy what he did for a living she got very defensive and started making excuses for his being unemployed. As if she's used to protecting *him*. Now that she's in crisis, his failing to come through for her could be traumatic. Another abandonment's the last thing she needs."

"Should I visit her?"

"Embrey suggested you take a low profile for now, and I agree."

"Meaning?"

"You don't volunteer, but if she approaches you, don't turn her away."

"When's she getting out?"

"Tomorrow."

"All right, you're the doctors. . . . Anyway, what I was calling about is I talked to Malibu Sheriffs and they faxed me—if you're still interested in the dream."

"One way or the other, it's relevant to Lucy's mental state."

"Well, nothing juicy. No homicides or attempted homicides of females in the entire beach area from June to November of that year. And of the eight rapes they've got, seven were up in Oxnard, no victim matches to the long-haired girl. Two of them were probable domestics—middle-aged women—two were little kids, and the other three were Mexican bar scenes with hookers, all charges dropped. The eighth one *was* Malibu, but nowhere near Topanga. Ranch up in Decker Canyon, some cowboys getting drunk and assaulting a lady horse groom."

"Did the lady have long hair?"

"The lady was fifty-five, two hundred pounds and gray-haired. No Topanga missing females, either, during that time span. They did send me paper on four missing persons cases in the area that never got closed, but once again they were all north, Oxnard and Malibu. Given the flavor of the times—flower children hitchhiking—four doesn't seem like a lot."

"Do any of the four match the girl in the dream?"

"I didn't really study them, Alex. Hold on, let me pull them out. . . . Number one is Jessica Martina Gallegos, Oxnard. Sixteen years old, high school sophomore, black hair, brown eyes, five one, hundred and fifty—doesn't sound long and leggy to me —last seen waiting for a bus at ten P.M. in front of the Teatro Carnival on Oxnard Boulevard. The pictures came through the fax pretty grainy, but I can see enough to tell you she doesn't have long flowing hair. Short and curly and light with dark roots.

"Number two, Iris Mae Jenrette, thirty-two, five-four, one-ten, blond and green, last seen at the Beachrider Motel, Point

Dume. . . . Apparently this one was out from Idaho on a honey-moon, had a fight with hubby, took the car, and split, didn't come home. . . . Long hair, but it's ultra-platinum and teased. Want the other two?"

"Why not."

"Karen Denise Best, nineteen, five-seven, one-seventeen, blond and blue. . . . Waitress at The Sand Dollar Restaurant in Paradise Cove, last seen working the dinner shift . . . reported missing by parents from New Bedford, Mass.; they didn't get their weekly phone call. . . .

And number four, Christine no-middle-name Faylen, also nineteen, five-five, one-twenty, brown and brown, freshman at Colorado State . . . another tourist, traveling with two friends, staying at a rented place in Venice. Says here she went for a Coke on the beach at Zuma and didn't return to her buddies. Both of those have long straight hair, but only Faylen's is dark."

"Five-five, one-twenty," I said. "Slender. She could be leggy. And the circumstances are interesting. Going for a drink in broad daylight and not coming back?"

"And what? She ends up in Topanga, ten, fifteen miles away, at a party? For all we know, she showed up the next day and the friends never bothered to let the sheriff know. Missing persons cases are like that. And no red flags on any of these. My vote is Lucy never witnessed any crime, Alex. Either she saw people having sex, and misconstrued it, or Daddy and/or Scumbag Trafficant did something to *her*. Or the whole thing's total fantasy."

"I'm sure you're right."

"But?"

"But what?"

"There's a 'but' in your voice."

"Would you mind if I did a little follow-up?"

"What kind of follow-up?"

"Calling the families of the four missing girls. Especially Faylen."

"Why, Alex?"

"To eliminate as many variables as possible for whoever ends up doing therapy with Lucy. For Lucy herself. She's sounding more and more confused. The clearer the information we have, the more likely we are to get close to the truth."

"What if no one ends up doing therapy with Lucy? You said she wanted to drop out."

"Then I wasted a few phone calls. Let's say she ends up on *your* doorstep. Wouldn't you want to know as much as possible if she starts convincing herself she witnessed a murder?"

"Guess so. . . . Okay, here're the numbers, I hope for your sake all of them did show up. Twenty-one years of grief ain't a pleasant thing to dig up."

I'd copied down:

Jessica Gallegos. Last Seen: 7/2. Parents, M/M Ernesto Gallegos.

Iris Jenrette. 7/29. Husband, James Jenrette.

Karen Best. 8/14. Parents, M/M Sherrell Best.

Christine Faylen. 8/21. Shelley Anne Daniels, Lisa Joanne Constantino. Parents, M/M David Faylen.

I sat for a long time trying to figure out how to cushion the shock of each call.

Then I punched buttons.

The Gallegos home number was now Our Lady of Mercy Thrift Shop. The Ventura/Oxnard directory listed a couple of dozen Gallegoses, none of them Ernesto or Jessica. The high school student would be close to forty now, maybe married, maybe with kids of her own. . . .

I turned to the next number. Iris Jenrette. Boise. A woman answered.

"Is James Jenrette there?"

"He's at work. Who's this?"

"I'm calling about some information he requested on homeowner's insurance."

"He never mentioned anything about that. We're already insured up the hilt."

"Is this Mrs. Jenrette?"

"Iris," she said impatiently. "I don't know what he's up to now. You'll have to call him back after nine. He's working late at the store."

"Sure," I said.

Dial tone.

The Best family's number in Massachusetts was busy, and at the Faylen household I got a recorded message: an older woman's voice softened by an undertone of laughter.

"Hi, you've reached the home of Cynthia and Dave, we're not in or maybe we are and are just too darn lazy to get off our butts and come to the phone. So if you're one of those persistent types, wait for the proverbial beep and speak your proverbial piece."

I tried Denver Information for a listing on Christine Faylen and got one immediately.

"Law offices."

"Christine Faylen, please."

"The office is closed, this is the exchange."

"I'd like to reach Ms. Faylen. It's important."

"One moment."

A few minutes later a woman came on.

"Chris Faylen."

"Ms. Faylen, I'm calling from the Records Department at the City of Malibu. We're going through our old files, and your name came up as the subject of a missing persons report twenty-one years ago."

"*What?*"

I gave her the exact date and time. "A Christine Faylen was reported missing from the Zuma Beach by Shelley Anne Daniels and Lisa Joanne Constan—"

"Shelley and Lisa, sure, sure, what a hoot. You're kidding, that's still on the *books?*"

"I'm afraid so."

She broke into loud, hearty laughter. "Unbelievable. Well, I can assure you I'm not missing—maybe a little mentally, but the bod's right here, safe and sound. Ha-ha."

"That's good to hear."

"All this time . . . no one's been looking for me, have they? God, this is so—" Guffaws.

"Not recently, it's just a matter of—"

"Unbelievable," she repeated. "What a scream. Do I have to fill out any forms or anything?"

"No, your verbal assurance is—"

"You're sure, now? Because I'm an attorney, it wouldn't do to be a nonentity. And I've seen all sorts of screw-ups when the paperwork's not complete—for all I know I haven't been accruing my Social Security all this time . . . unbe*liev*able."

"None of our records are sent to the federal government."

"You're sure?"

"Absolutely."

Giggles. "Missing persons. Ha ha ha. I was only gone for three *days,* met a—ha ha, no need to get into that. Anyway, thanks for calling."

"Pleasure, Ms. Faylen."

"Back from the Land of the Missing. Ha ha ha."

I tried Karen Best's number again. This time the phone rang three times before a woman said, "Hello."

"Mrs. Best?"

"Yes?"

"Mrs. Sherrell Best?"

"No, this is Taffy. Who is this?"

"I'm calling from California, trying to locate Karen Best."

Silence.

"Who *is* this?"

Her voice had ratcheted tight. A phony story wouldn't work.

"My name is Dr. Alex Delaware. I'm a psychologist who sometimes works with the Los Angeles police. Karen's name came up in a review of missing persons cases that I've been following up."

"Following them up how?"

"Checking whether or not the person ever showed up."

"Why?" More tension. My gut was tight, too.

"Because they may relate to a current case. I'm sorry, but I can't say any more, Mrs.—"

"What'd you say your name was?"

"Delaware. You can call Detective Milo Sturgis at the West Los Angeles Substation for verification."

I started to recite Milo's number.

She broke in. "Hold on."

The phone clanged down.

Moments later, a man said, "This is Craig Best. Karen was my sister. What's going on?"

I repeated what I'd told his wife.

"No, she was never found. What is this, some sort of a research project?"

"Your sister's name came up in relationship to another case."

"What kind of case?"

"An individual here in L.A.'s having memories of seeing a young woman abducted at a certain time and place. We've been reviewing missing persons cases that might be related."

"Memories? What, some kind of psychic? 'Cause we went through all that."

"No. This is a possible witness, but I have to emphasize it's very tenta—"

"What time and place are you talking about?"

"The Malibu area. Mid-August. Your sister was working as a waitress at a place called—"

"The Sand Dollar. Before that she worked in Beverly Hills."

"Waitressing?"

"Yeah, a Chinese place, Ah Loo. She got jobs in the fancy neighborhoods because she wanted to be an actress and thought she'd run into movie stars. God knows who she *did* run into. What makes you think it was Karen this witness saw?"

"We don't think anything of the sort, Mr. Best. The investigation's still at a very early stage, and I'm sorry if this—"

"Investigation?" he said. "We could never get Malibu Sheriffs to do a serious one. So what are *you* investigating?"

"Would you mind verifying a few things for me?" I read off Karen's height and weight.

He said, "Yeah, that's right."

"Blond hair—"

"*Jesus,*" he said. "I can't believe that's still on there. We told them she dyed it brunette that summer. Brilliant!"

"Why?"

"Why what?"

"Why'd she go from blond to brunette? It's usually the other way around."

"That was her point. *Everyone* in L.A. was blond. She wanted to stand out. Her natural hair was gorgeous; my parents thought it was—what color hair did this supposed witness see?"

"It's by no means a clear memory, but the girl's described as having long dark hair and long legs."

Silence.

"Karen had *really* long legs; everyone said she should model —Lord Jesus, are you telling me we might finally *get* something here?"

"No, I'm sorry," I said. "Everything's very tentative."

"Yeah," he said. "Of course. Sure. No reason to start hoping now. Nothing to hope for anyway. She's dead. I accepted that years ago, haven't thought of her as alive in a long time. But my father . . . it was him you were calling, wasn't it? He'll freak out."

"He still thinks she's alive?"

"At this point, I don't know what he thinks. Let's just say he's not the type to let go. Looking for Karen wiped him out financially. We bought the house from him as a favor, after my mother died and he moved to California."

"He lives out here?"

"Highland Park."

An hour and a half drive from Malibu. I said, "Did he move in order to look for Karen?"

"That was the official reason, but he's . . . what can I say? He's my dad. Speak to him, see for yourself."

"I don't want to upset him."

"Don't worry—you couldn't. Here's the address and number."

I thanked him.

He said, "Now what do you mean by abducted? Kidnapped, something worse?"

"The witness remembers seeing a girl being carried off by some men, but the witness was very young at the time, so the details may not be accurate. It may not even have been Karen. I'm sorry for having to make this call without giving you something more concrete. We're a long way from hard evidence."

"Very young. You mean a *kid*?"

"Yes."

"Oh. So this really *is* pretty weak. Are there other girls involved, too? Because I can't believe you'd go to the trouble just for Karen. Is this some sort of serial killer thing?"

"There's no reason to believe that, Mr. Best. I promise to let you know if anything comes up."

"I hope you mean that. Karen was my only sibling. I've got six kids of my own . . . don't know what that has to do with anything."

I did. Replacement.

"Is there anything else," I said, "that you want to tell me about her?"

"What's to tell? She was beautiful, sweet, a real good kid. She'd be forty next month. I thought about that when I turned thirty-eight. She's dead, isn't she?"

"I'm not in any—"

"Bottom line," he said sadly. "She has to be. I knew something bad happened when she stopped calling—she always called, at least once a week on Sunday, usually other days too. She'd never have let us dangle all these years. If she was alive, we'd have heard from her. She got involved with something terrible out there. If you find out what, no matter how bad it is, call me. Don't rely on my dad to tell me. Give me your number."

I did, along with Milo's.

Before I hung up, he thanked me, and that made me feel low.

14

Twenty-one years of grief.

Sherrell Best's number stared up at me. It wasn't going to get easier.

A woman's taped voice answered.

"Welcome to the Church of the Outstretched Hand. If you're calling about food donations, our warehouse is located on Sixteen-seventy-eight North Cahuenga Boulevard, between Melrose and Santa Monica. Our dropoff chute is open twenty-four hours a day—"

Figuring it for a wrong number, I hung up, redialed, and got the same tape. This time I listened to the end.

". . . specially canned goods, powdered milk, and baby formula. If you're calling for spiritual guidance, our twenty-four-hour Help Line is . . ."

I copied that number down. The tape ended with a quote from First Corinthians:

"Christ our passover is sacrificed for us: Therefore let us keep the feast, not with old leaven, neither with the leaven of malice and wickedness; but with the unleavened bread of sincerity and truth."

The Help Line was answered by another woman. I asked for Sherrell Best.

"The Reverend's out in back with the packages. Can I help you?"

I gave her the police psychologist semi-truth.

"The police?" she said. "Is there some problem?"

"It's concerning the Reverend's daughter."

"Karen?" Her voice jumped an octave.

"Yes."

"One *minute.*"

Seconds later, a man said, "Sherrell Best. What about Karen?"

I started to give him my intro.

He said, "*Please,* sir. Tell me about *Karen.*"

I repeated the story I'd told his son. When I was finished, he said, "Praise the Lord, I knew she'd be found."

"Reverend Best, I don't want to—"

"Don't worry, sir, I don't expect her to be restored. There was only one Rebirth. But the truth—I knew it would out. 'In your patience possess ye your souls.' "

"We don't really have the truth, Reverend. Just—"

"This is the *beginning,* sir. What does this witness remember?"

"Just what I told you. Sir."

"Well, I have things for *you.* Names, dates, clues. May I show them to you? It may sound stupid, but, please, would you humor an old maniac?"

"Certainly," I said.

"When can we meet? I'll come to you."

"How about tomorrow?"

Pause. "If need be, sir, I'll wait until tomorrow, but today would be better."

"I could meet you tonight," I said. "Around nine."

"Nine would be perfect. Where shall it be? The file's at my home."

"Your home's fine."

"I live in Highland Park." Repeating the address his son had given me. "Where are you coming from?"

"The west side."

"If you'd like I can come to you."

"No, it's no problem."

"You're sure? All right, then. I can have it all organized for you by the time you get there. Will you have time for dinner? I can prepare something."

"That won't be necessary."

"Coffee, then? Or tea?"

"Coffee."

"Coffee," he said, as if committing a menu to memory. "I look forward to it, sir. God bless you."

*   *   *

At eight-fifteen, I left Robin and Spike in the garage workshop and drove over Malibu Canyon to the 101. Midway through the Valley it turned into the 134, and a few miles later I connected to the Glendale Freeway south and got off just past Eagle Rock, in Highland Park.

The streets were dark, hilly, and tilting, crowded with small houses, duplexes, and apartment buildings on scratch lots, suburban silence broken by a constant freeway dirge. Runt lawns hosted old cars and trucks. The neighborhood had once been working-class white; now it was mostly working-class Hispanic. Gangs had made some inroads. A police chief had lived there, but that hadn't made much difference.

Sherrell Best's home was a single that overlooked a dry wash and the six lanes of asphalt that paralleled it. A box with a low-pitched tar roof. The stucco was sprayed on and looked pink in the nightlight. The grass was split by a concrete walkway. Iron grating shielded the windows.

Spanish music came from the place next door. Best's place was silent but all the lights were on—custard-colored patches behind woven curtains. A twenty-year-old Olds 88 sat in the driveway.

He was at the front door before I got there, a small round man with a small round head. He wore black-rimmed glasses, a wash-and-wear white shirt, and a narrow gray clip-on tie.

"Dr. Delaware?" he said, holding the door open, then closing it behind us and double-bolting. The house smelled of canned vegetable soup. The front was divided between a low narrow living room and a dining area even more pinched. The furniture was old and fussy-looking and arranged very neatly: polished wood tables with Queen Anne legs, beaded lamps with floral shades, overstuffed chairs sleeved with doilies. A gray hooked rug spread on the vinyl floor like a sleeping pet. The walls were covered with framed posters of biblical scenes. All the characters looked Nordic and on the brink of emotional collapse.

"Here's our coffee, sir. Please sit down."

The dining table was bridge-sized and metal-legged, crowded with an electric percolator, two plastic cups on saucers, a box of sugar, a pint container of half-and-half, and a plate of Oreo cookies. Next to that was a two-foot-square cardboard box labeled KAREN in black marker.

We sat down facing each other and Best picked up the pitcher and started pouring. His complexion was florid and mottled, like raw sweetbreads, and his blue eyes popped behind thick lenses. Furrows scored his brow, as if the flesh had been plowed. The rim of his collar bit into his neck flesh like a knife in shortening. His mouth was thin, his nose wide and bulbous with large pores. The little hair he had was slicked and black.

"Karen looked like her mother," he said. "Cream and sugar?"

"Black is fine." I took the cup.

"Mrs. Best was beautiful," he said. "Talk of our town was what did she ever see in me."

Short laugh. Wide spaces between brown teeth, lots of silver fillings.

"My son Craig took after her too. Here, have an Oreo— Karen used to break them apart and eat the filling first. She could spend half an hour on one cookie."

Behind him, against a backdrop of fruiting trees and golden wet sheaves, a wet-eyed Ruth embraced Naomi.

He filled his own cup. "So what, exactly, led you to Karen?"

"Just what I told you, Reverend."

"Memories? Do you have children, doctor?"

"No."

His lips puckered and his eyes closed for a moment. "Here." Reaching for the box. "Let me show you what I've got, and you tell me if any of it helps you."

Standing, he shoved his hands deep into the carton, like a surgeon rearranging viscera. What little space was left on the table quickly filled with spiral notebooks, bound stacks of newspaper clippings, and other papers.

He untied the clippings first and passed them to me. The newsprint was brittle and dry, the color of weak tea. The cutouts were twenty-one years old, all from a beachside throwaway called the *Shoreline Shopper*.

Best ate a cookie, then another, as he watched me read.

The first pages were taken from the classifieds. Two months' worth of a Personals ad, circled in blue:

Lost. Reward. Karen Denise Best, 19 y.o., 5-7, 117, blond hair maybe dyed brown, blue eyes, speaks with a New England accent, appendectomy scar. Our daughter was last seen walking up the road to PCH at the Sand

Dollar Restaurant in Paradise Cove. We love her very much and miss her and we are worried. Please call collect, any hour, to 508-555-4532. Any information leading to finding her will be $$$ rewarded.

"Did anyone ever call?" I said.

"Lots of people called. Liars and practical jokers, and some well-meaning people who thought they'd seen her. I paid out eighteen hundred and fifty-five dollars." He poked a finger under his glasses, rubbing his eye.

I turned back to the clippings. The last was an article from the op-ed page, written by the editor of the paper, a woman named Marian Sonner, and surrounded by ads for local shops. A poor-quality photo of a beautiful fair-haired girl was set in the middle of the text. Even the blurred reproduction couldn't hide the innocence and enthusiasm on the heart-shaped face.

FATHER TRAVELS FROM EAST
IN QUEST FOR MISSING DAUGHTER

MALIBU. *Special to the Shopper.*

Sherrell Best is a determined man. Maybe even stubborn, but who's to blame him? Isn't stubbornness part of the American Dream, Malibuites?

Raised in the midst of the Great Depression, he fought in World War II, rising to the rank of sergeant, came back and married his high school sweetheart, the lovely Eleanor, and built up a plumbing supplies business from scratch. To top it off, he and Eleanor had two young'uns: beautiful blond Karen and, two years later, freckle-faced Craig.

So far so good. Then it crumbled.

Out here, no less. In golden So Cal, where the waves are blue and the sky is too, and sometimes what happens to people isn't all sun and prettiness.

Malibu. The golden heart of a golden state. Where peace and freedom and love are the bywords of a new generation that's never experienced the hardships of its forebears.

Karen, beauty of face and form and heart. Prom queen and volleyball player and lover of dogs, left vying suitors in New Bedford, Mass., to chase the Dream.

Hollywood. The Silver Screen.

She came on Greyhound and learned that the Dream was played out in Beverly Hills. And Malibu. To some of us, those places are just home. But to Karen they were Glamour and Excitement. The Dream.

Like so many others, she ended up slinging hash—or should I say Catch of the Day—sorry, Marv and Barb D'Amato of Sand Dollar fame.

Like so many others.

But then . . . *unlike* so many others . . . she disappeared.

Vanished.

Like the smog when the beach breeze hits it.

She was last seen six months ago. Leaving Marv and Barb's S.D. on foot after the night shift.

And that's the last anyone saw of her.

Vanished.

The sheriffs looked for her. They did their best, we're proud of our men in tan.

But they didn't find her.

Neither did a gumshoe hired by Sherrell and his beloved Eleanor.

So Sherrell's out here from Massachusetts. Staying at the Beachrider Motel and living off savings.

Trying to find his princess.

This is her picture.

Karen Best. Her hair might be dark. She wrote home that she was dying it.

To look more exotic.

Vanished.

Sherrell's a determined man.

He's not rich, but he'll pay a hefty reward to anyone who can find Karen.

Maybe you've seen him, handing out flyers in the parking lot at Alexander's market. Or in front of Bill and Sandy Levinger's Shell Shack or the Frostee Kup, down by Cross Creek.

Asking his questions.

"Have you seen this girl?"

Maybe you've walked right by him.

Maybe you just shook your head and said, Poor guy.

No matter. He's a determined man. He won't give up.

Help him, Malibuites.

If you can.

Maybe this story can have a happy ending.

Maybe this really is a generation of peace and freedom and love.

Maybe . . .

I put the page down.

Best said, "She meant well. She was a sweet old woman, died a few months later and the paper went out of business."

"Did you pay for the article?"

"I paid for many things. No regrets."

He took off his glasses and rubbed his eyes some more. "More coffee?"

"No, thanks. Did the sheriffs do a thorough job?"

"I suppose they did their job. Asking questions of the same people I'd spoken to. Finally, they mounted a real search. For one day, in the canyons and gullies. Then they flew a helicopter over the coastline for an hour or so. They said the layout made it impossible to do much more. Too much brush, places that were hard to get to. I don't think they really believed she'd be found there. They were convinced she'd run away with a boy."

"Was any of this in the major newspapers?" I said.

"The papers weren't interested. I phoned all of them, over and over. They never returned my calls. Part of it was the way things were, back then. All those hippie boys and girls dropping out. But Karen wasn't like that. I'm not saying she was a perfect angel. But she was no hippie."

"When did you hire the private detective?"

"After the sheriffs stopped returning my calls. I hired two of them, really. It's all here."

He handed me a white sheet of paper, perfectly typed.

KAREN: PEOPLE INVOLVED

I. LAW ENFORCEMENT
    A. L.A. County Sheriffs Dept., Malibu Station.
        1. Deputy Shockley (took the call but nothing else)
        2. Dep. Lester (took report)
        3. Sgt. Concannon—in charge of search. His superior: Lt. Maarten, but never met him.
        4. Various eagle scouts under Sgt. Concannon, along with other deputies, whose names weren't given.

    B. PRIVATE INVESTIGATORS
        1. Felix Barnard, 25603 Pacific Coast Highway, Malibu, CA.
           (October–November. Spoke to staff at Sand Dollar: Sue Billings, Tom Shea, Gwen Peet, Doris Reingold, Mary

Andreas, Leonard Korcik. Karen's landlady: Mrs. Hilda Johansen, 13457 Paso de Oro, Pacific Palisades.)

2. Charles D. Napoli, 6654 Hollywood Boulevard, Hollywood, CA.

   (December–Jan. Re-interviewed F. Barnard's subjects, met with sheriffs, brokered purchase of membership in PeopleFinders.)

"What's PeopleFinders?" I said.

"Napoli told me there was a national network of detectives who specialized in looking for missing children. Subscription was a thousand dollars for the first year, five hundred every year after that. The money was supposed to buy access to hundreds of files and contacts. No such outfit existed. Napoli took the money, and another thousand I paid him for investigation, and left town."

He smiled. "I don't regret my foolishness. 'Hope maketh not ashamed.' After Napoli swindled me, I went to a third firm, one that advertised finding missing people within forty-eight hours. They took a consultation fee and said all that could be done, had been."

"After the first one, why'd you hire someone out in Hollywood?"

"I was hoping someone from the outside could see clearer. Barnard was slow. Very easygoing. All of Malibu seemed that way, people smiling but moving very slowly. I'd never been to California, wasn't used to it."

"When did you move out here?"

"Two years later. Permanently, that is. Before that, I was coming out every two months for a couple of weeks at a time. I stayed in motels or lived in a rented car, driving up and down the coast every day, from Manhattan Beach to Santa Barbara. Once I went as far north as San Simeon. Every canyon or state park I'd pass, I'd drive through, walk around, talking to the rangers, ground crews, campers, anyone. It became my job. My business suffered. Then Mrs. Best developed an aneurysm and died and I sold what was left of the business and came here to settle. Craig and Taffy were starting out, and I let them live in the house. A few years later, they bought it. It was a good time for me to leave —they needed their own life and I wanted to devote myself to looking for Karen. I spent ten hours a day in the car. Hoping one day I'd run into her somewhere. Maybe she'd lost her memory and was . . . somewhere."

He pushed the cookies away. "What does your witness remember?"

"Just what I told you, Reverend."

"A young girl being carried away by some men. That's vague."

"Yes, it is, and I'm sorry I can't promise you it means anything."

I tried to return the data sheet.

"No, that's a copy. Take it, I've got plenty."

I folded it and put it in my pocket.

"A young girl," he said. "Long dark hair, long legs—when Karen was a little girl we used to call her Storkie. For Stork. Where does your witness—is it a man or a woman?"

"I'm not at liberty to say."

He frowned. "Where does this witness think this *abduction* occurred?"

"Some sort of rustic site. Maybe a log cabin. Trees all around."

He pressed his belly against the table edge. "You're a police psychologist. You could hypnotize this person, couldn't you? That helps with memory."

"That's a possibility."

"Why not a probability?"

"The witness is in a fragile state of mind."

"How fragile?"

"I'm sorry, I can't say any more."

"Yes, yes, of course, sorry . . . but you *are* going to follow up."

"I'll do whatever I can, Reverend."

"You work *for* the police department?"

"I'm a private consultant. The witness is a patient of mine. A police detective is aware of what I'm doing, but it's not official yet."

The bulging eyes narrowed. "Why are you going to all this trouble?"

"To help my patient."

He looked at me for a long time.

"You're a devoted fellow."

I shrugged.

He fiddled with his glasses, looked at his coffee, but didn't touch it.

"I highly advise that you find some way to talk to Gwen and

Tom Shea. On the sheet she's listed by her maiden name, Peet, but they're married now. They worked with Karen at the Sand Dollar. Worked with her that last shift. I've always felt they knew more than they let on."

"Why's that?"

"The way they acted when I spoke to them—shifty, nervous. Felix Barnard said they seemed innocent to him. So did the sheriffs. They were both local kids, good reputations, neither had any sort of criminal record. But I'll tell you one thing: When I asked them about Karen, they couldn't look me in the eye. They'd been friends with her; Gwen waited tables, Tom tended bar. Why would talking about her make them uncomfortable? And they left the restaurant just a few minutes after Karen did. Karen was walking, but they were in a car. Doesn't it make sense that they would have overtaken her?"

"Maybe someone picked her up."

"Who would she have allowed to pick her up? She wasn't dating anyone, had no close friends. And she never would have hitchhiked. We talked about that before she left Massachusetts."

His voice remained low, but his eyes bulged even more and the ridges in his forehead were wet.

"I'm sure they're hiding something. I know what guilt looks like."

I pulled the paper out of my jacket, unfolded it, and circled the two names.

"I kept going back to them," said Best, "offered them money —the last of my cash before I started selling off the stocks and bonds. They wouldn't even talk to me. Finally Tom called the sheriff, complained I was harassing them. I returned a few days later anyway, wanting to catch Gwen alone. She wouldn't open the door, and the next day Tom came to my motel and threatened to beat me up if I didn't leave them alone."

"Was that the end of it?"

He sighed. "I did drive by their house, once or twice a week. Then they upped and left—moved out of Malibu. If that isn't guilt, I don't know what is. I called up the restaurant, pretending to be a friend, and was told they'd gone to Aspen. But they've been back in Malibu for over sixteen years. Own a place called Shooting the Curl—surfing supplies shop, near the pier. Doing very well, I might add. Tom drives one of those BMWs and Gwen has a fancy van."

"You still drive by."

"Only once a year, Dr. Delaware. On the anniversary of Karen's disappearance."

"Do you do anything else?"

"Do I try to talk to them? No, what would be the use? For me, it's a day of reflection. I drive from Santa Monica to Santa Barbara. If I see a homeless person, I stop and give them food. Sometimes I pull over at a campsite, but I don't talk to anyone or show Karen's picture. What would be the sense showing the picture of a nineteen-year-old girl?"

He looked down. Hooked his fingers under his glasses and rubbed his eyes again. "She's almost forty by now, but I still think of her as nineteen. . . . Don't worry, doctor, I don't bother the Sheas. Whatever they did, they have to live with. And they have their own troubles now: a crippled child. Maybe one day they'll come to see that Providence and Fate emanate from the same place. When you approach them, don't mention my name, I'm sure they think of me as a raving lunatic."

"How long was Karen out in California before she disappeared?"

"Five months."

"How often did she write?"

"She never wrote. She phoned. Always on Sunday, and sometimes on Wednesday and Friday. That's why we were alarmed that first Sunday. She was like clockwork when it came to those Sunday phone calls. We phoned the restaurant, and they said she hadn't shown up for work."

"I assume she never said anything on a previous call that hinted at her disappearance."

"Nothing. She was happy, enjoying the weather, enjoying her job, everything was fine. She was trying to earn enough money to enroll in acting school."

"Did she say which school?"

"No, it never got that far."

"How did you feel about her becoming an actress?"

"We didn't really think she'd become one. We thought she'd try awhile and come back, go to college, meet someone nice."

His lip quivered.

"My wife took most of the calls. I was usually at the store. After Karen disappeared, I grew to hate the store. Gave it to Craig, but he sold it and got a job with the state. Building and Safety. After I moved here, my first year was taken up completely by looking for Karen. The second year too, but nothing was turning up. I had time on my hands and started to read the Bible. Till then I wasn't a religious man—I'd gone to church but I thought about profits and losses while pretending to worship. This time, the Bible started to mean something to me. I found a seminary in Eagle Rock and enrolled. Got ordained five years later and started the church. Do you know what we do?"

"Distribute food to poor people."

"To *anyone*, we don't ask questions. No one gets paid. I live off my Social Security and the few bonds I have left, and the others are all volunteers. Restaurants donate the food. It's a good life. I only wish Karen were here to see it."

He gobbled a cookie and swallowed coffee that had to be cold.

I looked at the cardboard box.

He emptied the rest of the contents onto the table. "I'm going to clean up."

Clearing the dishes, he began washing them.

I opened the first of four photograph albums covering Karen Best's development from infancy to young womanhood. Taped to the second was a tiny envelope labeled *First haircut.*

Holding the packet up to the light I saw several curly snippets inside.

Grade school graduation program. Karen, the winner of a Good Citizenship award.

High school yearbook, Karen in French Club and Song Girls. *Karrie. Her eyes speak volumes.*

A prom shot: Karen beautiful and mature-looking by now, her blond hair long and silky and curled at the ends. On the arm of a gawky boy with a dark Beatles do and a struggling mustache.

A dessicated orchid corsage in a stiff plastic packet embossed with the name of a New Bedford florist.

A hundred or so copies of the sheet Best had given me, bound by rubber bands.

A copy of the Lord's Prayer.

I put it all back. Best was standing over the kitchen sink, hands in plastic gloves, the water full blast and steaming.

I went in.

As he washed, he stared at something over the faucet.

Another Bible picture, this one a black-and-white etching.

A young woman being dragged by her hair.

Dinah's Abduction by Shechem.

Best's gloved hands were clenched. The steam had fogged his glasses and his lips moved rapidly.

Praying.

15

When I got back, I read the Bible. What I learned made it hard for me to fall asleep.

The next morning, Robin and I had breakfast in town; then I drove back to the library and had a second look at the newspaper account of the Sanctum party. August 15. Karen Best had been last seen the night before.

After xeroxing the article, I called Milo. He was out but Del Hardy picked up. The black detective was Milo's occasional partner, but they hadn't worked together recently.

"Hey, doc, how's it going?"

"Pretty good. How's the guitar?"

"Sitting in a closet, no time to play. Listen, Bigfoot's finishing up a robbery at the Smart Shop on Palms, maybe you can catch him."

He gave me the number, and I talked to a female officer who finally put me through to Milo.

"Morning salutations." He sounded distracted.

"Don't want to bug you but—"

"Nah, I'm finished here. What's up?"

I told him.

"The Best girl," he said. "Wasn't she a blonde?"

"She dyed her hair that summer. And according to her brother she had very long legs. It may turn out to be nothing, but I just—"

"It—uh-oh, TV crew just drove up, gotta split. Where are you?"

"Westwood."

"Meet me at Rancho Park, on the north end, past the baseball diamond—take the first entrance past the golf course and go as far as you can. You'll know me 'cause I won't be feeding the ducks."

I got there a quarter hour later and found him on a bench, near a cement wading pond that had been drained but was still streaked with algae. A stray retriever was nosing the grass. No ducks or people in sight. I showed him Best's data sheet and the clipping and pointed out the date of the party.

"Night before she missed her call home, for what it's worth."

He skimmed and handed it all back to me. "You actually met with the father?"

"At his request."

"How does he grab you?"

"Devoted. Obsessive."

"So you two got along great."

"There was a certain rapport there." I summarized what Best had told me about the search for Karen, ending with his suspicion of the Sheas.

"So what does that have to do with Lowell and Trafficant? Paradise Cove is—what?—ten, fifteen miles up from Topanga."

"She worked in Paradise Cove, but she lived near Topanga Beach. I passed the address coming into town. Just a hop and a jump from Topanga Canyon Road. Then there's the time frame and her physical similarity to the girl in the dream."

Crossing his long legs, he looked up at the sky. An airplane was writing something illegible. He shook his head. "This father sounds obsessive to the point of nuttiness. The way he's been bugging those people."

"He says he hasn't done it for years. If that's true, it indicates self-control."

He continued skygazing. "Actually, that does amaze me. Living in the same city with them, believing they know something, and letting it go."

"Maybe his work keeps him going. He fills his days with good deeds."

"Food to the poor, huh?"

"Could be I'm a chump, but he impressed me as a good guy, Milo. Trying to deal with his loss by finding some higher meaning. The only thing that bothered me was a picture he had hanging up in the kitchen over the sink. A Bible print—Dinah being abducted by Shechem. He was staring at it as he washed the dishes. I looked up the story when I got home. It's in the book of Genesis. Dinah was Jacob's daughter; Shechem was a Canaanite prince who kidnapped her and raped her. Two of her brothers took revenge by slaughtering him and his whole village."

"Nice image for a man of the cloth to meditate on."

"I don't want to light any fires under him. I know what revenge can do."

He lowered his eyes and looked at me.

"So what's the theoretical scenario here? She took a nature hike on Friday night, ended up at Lowell's place the day before the party, and got invited in?"

"Not unless she was a serious hiker. We're talking several miles up to the top of Topanga. But maybe she was hitchhiking and got picked up. And maybe the party started early—or it was informal. People drifting in at all hours." I held up the clipping. "This makes it sound like a loose scene rather than some formal bash."

"All those big shots and people are just wandering in?"

"You remember how things were back in the seventies. Peace, love, people playing at social equality. Best said that was one of the reasons the sheriffs didn't take Karen's disappearance seriously. Times were casual, kids on the road, everyone into free-and-easy."

He looked out at the baseball diamond and the rolling lawns beyond. "I spent the seventies grinding away in college, then shooting at guys in black pajamas, but I take your word for it."

"I was a grind too," I said. "But I remember hitchhikers thicker than gulls on PCH. Best says Karen was a good girl, but she'd been away from home for almost half a year, and kids can change fast when they taste freedom. Plus, she wanted to be an actress. What if she was thumbing—or just taking a short walk up the canyon, unwinding after work. And a person with a famous face pulled alongside her—in a stretch limo. Telling her there's a hot party up the hill, lots of other showbiz types, hop in. Would an aspiring actress turn that down?"

"Guess it's plausible," he said. "If the partying started early. But even then, all you've really got is a dream and a missing girl."

"A girl who called home every week and then stopped. And was never heard from again."

He faced me once more. "I'm not saying she's not dead, Alex. Sounds like she probably is. But that doesn't mean she died up in Lowell's place, and after all these years I don't see how you're gonna get any closer to it."

"I don't either. God, I really hope I haven't lit a fire under Best. At the very least, I'm giving him false hope."

"Well," he said, "if you're right about his being a man of faith, maybe it'll carry him through."

"Maybe." I sat forward on the bench. A tiny colorless spider had crawled onto my knee. I picked it up carefully, and its thread legs wriggled frantically. Placing it on the grass, I watched it disappear among the blades.

Milo said, "Something *has* been bothering me, though. What you told me about brother Peter. Guy never travels, but he just *happens* to be out of town when she sticks her head in the oven? Unemployed, but he's too tied up with *business* to get back? Then he takes the time to call Embrey and a half brother he hasn't seen in twenty years but not Lucy? *Then* you tell me he's weird. And now Lucy's saying someone swiped her underwear, and he has a key to her apartment."

"You think he did it?"

"I think it sounds like he's running from something. Maybe nasty impulses. Maybe he's close to her in a way that scares him, so he split to the desert to be alone with his goddamn thoughts."

"Oh, man," I said. "Just what Lucy needs."

I thought about my brief meeting with Peter, trying to remember as much as I could about him. Pale face, sleepy voice. Cold hands. Bulky sweater on a hot day. Eager to get back to the car. Looking down at his lap. . . .

"What if he's running from something else?" I said.

I described the brother.

Milo looked at me. His big black eyebrows were up.

"Junkie?"

"It fits, doesn't it? His unemployment, Lucy's defensive attitude—evasive, actually. I remember her saying he was always trying to protect her *'even though he'*—and then she broke off the sentence. When I pressed she said, Even though he isn't the toughest guy in the world. But it wasn't what she started to say. I know it's conjecture, but he *really* wanted to get back inside that car. When I glanced back, he was sitting low in the seat. As if he was doing something. Lucy looked back too, and that session she dropped her chronic smile. He could have been fixing right there. She could have known."

"Junkie," he repeated. "Could be. Hungry hypes don't wait for a corner suite and fresh linens."

"It would explain his cutting out on Lucy in her time of need. Talking to everyone else *but* her because she'd know he was traveling to make a buy, and he didn't want to have to explain. Doesn't lots of stuff come into New Mexico from the border?"

He nodded. "But no shortage of stuff right here in L.A."

"Maybe he couldn't buy here. Because he'd run up some serious debts—*that* could be why he left town. Avoiding creditors. The kind who don't send overdue notices." My stomach tightened. "For all we know, the creditors know about Lucy and are trying to use her as leverage. Maybe those phone hang-ups *were* real. Maybe someone really did break in and mess with her underwear."

"No one broke in," he said. "She said there was no evidence of that."

"Okay, so they tossed Puck's place and found the key to Lucy's apartment."

"That's awfully subtle for people like that," he said. "They'd enjoy breaking in."

"Maybe it's at a subtle stage. Intimidating him so he makes a big score for them and settles up. Maybe he's a longtime seller. How else would he pay for his habit without a job? Lucy's got a family trust fund that pays her a thousand dollars a month, so he might too. But with any kind of habit, a thousand a month wouldn't go very far."

"Trust fund from Lowell's side of the family or the mother's?"

"Lowell's."

"Daddy abandons the kids, but supports them?"

"It's a generation-skipping thing set up by *his* mother for taxes. He may have no control over it."

"Leverage," he said. "Yeah, be nice to blame it all on the dope demons and restore her credibility. But I still don't see any connection to her head in the oven."

"What if someone drugged her and put her there? She's a creature of routine, has a drink of juice, every night, watches PBS. That would explain the drapes being open—they wanted her to be found. Wanted to send a message to Puck. Wouldn't *that* be something? We're all assuming she's lying or denying, and she's telling the truth?"

He rubbed his face. "It would *absolutely* be something, Alex. It would be Fantasyland, 'cause there's no knot on her head and the hospital found nothing on her dope panel."

"What if they gave her something the panel doesn't test for, like chloroform?"

"Hey," he said, "you wanna theorize, I say it's more likely Pucky himself tried to gas her—pissed 'cause she wouldn't give him dope money. Or maybe he's just after her chunk of the trust fund and split town to give himself an alibi. And he's calling Ken to find out if she's dead. You like that one, I can make up six more like it for a quarter. Couple more quarters, I'll fill your *day* with fantasy."

Off in the distance, the retriever sniffed the air and bolted off after something. "You're right," I said. "I'm lapsing into wishful thinking because I'd just love it if she didn't try to destroy herself. But she did. And for all I know, Puck never touched dope. Just a shy guy with circulatory problems."

"No," he said, "there's something off about him. I wanted to check him out on the computer this morning, but I got called to the market two-eleven at six-thirty. First thing I do when I get back is play computer games. Got an address for him?"

"Ken said Studio City. Are you still going to check out Trafficant?"

"Sure, why not? I'm already pushing buttons."

"Poor Lucy," I said. "Another hurt."

"Yeah," he said. "Hurt seems to be on her dance card."

It was 1 P.M. when I got back to Malibu. While stopped at a red light near the pier, I caught a look at Shooting the Curl's facade. White building, blued windows. A sign with fat white letters spelling out the name over a mural of a wet-suited surfer riding a big wave.

Paradise Cove was ten miles later. A neon sign on a tall pole pointed toward the beach. THE SAND DOLLAR *Breakfast Lunch Dinner.* Impulsively, I turned off.

A dipping road took me past an acre or so of wildflowers, then a trailer park shaded by huge shaggy eucalyptus. Between the trees, the water was flat and silver. Another hundred feet and I came up against a guardhouse and a lowered wooden arm. A sign said the beach was private and it would cost $5 to go any farther unless I was eating at the restaurant.

The kid in the guardhouse stuck his head out. His nose was peeling and his sunglasses were mirrored.

"Sand Dollar," I said.

"Five bucks." He handed me a ticket. "Get this stamped and I'll give it back to you when you leave."

I drove down the final slope to a big wide parking lot. The restaurant was down at the bottom, set on the sand, a wood-shingled shuttered thing with a Happy Hour banner above the door.

Inside was a dark waiting area carpeted in red felt, paneled in cheap wood, and hung with salt-eaten nautical gear. No one was waiting, but a cigarette was smoldering in an ashtray. To the right was a cavelike bar with a couple of people bellying up and watching stand-up comedy on cable. Straight ahead was an empty host's stand and, beyond that, the restaurant.

The main room was gigantic, the way L.A. restaurants used to be before the land boom, with two long rows of red brass-buttoned booths and the same felt carpeting. The entire beach wall was glass. A big storm, several years ago, had sheared off one third of the pier. The remains jutted over the water. A few tourists sat on the beach. The people in the restaurant looked mostly like locals, but there weren't many of them and they were distributed thinly.

A couple of waitresses were working, one young and red-headed, the other in her fifties with a squat face and cropped gray hair. Both wore pink blouses, black pants, and red aprons, their sleeves rolled up, their eyes tired. A busboy collected dishes from a table in the far corner.

The host was a tall, heavy, white-bearded man. He noticed me and stopped talking to a busboy.

"Lunch for one," I said, and he took me to a window booth.

The older waitress showed up a few minutes later, all business. I ordered the Angler's Breakfast, $10.95 (Served All Day): deep-fried red snapper, eggs, hash browns, juice, and coffee. The food was good and I tried to eat slowly. By the time I finished, the restaurant was nearly empty and the waitress was nowhere in sight. I finally spotted her in the bar, smoking and watching TV, and gave a wave.

She came over, looking peeved. Her name tag said DORIS.

I handed her a twenty and the parking stub and she went to

get change. Pulling out Best's data sheet, I scanned the names of the restaurant staffers.

Doris Reingold?

When she returned, I said, "Keep five for yourself," and got a big smile.

"Thank you, sir, how was your meal?"

"Excellent."

"The Angler's one of our popular ones."

"I can see why . . . looks like things are pretty quiet today."

"It goes up and down. On Sunday no one gets in without a reservation."

"That so?"

"All the Hollywood people show up—they're over at their beach places for the weekend. Barbra Streisand sits in that corner. She's tiny. We get chefs, too, like the guy who runs La Poubelle. They bring their kids. I keep telling Marvin to raise prices, but he won't."

"Why not?"

She shrugged. "Old habits. We'll probably be closed down by next year anyway. Marvin's not healthy, and they keep after him for the land. It's worth a fortune."

"Too bad. I'll have to come here more often while you're still open."

"You do that. I could use customers like you." She laughed. "Live around here?"

"Just moved in," I said. "Near the county line."

"On the beach?"

I nodded.

"Ooh, that's pretty. I pass by there on the way home to Ventura. Own or rent?"

"Rent."

"Me too. Only the millionaires own, right?"

"Better believe it. Been working here for a while?"

She pulled on a jowl and grinned. "It shows, huh? But I won't tell you exactly how long, so don't even ask."

I smiled back. "So what'll you do if it closes down?"

"I don't know, maybe catering. All those chefs, there's always something comes up. Not that I look forward to that."

"You don't like catering?"

"Big hassle. Used to do it years ago. Friend of mine—she worked here too—used to get catering jobs for herself and anyone else who wanted them. Good money, but a big hassle." She winked. "Marvin never liked our moonlighting. We did it behind his back."

"I'm thinking of throwing a housewarming party, could use a good caterer. Who's your friend?"

She shook her head. "She doesn't do it anymore. Got rich— owns her own business."

"Lucky her."

"Yeah."

"What kind of business gets you rich nowadays?"

She smiled at me. "You're living on the beach, what do you do?"

"Psychologist."

"Oh." She winked again. "So maybe I shouldn't be talking to you."

"Don't worry, off duty," I said.

"You know," she said, "I wouldn'ta tagged you for that. I figured you for a lawyer or the music business or something." Fingering her apron pocket, where the tip had gone.

"I used to play in a band," I said. "Cocktail lounges. I know what it's like to depend on people's generosity."

"Ain't that the truth. And most of the time, people aren't. That's what I hated about catering parties. You see people at their worst; to them you're a stick of furniture. And no tips. One collective service charge. If the boss isn't honest, you're sunk."

"Was your friend honest?"

"Which—oh, her. Yeah, honest enough."

"You must have seen some interesting parties, though. Working around here."

She reached for a cigarette. "Mind?"

I shook my head. She lit up.

"Maybe to some it was interesting. All it was to me was serving and clearing and people sticking their hands in my face." She shook her head and looked back. "Want more coffee? Maybe I'll have some myself. Marvin's in the john, as usual."

"Love the company," I said.

She got the pot and another cup. Sitting down opposite me, cigarette fuming, she poured for both of us.

"It's been real nice working here," she said. "So close to the ocean."

"How're things in Ventura?"

"Dying. Who knows, maybe I'll move. Got two grown boys, both in the army. One's in Germany, the other's near Seattle. Or Nevada. I like Nevada; things are booming there."

"Your rich friend can't help you find anything?"

"Nah, like I said, she's out of it. She and her husband own a surf shop—nothing for me to do there."

"Shooting the Curl?"

"Yeah, you know it?"

"I've passed by. Doesn't look like a big business."

"Believe me, it is. They've got a place right on the sand at La Costa—own, not rent—and that ain't Spam salad."

She took a deep drag as her eyes swung toward the window. "Here we go again."

I followed her eyes to the beach. A camera crew was setting up, sound trucks and vans were parked in the background, and a couple dozen people were standing around.

"Commercials," she said. "They come here all the time: sun-tan lotion, cars, Coca-Cola, you name it. Pay Marvin so much he doesn't have to raise his prices—speaking of the devil."

She looked out toward the front of the restaurant. The white-bearded man was coming toward us, head down, scowling, arms swinging.

She stood and held out a hand to him, smiling and mutter-ing, "Hold your horses, Marvin." He stared at her, then at me, finally turned around and returned to his booth.

"Back to base," she said, stubbing out her cigarette. "Nice talking to you."

"Nice talking to you too."

"Doris," she said, touching her badge. "Ask for me the next time you come in. I'll get you a beach seat. . . ."

Catering jobs, contracted by Gwen Shea.

For anyone who wanted them.

All those chefs . . . contacts.

Had Karen Best gotten a job at the Sanctum party?

Gone up early to set up and never come back?

I sat in the car and had another look at Best's data sheet.

Felix Barnard, the private eye, hadn't noted anything about moonlighting.

The others not telling him in order to hide it from Marvin?

Or maybe Barnard just hadn't asked the right questions.

Best had said the detective was slow-moving, too laid back.

Flipping through the Rostale directory, I looked for his name in both the yellow pages and the personal listings but found nothing.

House of cards.

But what Doris had just told me tightened the connection between Karen Best and Sanctum one tiny notch.

Maybe Sherrell Best's intuition about the Sheas was right on target.

Doris was an eager conversationalist. There'd been no way to bring up Karen's disappearance with her, but it was worth another try.

No telling what a little positive reinforcement could accomplish.

16

The names of the other Sand Dollar people:

Sue Billings
Mary Andreas
Leonard Korcik

I got home and looked them up. Neither of the women was in the book, but Korcik, L. T., was listed in Encinal Canyon.

A man answered. "Tree farm."

"Leonard Korcik, please."

"This is Len."

"Are you the same Leonard Korcik who used to work at the Sand Dollar?"

"No, that's my dad. Who's this?"

"I'm working with the police clearing some old missing persons cases. A girl named Karen Best disappeared a number of years ago. Your dad was questioned about it, and I just wanted to check a few things out."

"My dad died three years ago."

"I'm sorry. Did he ever mention Karen Best?"

"Who?"

"Karen Best."

"How long ago was this?"

"Twenty-one years."

He laughed. "I was seven years old, then. I never heard nothing."

"What did your dad do at the restaurant?"

"Worked the bar part time and cleaned up. We got a tree farm. You need any trees, call me."
Click.

Wendy Embrey phoned just before five. "Can't be sure, but my bet is she'll be back in your court."

"Why's that?"

"The minute I told her I was authorizing her release, she closed up—friendly but clearly nothing to say."

"What makes you think she'll want to see me?"

"I asked her if you'd visited and she lit up. If I were you, I'd be checking my transference meter regularly." Straining for graciousness, but an edge had come into her voice.

"I'm not so sure," I said. "When I was there she said something about not needing any therapy at all."

"Great," she said. "There's some A-plus reality testing for you. Well, you can only lead them to water—lack of insight isn't grounds for extending the seventy-two. Anyway, her father called me. Since I'm probably out of the picture, I thought I'd pass that along."

"When did he call?"

"This morning." She read off a number very quickly.

"Was there a message?" I said, copying.

"Nope, just to call him. Good luck. She's getting out tonight."

A woman answered. "Yes?"

"Dr. Delaware returning Mr. Lowell's call."

"Who?"

"I'm his daughter's psychologist."

"I thought she was seeing Dr.—"

"Embrey. She's off the case."

"Oh. . . . Well, if you're the doctor, Mr. Lowell will have a meeting with *you.*"

"About what?"

"Lucretia, I assume."

"I couldn't do that without Lucy's permission."

"Hold on."

A few seconds passed; then a very loud, deep voice said, "Lowell. Who're you?"

"Alex Delaware."

"Delaware. The first state, an ignoble little backwater. What are you, French Canadian? Acadian? Coon-ass?"

"How can I help you, Mr. Lowell?"

"You can't help me at all. Maybe I can help you. My boy snitched on the girl's attempt to snuff herself, the implication being, of course, that it was my damned fault, nammer, nammer, nammer. I doubt she's changed much, the constipated squall, basic character never does, so I can give you some piercing insights. Unless you're one of those biopsychiatric Frankenmaniacs who believes character is all a matter of serotonin and dopamines."

"Which of your sons called you?"

"The opium fiend, who else?"

"Peter?"

"Selfsame."

"Where'd he call from?"

"How would I know? My girl took it. And don't try arraigning me at the Tribunal of Ruined Progeny. Guilt may be your stock in trade, but it's not my currency. I'll see you not tomorrow but the day after. An hour at the most, significantly less if you annoy me. You'll come to me; I don't travel."

"Sorry," I said. "I can't talk to you without Lucy's permission."

"What?" He laughed so loud I had to move the phone away from my ear. "*Bedlam* is the New Olympus? The *lunatics* rule the asylum? What the fuck are you talking about?"

"Confidentiality, Mr. Lowell."

"There *are* no secrets, boy. Not in the massage-message age. McLuhan's books are a shitbin—*furor loquendi*—but it's true we're all staring up each other's assholes. . . . Very well, you've lost your chance. *Salaam,* as the Arabs say, to hell with everyone."

"If Lucy does consent, I would like the opportunity to talk to you. May I call you back?"

"*May* you?" He laughed again. "At your own risk. You may also pass Go or eat raw fish with the Japs or take three baby steps or fuck yourself with a garden tool."

Robin and I had dinner out on the deck. The tide had whipped the sand like cream, and the beach at twilight was a graying plane of peaks and troughs. I couldn't stop thinking of my conversation with Lowell.

Had he missed a dose of lithium, or was he cultivating nuttiness for attention?

He probably didn't get much attention anymore.

Why had he called? His offer to provide insights was almost
comical.

The opium eater. The hunch about Peter confirmed.

Maybe a shattered career and old age had finally caused
Lowell to survey the ruins of his family.

One child dead, the other three estranged.

An addict, an attempted suicide. . . .

Ken seemed a nice enough fellow, but his antipathy for his
father was right on the surface.

"What's on your mind, honey?" said Robin.

"Nothing much."

She smiled and let her hand rest on my bicep. I tried to chase
away clinical thoughts and turned to her. A trace of color remained in the sky—a paint smear of salmon, capping the sinking
sun. It played on the auburn in her hair and made her eyes cop-
pery and catlike.

"Still at work?" she said, stroking.

"No more."

I drew her to me and kissed her deeply. Her tongue lingered
in my mouth.

"Carpe foxum," I said.

"What's that?"

"Seize the babe."

17

Despite a decent night's sleep, my first thought upon waking was: Lucy's out of the hospital.

I wasn't happy with the idea of her trying to make it on her own. But if I pushed she'd probably back away, so I decided to give her till noon before calling.

In the meantime, I'd catch Milo up on what Doris Reingold had told me.

He hadn't come into the station yet and no one picked up at his home. I called the business number he used for his private moonlighting and the tape answered: "Blue Investigations." I left a message.

It was just after nine; Robin and Spike had been gone for over an hour. I drove to the market at Trancas and bought groceries, thinking about all the places off the highway where a girl could disappear. Just as I got home, Milo phoned.

"I'm at Lucy's place. Can you come out right now?"

"Is she okay?"

"Physically, she's fine. Just come out; we'll talk once you get here. Here's the address."

The street was three blocks north of Ventura Boulevard. The block was treeless and sun-fried, all apartments, mostly mega-units with underground parking and security gates that would give an experienced burglar pause for about twenty seconds. FOR RENT banners and real estate brokerage signs on most of them. Promises of "move-in incentives."

Lucy's building was older and smaller, a two-story quadriplex of flesh-tone stucco and dark red wood. Two units on top, two below, each open to the street, with individual entrances set back from a covered walkway. Another FOR RENT sign staked in the lawn near the ground-level mailbox.

Her apartment was number 4, upstairs. Number 3 was vacant. Her welcome mat featured a chipmunk saying "Hi!" The windows through which Ken had seen her kneeling in the kitchen were masked by shades. The doorjamb around the hinges was splintered a bit and nailed together—Ken's breaking in to save her—but the door was locked. I rang the bell and Milo parted the shades, then let me in.

The front of the apartment was divided into living and dining areas. The kitchen was a cubby with avocado cabinets and white appliances. Barely enough room to kneel. All the walls were off-white, not that different from the Psych unit at Woodbridge.

The oven was a squat little two-burner Kenmore, maybe fifteen years old. The dining room table was fake oak surrounded by three folding chairs. In the living room were a tufted blue velvet love seat and two matching chairs, a glass-topped coffee table, and a 14-inch television and a VCR on a rolling stand.

On top of the TV was a single photo, of Lucy and Peter. Head shots, no identifying background. She was smiling, he was trying to.

Lucy sat on the blue couch, barefoot, wearing jeans and a baggy gray sweatshirt that said L.A.'s the One. Her hands gripped each other, and she looked up and gave me a struggling smile. Milo went and stood behind her. His jacket was over a chair. He wore his revolver in a waist holster.

He looked at the coffee table. "Look, but please don't touch."

A short stack of magazines had been pushed to one side. Next to it was a sheet of yellow ruled legal paper; next to that, a white envelope.

On the paper was a note, typed off-center, crowding the left margin and the top of the page:

FUCK YOU BITCH IN HELL
JOBE DIES, YOU DIE TWICE

Below that was something affixed to the page with transparent strips of cellophane tape.

Dark shriveled things, the size and shape of olive pits.

"Rat turds," said Milo. "Pending lab analysis. But I don't need a tech to tell me."

"Mailed or delivered?"

"Delivered."

"Delivered right inside," said Lucy. "I found it on the table when I got home last night."

"What time was that?"

"Three in the morning. They let me out at one, but then there was paperwork and I left some clothes up in my room and had to go back. When I got here, the door was unlocked, but I just figured Ken or the paramedics had forgotten to lock it." Trying to be calm. Her hands were white.

"You came home alone?"

She nodded. "I didn't notice it because I was tired, just wanted to sleep. I fell off, then I woke up around five to get a glass of water and saw it."

"Who has keys to the apartment?"

"Just Peter and myself. And the landlord, I guess."

"Who's the landlord?"

"Some old woman who lives in Port Hueneme," said Milo. "Her handyman patched the jamb. I just spoke to him, and he claims he locked it when he was through."

"Anything weird about him?"

"Mr. Gonsalvez?" said Lucy. "No, he's a sweetie—and he couldn't have written that, he barely speaks English."

Milo nodded. Lucy hugged herself.

I found his eye. "Is the lab on its way?"

"Not yet." To Lucy: "Why don't you pack those few things."

"Can I take a shower? I really don't think anyone was in the bathroom."

"Sure."

She left. A door closed and a few moments later the sound of the shower filtered through, like heavy distant rain.

Milo sat down where she'd been. He pointed to the chair without the jacket, and I took it.

"What do you think?" he said softly.

"The timing is pretty convenient," I said. "Out of the hospital a few hours and she gets you right back here. But what about our theory about Peter's loan sharks?"

"Loan sharks tend to escalate the violence. Why would they gas her, than regress to this?"

"Maybe they came to do serious harm but didn't find her home. Or maybe they and Peter have nothing to do with it. What if it *is* someone connected to Shwandt—remember how the Bogettes threatened justice? Or some other nut who's latched on to Lucy—someone who noticed her at the trial."

"How would anyone know she was away?"

"They watched her—stalked her. Remember, she leaves her drapes open." Tension in my voice. "Is there anything that makes you doubt her?"

"No, that's the thing. She's calmed down now, but when I first got here she was petrified. Shaking. Either genuine terror or great acting, Alex. And she doesn't have a typewriter, so the note couldn't have been written here. Where else would she write it between two and five in the morning? Where the hell would she get *rat* shit?"

"That's reminiscent of Shwandt."

He nodded.

"Was anything else disturbed?" I said.

"No."

I took in the skimpy decor.

"You should see the bedroom," he said. "Single mattress on a board, a cheapie end table, nothing on the walls. Her clothes aren't bad, but she doesn't have much."

"Nunnish."

He looked at me sharply.

I said, "So what's bugging you about it?"

"I just don't trust my instincts with her."

He dropped his chin into one palm. Black and gray stubble popped through the pockmarks.

"How long have you been here?" I said.

"Since five-forty."

It was after eleven.

"Why'd you wait so long to call me?"

"Didn't want to interrupt your beauty sleep."

"Seriously."

He frowned and pushed hair off his forehead. "After I calmed her down, we talked. Capital T. I told her I was gay—I know you warned me, but it just seemed right. I followed my instincts; once in a while it works." Looking at me.

"Okay. How'd she take it?"

"Almost as if she was relieved."

"Maybe she is," I said. "On two counts. She's not personally rejected, and she can be with you while avoiding the mess of a sexual relationship."

"Whatever. . . . Sorry if I jumped the gun, Alex. I didn't want to screw anything up. But sitting there, holding her, she's crying, her head on my shoulder, I could just see something happening, and all she needed was another rejection. I figured—"

"Obviously, you figured right."

His smile was slow to form. "Mr. Validation—ever think of working with people?"

"Are you going to call the lab to do a crime scene?"

"If I do, this could get really messy. Once those wheels start rolling, it'll be impossible to keep it quiet. Someone's bound to talk: Bogeyman juror harassed. . . . It's only a matter of time before the press dogs find out and start peeing all over it. Then they start focusing on her and learn she tried to kill herself and got committed. Who'd *love* that?"

"Shwandt's lawyers," I said. "Mentally ill juror. Grounds for instant reversal."

"Especially coming on the heels of the copycat. My bet is they'd get the whole thing thrown out."

"Lucy would be humiliated," I said.

"Big time." He got up and paced.

I looked over at the note. "Is there any conceivable way this could be *related* to the copycat? Could the Bogettes or someone else in Shwandt's camp have hatched up some scheme to get his conviction reversed?"

"Who the hell knows? Those girls are crazy as shit. Low-IQ fanaticism, the worst kind."

"It would sure be a low-IQ plan. No other jury will ever let Shwandt walk the street again."

"Yeah, but if he's in court, they get to *see* him. For all I know, they're planning to *liberate* him out of there."

I read the note again. " 'Die twice.' Could that mean humiliation as well as the real thing?"

He shrugged. The shower stopped.

"Okay," he said. "Till we clear this up, priority one is keeping her safe. If she manufactured this, the worst thing is I get snookered. So where do I stash her? She says she's got no close friends and no family other than him." Glancing at the picture on the TV. "And he is a junkie, by the way."

"I know," I said. "His father told me."

"When did you speak with *him*?"

"Yesterday. I tried to get hold of you to tell you. I have some other stuff to talk about too, but let's figure out what to do with Lucy first."

"I could put her in a hotel, but any place above a fleabag is gonna eat into her money pretty damn fast."

"What about Ken? He's in real estate—deals with distressed properties. Even if he doesn't have anything himself, he might know of a low-cost, short-term rental. Here or up in Palo Alto. Maybe she should go out of town for a while."

"It's a thought," he said. "She talked about him a little, wanting to thank him for saving her but not knowing how to approach him. How weird it was having a brother she didn't know. Then she changed the subject to the Puckster. Worried that he hasn't called."

"Worried, not angry?"

"Worried. I got the feeling she's been worrying about him for a long time."

"I'm sure she has," I said. "She say anything more about him?"

"No, and I didn't push. . . . Okay, can you reach Ken?"

"I've got his card."

The bedroom door opened and Lucy came in the room, toweling her hair.

"Definitely nothing else missing," she said. "My stuff's all intact."

"Good," said Milo. He got up and held out a chair for her.

18

"Another trial," she said. "Carrie's poor parents going through it again—all the families. You really think those horrible girls could be behind this?"

"We don't know," said Milo. "But publicity's their meat. That's why we want to keep you safe and do it quietly."

"My—" She bit her lip.

"What, Lucy?" I said.

"The . . . oven. I'd been starting to wonder if I really—but do you think someone could have done that to me? Drugged me somehow? Remember how I mentioned feeling drugged to you, a couple of sessions ago?"

I nodded.

"I thought I was just tired," she said. "Too much work, not enough sleep. But—could it be?"

"Anything's possible," I said.

She raised her knees to her chin. Her arms were around her legs and her body looked very small. "Well, do what you need to get to the bottom of it. Don't worry about me, I'll handle whatever comes along."

"Publicity would mean more than just a new trial," I said. "Instant celebrity, including the three days you spent at Woodbridge."

That made her flinch. "Oh . . . the crazy juror . . . oh, boy."

Looking at Milo.

He said, "I'm going to fingerprint your apartment myself instead of calling in the lab. It'll take longer, but I'll be able to keep it under wraps. Depending upon what I find, we'll take it from there. Has anyone visited you recently?"

"No. No one."

"I'll also find you a temporary place for the next day or so. After that, we thought we'd ask Ken to look into something 'cause he's in real estate. You okay with that?"

"Guess so. Sure." To me: "Would he want to?"

"At the hospital he mentioned wanting to meet you. Though I'm sure he's a little nervous about it."

She smiled. "Like I'm really scary."

"The unknown is scary."

The smile faded.

She began packing, and I returned to Malibu and called Ken's office. No secretary. I spoke to his answering-machine tape, and he came on the line as soon as I mentioned my name.

"Hi, doc, what's up?"

I told him.

"Someone broke in?"

"Lucy said she found the door open when she came home."

"Shit. I bet *I* left it open. I was in such a hurry to get her to the hospital—"

"No, the lock was fixed after that, and the handyman claims the door was locked. So either he was careless or someone jimmied it."

"Why would—maybe someone was casing the neighborhood, knew she was out. Did they take anything?"

"No, they just left the note. Detective Sturgis is looking into it, but we need to keep it quiet. To avoid publicity that might hurt Lucy and give Shwandt a retrial."

"Hurt her how?"

"If the story gets out, someone could do some checking and find out about her seventy-two hours at Woodbridge."

"Oh. Yeah, I see what you mean. That would be terrible."

"In the meantime, we're trying to find a safe place for her to stay. Your brother's still out of town, and we wondered if you could put her up in Palo Alto."

"That's okay with Lucy?"

"She's a bit nervous about meeting you, but you'd be doing her a great favor."

"Then, sure. But she doesn't even need to come up here. The

company's got lots of vacant properties in L.A. Most are low-income, but some are pretty nice. . . . I think there's a really good one in Brentwood, totally furnished. I was planning to fly down tonight anyway; let me check—unless you think she should leave town."

"No," I said. "A secure place down here would be fine."

"I could stay with her, if that'll help. I couldn't stick with her every moment, but I'd be home most nights."

"Sounds good. Thanks, Ken."

"Sure, no problem. Glad to be useful."

Milo called at three-thirty to say he was on the way over. He arrived just after four.

"Got her over at the Ramada on Beverly Drive and Pico, registered under my name." He gave me the room and the phone number.

"She okay by herself?"

"Seems to be. I gave her all the usual precautions, though I can't see how anyone could possibly find her there."

"After spending more time with her, any new thoughts about her credibility?"

"She seems *goddamn* credible, nothing shaky or flaky. If she's lying, she's either totally nuts or a stone psychopath, and I can't believe I'm that gullible."

"It's not a matter of gullible. All of us are like locks. No matter how strong the bolt, there's always a key out there that opens it."

"So what're you saying? I'm a sucker for her? *You* think she's lying?"

"I think she's a very confused young woman. The dream, now this. *I'm* having trouble sorting out reality, so I imagine it's pretty tough for her."

"You only answered one question."

"Do I think you're a sucker for her? I'd term it emotionally susceptible, and, yeah, you sure are. Do I think it's bad? No. She needs help and you're providing it. Like you said, the worst that can happen is you get snookered. Any more discussion about your being gay?"

"Nope, it didn't come up." He looked burdened.

"What?" I said.

"What's the other stuff you said you wanted to talk to me about?"

"The Karen Best scenario looks a little less theoretical. I was over at the Sand Dollar yesterday and happened to get served by a waitress named Doris Reingold. She was on Best's list—been working there all this time. She told me Gwen Shea recruited staffers regularly for nighttime catering gigs. Karen's name didn't come up—there was no way to work it into the conversation. But Best did say Karen was friendly with the Sheas. It's logical they'd have thrown some work her way. So maybe she worked the Sanctum party."

"Why didn't the private eye find any of this out?"

"Maybe he was incompetent and didn't ask the right questions. The staff kept catering gigs quiet. The Dollar's owner didn't approve."

He pushed back from the table and stretched his legs. "You just happened to get served by her, huh?"

"Scout's honor."

"And you just happened to be eating there."

"Place has a great view," I said.

He looked at the glass doors. "Like you need to go somewhere for that."

"I didn't turn any rocks over," I said. "Doris thinks I'm just a friendly guy who tips big. And it's at least thought-provoking, isn't it? Karen fits the girl in Lucy's dream, she disappears the night before the party. Big bash like that could have taken a couple of days to set up. Maybe she went up early. If the Sheas hired her and something happened to her, that would be a fine reason for them to act evasive with her father. Throw in Trafficant and *his* disappearance, and it's a little more than random numbers, wouldn't you say?"

He walked over to the window. "Okay, my thoughts are provoked, but let's not forget the only reason this came up in the first place is Lucy's *dream*. And we still don't know how much of *that* is real."

"Karen Best's disappearance is real. And there'd be no easy way for Lucy to know that. Unlike the party, it wasn't covered in the *Times*. Best said all the major papers shined him on."

I got the copy of the *Shoreline Shopper* and handed it to him.

"He paid for this. The paper went out of business shortly after. I doubt it's catalogued in any library."

He read as I looked at the gulls. "Says here no one saw her after she left the restaurant at eleven P.M. on Friday, never came home that night. So you're saying she went up to Sanctum and spent the night?"

"Maybe she had a one-night stand with a guy. A guy who picked her up and hurt her."

"Trafficant?"

"He was famous."

"Then what? He offs her Friday night? Or parties with her again on Saturday and then offs her?"

"In the dream, Lucy remembers lights and noise. Maybe that was the staff setting up, but it sounds more like the party itself."

"The dream," he said, shaking his head. "So she's there working on Saturday. Slinging designer hash to hundreds of people and no one remembers her."

"There's no indication either the sheriffs or Barnard made any connection to the party."

"Maybe because Karen wasn't there." He waved the clipping. "This *is* major coverage, locally. You'd think someone around the beach area would have seen it."

"That piece ran six months after the disappearance. Who's going to remember a waitress who served them half a year ago? With Lowell and movie stars at the party, who'd notice the staff, period? It would be nice to get hold of Felix Barnard and see if he has any of his old records, but I can't find a listing on him. Some background on the Sheas would be useful too. Like, have they gotten involved in anything shaky since then? I can pay another visit to the Sand Dollar and try to get more out of Reingold. The chef who catered the party would be another potential source. For old time cards or personnel records that could verify Karen's presence. Some guy named Nunez. Scones Restaurant."

"Dead," said Milo. "AIDS, couple of years ago."

"You knew him?"

"Rick knew him. Patched up a sliced finger in the ER. We went to his restaurant a couple of times and got comped. Vegetables I'd never seen before and the portions were too small." He tapped the glass lightly.

"Have you punched Trafficant into the computer yet?"

He nodded. "Nothing on NCIC. Haven't had a chance to look into his tax returns. Have you called his publisher?"

"No, too late to do it now, I'll try tomorrow. I may also get a chance to sound out his patron."

I described my conversation with Lowell.

He said, "Sounds like the asshole Lucy says he is. Why his sudden interest?"

"Good question. Peter phoned him from New Mexico, too, and told him about Lucy's suicide attempt. Lowell implied it was an attempted guilt trip that didn't work. He claims he has insights to offer on Lucy, though his tone was more contemptuous than concerned."

"Insights? After all these years?"

"He's sure she hasn't changed much. The only thing I can think of is he's trying, in a bizarre way, to get some kind of relationship going."

"By being contemptuous?"

"He's a real piece of work, Milo. Spews out words nonstop. He made such a point about not feeling guilty, it could mean on some level he *does* feel responsible."

"Weird," he said. "So old Pucko continues to call everyone but Lucy. Guy gives me *a definite* bad feeling—like that picture on her TV. She's smiling, but he looks like he can't wait to get the hell out of there and jam a spike in his arm. And he's more than a penny-ante addict. Three arrests for possession of heroin and two for selling, all within the last six years. There's also a sealed juvenile record back in Massachusetts and some misdemeanor stuff with Boston PD. The biggest bust was three years ago. He tried to peddle thirty grand worth of smack to an undercover cop. Got off on technicalities, case dismissed. Gary Mandel was his lawyer. Ever hear of him?"

"No."

"Ex-prosecutor, specializes in serious dope cases, very big retainer."

"Think Puck's connected?"

"Thirty g doesn't make him King Smack, but it does make him more than a street-corner pusher. If he was playing with the big-tentacle crowd and offended someone, that would explain the quick escape. Whatever, Lucy ain't winning any family values sweepstakes; hope Ken turns out to be a good egg. When you gonna go see Daddy?"

"I'm not unless Lucy wants me to. And I'm not going to bring it up until I'm sure it won't agitate her."

"Yeah." He turned toward the tide pools. A couple of skiffs were floating out near the kelp beds. "God, it's gorgeous here. You could forget what planet you're on."

"Sure could," I said, but I was thinking of log cabins and the crushing terror darkness could bring to a small child's mind.

The phone rang, jolting both of us. I picked it up.

"Doctor? Ken Lowell. I'm still in Palo Alto, but I wanted you to know I got that Brentwood place set up for Lucy. I'm catching a seven o'clock flight, should be able to be there by eight-thirty, nine. Do you want me to come by and pick her up or should I just meet you there?"

I asked Milo.

"Tell him to meet us."

I did.

"See you then," said Ken. He gave me an address on Rockingham Avenue. "How's she holding up?"

"Fine."

"Good. We Lowells are tough—built to take it."

He hung up. I gave Milo the address and he wrote it down. He returned to the table, glanced at the *Shoreline Shopper* piece, and headed for the door. "I'll see what I can do about locating the PI. Regards to Beauty and the Beast."

"Where are you off to?"

"Get Lucy some dinner, and then we'll drive over to Brentwood, get her set up. I'm glad he came through."

"Finally someone in the family does."

"Yeah. . . . I was planning to spend the night with her. Rented a suite—two separate bedrooms and all."

19

No one had called by ten the next morning, so I phoned the Brentwood house. Ken answered, yawning.

"Oh, hi. We didn't get to sleep till late. Hold on, I'll get Lucy."

Seconds later: "Morning, Dr. Delaware."

"How's everything?"

"Fine. I just got up. Ken and I were up late, talking. Hold on, please—'Bye, Ken—he just left to buy some groceries. He's nice. . . . I keep thinking about Puck—I'm sure he'll be back any day but . . . I guess the last few days are a jumble. It's hard to believe any of this is really happening."

She managed a brief, tight laugh.

"Would you like to come in?" I said.

"I would, but my car's still back at my place. I need to get it towed here."

"I can come out."

"No, I don't want to put you through any more bother."

"No bother."

"No, Dr. Delaware, I can't keep imposing."

"Don't worry about it, Lucy. How about noon?"

"Sure," she said. "Noon's fine." Another small laugh. "I'm not going anywhere."

Just as I was getting ready to leave, Sherrell Best phoned. "I'm sure there's nothing new, doctor, but—"

"Nothing yet, Reverend, though the police are interested in

speaking with Felix Barnard. He's not in Malibu anymore. Any idea where he went?"

"Why do they want to speak to him?"

"Normal follow-up."

"Oh. Of course. No, I'm sorry, I don't know where he is. Probably retired. He was in his sixties back then, and he closed up shop right after he mailed me his report."

"Your case was his last?"

"The very last—at least that's what he told me. I thought his age meant experience, but maybe a young man would have done better. Some people get to a certain age, it's hard for them to feel inspired."

I got on the highway at eleven. The beach was placid, the land-side hills upholstered with yellow poppies. Reaching the pier and passing it, I spied the fat white letters of Shooting the Curl's facade and turned left, impulsively, into the shopping center.

Up close the painted sign was cartoonish, the surfer hyper-muscular with a massive head topped by brass-colored hair and a grinning mouth big enough to swallow a shark. He balanced on a swirl of foam while giving the thumbs-up sign with a swollen red digit. The white letters had been touched up recently, and they sparkled in the sun.

I found a parking space in front of the shop, next to a char-coal-gray BMW coupe with chromed wheels and a rear spoiler. Despite the customization, the car hadn't been washed in a while and the marine air had done its job on the paint. The license plate read SHT CRL. A bumper sticker said SAVE THE COAST, and a blue handicapped-parking permit rested atop the dashboard.

A cement ramp with metal railing led to the entrance of the store. Brass wind chimes tinkled as I stepped in; then I was as-saulted by the drum solo from *Wipeout*. The store was double-width, with one half devoted to surfboards, custom wet suits, and surfing paraphernalia, the other to beachwear, suntan lotion, and posters, mostly variations on the tiny-man-rides-monster-wave theme or flesh-in-your-face shots of overripe women in micro-bikinis. Logos filled the rest of the wall space: BODY GLOVE. ONE WAVE. NO FEAR.

A few girls in their late teens browsed the poster bin, gig-gling, and a middle-aged couple stood by the swimwear, fascinated by the neoprene bathing suits. No one worked the clothing counter, but a man in his forties sat behind the surfboard register, eating a fast-food breakfast from a Styrofoam box and looking down at something. Above him a pink banner screamed SEX WAX!

Without glancing up, he said, "What can I do for you?"

"Just browsing."

He forked something into his mouth, and I noticed the sports section in his other hand. His hair was longish, very thin, minnow-silver, combed across his forehead but unable to hide the sunburnt skin of his brow. He had well-proportioned features, except for light-brown eyes that were set too close. His skin had loosened its hold on the bones below. The eyes were bloodshot and bagged and, though he was lean, a second chin tugged at his first. He wore a lime-colored polo shirt with sleeves that reached his elbows. His shoulders were broad, his forearms chunky and furred with gray hair that nearly obscured an anchor tattoo.

The music switched to the Beach Boys' "In My Room." One of the browsing girls brought a rolled poster over to the clothes counter and looked around as she fished money out of her jeans.

The man said, "I'll take that here."

He put down his paper. The girl came up and paid for her poster and left with her friends, laughing.

The man swallowed a mouthful of egg-muffin and watched the girls wiggle the glass doors.

"Having fun," I said.

"Yeah," he said. "You see what she bought? Stud poster—centerfold from *Pretty Boy*. It's meant for gays, but they put out a calendar and it sold so well to women, they decided to market the months separately." He grinned. "In our day, girls weren't like that, huh?"

"Not the ones I knew."

"So what is it for you?" he said. "Reincarnation, or just passing through from Chicago?"

"Reincarnation?"

"Second childhood. Second chance at the big wave. That's what it usually is when a guy your age comes in. Or a tourist wanting to bring home a little piece of California for Aunt Ethel."

I laughed. "I'm looking for bathing trunks."

He hit his forehead and gave another grin. "Wrong again. Good thing I don't gamble. Suits are over there."

I went over to a rack marked DUDES and flipped through the merchandise. A pair of baggy black trunks caught my eye because of a square patch with a Saint Bernard over the pocket bearing the legend BIG DOG. The mutt's tongue was out and he looked mischievous. Clearly a spiritual brother to Spike. I pulled the shorts off the rack and brought them up.

The man said, "Cool baggies," and rang up the sale.

I said, "What do the guys having a second childhood usually buy?"

"The works: board, board cover, leash, wet suit, wax, sport sandals, zinc, hair dye. We have the suits custom-cut for us; usually they're freaked out to see what size they take now. Plus all the changes in board technology. A guy your age might have rode something as big as a tree trunk. Name of the game now is minimum weight."

Turning his hand into a blade, he sliced air.

"The new stuff, once you get the feel, it's like hydroplaning. You can drive out to Zuma or County Line and see kids that are basically Jesus walking on water."

"Sounds like you did a bit of water work yourself."

"Still do." He grinned and handed me my receipt. "No second childhood for me, 'cause I never got out of my first."

The chimes sounded. A dark-haired woman had opened the door and stuck her foot in.

"I need help, Tom."

She was tall and nice-looking with a narrow, graceful figure and long thin arms with some muscle definition. Her hair was wavy and very short, almost black, her eyes so light they seemed pupil-less. The sun had cured her face to tight bronze leather. She wore high-cut pink shorts that exposed long smooth legs. Her blouse was white and sleeveless and tucked in snugly.

Tom said, "Just finishing up a sale, babe."

She didn't smile or answer, just kept standing there in the door. I heard a powerful engine idling and looked out to see a white Ford van conversion, smoke puffing from its rear.

The woman cleared her throat.

Tom said, "Here you go, pal, enjoy 'em."

I left the store, taking as long as possible to get back to the Seville. Once in the car, I sat behind the wheel pretending to look for something. A few seconds later Tom Shea came out of the shop and followed his wife to the van. She got behind the wheel and closed the driver's door and a metal ramp slid out from the rear of the vehicle. It touched the asphalt and I heard it scrape. Tom opened the rear door and reached in, back muscles bunching, as he pulled on something. A moment later an electric wheel-chair appeared in the doorway, bearing a slumping, bronze-haired boy.

Tom guided the chair down the ramp. I started the Seville and inched out, watching. The boy could have been anywhere from twelve to twenty. His head was large and it lolled, eyes wide, tongue extended. His shrunken body was belted into the chair. Despite the restraint, he slanted sharply to the right, the head almost touching his right shoulder. One arm was belted, too. The other clutched a joystick at the front of the chair.

Tom wasn't smiling. He said something, and the joystick hand moved. The chair rolled down the ramp, very slowly, and when it was on the asphalt Tom closed the van door. Then he got behind the chair and guided it up the cement slope toward the store. The van's engine cut off and Gwen Shea came around, sprinted up ahead, and held the store door. As Tom eased the chair through, I caught a glimpse of the boy's face. Sleepy, but grinning. Big grin, almost voracious.

His hair a thick, straight mat, the kind that might turn silver-minnow when it aged.

But he reminded me of more than his father.

As I drove away, I realized what it was.

The grin. Triumphant, cartoonish.

He was an atrophied version of the surfer on the sign.

20

Years ago, the mother of a severely brain-damaged child sat in my hospital office and cried for half an hour without break. When she finally stopped, she said, "I love her, but God forgive me, sometimes I want her to die." She never cried again in my presence, and whenever we passed in the hall she looked away from me with a face that was part despair, part rage.

The same face Gwen Shea wore.

The idea of approaching her about a twenty-one-year-old disappearance seemed ridiculous and cruel. What reason did I have to believe Best wasn't just an old man deluded by hope?

I caught a green light and sped out of Malibu into the Palisades, making my way to Rockingham Avenue and possibly more delusions.

The house was a sizable two-story Tudor with pink roses and blue agapanthus along the front and a low hedge of waxy privet bordering the brick walkway. A white Ford Taurus with a rental sticker sat in the driveway. Ken Lowell answered the door wearing a blue suit and holding a Filofax. His shoes were shined and his hair was wet.

"Morning, just on my way out."

He let me into a parqueted foyer. A statuary-marble center table held a black vase full of white silk flowers. Behind it, the stairway was a softly curving arc of polished oak.

The front rooms on either side were dark and vaulted,

shaded by heavy cream damask drapes and filled with gleaming furniture.

"Nice repo," I said.

Ken nodded. "The owners cut out to Europe overnight. Food in the fridge and clothes in the closet. Some kind of shopping center deal that went bad. People are looking for them."

"Been seeing a lot of that lately?"

"More than usual for the last couple of years. It's what we specialize in. We pick them up from the bank, rehab them, and turn them around. I guess that makes us capitalist exploiters." He smiled and picked out one of the silk flowers. "It's not what I thought I'd be doing when I was in Berkeley."

"What were you interested in then?"

"My sister Jo was an archaeology major; she turned me on to old bones. After she graduated, she went to Nepal to climb around and explore. I flew there to be with her and we hung out together in Katmandu—place called Freak Street, Telegraph Avenue transplanted to the Himalayas." He shook his head and looked at the flower. "I was with her when she died."

"What happened?" I said.

"We were hiking. She was experienced, very athletic. This was just a stroll for her. But she put her foot down and something gave way and she fell over a hundred feet. I was way behind. She passed right by me as she went down, landed on a ledge full of sharp rocks." He touched his eyes and pressed down on the lids. Then his hands flew to his lapels.

A door opened on the upstairs landing, and Lucy came down the stairs.

"Morning," she said, looking at Ken. "Everything okay?"

"Everything's great." He smiled and buttoned his jacket. "I should be back around six. Don't worry about your car, I'll have it brought over." A wave, and he was gone.

"Looks like you're being well taken care of," I said.

"He's a sweet guy." She looked at the living room. "Not too shabby for a hideout, huh? Can I get you something to drink?"

"No, thanks."

"Would you like to talk outside? It's nice in here, but I find it a little gloomy."

The backyard was generous, with a pork-chop-shaped swimming pool and waterfall spa. A brick patio running along the rear of the house contained a table and chairs and potted plants that needed watering. The neighboring properties were blocked from view by tall honeysuckle hedges and billowing mounds of plumbago.

We sat. Lucy crossed her legs and looked up at the sky. Her eyes were tired, and she seemed to be fighting tears.

"What is it?" I said.

"I can't stop thinking about Puck."

After a second's debate, I said, "He called your—called Lowell two days ago to tell him you were in the hospital. He obviously cares about you, but something's keeping him out of town."

Her legs uncrossed and her head shot forward. "Why would he call *him*—how do you know this?"

"Lowell phoned me, wanting to talk about you. I told him I couldn't without your permission."

"That's crazy. Why would Puck call *him*?"

"He knew you were at Woodbridge."

"He must have found out some—absurd. I don't understand *any* of this."

"I got the impression Puck had been in contact with him."

She stared at me, then lowered her head, as if ashamed.

"He told me Puck had a drug problem," I said. "I didn't assume it was true, but Milo checked it out."

Her mouth opened, then closed. Her fingernails scraped the glass top of the table, and my short hairs rose.

"*Damn* him. He had no right—why did *Milo* have to do that?"

"For your sake. And Puck's. We couldn't understand why he couldn't come back to see you, figured he might be in some kind of trouble. How long's he been addicted?"

"He—I don't know, exactly. He started smoking grass in prep school. By the time he started Tufts he was already into . . . the bad stuff. He had to drop out in his junior year because a campus policeman caught him shooting up in a dorm room. After that he didn't care and just hit the streets. The police kept picking him up for vagrancy, and the system kept spitting him back. He tried to get help—student health, free clinics, private doctors. Nothing worked. It's a disease."

Her fingers ran down the glass again, but silently.

"Even with all his problems," she said softly, "he was good

to me—he cares about me. *That's* what scares me. He must be in trouble. It would have to be something serious for him not to be here."

"He's been telling everyone it was business."

She gave a miserable look. Covered her face. Exposed it. "Yes, he sold. Once in a while. Only to get his own stash. I know it's wrong, and I'm sure in some part of his brain he does too. But he felt he had no choice. He was broke, and *he* wouldn't give him more than pennies. I tried to help him, but most of the time he wouldn't take anything from me—not unless he was hurting really bad. He's the one who suffers . . . the way he lives—a hole over a hairdresser's."

She looked out at the landscaped yard.

"It's not like he sold to little kids or anything like that. Just to junkies, and they'd have to get it one way or the other. . . . It's the heroin. All this talk about crack, and heroin goes on eating people up."

She began to cry.

I patted her shoulder.

"So many times I offered to have him come live with me. To try another program. He said he was beyond hope and didn't want to drag me down. Didn't *want* treatment—he *liked* junk, it was his lover, he'd never give it up. But still he was always there for me. If I called him to talk about something, he'd always listen. Even if he was stoned, he'd try. Sitting there, pretending to be normal—he'd be here now if he wasn't in some kind of major trouble."

"What kind of trouble?"

She squeezed her hands together. "The people he hung out with."

"Who are they?"

"That's the thing, I don't know. He made a point about shielding me. Whenever I came over, he rushed around, cleaning up, putting his kit away. Lately, he didn't even want me over at his place—too depressing, he said. So we had coffee in restaurants. He'd come in looking half dead, trying so hard to act okay. I know he sounds like just another stupid junkie, but he really is a wonderful brother."

I nodded, thinking of Puck's dinner date with Ken, how an addict might have viewed the sudden appearance of a wealthy half brother. Yet he hadn't shown up.

"Milo's not going to call the police in Taos or anything like that, is he? I don't want to put him in any more danger."

"No," I said. "Milo's main concern is you."

"Yes, I can't believe all he's done. You, too. And now Ken." She wiped her eyes.

"I must bring it out in people, like a wounded bird. Puck told me that, once. That he'd always seen me as wounded. I didn't like that. I wanted him to perceive me as strong."

"You are strong."

She spread her fingers on the glass. Looked through the tabletop, studying the pattern of the bricks. "Milo told me, you know. About being gay. It shocked me. . . . Now I understand the position you were in. I really put you in the middle. I'm sorry."

"It was one of those things that couldn't be helped."

She shook her head. "I'd never have suspected it. A big, burly guy like that—that's stupid, of course, but still, it was the *last* thing I'd have guessed. It must be so hard for him. The job."

"How did finding out affect you?"

"What do you mean?"

"How do you feel about his being gay?"

"How do I *feel* about it? Well . . . I'm certainly glad I know the truth now."

She looked away.

"Anything else?" I said.

"I guess—on a selfish level—I guess I'm disappointed." She shook her head.

"Maybe it was just a stupid crush, but it sure—I mean, the feelings are still there. How can you kill feelings, right?"

I nodded.

She stood and walked up and down the patio.

"He and I both do this," she said. "Pace when we're nervous. We found out when we were at the hotel. All of a sudden, we started doing it simultaneously; it was a riot."

She looked at me. "You know how I feel? Cheated. But I'll get over it. And I'm still grateful to have him as a friend. Don't worry about me, I may look wounded but it's an illusion. All done with mirrors." Smile.

She sat down. "Now let's talk about the Great Man. What does he *want*, all of a sudden? What's his game?"

"I don't know, Lucy. Maybe to connect with you, somehow."

"No," she said angrily. "No way. He's up to something, believe me. He's a master manipulator, you have no idea. He loved hitting Puck when he was down."

"Puck went to him for money?"

"After he cut off the trust fund."

"He has that power?"

"Not officially, but the lawyers work for the family trust, and they do. One call from him." Snapping her fingers. "They invoked some sort of spendthrift clause. After that, Puck had to go to him. Only a few times, as a last resort. And of course he demeaned Puck and made him beg for every penny. Lectured him about financial responsibility, as if he's some expert. He lives off a trust fund, too. His mother's father owned textile mills all over New York and New Jersey, made a fortune before income taxes. He's never had to work a day in his life. If he did, he'd be sunk. He hasn't published or sold a painting in years."

She slammed a fist into a palm. "*Forget* him. Forget whoever played around with my undies and hung up on me and wrote that stupid *note*. No more fear, no more bullshit. I'm *evicting* it all from my mind. I don't care what it looks like, I never tried to kill myself. I love life. And I want a *real* life—a regular, boring, ordinary life. This is a nice place, but in a few days I'm out of here."

"Where to?"

"I don't know. Somewhere on my own. I'm *not* going to spend my life looking over my shoulder."

She got up again. "Had the dream again last night. Ken came in, said he'd heard me crying out. I was sweating. It's as if that damned incubus is sitting back there, just waiting to torment me. As if there's a big pile of garbage stuck in my memory banks. I want to evict that, too. Get my head clear. How do I do that?"

I considered my answer. The delay brought panic to her eyes.

"What is it? Is there something wrong with me—did they find something on those tests in the hospital?"

"No," I said. "You're perfectly healthy."

"Then what?"

Timing: the art of therapy.

Mine was off. I felt out of balance.

Her nails scraped the table.

"The dream," I said. "Has it changed in any way?"

"No. What are you holding back from me?"

"What makes you think I'm holding back?"

"Please, Dr. Delaware, I know your intentions are good, but I'm tired of being protected."

I thought of her head in the oven.

"Sometimes there's nothing wrong with being protected."

"Please. I'm not crazy—or do you think I am?"

"No," I said.

"Then what is it? What aren't you telling me?"

I continued to deliberate. She looked ready to jump out of her skin.

Feeling like a first-time skydiver about to step into space, I said, "Some things have come up. They may be related to your dream, or they may mean nothing. Given all your stress, I'm not comfortable dropping them on you, unless you can promise you'll take them calmly."

"What things?"

"Can you promise me?"

"Yes, yes, what?" Her hands were flexing. She stilled them. Forced a smile. Sat.

Waiting, like a child not knowing if candy was coming or the strap.

"You don't remember any contact with Lowell," I said. "But Ken says you spent a summer with him at Sanctum. All four of you did: you, Ken, Puck, and Jo."

"*What?* When?"

"The summer the retreat opened. You were four years old."

"How could—when did he tell you this?"

"The night he brought you into the hospital. I asked him not to discuss it with you. I wanted to pace things."

"Four years old? How can that be? I'd remember that!"

"Your Aunt Kate had just gotten married and gone on her honeymoon. Does the time frame fit?"

She stared at the lawn. Slumped low in her chair.

"I—" she said, very softly. "I still can't see how I couldn't remember something like that."

"Memories from any age can be blocked out."

"Four . . . that's the age I feel in the dream."

I nodded.

She started to reach for my arm, then stopped herself. Her face had gone gray-white, like skim milk. "You think it could be *real*?"

"I don't know, Lucy. That's what we need to figure out."

"Four . . . I'm so confused."

"Some parts of the dream seem to match reality," I said. "There was a big party that summer. That could explain the sounds and lights. And the buildings at Sanctum are made of logs."

Her hands fisted. Her eyes were cold yet electric. "What about the rest of it—what I saw?"

"I don't know."

She started to shake, and I held her shoulders till she stopped.

Finally she was able to take a deep breath.

"Calm," she said to herself. "I can handle this."

Another breath. She closed her eyes, her shoulders loosened, and I let go. A few more inhalations, and for a moment I thought she'd lapse into the semihypnotic state I'd seen a few days ago. Then her eyes opened. "I don't feel anything. No big insights . . . but could it—the girl? What do you think? Do you know anything else that you're not telling me?"

I studied her face. No muscles moved. Her eyes were still and dry and piercing.

"Yes," I said. "After Ken told me, Milo and I did some research, looking into crimes in that area. We found no murders or rapes that matched, but we did come across a missing persons case involving a girl who was never found. She did have long dark hair and long legs, but that could apply to lots of girls. So let's not assume anything for the moment."

"Oh, God."

"It may very well mean absolutely nothing, Lucy, and latching on to it may distort your memories. That's why I didn't want to rush into it."

"It's okay," she said. "I won't rush into anything either." Putting her hands in her lap. Smoothing her hair. "What else do you know about this girl?"

"Her name was Karen Best. She disappeared the night before the party—which *wouldn't* fit with the dream. She was last seen in Paradise Cove, fifteen miles from Topanga. And there's no evidence she was ever up at Sanctum. The only thing that does match is her physical description, and there's nothing very distinctive about it. As I told you before, dreams can be mixtures of reality and fantasy. You were four years old, may very well have seen something a child's mind couldn't process."

"Such as?"

"Something sexual, like you initially assumed. Small children who witness the sexual act often interpret it as an assault."

"But the scraping sounds—the last couple of times, like last night—it was definitely shovels digging. Burying her."

Hunching her back, she bit her finger.

"Lucy—"

She removed the finger and rubbed the upper joint. "Don't worry," she said softly. "I'm not going to fall apart. I'm just trying to put this into place."

"Don't try to do it all at once."

She nodded. Breathed deeply again, and placed her hands on the table, as if summoning a spirit at a séance.

"Why now?" she said. "If I've forgotten it all these years, why now?"

"Perhaps the stress of the trial," I said. "Hearing about all that sexual violence. Or maybe you're strong enough to deal with it now."

She expelled air. "What does Milo think about this?"

"He's open-minded but skeptical."

"But he didn't dismiss it . . . the girl. Karen. Do you have a picture?"

"Not with me, but I can get one."

"I want to see her."

I nodded.

"Does she have a family?"

"A father and a brother."

"Have you met them?"

"The father. The brother lives back east."

"Was she originally from back east?"

"Massachusetts."

"*Boston?*"

"New Bedford."

"I've been there *plenty* of times—used to go out there with Ray to buy squid from the Portuguese fishermen. What was she doing in L.A.?"

"She came out to be an actress and ended up waiting tables."

"Poor thing," she said. "Poor, poor thing. . . . Does her family know about me?"

"I told the father someone had a distant memory of a girl who resembled his daughter being abducted."

"How did he take that?"

"He hopes something will come of it."

"What's he like?"

"He's a minister. Seems nice."

"Does he want to meet me?"

"At some point," I said. "If we learn more."

"So he hasn't given up on finding her?"

"He's not doing anything active anymore."

"No, of course not—all these years. What about right after it happened?"

"He mounted an intensive search."

"He loves her," she said flatly. "A minister. Which church?"

"It's a group that feeds the poor."

"A good man—maybe I can help him. Can you hypnotize me or something? I've heard that can unlock memories. I'm sure I'd be an easy subject. Sometimes I feel as if I'm walking around in a trance anyway."

She gave an angry, nervous laugh.

"When I hooked for Raymond, I used to trance out all the time—see how tough I am? I haven't repressed any of *that*. I even told Milo. The slate is clear. So let's get into my head. I want to get rid of all the garbage."

"Hypnosis isn't just something you jump into, Lucy."

"It's dangerous?"

"Not when done with a properly prepared patient."

"You're worried about my mental stability?"

"I'm concerned about your stress level."

She sat back, as if studying me. "Tell me honestly. Do you think I tried to kill myself?"

"I really don't know, Lucy. Ken saw you with your head in that oven."

"Okay, it was there," she said. "I'm not going to deny reality. But the phone calls, the undies, the note—I know it sounds paranoid, but all that happened. I didn't put those horrible rat things there. Tell me you believe that."

I nodded.

She said, "Maybe one of those crazy girls is out to get me. Or some other nut, who knows? I'm even willing to consider the possibility that I did it while I was sleepwalking—like the first time I ended up on the kitchen floor. But I wouldn't *willfully* try to kill myself. Life means too much to me, and killing myself would be giving in to *him*. Confirming his preconception that we're all weak and useless. That's what he told Puck every time

Puck came to him. We were weak, spineless, useless. *Banal.* I'd never do myself in, give him the satisfaction. Do you understand?"

"Yes."

A distant look came into her eyes. "Sleepwalking. The more I think about it, the more I'm sure that has to be the key. From the beginning. I must have gotten up in the middle of the night and left that cabin and seen something . . . sex and violence, just like you said. I can't put it in words, but that *feels* right—there's an internal logic." She smiled and exhaled. "It's good you told me about all this. I won't disappoint you and misuse it. You've really helped me today, Dr. Delaware."

I nodded.

"Not that it's easy," she went on. "I'm still shaking inside." Touching her belly. "But things are finally starting to make sense. *Viscerally.*"

She touched my arm.

"Keep helping me. Please. Help me get into my head and find out the truth. Help me get back in control."

21

A hummingbird shot up in the air, a tiny rocket. A gardener's air gun blasted from somewhere down the block.

Her eyes were fixed on me.

"I'll help you any way I can, Lucy."

"What about hypnosis?"

"Right now?"

"Yes. I feel ready. I don't even care if it works, just that I tried my best. If I don't *do* something, I'll just sit around here feeling helpless. So much has come down on me."

"That's exactly why I don't want to jump into anything."

"I understand," she said. "But if hypnosis could help clarify things, wouldn't that help *unload* me?"

"What do you know about hypnosis?"

"Not much—I mean, I saw stage shows in college but they were rather silly, people quacking like ducks. I have heard that when you go under in therapy sometimes you can unlock memories."

"That's true," I said, "but any time you work with the unconscious, there's a risk of unleashing unpredictable things."

"I'm a veteran of that already, wouldn't you say?"

"All the more reason," I said.

"Okay," she said. "You're the expert. But I also know that what's stressing me is carrying around all this stuff and not understanding it."

I looked at her, trying not to appear coldly clinical.

Her posture was loose, receptive. She seemed calmer than ever before. Purposeful.

I gave her my preinduction lecture, explaining that hypnosis was deep relaxation combined with focused concentration, nothing magical. How it didn't weaken the patient's control but was merely the harnessing of a process that occurred naturally for most people. That all hypnosis was self-hypnosis, and the more she did it the better she'd get.

As I spoke, her body pitched progressively forward and her lips parted.

When I finished, she said, "I understand."

Her fingertips were inches from mine, her face close enough for me to see my reflection in her pupils. I looked worried.

"I want to help someone else," she said.

"All right, we'll start out with some simple muscle relaxation exercises. But we may not go any further today."

"Whatever you say."

I had her tense and loosen muscle groups, moving from her head to her toes. She closed her eyes and her body swayed in time with my voice. I was sure she'd go under quickly.

Instead, she fell asleep.

At first I didn't realize it and kept talking. Then I saw her head tilt back and her mouth open, letting out soft, delicate snores.

No more body sway.

No movement at all but the heave of her chest.

"Lucy, if you can hear me, lift your right index finger."

Nothing.

I picked up her hand. Limp.

I flexed her head. No tension.

"Lucy?"

Silence.

Her eyes moved rapidly behind their lids, then stopped.

Sleep. The ultimate resistance.

I put her hand down and made sure she didn't slip off the chair. The air gun had stopped. The yard was too quiet.

She dozed for a while; then suddenly her body began jerking and twitching.

Crunching her facial features.

Grunting.

Fragmented REM, the kind associated with nightmares.

I stroked her hand, told her everything was okay. She fell asleep.

A moment later, the same pattern.

After two more episodes, I said, "Wake up, Lucy." She didn't till a minute later, and I wasn't sure it was in response to my voice.

Sitting up, she opened her eyes. Looking at me but not seeing me.

She closed them and went slack.

Oblivious, once more.

I tried to shake her awake, gently.

Each time I got her to open her eyes, she rolled them drowsily and the lids closed.

Finally, I managed to bring her out. She blinked and stared and muttered something and rubbed her eyes.

"What's that, Lucy?"

"What happened?"

"You fell asleep."

"I did?" Yawn.

"You've been sleeping almost half an hour."

"I—we—we were doing hypnosis, weren't we? I wasn't dreaming about that, was I?"

"No, we were doing hypnosis."

"Was I hypnotized?"

"Yes. You were right about being good at it."

"Did I do—say anything?"

"No, you fell asleep."

She stretched. "I feel refreshed. Was that supposed to happen —falling asleep?"

"It needed to happen."

"I didn't say anything at all?"

"No, but we're just starting out. You did great."

"But I'm a good subject?"

"You're an excellent subject."

She smiled. "Okay, I guess I'd better just let it play itself out —but I do feel *good*. Hypnosis is great. You should do it with Ken."

"Why's that?"

"He's going through some very tough times. His ex-wife is really vindictive, out to take him to the cleaners, doesn't let him see his kids. He has visitation, and the court keeps ordering her to comply. But when she doesn't, they don't enforce it."

"When did they get divorced?"

"A year ago. He didn't come out and actually say so, but I get the feeling she had an affair. He's real cheerful all the time for my sake, but he's feeling it—very restless at night. I heard him go downstairs twice. This morning I got up at five-thirty and he was dressed and doing paperwork."

"Sounds like a hard worker."

"Very. He got into real estate right out of college. Started off as a clerk and worked himself up. But it's taken a toll. He's got a bottle of Maalox in his briefcase."

She was silent for a moment. "One big happy family, huh?"

Closing her eyes, she tilted her head back again.

"You know, it's strange, but as we talk right now I'm starting to get in touch with bits and pieces of memory—about being sent to California that summer."

"In touch how?"

"Like bits of—light. Poking through a piece of fabric. I can't really explain it . . . it doesn't feel bad."

"What do you remember?"

"Nothing specific, just the bits and pieces—like something on the tip of your tongue? It's almost as if the corners of my mind are being pulled back and I'm peeking through but I can't see clearly. . . ."

She frowned. Her forehead knitted.

"Nothing more," she said, opening her eyes. "But it doesn't seem weird anymore—being up there and not remembering. It's as if I'm getting in touch with my own history."

I thought of the nanny Ken had mentioned. Enough for one day.

"When can we do this again?" she said.

"I can see you tomorrow. Two o'clock at my house."

"Great."

"In the meantime, I assume you want me to ignore Lowell's invitation."

I expected a quick reaction, but she put her finger to her lip and thought. "I guess the only reason to talk to him would be to find out what he's up to. And maybe I should do that myself."

"That's a lot to bite off, right now," I said. "If you want to scope him out, I could listen to what he has to say and report back to you."

"Believe me, I'm not rushing off to have a tête-à-tête with him. But if I send you to represent me, that'll just show him I'm weak."

"He already knows you're seeing me. And why should we care what he thinks?"

"True," she said. "But I don't want anything to do with him, directly or indirectly. I'd rather put my head in the oven—just kidding."

We went back into the house.

"You know," she said, "maybe I'm being too rigid. I guess it would be okay for you to meet with him if you think it could do any good."

"I can't promise you it would."

"Are you interested in meeting the Great Man?"

"I'm interested in meeting someone so destructive."

"A psychological specimen, huh?"

That wasn't what I'd meant, but she went on.

"Putting him under the microscope—okay, go ahead. Meanwhile, I'll concentrate on relaxing. Getting comfortable with my unconscious."

I was surprised to find Robin and Spike home.

"The electricians didn't show up," she said. "The truck broke down."

"Probably in the parking lot at Dodger Stadium."

"No doubt. I left the drywallers there, figured I'd get some work done here, and then maybe you and I could go out and have some fun."

"Fun? What's that?"

"I think it's something the Chinese invented. They invented everything, right?"

She put her arms around my waist and her face against my chest.

"Actually," she said, "I'm glad the turkeys flaked out. I've been thinking about how little we've seen of each other lately."

"When it's all done," I said, "let's go away somewhere."

"Where?"

"Some remote island without phones or TV."

Something bumped my ankle. I looked down and saw Spike staring up at us. He cocked his head and snorted.

"But with air-conditioning for the pooch," I said.

Robin laughed and bent to pet him.

He began breathing hard, then rolled over on his back, paws up, offering his beer gut. As Robin scratched him, he grumbled with pleasure.

Once in a while, things are simple.

22

At nine-thirty that evening they got complicated.

We were watching a bad old movie, laughing at the dialogue, when the phone rang and Milo said, "There's someone I thought you might like to meet. Right in the neighborhood, actually."

"My neighborhood?"

"Must be. I see the ocean." He gave me a name, then an address in Paradise Cove.

"Oh."

"Trailer park, right near the Sand Dollar."

"Are you there now?"

"Actually, I'm at the Sand Dollar bar—is this a bad time?"

Robin sat up and mouthed, "Patient?"

"Milo," I told her. "He's got someone he'd like me to meet."

"Now?"

I nodded.

"Go," she said. "But *definitely* no phones on the island."

The road down to the cove was unlit and hemmed in by hillside and sky. The guardhouse was empty and the gate was up. Beyond the Sand Dollar lot, the ocean was a tight stretch of black vinyl. The lot was nearly empty, and the restaurant's neon sign was suspended in the darkness.

I turned right and drove up a short steep road to the trailer park. The mobile homes were stuck into the sloping terrain like metal studs in leather. To the left was a small flat parking area atop a low bluff. Rick's white Porsche 928 was parked there and I

pulled in next to it, under the grasping branches of a huge pit-
tosporum tree.

The units were numbered in a system that defied logic, and it
took a while to find the address Milo'd given me.

I climbed nearly to the top of the park, walking on asphalt
paths lined with rock and seashell borders. Most of the trailers
were dark. Blue TV light seeped from behind a few curtained
windows.

The address I was looking for matched a white Happy
Tourister with aluminum siding and a bolt-on carport. A barbecue sat in the port. Geranium ivy grew around the wheel wells.

Milo answered my knock. A short, solid-looking woman in
her mid-sixties stood behind him. Her hair was tinted the color of
ranch mink and permed, and she had a small square face and
searching dark eyes. She wore a pea-green sleeveless blouse and
stretch jeans. She wasn't fat but her arms were heavy. Eyeglasses
hung from a chain around her neck.

Milo stood aside. The trailer's front room was a gold-stained
pine kitchen with a brown linoleum floor and white Formica
counters. It was sweet with the smell of baked beans.

The woman met my smile with one of her own, but it
seemed obligatory.

Milo said, "Mrs. Barnard, this is Dr. Delaware, our psychological consultant. Doctor, Mrs. Maureen Barnard."

"Mo," said the woman holding out a hand. We shook.

Milo said, "Mo was married to Felix Barnard."

The woman acknowledged the relationship with a sad look
and led us into the living area. More pine, gold carpets, a quilted
white sofa specked with gold, and a matching recliner. Big TV
and a very small stereo. The place was immaculate.

Mo Barnard took the recliner and Milo and I shared the
couch. The ceilings were very low, and Milo's bulk made the
room look even smaller than it was. On the coffee table was a
year's worth of *Reader's Digest* along with a thick bound stack of
supermarket coupons and a sandpiper carved out of driftwood.
Next to Mo was an octagonal pressed-wood table bearing a remote control and a cut-glass bowl of miniature candy bars: Hershey's, Mr. Goodbar, Krackel. She picked up the remote and put
it in her lap, then handed the bowl to Milo.

Unwrapping a Mr. Goodbar, he said, "As I told you, it was
Dr. Delaware who got us involved in the case that led us to look

into your husband's death." To me: "Mr. Barnard was murdered a year after Karen Best disappeared."

Mo Barnard was looking at me.

"I'm sorry," I said.

"Quite a shock when it happened," she said, "but it's been a long time. Strange to be hearing about it after all these years, but you never know, do you?"

Despite living at the beach, her skin was white and putty-soft. Her eyes had the flat, dark cast of a Grant Wood matriarch. She fingered the remote control and looked at the blank TV screen.

Milo gave me the candy bowl.

As I unwrapped a Hershey bar, he said, "Felix's killer was never found. He was shot in a motel on La Cienega near Pico. West side of the boulevard."

La Cienega was the border between Wilshire Division's jurisdiction and West L.A.'s. The west side of the street made it Milo's territory.

Mo Barnard sighed. Milo smiled at her, and the way she reciprocated it let me know he'd been here with her for a while.

"Strange," she said. "All these years. I thought he was with a whore, didn't know whether to be sad or mad. After a while, I forgot about that part of it. Now you come and tell me it could have been something else. You just never know, do you."

"Just a possibility," Milo reminded her.

"Yes, I know, it'll probably never be solved. But just the chance that he wasn't with a whore cheers me up a bit. He wasn't a bad guy—lots of good qualities, really."

Milo told me, "The motel was one of those places rented by the hour. So you can see why Mo assumed that."

"The *police* assumed it," she said. "Even though the motel clerk said he hadn't seen any woman go in with Felix. But of course, he could've lied. Felix was once a policeman himself. Just for a short time, in Baltimore; that's where he grew up. I met him in San Bernadino. He was working for an insurance company, investigating accident claims. I was a records clerk at city hall. He got let go right after we got married, and we moved to L.A."

"Did you work for the city here, too?" I said.

"No, I got a job doing the books for Fred Shale Real Estate, over in Pacific Palisades. I did that for thirty-one years. Felix and I lived in Santa Monica, near the Venice side. Felix's office was out here in Malibu, but this last year's the first time I've actually *lived* in Malibu. My sister and her husband own this place, but he's got bad lungs so they moved over to Cathedral City, near Palm Springs."

Milo said, "The interesting thing is, Mo feels Felix may have come into some money about a year before he was killed."

"I'm pretty sure of it," said Mo. "He denied it but the signs were there. I thought he was keeping someone on the side." Her cheeks colored. "Truth be known, he'd done that before, more than once. But in his younger days. He was sixty-three by then— ten years older than me, but when I married him I thought he was mature." She chuckled and said, "Hand me a Krackel bar, will you?"

Milo did.

"What signs did you notice?" I said.

"First of all, his retiring. For years he'd talked about it, but he always complained he couldn't get enough money together—always griped about my having health benefits and a pension from San Berdoo and from Shale, and he was out on his own with nothing. Then, all of a sudden, he just walks in and announces there's enough in the kitty. I said, 'What pie dropped out of the sky, Felix?' He just smiled and patted my head and said, 'Don't you worry, Sugaroo, we're finally going to get that place in Laguna Niguel.' We were always talking about buying a condo down there, but we didn't have the money. We might have been able to afford one of those retirement communities, but Felix never saw himself as old. When he turned fifty, he bought himself a *too*pay and contact lenses. I guess he figured being so much older than me—I used to look like a kid, people would sometimes mistake me for his daughter—he should do something about it. The other thing he did that made me suspicious was get a new car, a cherry-red Thunderbird, the Landau model, the vinyl top. Which was their top of the line. We had a big fight over that, me wanting to know how we could afford it and him saying it was none of my business."

She shook her head. "We fought a lot, but we stayed together thirty-one years. Then he got himself killed and there was no big money in his bank account, just a little over three thousand dollars, and I figured he'd spent whatever he had on the car. And whores. I drove that car for fifteen years, finally junked it."

"Did he leave any business records behind?" I said.

"You mean his detective files? No, I told Mr. Sturgis he

wasn't much for keeping records—truth is, he was pretty disorganized in general. After he died, I went through his things and was surprised how little there was—just scraps of paper with scrawls. I figured, his line of work, there might be things there that would embarrass people. I threw everything out."

"What kind of cases did he work on?"

She looked at Milo. "Same questions—no, I don't mind. I don't really know what kind of cases. Felix didn't talk about his work. Truth is, I don't think there were too many cases, toward the end. I know he did some work for lawyers, but for the life of me I can't remember the names of any of them. I wasn't part of his work, had my own job to do. I'm no feminist but I always worked. We never had kids, both of us just went and did our own job."

I nodded.

She said, "I don't mean to paint him as some kind of bum. Basically, he was a nice guy, didn't raise his voice, even when we fought. But he could be a little . . . easy around the edges, know what I mean?"

"Cutting corners."

" 'Zactly. The first time I met him he tried to pay me five dollars to release an accident record to him without filling out the proper forms and paying the county fee. I turned him down and he was real good-natured about it. Laughed it off—he had a great laugh. I was only nineteen, should have known better anyway, but I didn't. He came back the next day and asked me out. My parents hated his guts. Six months later we were married. Despite all the problems, he was a pretty good husband."

"So he never discussed Karen Best?"

"Never," she said. "Truth is, we didn't discuss much, period. We kept different hours. I'd be up at six, walking the dogs—we used to have miniature poodles—in the office at eight, back by five. Felix liked to sleep late. He claimed a lot of his work had to be done at night, and maybe it was true. He was gone a lot when I was home and vice versa." She grinned. "Maybe that's how we stayed together thirty-one years."

The grin dropped from her face.

"Still, his being killed was the worst thing ever happened to me after my parents passing away." To Milo: "When you first called, I didn't want to talk about it. But you were a gentleman, and then you told me maybe Felix didn't die because of whoring around. That would be nice to know."

23

She showed us two pictures of herself and Felix, saying, "These are the only ones I have. When you go mobile, you keep things to the minimum."

The first was a wedding portrait, the young couple posed in front of a painted backdrop of the Trevi Fountain. She'd been a pretty dark-haired girl, but even at nineteen her eyes had been wary. Felix wasn't much taller than his bride, a spare man with slicked hair and Clark Gable ears. He'd worn a pencil mustache, like Gable, but had none of the actor's strength in his face.

The second snapshot had been taken two years before Barnard's murder. The mustache was gone and the PI was stooped, his face lined, the toupee embarrassingly obvious. He wore a gray sharkskin suit with skinny lapels and a white turtleneck and held a cigarette in a holder. Mo's hair was bleached blond and she'd put on some weight, but despite that she did look young enough to be his daughter. The picture had been taken in a back yard, their faces shaded by a big orange tree.

"Our place in Santa Monica," she said. "I rent it out now. The income along with my pension's what keeps me going."

Milo asked to borrow the more recent photo, and she said, "Sure." We thanked her and left. As we stepped out of the trailer, she said, "Good luck to you. Let me know if you find out anything."

"Nice lady," I said, as we walked down to our cars.

"She fed me dinner," said Milo. "Beans and franks and potato chips. I was ready for camp songs. Before she really opened up, we watched *Jeopardy.* She knows a lot about presidents' wives."

"How long were you there?"

"Since six."

Four and a half hours. "Dedication."

"Yeah, beatify me."

"How'd you learn about Barnard's murder?"

"Social Security said he was deceased, so I checked county Death Records and it came up homicide, which needless to say surprised me. According to the autopsy report, he got shot in the back of the head in that motel, just like she said. What she doesn't know is that his pants were down around his ankles, but there was no evidence of sexual activity and he hadn't ejaculated recently."

"Was the place an outright bordello?"

"More of an anything-goes place. I knew it well from when I used to ride Westside patrol. Drugs, assaults, all-around obnoxious behavior. The detectives on the case assumed Barnard was a john who got in trouble."

"He was shot," I said. "Wouldn't a hooker have been more likely to stab him?"

"There are no rules, Alex. Some of the girls pack fire, or a pimp could have killed him; lots of them carry."

"Did anyone hear the shot?"

"Nope. Clerk discovered his body, cleaning up. By the time he called it in, place was empty."

"Deaf clerk?"

"It's a busy street, he had the TV blasting, who knows? There was no reason to think it was anything more than Barnard picking the wrong time and place for a blowjob."

"And now?"

"Maybe still. I called you because the fact that he was murdered knocks the Karen Best case up another notch on the Intrigue Scale. As does Mo's feeling that he came into dough."

"Best told me Karen was Barnard's last case," I said. "And Barnard was killed a year after Karen disappeared. You think he could have been blackmailing someone about Karen and they finally got tired of paying?"

"Or he got too greedy. On the other hand, he could have been blackmailing someone about another case totally *unrelated* to Karen. Or maybe he got the T-bird by saving pennies behind his wife's back. Or at the track. She said all he left her was three thousand bucks—how much would a T-bird have cost back then?"

"Probably six, seven thousand."

"Not major-league blackmail. We're still a long way from evidence. Barnard could have been shot simply because some whore *did* get mad at him."

"So where do we go from here?"

"I'll see if I can turn up anything more on him. Then I guess the logical thing is to try to find those Sand Dollar people and see if they remember anything about Karen."

He looked through the trees at the restaurant. No cars in the lot and only a few lights were on.

"I went in there tonight looking for Doris Reingold, but she's off for a couple of days. . . . The thing that bothers me about Barnard's investigation is if Karen was hired by the Sheas to work the Sanctum party, why wouldn't anyone at the Dollar have mentioned it?"

"You think someone told Barnard and he left it out intentionally?"

"Who knows? Like you said, maybe he was just an incompetent boob and didn't ask the right questions. Or he got answers and didn't think they were important."

"Malibu Sheriffs interviewed the same people," I said. "If Karen was working the party, why wasn't it in their reports?"

"Maybe she never was at the party. Or could be the sheriffs found out she was and didn't think it was important either."

"The last place she was seen wasn't important?"

"Her serving hors d'oeuvres to five hundred people isn't much of a lead, Alex. She could have been picked up by some party animal and run into trouble later. What reason would anyone have to suspect she was somewhere on the grounds, six feet under?"

We reached the bluff and I walked him to the Porsche. He opened the driver's door and fished for car keys.

"I told Lucy about Karen," I said.

"Oh?"

"I'm still not sure it was right, but I followed *my* instincts. It was either continue to hold back information from her, and take the chance it would destroy our rapport, or be straight."

"How'd she react?"

"Initial shock. Then she warmed to the idea that the dream

might actually mean something. Learning the truth's become her mission."

"Great."

"I'm doing my best to keep the lid on. So far, she's being reasonable. She asked for hypnosis to enhance her memory, and I agreed to try some basic relaxation. I thought she'd be really susceptible, and at first she seemed to be. Then she fell asleep. Which means she's resisting strongly. She slept very deeply and her dream pattern's fragmented. I actually watched her go in and out of several phases. I'm not surprised she's a sleepwalker and has chronic nightmares. She'd like to believe she sleepwalked her way into the kitchen and put her head in the oven, and I guess it's possible. Sleep's her great escape. She blocks things out by dozing off."

The keys came out of his pocket, and he jangled them. "Did it bother her, falling asleep?"

"I downplayed it, made it sound routine. I was worried about getting into too much too quickly, but overall the session seemed to help her. She left in good spirits. Other than the dream, her main concern's Puck. She's well aware of his addiction, defends him as a sick guy. And thinking about him helps her forget about her own troubles. You had any thoughts on the note?"

"Not really."

"Anything new on the copycat?"

"Not a thing, but I'm gonna check out the Bogettes very seriously." He got in the Porsche, started it, and lowered the window.

"I went by the Sheas' surf shop today," I said. "Bought a pair of shorts. Gwen arrived with their son. He's got severe cerebral palsy, needs constant care. Tom Shea drives a newish BMW 735, Gwen's got a customized van for transporting the boy, and both Best and Doris Reingold said the Sheas have a house on the beach at La Costa. Even years ago that was serious money. Not to mention all the medical expenses. The shop didn't look like any big cash cow, but even assuming it is, how'd they get the capital to start up a business by tending bar and waiting tables? Now that we're thinking about Barnard getting paid off, it makes me wonder if they did, too."

"Gwen was obviously an enterprising lady, subcontracting catering. Maybe she had other things going."

"It's still quite a leap from moonlighting to living on the sand. Coming into a little venture capital twenty-one years ago would have helped. Be interesting to know what transpired between the time the Sheas left for Aspen and returned. And why they left in the first place. If it was just because Sherrell Best was bugging them, that would imply some kind of guilt."

"Well," he said, "I gave the widow Barnard plenty of information. Malibu's still a small town, there should be some whispering. Break a few eggs, and who knows?"

"Flushing out the prey?"

He turned his hand into a pistol and pointed it at the windshield. "Boom."

"I may have a shot at big game," I said. "Lucy and I decided I should accept Buck Lowell's invitation to chat."

His hand lowered. "Where you going to meet with him?"

"Sanctum."

"Don't go snooping around the dirt looking for burial plots."

"I promise. Dad."

"Listen, I know you. . . . Meanwhile, you want to talk to Doris Reingold again, or should I try?"

"I can do it; we're already pals. If she's got nothing to hide, another big tip might be enough to pry something loose."

"Hoo-hah, Daddy Warbucks."

"I expect to be reimbursed by the department."

"Oh, sure, absolutely. Officer Santa Claus'll deliver it to you personally. And no new taxes."

24

The next morning, feeling like a hunter, I called Sanctum. The same woman who'd answered the first time picked up. Before I finished introducing myself, she said, "Hold on."

Several minutes later: "He'll see you here, tomorrow at one. We're hard to find, these are the directions."

I copied them and she hung up.

I got Terry Trafficant's book from the bedroom and searched for mention of his editor, but there was none. At his publisher, a confused receptionist said, "There isn't anyone here by that name."

"He's an author."

"Fiction or nonfiction?"

Good question. "Nonfiction."

"Hold on."

A moment later, a man said, "Editorial."

"I'm trying to locate Terrence Trafficant's editor."

"Who?"

"Terrence Trafficant. *From Hunger to Rage.*"

"Is that on our current list?"

"No, it was published twenty-one years ago."

Click.

A woman said, "Remainders."

I repeated my request.

"No," she said, "that isn't on our roster. When was it published?"

"Twenty-one years ago."

"Then I'm sure it's long gone to the pulp mill. Try a used bookstore."

"I don't want the book. I'm looking for the editor."

Click. Back to the same man at Editorial, very unhappy to hear from me. "I'm sure I have no idea who that was, sir. People come and go all the time."

"Would there be any way to find out?"

"Not that I'm aware of."

"Please connect me to your editorial director."

"That's Bridget Bancroft," he said, as if that ended it.

"Then that's who I'll speak to."

Click.

"Bridget Bancroft's office."

"I'd like to speak with Ms. Bancroft."

"Regarding?"

"Excerpting one of your authors. My name is Alex Printer, and I represent Delaware Press in California. We'd like to include some selections from Terrence Trafficant's *From Hunger to Rage* in a—"

"You'd need to speak to our Rights department about that."

"Could you tell me who Mr. Trafficant's editor is?"

"What's the author's name?"

"Trafficant. *From Hunger to Rage.* Published twenty-one years ago."

"I have no idea. People come and go."

"Would Ms. Bancroft know?"

"Ms. Bancroft's on vacation."

"Would you please ask her to call me when she gets back?"

"Certainly," she said. "Would you like to speak to Rights?"

"Please."

Click. Voice mail. I left another message and hung up.

Ah, fame.

Lucy arrived precisely on time for her afternoon appointment. She looked energetic, and her eyes were bright.

"I got plenty of sleep last night—no dream—so I shouldn't doze off. It's a little weird sleeping in someone else's bed, but Ken said I'd get used to it; he does it all the time."

Suddenly, she clamped her lips. Her eyes misted.

"Anything wrong?" I said.

"Nothing. . . . I was just thinking of the summer I worked for Raymond. Sleeping in that bed. . . . I used to have to put on stuff for the customers: lots of makeup, skimpy outfits, sometimes wigs. Costume jewelry, so they could pretend they were rich."

She hunched and dropped her head. Each hand gripped a bicep and she hugged herself very tightly.

"They had their fantasies," she said.

The ocean roared. She didn't move.

"I hated it," she said softly. "I really *hated* it. Being *invaded*, hour after *hour*, day after *day*! I put myself somewhere else—like hypnosis, I guess. Maybe that's why it's easy for me."

"Cutting yourself off."

Nod.

"Where'd you go?"

"To the beach." She laughed. "How's that for karma? Usually it worked. But sometimes I'd come back to the real world, lying there— someone *on* me. I don't want *ever* to lose control like that again."

Straightening her back, she said, "No offense, but no man can ever really understand. Men don't get invaded. Maybe that's why the dream's coming back. All those years ago I saw *Karen* invaded and it stuck in my head, and somehow . . ."

She reached for a tissue.

"So," she said, "time for hypnosis? I won't go bananas on you, I promise."

"Scout's honor?"

"Scout's honor."

I had her relax and stare at the ocean as I explained that age regression wasn't always effective or accurate. How some people couldn't get in touch with childhood memories, even under the deepest hypnotic trance. How others imagined or manufactured false memories.

She nodded, dreamy already.

I began the induction and she went under almost immediately, achieving waxy limbs and surface anesthesia to a pinprick.

I had her go to a "favorite place" and left her there for a while. She looked serene.

I said, "Lucy, can you talk to me?"

Her "yes" was low and throaty, nearly inaudible over the waves.

"You can," I said, "but talking's hard work, isn't it?"

"Yes."

"But you're comfortable."

"Yes."

"And you want to communicate with me."

"Yes."

"Talking's hard work because you're so relaxed, Lucy. That's good. To make it easier for you to communicate, you can answer yes or no with finger signals. If the answer's 'yes,' raise your right index finger. If it's 'no,' raise your left index finger. Do you understand?"

She mouthed something. Then her right finger rose.

"Very good. Put it down now; from here on, you just have to leave it up for a second. Now, let's try a 'no' for practice—good. You're going to stay deeply relaxed and be able to say what you need to say. Understand?"

The right finger rose and dropped.

"Do you want to stop our hypnosis right here?"

Left finger.

"You want to go on."

Right finger.

"Do you remember what we discussed about age regression?"

Right finger.

"Would you like to try that now?"

Right finger.

"Okay, take a nice deep breath and get even more relaxed, more and more peaceful, very much in control, hearing the sound of my voice but staying totally in control of your own feelings and perceptions. Good. . . . Now I'd like you to picture yourself in a room with a giant TV screen. A very pleasant, comfortable room. You're in a comfortable chair and the screen is in front of you. You're watching the screen and feeling very relaxed. On the screen is a calendar with today's date on it. A desk calendar, the type with pages that flip. Can you see it?"

Right finger.

"Good. This calendar is special. Instead of each page being a day, this calendar holds the same date and changes years. The top page is today's date, this year. The one under it is today's date, last year—watch as I flip it."

Her right hand twitched and her eyes moved.

"Can you see last year's date?"
Right finger.
"Now I'm going to flip the next page."
Twitch.
"What date is it?"
Her lips moved. "Two . . . years ago."
"Right. Today's date, two years ago. Let's stay with that date for a minute. Take a deep breath and count to three, and at three you can go to where you were on that date. But you'll be watching yourself on the screen. As if you're watching someone else. Seeing what you need to see. But no matter what happens on the screen, it doesn't have to bother you. Understand? Good. Okay, ready: One. Two. Three."

She inhaled and let it out through an open mouth. The faintest of nods.
"Where are you now, Lucy?"
Pause. "Work."
"At work?"
Right finger.
"Where at work?"
"Desk."
"At your desk. Good. Now tell me what you're doing at your desk."
She tightened her face; then it loosened very slowly.
"Simkins . . . Manufacturing . . . accounts receivable."
"Doing the books on Simkins Manufacturing. Is it a big job?"
Right finger.
"A big accounting job. How do the books look?"
Pause. Her brows knitted. "Sloppy."
"Sloppy."
Right finger.
"But that doesn't bother you, because you're just watching it, you're not experiencing it."
Her brow relaxed.
"Good. Do you want to stay there for a while, working?"
Left finger. Smile.
"No?"
"Boring."
"Okay, let's go to another year. Take a deep breath, count to three, and we'll return to our calendar on the screen. One. Two. Three."

*   *   *

I took her back in time, gradually, careful to avoid the summer in Boston. She remembered her sixteenth summer, playing gin rummy with a cleaning maid in her summer school dorm room, no other children around. Twelve was similar isolation, reading *Jane Eyre* in a room with a single bed. As she felt herself younger, her posture loosened and her voice got higher, more tentative, displaying an occasional stammer.

I brought her back to the age of eight—a summer at yet another boarding school. Riding horseback with the headmistress but unable to remember any other children.

No mention of Puck or any other family member.

The loneliness she'd grown up with became more vivid. I felt sad and made sure to keep that out of my voice.

She sat very low in the chair, nearly supine, ankles crossed, knees slightly apart, a fingertip on her lip.

I changed the date on the calendar to August 14. Took her back to age six. Her eyes moved very fast and her voice assumed a slight whine as she told me about losing a favorite doll.

Breathing deeply and peacefully.

"Okay," I said, "now let's flip two more pages, Lucy. You're four years old."

Her breath caught and she knuckled her eyes.

"Deeper relaxed, Lucy. So, so peaceful. Watching the screen, so it doesn't have to bother you."

Her hands fell to her lap. Her legs spread more, the feet turned on their side.

"Four years old," I said. "What are you watching?"

Silence.

"Lucy?"

"House." Very soft, very high, almost a squeak.

"Watching a house on the screen."

"Uh-*hu*-uh."

"A nice house?"

Silence. "House."

"Okay. Do you want to keep watching that house?"

Left finger.

"You want to watch something else?"

Silence. Confusion. Then: "Dark."

"It's dark outside."

"Go out."

"You want to watch yourself going out."

"Lights. Far . . . go out."

"It's dark and you want to go to the lights."

"Uh-*hu*-uh."

"Have you been sleeping?"

"Uh-*hu*-uh."

"You can also tell me 'yes' with your finger."

Right finger.

"Very good. So you're in the house and you want to go out. Why don't you just tell me in your own words what's going on."

She fidgeted and touched her nose. Sniffed and blinked and opened her eyes. But she wasn't seeing me.

They closed again.

"Sleep . . . walk. Sleep . . . walk. Door . . . wood. Out . . . out, out . . . out . . .

She grimaced. Her breath quickened and her chest heaved.

"Relax, Lucy. Deeper and deeper relaxed, remembering what you need to remember, seeing what you need to see. . . . Good, very good. Just keep breathing deeply. No matter what you see or hear or touch or smell or remember, you'll stay deeper and deeper relaxed, watching yourself from the TV room, so safe and calm and in control . . . good. Okay, go on."

"Out . . . lights. People yelling." Puzzled look. "Not my fault . . ."

"Deeper and deeper relaxed."

She sighed and her head drooped. Said something I couldn't hear.

I moved my chair right next to hers. A carotid pulse was beating slow and steady. Her cheeks were pink. I touched the top of her hand. Warm. Her fingers curled around mine and squeezed.

"Walk," she said. "Trees—pretty."

She said nothing for a long time, but her eyes kept moving and her head bobbed.

Walking in place.

Her head moved from side to side.

Taking in the scenery?

Suddenly, I felt her hand go cold.

"What is it, Lucy?"

"*Father.*"

"You see Father on the screen?"

Long pause as she gripped my hand. Then her right index finger rose but the rest of her fingers stayed clamped.

"Deeper and deeper relaxed, Lucy."

Slow breathing, but louder and harsher.

"You can leave this place, Lucy. You can turn off the TV any time you want to."

She made a growling sound, and the left finger stayed up in the air for several seconds.

"You want to stay here."

Right finger.

"Okay, that's fine. Go ahead, do what you want to do and tell me what you want to tell me."

A long silence. "Father . . . men . . . carrying lady. Pretty. Like Mama . . . dark . . . hair. Pretty . . . carrying."

More silence. The pulse in her neck quickened.

I said, "Other men, too."

Right finger.

"How many?"

Concentration. Her head moved from side to side. "Two."

"Two besides Father?"

Right finger. Her hand remained cold. Sweat flowed from her hairline, trickling down her cheek. She seemed impervious as I wiped it.

"You're just watching it," I whispered. "You're safe."

"Two," she said.

"What do they look like?"

Silence.

"Can you see them?"

Right finger. "Carrying the lady."

"Is she saying anything?"

Left finger.

"What's she wearing?"

"Blouse . . . white blouse . . . skirt."

"What color skirt?"

"White."

"A white blouse and a white skirt. Any shoes?"

Left finger. "Toes."

"You see her toes."

Right finger.

"Is she moving them?"

Left finger. "Not moving."

"Can you see her face?"

Silence. "Pretty. Sleeping."

"She's sleeping."

Confused look. "Not moving."

"She's not moving at all?"

Right finger.

"So you think she's sleeping."

Right finger. "Carrying her."

"The men are carrying her. Is Father carrying her?"

Left finger. "Hair . . . hairy lip."

"A man with a hairy lip is carrying her?" I thought of Terry Trafficant's bearded, skeletal face.

Right finger.

"You can see the men now."

She puckered her face. "Hairy Lip . . . other man turned around."

"The third man is turned around. You see his back?"

Right finger.

"Can you see what the other men are wearing?"

Silence. "Father . . . white . . . down to ground." Confused.

"Down to the ground. Long. Like a robe?"

Right finger.

"And the other men?"

"Dark . . . clothes."

"Both of them?"

Right finger. "Dark outside. Too."

"It's dark outside and it's hard to see. But you can see Father's white robe and the lady's white blouse. The other two men are wearing dark clothes."

Another look of confusion. She pouted. "*Ha*-ard."

"It's okay, Lucy. Whatever you see is okay. Just tell me whatever you want to."

She squinted, as if trying to focus. Tensed and sat up.

"Shovel . . . digging . . . Hairy Lip . . . Father holding the lady. Hairy Lip and the other man are digging. Digging fast, digging. Digging and digging. Digging. Father holding . . . heavy. Says 'Heavy' . . . 'Hurry the hell up!' Angry . . . puts her down. . . ."

She shook her head and sweat flew.

I dabbed her again. "Father put the lady down on the ground?"

Right finger.

"Digging . . . and digging and digging. . . . 'Roll it.' "
Her voice deepened. 'Roll it, *roll* it!' "

"You're watching it, Lucy. On the screen. You're sa—"

Her fingernails dug into mine. The child's voice returned.
"Lady . . . gone. Lady gone! Lady gone! *Lady gone!*"

25

She slipped into inert silence as I flipped the calendar pages back to the present.

Before I brought her completely out, I gave her posthypnotic suggestions to feel refreshed and successful and to be able to remember anything she'd seen that night while remaining relaxed.

She came out smiling and yawning. "I'm not sure what happened, but I feel pretty good."

I had her stretch and walk around. Then I told her.

"Three men," she said.

"You described one as having a hairy lip."

She rubbed the rim of her water glass. "A mustache? I can't really remember that—can't remember anything—but that *feels* right. Hints of memories, distant but right. Am I making sense?"

"Perfect sense."

"Can I go back under and try some more?"

"I think we've done enough."

"What about tomorrow?"

"All right," I said. "But promise me not to try anything by yourself before then."

"I promise. Now can I see that picture of Karen?"

I went and got the clipping from the *Shoreline Shopper*.

The moment she looked at the photo her hands began to shake.

She took the paper from me, stared at it for a long time. As she began to read, her hands stilled. But the color had left her face and her freckles stood out like Braille dots.

Handing the clipping back to me, she nodded. Then she cried.

At four, I drove to the Sand Dollar. The film crew was there again and a blond beach goddess in a black thong bikini was posing on the sand with a sweating can of beer.

As I entered the restaurant, I spotted Doris Reingold at the bar. She got off her stool. "Hi, there." After seating me near the window, she said, "Back in a jiff."

I was the only customer in the place. The beach was unpopulated. A busboy brought me coffee and I watched the blonde smile on command, flipping her hair, turning herself slowly like a chicken on a spit.

"Good view?" said Doris, pad in hand.

"Hooray for Hollywood."

She laughed. "Good to see you back. Early dinner? We just got in some fresh local halibut."

"No, just a snack. What kind of pie do you have?"

"Lemme see." She ticked her pad with her pen. "Today we've got apple and chocolate cream and, I think, pecan."

"Apple with vanilla ice cream."

She brought me a double wedge under two dollops of ice cream.

"Feel free to sit down," I said.

She touched her gray hair. "Sure. Marvin's not in for a while, why not?"

After pouring coffee for herself, she slid into the booth, the way she had the first time. Looking out at the blonde, she said, "Girl like that, gonna get herself one of two things: rich or in trouble."

"Or both." I cut into the pie.

"True," she said. "One doesn't eliminate the other. You have kids?"

"No, I'm not married."

"That doesn't mean anything. You know the definition of a bachelor? No kids—to speak of."

We both chuckled.

I said, "You said you had two, right?"

"Two boys, both grown, both army master sergeants, both married with kids of their own. Their dad was an army man, too.

I divorced him when they were little, but somehow it rubbed off."

"Must have been tough raising them by yourself."

"Wasn't a picnic." She freed her pack of cigarettes and lit up, then took in a mouthful of coffee. "Tell you what I do enjoy, being a grandmother. You buy them stuff, play with 'em, and then you go home."

"So I've heard."

"Yeah, it's great." She smoked and stirred some sugar into her coffee.

"I'd like to have kids of my own," I said.

"Why not, you're young."

"It's a little scary. All those things that can go wrong. I used to work in a hospital, saw plenty of misery."

"Yeah, there's plenty of that."

"I was over by your friends' surf shop the other day and saw their son. Really sad."

She appraised me, through the smoke. "What made you go there?"

"Needed some swim trunks. When I passed by I remembered your telling me about it. Nice place, but how'd they get a house on the beach with that?"

She shrugged and gave a sour look.

"Still," I said. "That kid. No money in the world can make up for that. What is it, cerebral palsy?"

"Birth accident," she said, but wariness had crept into her voice. "I think he twisted his neck coming out or something."

"How old is he?"

"Sixteen or so. Yeah, it's tough, but we've all got our crosses to bear, so why dwell on it?"

She kept smoking and pretending not to study me. I ate some more pie.

After dragging half her cigarette down, she put it in the ashtray and watched it smolder. "I *do* feel sorry for them. It's a good example of what you just said—money *and* trouble."

Looking at the film crew again, she said, "Why all the interest in Gwen and Tom, handsome?"

All friendliness gone from her voice.

"No particular interest. They just came up."

"That so?"

"Sure. Is something the matter?"

She stared at me. "You tell me."

I ate pie and smiled. "Everything's fine with me."

"You some kind of bill collector? Or a cop?"

"Neither."

"What are you then?"

"What's the matter, Doris?"

"That's not an answer."

"I'm a psychologist, just like I said. Are Gwen and Tom in some kind of trouble?"

She pocketed her smokes and her lighter and got up. Standing over me, one thigh pressing into the rim of the table, she smiled. To a casual observer she would have looked like a helpful waitress.

"You come on real friendly, and then you ease the conversation around to Tom and Gwen. That just seems a strange thing for a guy to talk to a gal about."

Turning her back on me, she walked back to the bar. The restaurant was still empty.

I ate a few more bites of pie and then I saw her leave the restaurant. Throwing bills down on the table, I went after her.

She was heading for a shopworn red Camaro parked near the movie crew trucks. Cables were strewn across the parking lot, and one caught her heel and she went down. One of the grips picked her up, and other film people gathered around her. The blond model stopped posing.

I was within twenty feet of her when she saw me. She pointed and said something that made the people look at me as if I was slime on bone china.

A human knot closed around her, protectively.

I turned around, walking, not running, but when I made it to the Seville I was breathless.

I got in the car. No one had followed me but everyone was still looking at me. They kept on looking as I peeled out.

26

I reached Milo at work and told him what had just happened. "Didn't have a chance to get to Karen. Just talking about the Sheas—how they made their money—upset her."

"Jealous?"

"There was some kind of hostility there. She wasn't sympathetic about their having a kid with CP. What if she and the Sheas all got paid off to keep quiet about Karen, but the Sheas used it to build up a personal fortune and she blew it? I know it's a big jump, but she did say she worked catering gigs for Gwen. If the Sanctum party was one of them, she could very well have been there."

"Huge jump," he said, "but I'll see what I can find out about her. Meanwhile, stay away from there."

"Something else: Lucy and I did hypnosis again, and this time there was no resistance. I age-regressed her back to four years old, and she was able to make out more details of the dream. Definitely two other men besides Lowell. One's back was to her the whole time; the other had what she called a hairy lip, which I assume is a mustache. Trafficant wore a mustache and goatee, back then. Anything come up on him yet?"

"Haven't learned a damn thing except he stopped filing tax returns the year he vanished. As far as I can tell, he hasn't shown up in any major penal institutions. No death records either, but a guy like that would know how to work the system."

"I tried to trace him through his publisher. No one seemed to remember him at all. I didn't get the feeling they were trying to stonewall, just that he'd really faded from the scene."

"Yeah. Well, for all we know he's in Algeria or Cuba or something, still getting his royalty checks. Meanwhile, I've got something more immediate to deal with. Another copycat, discovered this morning. We've kept the media at bay, but you'll see it on the eleven o'clock news. Fourteen-year-old kid named Nicolette Verdugo. Walking home from school yesterday, never showed up. Cal Trans crew found her at daybreak in a drainage ditch out in Diamond Bar, near the Orange County border."

"Fourteen," I said. "Oh, Jesus."

He coughed and cleared his throat. "So now it's a new task force, the FBI's probably going to be called in, and guess who's representing Angel City? When Shwandt's lawyers find out about this, I promise you it's war. But the whole thing stinks. Keep this confidential: Both Shannon and Nicolette were defecated on, but neither had any semen in or on or near them. Ejaculation was a *major* thing for Shwandt; sometimes he did it more than once on a victim. In fact, the only time he *didn't* ejaculate was with Barbara Pryor, because he was too stoned to get an erection. Now why would someone pull off a first-rate copycat, cover all the details, and leave that out?"

"Someone who can't ejaculate," I said. "A woman? You think the Bogettes really could be behind it?"

"Who the hell knows? It's pretty hard to imagine women butchering another woman that way, but Manson's hags were pretty good with forks and knives. Problem is, how do we get close to them? There's absolutely no grounds for warrants; all we can do is try to interview them, and if they say fuck you, as they did today, we say thank you, ladies, and go home. That leaves surveillance, and with their level of paranoia they'll probably burrow deep underground. Anyway, it means eighteen-hour days for me. So do me a favor and keep an eye on Lucy. I'm not going to be much of a guardian angel."

"Anything specific I should do?"

"Keep her away from her own apartment till I clear up that goddamn note. Given this new murder, I'd rather err by being too cautious. The turds, by the way, were of *Rattus rattus* origin— our little black scurrying pal. And speaking of rats, all I've been able to learn about Brother Puck was that he had some dealings a few years ago with a dope group from Montebello. Small-time buys and sells; then they handed him thirty grand to peddle to other junkies, and he got busted. After that they cut him off, and he's been going to East L.A. for bits and pieces."

"Who paid for his defense?"

"Haven't found that out yet. If he comes back to town, I'll have a little talk with him. Meanwhile, give Lucy my best."

"One more thing," I said. "I showed Karen's picture to Lucy, and she's sure Karen was the girl in the dream. It's possible she's confabulating—wishful thinking because she hates her father and is on a mission to learn the truth—but her reaction was pretty extreme: She went white, started shaking."

"Your intuition tells you it's genuine?"

"My intuition's been rather quiet recently."

"Mine, too, when it comes to her."

"Maybe we can get corroboration of Karen's presence at the party from someone who worked that night."

"Someone who wasn't paid off? You know, Alex, the more I think about it, the whole idea of payoffs doesn't really cut it, logically. All you've got on the Sheas is that Best doesn't like the look in their eyes and they were lucky enough to make some money over a twenty-year period. All you've got on Doris is *she* doesn't like the Sheas. No indication of any collusion. If something happened that the three of them *and* Felix Barnard found out about, what's the theory? The whole bunch of them put the arm on Lowell or Trafficant or whoever had something to hide? And if Barnard's death was tied in with blackmail, why would the others be allowed to live?"

"They didn't break the rules; Barnard did."

"Still, to leave all those loose ends for so long? People living down the road from you knowing you were involved in *killing* a girl?"

"Maybe they didn't know the gory details. Just that Karen was last seen at the party. Lowell could have told them she had a bad drug trip and left early, something like that."

"So why pay them off?"

"To avoid bad publicity for Sanctum. Trafficant's presence had already created controversy. Trafficant killing Karen would have finished Lowell off."

"So who's our corroborator, some other server? What do we have here, a whole *platoon* of people who knew Karen had worked the party? With Best looking for her obsessively, all those fliers he put up, cornering people at the shopping center, you mean to tell me *no* one came forward?"

"They might not have if they really didn't believe she'd been harmed. What if the other servers were told she'd run off with a boyfriend and didn't *want* to be found? Or that Best was an abusive father and Karen was scared to death of him? Maybe spinning *that* yarn was what the Sheas got paid for. Which would make them collaborators and help ensure their silence."

"A yarn," he said.

"Convincing young people it was true wouldn't have been too hard. Remember the times: Don't trust anyone over thirty."

"Maybe," he said doubtfully.

"Locating the other servers would help," I said. "Especially those other women from the Dollar—Andreas and Billings."

"Nothing on them yet, and I can't promise you I'll have time to do a comprehensive in the near future. So do me a favor and don't launch Lucy on any trajectory you can't control. Keep yourself safe, too. I've got enough to worry about."

27

A warm quiet morning, lit by a primrose-yellow sun. Hypnosis session number three. Induction was effortless. Within minutes Lucy was four years old and watching herself wander through the forest.

Once again, Hairy Lip's and Lowell's faces were visible, but the third man kept his back to her and she could produce nothing more about him.

I questioned her more about the mustache.

"Is the hair on his lip dark or blond?"

She looked confused.

"Is Hairy Lip's hair brown, Lucy?"

"Don't . . . know."

"Is it blond—yellow?"

Consternation.

"The hairy lip, is it just a mustache—is the hair only on the top lip? Or does he have a beard, hair all over his face?"

"Um . . ." Shrug. "Hairy lip."

"Just a hairy lip?"

Shrug.

When she came out, I reviewed what she'd told me.

"Didn't do very well this time, did I?"

"You did fine. It's not a performance."

She knuckled her forehead. "I know it's all in here. Why can't I bring it out?"

"Maybe there's nothing else to remember. You're seeing

things the way you saw them then. Through a four-year-old's eyes. Certain concepts wouldn't have been available to you."

"I was so excited about today, I thought we'd make real progress."

"Give it time, maybe more will come out."

I let her sit quietly for a while.

"Actually," she said, "there *was* something. The trees where they buried her. I noticed something about them but you didn't ask me so I couldn't tell you—didn't have the words." Her eyes closed. "The image keeps coming back to me. Lacy."

"Lacy trees?"

Nod.

"What kind?"

She frowned. "I don't know."

"Just that they were lacy."

"And pretty. It's like"—her eyes opened—"I guess what you said was true. I didn't have the word 'lacy' when I was four, so I couldn't put it into words. But now that I'm an adult again, it came back to me. Pretty, lacy trees. Does that make sense?"

"Yes."

She shook her head. "Lacy trees. That's all I can say. Do you have time for me tomorrow?"

"Tomorrow morning?"

"Any time. I've got nothing to do but read old magazines and watch TV. Being alone in a big house is a lot more solitude than I'm used to."

"Ken's not around much?"

"Hardly at all. We're planning to spend some time together over the weekend, maybe take a drive somewhere."

Her hands were busy, fingers rubbing against one another.

"The third man," she said. "He keeps his back to me the whole time. It's frustrating. And all I can really see of the other one is the mustache."

I went and got the copy of Terry Trafficant's book, opened it to the rear flap, and showed her the author photo.

"No, definitely not. Sorry. His mustache is wimpy. Hairy Lip's was big and dark and thick."

She put the book down.

I said, "Could you describe him so someone could draw him?"

Her eyes closed again. Her squint looked painful. "I can see him but I can't really describe his features—it's as if I'm . . . *handicapped.* As if part of my brain is working, but I can't translate what I see into words."

She opened her eyes.

"I think I'd know him if I saw him, but I just can't tell you anything more about him other than the mustache. I'm sorry—it's not like actually seeing. More like images making their way into my mind. That sounds flaky, doesn't it? Maybe I'm totally off base on all of it."

"We'll just take it as far as it goes, Lucy."

"But I want to find out—for Karen's sake."

"It's possible Karen has nothing to do with the dream."

"She does," she said quickly. "I *feel* it. I know that sounds as if I'm letting my imagination get out of control. But I'm not. I didn't wish this upon myself. Why would I want to be dreaming about *him*?"

I didn't answer.

"Okay," she said. "We'll just take it as it comes. Is today the day you go up to see him?"

"Today at one."

She scratched her knee.

"Has that been on your mind?" I said.

"A bit."

"Any change of heart about my meeting him?"

"No. . . . I guess I'm a little nervous—though why should I be? You'll be dealing with it, not me."

I left the house at twelve-thirty, turned off PCH at the red clapboard buildings of the Malibu Feed Bin, and headed up Topanga Canyon Road, cutting through the palisades.

The drought had stripped the mountains down to the chapparal, but last month's freak rains had brought back some tender buds and the granite was freckled with weeds and wildflowers. Randomly planted eucalyptus appeared on the west side of the road. To the east was a gorge that deepened and darkened as I gained altitude.

There was little to break up the scenery for the first few miles other than an occasional shack or abandoned car. Then a scattering of small businesses appeared among dry, yellow clearings: a lumberyard, a general store and post office, a lean-to advertising magic crystals at discount.

At the top of the road was a fork that separated Old Topanga Road from the newer highway that led into the Valley. Both routes were empty.

The original Topanga settlers had been Californio homesteaders and New England gold panners, asking for little but beauty and riches and privacy. Their descendants still owned land in the canyon, and individualism remained the Topanga way.

During the sixties and seventies—the time of the Sanctum party—the hippies had invaded in giddy droves, living in caves, scrounging for food, and eliciting outrage the natives hadn't known they had in them. Gary Hinman had a house in Topanga back then, as did lots of other musicians, and he was recording rock 'n' roll tracks in his home studio when the Manson family murdered him.

No more hippies now. Most had wandered off, some had died from overdoses of freedom, a few had become transformed to Topanga burghers. But the canyon hadn't turned into Levittown. Artists and writers and others who didn't keep regular hours continued to homestake here, and I knew several professors and psychotherapists willing to brave the hour-plus drive to the city in order to return here at night. One of them, a man who studied the biochemistry of rage, once told me he'd come across a mountain lion in his back yard one night, savaging a raccoon and licking its chops.

"Scared the shit out of me, Alex, but it also took me to a higher spiritual level."

I turned left onto the old road. The next couple of miles were darker and greener and cooler, shaded by sycamores, maples, willows, and alders that arched over the blacktop.

Pretty, lacy trees.

Houses appeared every hundred to two hundred feet, most of them modest and one-storied and set into vine-crusted glades. Those on the left side of the road sat behind a dry wash, accessible by footbridge or through old railroad boxcars turned into tunnels.

Mine was the only car on the road, and though I could smell horse manure, there were no steeds in sight. I pulled over and read the directions the woman had given me.

Look for a private road around three miles from the bridge, and a wooden sign to the east.

I drove a slow mile. There were several dirt paths cutting

into the hillside on the east, all unmarked, and I made a couple of false starts before spotting a wooden sign nearly obscured by a heavy bank of scarlet honeysuckle.

S NC M

The road, if you could call it that, was an acutely slanting dirt path lined with elderberry and ferns and sugar bush. I traveled a thousand feet of kidney-jarring, hairpin solitude. The trees, here, were thick-trunked and hypertrophied, the brush beyond them impenetrable. The growth was so thick that branches scraped the roof of the car, and in some places the vegetation sprouted in the center of the road and brushed the Seville's underbody.

Soon I heard the high-note trickle of a stream. Groundwater. That explained the lushness during the drought. Looking for trees here would be like searching for pedestrians in Times Square.

A couple of turns, then I saw a two-piece gate up ahead. Heavy-duty chicken wire framed by planks of weathered redwood.

Latched, but not locked.

I got out, freed the bolt, and swung both gates open. They were heavy and rusty and left brown grit on my hands.

Another five hundred feet. Another gate, a twin of the first. Beyond it was a big, low-slung, lodge-type building flanked by enormous bristlecone pines and backed by a forest of more pines and firs and coast redwood. The roof was green asphalt shingle, the walls, logs.

I parked in the dirt, between a black Jeep Cherokee and an old white Mercedes convertible. A row of iron hitching posts fronted the lodge. Behind it, wide wooden steps led to a wraparound porch shaded by the eaves of the building and set up with a few bent-willow chairs. The cushions on the chairs were blue floral and mildewed. The windows of the lodge were gray with dust.

Flat, thick silence; then a squirrel scampered across the porch, stopped, and shimmied up a rain gutter.

I climbed the stairs and knocked on the front door. Nothing happened for a while; then it was pulled open and a woman looked out at me.

Thirty-five or so, five-seven, with straight, shoulder-length black hair parted in the middle and painted with copper high-lights. Her face was a tan oval, the skin smooth as fresh notepa-per, the jawline crisp. She wore second-skin black leggings under a bright green, oversized, sleeveless T-shirt. Her arms were bronze and smooth, her feet bare, her eyes orange-brown.

She had the kind of face that would photograph beautifully: perfectly aligned, slightly oversized features. Both ears were double-pierced.

"Dr. Delaware?" she said in a bored voice. "I'm Nova."

She waved me into a gigantic main room furnished with sagging tweed couches and thrift-shop tables and chairs. To the right was a clumsy, narrow staircase. The grubby plank flooring was covered haphazardly with colorless rugs. The ceiling was beamed with more planks and raw logs, and each beige stucco wall bore two large windows. Plenty of furniture and still enough room to dance. Along the rear wall, beyond the stairs, what had once been a reception desk had been turned into a wet bar crammed with bottles. On either side of the bar were doors.

The walls were covered with scores of mounted animal heads: deer, moose, fox, bear, a snarling puma, lacquered trout with their vital statistics engraved on plaques. All the specimens looked moth-eaten and tired, almost goofy. One was particularly grotesque—a gray, lumpy, porcine thing with Quasimodo fea-tures and yellow mandibular fangs that hooked over a sneering upper lip.

"Wally Warthog," said Nova, stopping next to a serape-cov-ered couch.

"Good-looking fellow."

"Charming."

"Does Mr. Lowell hunt?"

She gave a staccato laugh. "Not with a gun. These came with the place and he kept them. He planned to add some of his own —critics and reviewers."

"Never bagged any, huh?"

Her face got hard. "Wait here, I'll tell him you've arrived. If you need to, fix yourself something to drink."

She walked off toward the left-hand door. I went over to the bar. Empty bottles lined the floor. Premium brands, mostly. On the counter were eight or nine cheap glasses that hadn't seen water recently. An old refrigerator was filled with mixers. I

washed a glass and poured myself some tonic water, then returned to the center of the huge room. As I sat on a needlepoint
rocker, dust shot up. In front of me was a coffee table with nothing on it. I waited and drank for ten minutes; then the door
opened.

28

His face appeared two feet lower than I expected. He was sitting in a wheelchair, pushed by Nova.

The famous face, long and hatchet-jawed, with a bulbous nose and deep, dark eyes under shelf brows, now white. His hair was gray-black, worn past his shoulders and held together with a beaded band: the Venerable Chief look. His skin, liver-spotted and creased, was as rough as the ceiling beams.

My eyes dropped to his body. Wasted and spindle-limbed, reduced to almost nothing above the belt-line.

He wore a long-sleeved white shirt and dark pants. Everything bagged and sagged, and though the trouser fabric was heavy wool, I could see his kneecaps shining through. His feet were encased in cloth bedroom slippers. His hands were huge and white and grasping, dangling from the thin wrists like dying sunflowers.

As Nova propelled him forward, he glared at me. The chair was an old-fashioned manual, and it squeaked and wrinkled the rug. She positioned him opposite me.

"Need anything?"

He didn't answer and she left.

He kept glowering.

I gave him a pleasantly blank look.

"Good-looking piece of veal, aren't you? If I was a fag, I'd fuck you."

"That assumes a lot."

He threw back his head and laughed. His cheeks were flaccid

and they shook. He had most of his teeth, but they were dark and discolored.

"You'd let me," he said. "Without *hesitation*. You're a starfucker; that's why you're here."

I said nothing. Despite his crippled body and the size of the room, I began to feel hemmed in.

"What's in the glass?" he said.

"Tonic water."

He gave a disgusted look and said, "Put it down and pay attention. I'm in pain, and I don't have time for any lumpen-yuppie bullshit."

I placed the glass on a table.

"Okay, Little Dutch Boy, tell me who the hell you are and what qualifies you to be treating my daughter."

I gave him a brief oral résumé.

"Very impressive, you now qualify for a variable-rate mortgage of your IQ. If you're so smart, why didn't you become a *real* doctor? Cut into the cortex and get to the root of matter."

"Why didn't you?"

He pitched forward, winced, and cursed violently. Gripping the armpieces of the chair, he managed to shift slightly to the left. "William Carlos Williams was a doctor and he tried to be a poet. Somerset Maugham was a doctor and *he* tried to be a writer. Both sour, pretentious fucks. Mix-and-match works only in women's fashions; something's got to ebb, something's got to flow."

I nodded.

His eyes widened and he grinned. "Go ahead, patronize me, pricklet. I can chew up anything you serve me, digest it for my own benefit, and shit it back at you as high-density compost timbales."

He licked his lips and tried to spit. Nothing came out of his mouth.

"*I'm interested*," he said, "in certain *aspects* of medicine. Cabala, not calculus. . . . A fool I knew in college became a surgeon. I met him, years later, at a party *teeming* with starfuckers, and the pin-brain looked happier than ever. His work; there was no other reason for him to be satisfied. I got him talking about it, and the bloodier he got, the more ecstatic—if words were jism, I'd have been soaked. And do you know what brought the greatest joy to his dysphemistic face? Describing the scummy details of exploratory surgery, while eating a *cocktail* frank. Cracking open the bones, tying off the veins, swan-diving into the heat and jelly of a stinking, cancerous body cavity."

He raised his hands to nipple level and turned the palms up. "He said the greatest fun was holding living organs in his hands, feeling their pulse, smelling their steam. He was a yawny idiot, but he had the power to flex a wrist and rip spleens and livers and shit-filled guts out of someone else's flesh-ark."

He let his hands fall. He was breathing hard, the remnants of his chest heaving. *"That's* what interests me about medicine. Dropping a nuclear bomb on certain individuals interests me, too, but I'd never waste my time studying *physics.* Man Ray once said perfect art would kill an observer upon first glance. Damned near close to universal truth. Not bad for a photographer, and a kike. Delaware . . . that's not a kike name, is it?"

"No. And it's not wop or nigger or spic, either."

His mouth ticced and he laughed again, but it seemed obligatory.

"Look what we have here, a wit—at least by half. A fucking yuppie halfwit—you're the *future,* aren't you? Off-the-rack Gentleman's Farterly suits pretending to be bespoke. Politically correct careerism masquerading as moral duty—do you drive a *Beemer?* Or a *Baby Benz?* Either way, Hitler would be proud, though I don't imagine you've ever studied history. Do you know who Hitler was? Are you aware that he didn't drive a Buick? That Eichmann worked for Mercedes-Benz while hiding out in Argentina—do you know who the fuck Eichmann *was?"*

Remembering the white convertible out front, I said, "I drive American."

"How patriotic. Did you get it from Daddy?"

I didn't answer, thinking suddenly of my father, never able to afford a new car. . . .

"Daddy's *dead,* isn't he? Was he a would-be doctor, too?"

"A machinist," I said.

"Tool and die—he tooled, then he died. Tut-tut. So you're a blue-collar hero. Shaky-kneed arriviste by way of the public school system. First in the family to go to college and all that, a Kiwanis club scholarship, no doubt. Mommy's *so* proud in her Formica prison—is she dead, too?"

I stood up and began walking to the door.

"Oh!" he bellowed after me. "Oh, I've *offended* him; five minutes and he's running off to puke in the bushes, the fortitude of a *mayfly!"*

I half turned my head and smiled at him. "Not at all, it's just boring. The shape you're in, you should know life's too short for small talk."

His face incandesced with rage. He waited until I'd opened the door and stepped out onto the porch.

"Fuck *you* and fuck your charwoman *mother* on a Formica *counter*! Walk out, now, and you'll eat my shit in a soufflé before I give you my insights."

"Do you really have any?" I said, with my back to him.

"I know why the girl tried to *kill* herself."

I heard squeaks, turned, and saw him wheeling himself forward very slowly. He stopped and spun the chair, finally managing to turn his back on me. His hair hung in greasy strands. Either Nova wasn't much of a caretaker or he didn't allow her to groom him.

"Fix me a drink, Cubby, and maybe I'll share my wisdom with you. None of that single-malt swill you yuppie pricks go for —give me blended. Everything in life is blended; nothing stands on its own." Spinning again, he faced me. I thought he looked relieved that I was still there.

"What's yellow and red, yellow and red, yellow and red?" he said.

"What?" I said.

"Jap in a blender, *huuuf, huuuf*—and don't give me that look of outrage, you buttoned-down pool. I fought in the only war that counted and saw what those scrawny-dicked monkey-men are capable of. Did you know they used to *peel* the faces off the Allied prisoners? Marinate human hearts and kidneys in teriyaki sauce and *barbecue* them? There's your sushi bar for you. Truman *dry*-roasted the buck-toothed capuchins, only good thing *that* exophthalmic rag-pimp ever did. Stop standing there, gawking like a virgin sailor at wet pussy, and fix me a fine blended drink before I tire of you beyond the point of forgiveness!"

I went to the wet bar and found a bottle of Chivas, almost empty. As I poured, he said, "Know how to read?"

I had no intention of answering. But he didn't wait for a reply.

"Ever read anything I wrote?"

I named a few titles.

"Did you have to write term *papers* on them?"

"A few."

"What grades did you get?"

"I passed."

"Then fuck you, you didn't understand a thing."

I brought him his drink. He drained it and held out his glass. I refilled it. He took longer with the second drink, staring at the whisky, sipping, lifting a leg, and passing gas with satisfaction. I thought of all he'd written about heroism and finally understood the word *fiction.*

He tossed the glass away. His throw was weak, and the tumbler landed near the wheel of his chair and rolled on the rug.

He said, "The girl tried to end it all because she's empty. No passion, no pain, no reason to keep going. So anything you do with her will be worthless. You might as well be psychoanalyzing a *tadpole* in order to prevent its froggy fate. *I,* on the other hand, have a surplus of passion. Spilling over, as it were." He made slurping sounds. "The *only* thing that can save her is getting to know me."

I tried not to laugh or scream. "Getting to know you will be her therapy."

"Not therapy, you limited *gowk.* Therapy is for moral anencephalics and hamstrung aerobi-geeks. I'm talking about *salvation.*"

Leaning forward. "*Tell* her."

"I'll let her know," I said.

He laughed and raised the pitch of his voice. "Does she *hate* me?"

"I'm not free to talk about her feelings."

"La *da* la *da* la *da* la *da.* You claim you read *Dark Horses.* What was the point there?"

"The racetrack as a mini-world. The charac—"

"The *point* was that we all eat horseshit. Some dress it up with béarnaise sauce, some nibble, some hold their noses, some stick their faces right in it and wolf, but *no* one plays hooky. Best novel of the millennium. *Flew* out of me; my cock tingled every day I sat down at the typewriter."

He looked at the glass on the floor. "More."

I obliged him.

"Pulitzer capons thinking they were *giving* me something." He finished the whisky. "She hates me. I don't give a shit about her feelings. Hatred's a great motivator. I've always hated writing."

I looked over his shoulder at the animal heads, the leering warthog.

He said, "No attention span, Veal-chop? They came with the place. I considered adding to the collection—critics with glass eyes. Know why I didn't?"

I shook my head.

"No taxidermist would take on the job. Too hard to clean."

He laughed and demanded another drink. The Chivas was gone, and I poured him cheap scotch. With his body weight, his blood had to be pickled, but he showed no effects of the alcohol.

"Have you ever looked into the toilet after you've shat?" he said. "The bits of crud that are left sticking to the porcelain? Next time, scrape some of that off and place it in a dish of agar-agar. Feed it more shit and anything foul you can find, and in no time at all you'll have cultured yourself a critic."

More laughter, but strained. "A criminal—the vilest child-fucking inchworm of a mother-raper—is entitled to a trial of his peers. Do you know what kind of justice artists merit? Trial by *cretin.* Dickless, decorticate, petty-ante pissbladders who'd give their glands to have the gift but don't, so they take out their frustration on the blessed. Those who can, do. Those who can't, teach. Those who lack the tongue motility to lick the arseholes of *teachers,* write reviews."

He'd finally produced saliva. A strand trickled down the side of his mouth.

He stared at me. I readied myself for another outburst.

But he grew very quiet and his eyelids started to droop.

Then he fell asleep.

I listened to him snore. Nova came in, as if summoned by the noise. She'd changed into a filmy, collarless white blouse that barely reached her waist and black shorts that showed off beautiful legs. Her breasts were large and soft and unfettered, the nipples darkly evident through the thin fabric.

She said, "No sense in your staying, he'll be that way for a while."

"Does he do that often? Just nod off?"

"All the time. He's tired all the time. It's the pain."

"Is he on painkillers?"

"What do you think?"

"What's wrong with him?"

"Everything. His heart and his liver are bad, he's had several strokes, and his kidneys are weak. Basically, he's just falling apart."

Her tone was matter-of-fact.

"Are you a nurse?"

She smiled. "No, his assistant. He won't accept nursing, would rather drink and do things his way. You'd better be going."

I walked to the door.

"Are you bringing the daughter back?" she said.

"That'll be up to the daughter."

"She should meet him."

"Why's that?"

"Every daughter should meet her father."

29

"A caricature," said Lucy, trying to smile. But there was fear in her eyes.

Outside, the sun hid behind a cloud bank and the ocean was a restless gray curdle. Very low tide. I heard the breakers die far back, slapping the sand like slow, monstrous applause.

It was eight in the morning; I'd just finished telling her about my visit. Nicolette Verdugo's murder was all over the news. Jobe Shwandt was giving death-row interviews, lecturing on astrology and utopianism and the proper way to cut up a side of beef. One of the Bogettes had told the *Times* the day had come for all victims to rise up and slaughter the oppressors. Lucy had come in holding the morning paper, but she hadn't wanted to talk about any of that.

"So what's his angle?"

"I don't know," I said. "In his own bizarre way, he may be reaching out. Or just trying to regain some control."

She shook her head and smiled. Then her mouth turned down. "See any lacy trees?"

"There are trees all over the place. The house is set into a forest."

"A log house."

"Yes," I said. "Like a giant log cabin. Ken told me that's where you and Puck slept. You were being cared for by a nanny. Any memory of that?"

"I know," she said. "He told me, too. Some woman with short hair, and he remembers her as being grumpy. But that didn't trigger anything for me."

"Has he come up with anything else about that summer?"

She shook her head. "Apparently we had nothing to do with each other. It's frustrating. Why would I block out something like a nanny?"

"Maybe she wasn't with you very long. Not every memory registers."

"Guess not." The tendons in her neck were stretched tight. "Maybe I should jog my memory directly—go up there. From what you've told me, I should be able to handle him."

"Let's not rush things," I said.

"I need to know the truth."

"He's old and feeble but far from innocuous, Lucy. Remember how manipulative he was with Puck."

"I understand that. I'll go in expecting a total monster. And no matter what he tries, it's not going to work. Because I'm not Puck. He doesn't have anything I need. I just want to look for those trees."

The tide broke thunderously and she jumped.

I said, "Humor an overcautious therapist, Lucy. Let's take our time."

She was looking at the water. "Does it get that loud often?"

"Once in a while. Is there anything else you want to talk about?" I said.

"I want to talk about putting together a battle plan. Going up there and learning what happened."

"Going up there doesn't mean you'll learn anything."

"But *not* going up there means I definitely *won't*. He's a crippled old man. What can he do to me?"

"He has a way with words."

"That's all a writer ever has."

"The point is, he may be reaching out to you because he's dying."

Her eyes flickered but she didn't move.

"I've seen it plenty of times, Lucy. The most abusive, neglectful parents wanting some sort of relationship before they die. You need to sort out your own feelings about that very carefully. What if you go up there expecting brutality and he turns tender?"

"I could handle it," she said. "He can't collect debts that aren't owed to him."

She fooled with her hair and looked out at the ocean.

"I just thought of something. It's horribly mean, but it's

funny. If he really gets obnoxious, I'll handle him by falling asleep. Doze right off. That'll get the message across."

More hypnosis.

I took her back to two days before the Sanctum party, Thursday morning. Despite my attempt to cushion her with the TV screen technique, she lapsed into a child's voice and began muttering about trees and horses and "Brudda." Questions about a nanny or baby-sitter or anyone else elicited puzzled looks and an upstretched left index finger.

Further questioning revealed that "Brudda" was Puck, whom she called Petey.

Petey playing with her.

Petey throwing a ball.

The two of them tearing leaves and looking at ladybugs.

Petey smiling. She smiled, as she told it.

Then her own smile melted away, and I sensed that the present was beginning to intrude.

"What's happening, Lucy?"

Frown.

I took her forward, past the dream, to Sunday. She remembered nothing.

Back to Saturday night.

This time she described her walk in the forest calmly. Even the "scared" look on the abducted girl's face didn't ruffle her.

I zeroed in on the three men.

Talking about her father made her eyes move frantically under her lids. She thought he looked angry. Described his clothing: "Long . . . uh . . . white . . . like a dress."

The caftan the society column had described; she could have read it.

I asked her if there was anyone else she wanted to talk about, waiting to see if she'd move on to Hairy Lip without prodding.

Left finger.

I repeated my question about mustache versus beard, using simple phrasing a four-year-old could understand.

"Is it a big mustache or a little mustache?"

Pause. "Big."

"Real big?"

Right finger.

"Does it hang down or go straight out?"

"Down."

"It hangs down?"

"Dig . . ."

She grimaced; I thought she'd shifted forward to the burial.

"Now they're digging?"

Left finger. Anguished head-shake.

"What is it, Lucy?"

"*Dig . . . Dig*gity Dog."

For a second, I was thrown. Then I remembered a cartoon character from the seventies. A lazy, slow-talking bassett-hound sheriff with a twenty-gallon hat and a drooping walrus mustache.

"The mustache hangs down like Diggity Dog's?"

Right finger.

"What color is it?"

"Black."

"A black mustache that hangs down like Diggity Dog's."

Right finger, rigid, jabbing upward. Hard.

"Anything else about the man with the mustache, Lucy?"

"Black."

"A black mustache."

She grimaced.

"Good," I said. "You're doing great. Now is there anything you can tell me about the other man, the one with his back to you?"

Contemplation. Eyes moving under the lids.

"He . . . he's . . . says . . . says, *In* there. *In* there, *in* there, *dammit*, Buck. Hurry. Roll it, roll it. *Hurrydammit rollit in-there!*"

30

After she left I sat thinking about her sudden change of heart.

Courage competing with self-defense.

Maybe courage *was* her self-defense.

No matter, I couldn't allow her to face him. I'd hold her off, try to get her to discover as much as she could on her own.

I thought about what she'd seen today.

Hairy Lip. Maybe someone other than Trafficant.

The third man, always with his back to her.

In there, dammit, Buck.

Was *he* Trafficant? Barking at his patron? From what I'd seen of Lowell I couldn't imagine his tolerating that. But maybe his relationship with Trafficant had been more complex than mentor and protégé.

As I thought about it, Ken Lowell called.

"I'm a little concerned about Lucy, doctor. She told me about this dream she's been having. Now I understand what's been getting her up at night."

"She hasn't been sleeping well?"

"She thinks she has, because when she asks I tell her she has. But she gets up two or three times every night and walks around. Usually she goes out onto the landing, stares at a wall for a second or so, then returns to her room. But last night was a little scary. I found her at the top of the stairs, about to step off. I tried to wake her, but I couldn't. She let me guide her back to bed, but it was like moving a mannequin. I didn't say anything because I didn't want to upset her. Aside from that, I guess I'd like to know if you think there's anything to the dream. I mean, he was no great shakes as a father, but a murderer?"

"What do you remember about that night?"

"Nothing, really. There was a party; it was loud and wild. Jo and I were stuck in our cabin, not allowed to come out. I do remember looking out through the curtains and seeing people laughing and screaming and dancing around. Some had paint on their faces. A bunch of rock bands were blasting."

"Sounds like a love-in."

"Yeah, I guess that's what it was."

"So you never saw anything resembling Lucy's dream?"

"Three men carrying off a girl? No. Just couples slinking off together. I remember Jo telling me, 'Guess what they're doing?' She was eleven, really into the facts of life."

"Can you recall anything about Lucy and Puck's nanny?"

"I've been trying to. Actually, she might not have been a nanny. Because I think she was wearing the same kind of uniform the waiters and waitresses were wearing—all white. So maybe she was just a waitress. To be honest, I don't trust my memory on any of this. But if something really happened . . . Is there anything I can do to help Lucy with her sleepwalking?"

"Just keep her bedroom as safe as possible—no sharp objects, lock the windows. If she doesn't object, have her lock the door before she goes to sleep."

"Okay," he said doubtfully.

"Is there a problem with that?"

"Not really. Just the thought of being locked in. I'm a little claustrophobic. Probably because they did it to us that summer: put us in a cabin and bolted the door from the outside. It was like being caged. We hated it."

Robin came home at six, kissed me, and went into the shower. I sat on the floor tossing a ball to Spike, going along with his retriever fantasies, until the phone got me up.

Sherrell Best said, "Sorry to bother you again, Dr. Delaware, but is there anything new?"

"Nothing concrete yet, Reverend, I'm sorry."

"Nothing *concrete*? Does that mean you've learned *something*?"

"I wish I could give you some real progress, but—"

"Could I *please* meet your patient? Maybe the two of us can put our heads together. I don't want to cause any problems, but it might even help ease the burden."

"Let me think about it, Reverend."

"Thank you, Doctor. God bless."

Robin and I took Spike for a chicken dinner and a drive. He wedged himself between her legs and the passenger door and stared out the window with a determined expression on his flat face.

Robin laughed. "He's guarding us, Alex. Look how seriously he's taking it. Thank you, Spikey, I feel so secure with you."

"Joe Stud," I said.

She put her hand on my knee. "I feel secure with you, too."

"Yeah," I said, "but he takes up less room and he doesn't get emergency calls."

The night sky turned violet. I'd driven north and, just like last week, ended up near Ventura. This time it was more than chance. Best's call had gotten me thinking about Doris Reingold and the Sheas. The discrepancy in their lifestyles. I turned off the highway and entered the city limits. Robin looked at me but didn't say anything.

We cruised the empty, quiet streets. The first thing open was a gas station. The Seville had a quarter tank left. I pulled in, filled up, washed the windows, then told Robin, "One sec," and went to the pay phone. The directory was on its chain, but half the pages were gone. The R's remained, though, and Reingold, D., was listed on Palomar Avenue.

The cashier told me that was ten blocks up.

When I got in the car, Robin said, "Home?"

"Please indulge me for a second. There's something I want to check out."

"Is it related to a patient?"

"Indirectly."

"You're going to drop *in* on someone?"

"No. I just want to see how someone lives. It won't take long."

"Okay," she said, stretching.

"Yeah, I know I'm a real fun date."

"It's all right," she said. "If you don't behave yourself, *he* can drive me home."

*   *   *

The address was a one-story bungalow court on a treeless street, three units on each side of a U. Security floodlights washed the stubble lawn. Some of the streetlights were out.

Six or seven college-age boys sat on the grass in folding chairs, drinking beer. Bags of potato chips and Fritos lay at their feet. They had long hair and, though the night was cool, all were shirtless. When I got closer, a couple of them mumbled, "Evening," and one of them gave me the thumbs-up sign. The rest didn't move at all.

I walked up to the thumber. His hair was dark and down to his nipples. His cheeks were hollow above curly chin whiskers.

"Hey, man," he said, in a slurred voice. "Police?"

I shook my head.

" 'Cause we been quiet after that time, man." He flicked hair out of his face and stared at me. "You with the management?"

"No," I said. "Just someone looking for—"

"We paid the rent, man. Cash to Mrs. Patrillo. If she din't give it to you, tha's not our fault."

"Doris Reingold," I said. "Do you know which unit is hers?"

He digested that. "Five. But she ain't here."

"Do you know where she is?"

He scratched his head. "She packed up some stuff and split."

"When was this?"

Frown. Another head scratch. "Yesterday—yesterday night."

"What time?"

"Um . . . I was just comin' home and she was leavin'. It was at night. I said, You wan' me to carry that stuff for you? but she i'nored me." He belched and I could smell the hops. Taking a swig, he said, "Why you looking for her, man?"

"I'm a friend."

He smiled. "Well, she's okay . . . ackshally she's a old bitch." Laughter from some of the others.

A crew-cut kid said, "You're just pissed 'cause she cleaned you out, Kyle."

Thumber moved his head fast and stared at him. The other boy said, "Face it, Kyle."

"Fuck you." Kyle looked back at me. "She cheats, the old bitch."

"At what?" I said.

"Everything. Poker, craps, dice. What'd *you* play with her?"

"Chess."

"Yeah? Well, hate to tell you, but maybe she got herself a new boyfriend."

"Really?"

"Yeah. She split with a dude."

Another of the boys said, "Pass the rinds."

Kyle bent and fumbled on the grass for a long time, to a chorus of derision, before finally picking up a bag of pork rinds. Rolling it up, he tossed it behind his head. Someone caught it. Someone else said, "Shit! Watch it, asshole!"

I said, "Do you remember what this guy looked like?"

"Nope, but he had a fine Beemerdubyou." To his friends: "Remember that Beemerdubyou? With the bitchin' spoiler on its ass?"

A round-faced boy with very long, wavy blond hair said, "Din't it have a bra?"

"Yeah," said someone. "For its tits."

Laugh track.

I looked back at the curb. The Seville was five cars down the block, under a working streetlight. The driver's window was open, and I was pretty sure I saw Spike's blocky head leaning out.

"A dark gray BMW?" I said. "Chrome wheels?"

"Yeah," said Kyle. He shifted imaginary gears. "Gonna get me one of them."

"Bullshit," said another boy. "First you got to get your license back. Then you gotta learn how to play cards not like some asshole."

"I'll get it back, fuck you," said Kyle. Suddenly, his shoulders were hunched and he was drawing his hand back, as if ready for a touchdown throw. He snapped his wrist and tossed his beer can. It flew by me and landed in the street, clattering and rolling, narrowly missing a parked car.

"Hey, man," said someone. "Chill."

"Fuck *you!*" Kyle was up on his feet. Both his hands were tight and he was bouncing on bare feet. He had nothing on but baggies. Tangles of tattoos on both arms.

He said, "Fuck you," again.

No one answered. The snoring boy was awake.

Kyle wheeled and looked at me.

"What do *you* want?" he said in a new voice.

I gave him the thumbs-up sign and left.

As I got back in the car, Robin said, "Was everything okay back there?"

"Fine," I said. "Oh, glorious youth."

31

I drove back to Malibu thinking of something Doris had told me.

"I like Nevada."

A serious gambler? Was that where the payoff money had gone? If there'd ever been any.

Her leaving town under Tom Shea's escort right after I talked to her made me sure I was on to something.

Giving Lucy's dream new credence, I thought about the three men. Lowell and two others, one of them almost certainly Trafficant. Probably the one with his back turned.

So who was Hairy Lip?

Maybe just another guest, but more likely someone who knew Lowell and Trafficant well enough to be invited to the private party.

Member of the club.

Another Sanctum Fellow?

When we got home, I reread the newspaper coverage of the Sanctum opening while Robin brushed her hair and got into her nightgown.

Three names, no pictures:

Christopher Graydon-Jones, the English sculptor.

Joachim Sprentzel, the German composer.

And Denton Mellors, the aspiring American novelist. The sole reviewer to praise *Command: Shed the Light*. He'd also lauded Trafficant's book. His fellowship payback, just as Trafficant's had been?

The more I thought about it, the more it made sense.

Lowell and his two star pupils.

Maybe he'd coached them in something other than writing. But where to go with it?

Robin was in bed, curled on her side.

I slipped out of my clothes and got in next to her, wrapping my arms around her.

She mumbled.

I held her and felt her drift off to sleep.

I woke up before sunrise, thinking about Lucy's dream. She and Ken were spending some time together today, and her next session would be tomorrow.

I made breakfast for Robin and myself and brought it to bed. While she showered, I called New York and made another attempt to locate Trafficant through his publisher. All I learned was that out-of-print authors don't garner much respect.

Robin was ready to leave for the jobsite at 8:30. As her truck pulled away, Spike's flat face pressed up against the passenger window. I was right behind in the Seville.

At Bel Air, she continued east and I turned off at the university. I walked into the research library at 9:25. A few early birds were studying, but plenty of computer terminals were available. I accessed the periodicals index and typed in names, starting with my most likely candidate, Denton Mellors.

Not a word. I checked *Books in Print*, academic journals, every sublist I could find.

Nothing. If he'd ever published his novel, there was no record of it.

I went on to Christopher Graydon-Jones.

Three citations, the first twenty years ago when the sculptor had received a commission from a company called Enterprise Insurance to create a bronze and iron piece for the lobby of its corporate headquarters in downtown L.A. Minor coverage in the *L.A. Times* arts supplement, no picture.

Two years after that, a business journal had him working for the same company as Assistant Deputy Director of Marketing, an interesting transition. Five years later, he'd advanced to Chief Operating Officer at Enterprise, and a publicity photo showed him looking older than his thirty-five years: balding, with a long face, wide pouchy eyes, and a weak chin. Clean-shaven.

Next: Joachim Sprentzel. The German had taught composition at Juilliard before committing suicide eight years ago, in Hartford, Connecticut. A *Hartford Courant* obituary cited a "protracted illness" and noted Sprentzel's "commitment to textural atonalism and chromatic adventure." His parents still lived in Munich. No wife or children.

A ten-year-old Juilliard faculty shot portrayed an intense-looking man with a very strong square jaw, bushy dark hair, and nervous eyes behind tiny wire-frame eyeglasses.

Above the jaw, a thick drooping mustache.

Remarkably similar in shape and color to Diggity Dog's.

Hairy Lip.

Suicide after a protracted illness. A single man.

My gut assumption was AIDS, but it could have been anything.

Dead. Another avenue closed off.

I photocopied all of it and checked in with my service. Messages from two lawyers, a judge, and Sherrell Best. I saved the Reverend for last. He wasn't home, and a woman at the Church of the Outstretched Hand said he was out making food deliveries.

I returned the phone to its cradle.

Three men at a gravesite.

Lowell, Trafficant, and Sprentzel?

All three out of reach.

I reviewed the photocopied articles.

It was a long shot, but maybe Christopher Graydon-Jones was still working downtown.

I looked up Enterprise Insurance in the Central L.A. book. No listing. But a scan of the yellow pages revealed an address on 26th Street in Santa Monica and the subheading "Specializing in worker's compensation plans and corporate liability."

I called the number and asked for Mr. Graydon-Jones. To my amazement I was put through to a happy-sounding secretary. When I asked to speak to her boss, she managed to stay happy while getting protective.

"What's this in regard to, sir?"

"Mr. Graydon-Jones's fellowship at Sanctum."

"What's Sanctum, sir?"

"An artistic retreat run by the novelist M. Bayard Lowell. Mr. Graydon-Jones was a sculpture fellow there, quite a while ago. I'm a freelance writer working on a biography of Mr. Lowell, and I'm attempting to reach—"

"An artistic what?"

"Retreat. A place where artists can go to pursue their art."

"You're saying Mr. Graydon-Jones was once an artist?"

"He was a sculptor. He did the sculpture in the lobby of Enterprise's corporate office downtown."

"We haven't been downtown for years."

"I realize that, but Mr. Graydon-Jones was commissioned back in—"

"Is this some sort of joke, sir?"

"No. Could you please give him the message? He may want to speak with me."

"He's out right now. Your name, sir?"

"Del Ware. Sandy Del Ware." I gave her my number.

"Very well, Mr. Del Ware," she said, too quickly. Then she hung up.

I looked at my watch. Twelve-fifteen. Graydon-Jones out to lunch? Or sitting behind a big desk shuffling papers, a busy, important man.

I had plenty of time.

Enterprise's headquarters was only a twenty-minute drive.

The building was just south of Olympic, in a high-end industrial park favoring electronics companies. Five stories, brick and glass, with a restaurant on the ground floor called Escape, specializing in expensive burgers and tropical drinks.

Enterprise was just a suite on the second floor. The door was locked and a sign dangling from the knob said OUT TO LUNCH UNTIL 2 P.M.

I went back down to the ground floor. No sculpture. The door to the restaurant was open, and the odors from within weren't bad. I decided to have lunch and then try again.

A hostess looked me over and said, "Just one?"

I gave her my best aw-shucks lonely-guy smile, and she put me in a tiny corner table near the rest rooms. The place was teeming with suits and smiles, the air ripe with alcohol and gravy. Paper palms on white walls. Gauguin prints hanging alongside travel photos of blue water and brown bodies.

I ordered a beer and a Tahiti Burger and was working my way down the foam when I saw him across the room in a booth with a woman.

Older, balder, the little hair he had left iron-gray. But definitely the same long face, mournful eyes, and a chin that had lost even more bone, receding into a stringy neck. He wore a dark blue suit and a tie so bright it seemed radioactive.

The woman was in her thirties, honey-blond and well put together. No food in front of them, just red drinks with celery sticks and piles of paper.

I ate and watched them; then the woman collected the papers, shook Graydon-Jones's hand, and left.

He ordered another drink and lit up a cigarillo.

I left money on my table and approached.

"Mr. Graydon-Jones?"

He looked up. The sad eyes were blue.

I repeated the pitch I'd given his secretary.

He smiled. "Yes, I got your message. Sanctum. How strange." English accent, tinged with working-class cadences that wouldn't mean much here but would pigeonhole him back in the U.K.

"What is?" I said.

"Hearing about that place after all this time. What was your name again?"

"Sandy Del Ware."

"And you're writing a biography of Lowell?"

"Trying to."

"Do you have a business card?"

"No, sorry. I'm a freelance."

He tapped ashes into an ashtray. "Trying? Does that mean you have no contract?"

"Several publishers are interested, but my agent wants me to submit a thorough outline before he negotiates a deal. I've been able to get all the basics on Lowell except for the time period when he opened Sanctum. In fact, you're the only Fellow I've been able to locate."

"That so?" He smiled. "Please sit down. Drink?"

"No, but I'd be happy to buy you one."

He laughed. "No, thank you. Two at lunch is my limit."

He called for the bill, ordered coffee for both of us, and scrawled something on the check.

"I appreciate your talking to me," I said.

"Only for a few minutes." Looking at a big Rolex. "Now, why on earth would you want to write a book about Buck?"

"He's an interesting character. Rise and fall of a major talent."

"Hmm. Yes. I suppose that would be nicely ironic. But to me he was rather a bore. No offense, but one of those eternal children Americans seem so fond of."

"Well, hopefully they'll stay fond and buy my book."

He smiled again and buttoned his jacket over his thin chest. The suit looked to be one of those highly structured English affairs that costs thousands. His shirt was white with horizontal blue stripes and a high white collar, probably Turnbull & Asser. The conspicuous tie was patterned with artist's brushes and palettes on black jacquard silk. Simulated dabs of paint supplied the color: scarlet and orange and turquoise and lime-green. "So what would you like to know about the Bug Farm?"

"Pardon?"

"The Bug Farm. That's what we called the place. It was infested with bugs: beetles, spiders, whatever. And we were all buggy back then. Bugged out—a bit crazy. The old man probably selected us for that. How's he doing?"

"Alive but ill."

"Sorry to hear that . . . I suppose. Anyway, there's not much I can tell you. The bloody farce only lasted one year."

"I know," I lied. "But no one's been able to tell me why."

"The old man lost interest is why. One year we were his prize pigeons, the next we were out on our arses. Best thing that ever happened to me. I learned about the real world."

"How were you selected?"

"I was an artist back then—or at least I thought I was." He looked at his hands, long-fingered, powerful. "Bronze and stone. I wasn't half terrible actually. Won some awards in England and got a contract with a gallery in New York. The owner heard about the retreat and recommended me to Lowell. In lieu of paying me for two pieces."

"From sculpture to insurance," I said. "Must have been an interesting switch."

He crushed out the cigarillo. "There's art in everything. Anyway, I'm sorry I can't be more helpful. As I say, it was a foolish year."

"Do you have any idea how I can locate the other Fellows? Not Joachim Sprentzel, of course. He's dead."

He scratched his neck. "Really? Poor chap. How?"

"Suicide. His obituary said he'd been ill for a long time."

"AIDS?"

"Was he gay?"

"As springtime. Not a bad sort. Kept to himself, writing music all day—no piano or violin, just scratching away at that funny lined paper."

"Is there anything else you can tell me about him?"

"Such as?"

"Personality characteristics that might be interesting in a book?"

"Personality," he said, touching the side of his nose. "Quiet. Withdrawn. A bit gloomy, perhaps. Probably because there were no boys to play with. And, of course, being German. . . . That's about it. He didn't socialize much—none of us did. Buck gave us each a little cabin and told us to 'wax brilliant.' Isolation was encouraged. It wasn't a sociable place."

"I've heard the grand opening party was pretty interesting."

"So have I—wine, women, song, music, all sorts of fun. One damned bit of ha-ha the whole year, and I was having my appendix out. Bit of bad luck, eh? When I healed up and got back, the old man wouldn't talk to me. Punishment for not being there. As if I'd defied him by bursting my bloody appendix. A few months later, I was out on my arse."

Removing the celery stick from his glass, he nibbled the edge.

"Gawd, this takes me back. You really think you've got a book in it?"

"I hope so."

"Send me a copy if it ever gets published."

"Absolutely. Speaking of getting published, I can't find anything on the two writing Fellows, Terrence Trafficant and Denton Mellors. Trafficant had a best-seller, then faded from view, and Mellors just seems to have disappeared without publishing anything."

"Terry the Pirate and Denny. . . . This is a hoot, haven't thought about them in ages. Well, Terry's probably in jail somewhere. I have no idea about Denny."

"You think Trafficant got into trouble again?"

"I wouldn't doubt it. Trouble was his *art*. Fancied himself a *bad* guy, bloody Wild West outlaw. Bloody *criminal* is what he was, used to walk around with a big hunting knife in his belt, take it out during mealtime, pick his teeth, clean his nails. He put it by his plate when he ate, protecting his food with one arm, as if we were out to steal it. He really gave poor Sprentzel a hard time. Removing his shirt, asking Sprentzel if he thought he was pretty. Imitating Sprentzel's accent, calling him a faggot and worse. Threatening him."

"What kinds of threats?"

" 'Make you my wife, faggot.' That kind of rubbish. The rest of us were scared witless, but Lowell always stood up for Terry. A bloody pet—one big cheery family we were. Where else could Trafficant be other than jail?"

"Still, it's odd," I said. "Achieving all that success and reverting back to his old ways."

"A criminal," he said, with some passion. His forehead was shiny and he licked his lips. "He was never anything but."

"What about Mellors?"

"Another charmer—very bright actually. Well-spoken, educated, but a bit of an arse-licker."

"Lowell's ass?"

"And Terry's. He got on with Terry better than the rest of us. Not as cherished as Terry, though. Number-two man on the ladder."

"Sounds like there was a hierarchy."

"Definitely. Terry first, then Denny. Then Sprentzel and me, vying for low rung. I'd have to say Sprentzel was at rock bottom because he was gay. Buck had no tolerance for that—man's man and all that, raw meat for breakfast."

"But he chose Sprentzel as a Fellow."

"He didn't know when he chose him. Sprentzel wasn't one of those nelly-fairy types, flouncing around. In fact, I'm not sure how we all found out about him. Probably from Terry. Terry always made a big point of it." He looked downward. "All that bluster. That knife. . . . Yes, poor Sprentzel was definitely low man."

"Was Mellors a tough guy, too?"

"No, not really—university type. Devious, but not nasty."

Trying to figure out how to ask what he looked like, I said, "I've seen pictures of Trafficant, but none of Mellors."

"Yes, Terry became quite a celebrity for a while. The book."

"What about Mellors? Did he ever publish his book?"

"I have no idea." Shrug. "As I said, Buck encouraged isolation."

"What did he look like—just to help me form a mental picture."

"Big. Muscular. Light for his race."

"He was black?"

"Tan," he said. "What the South Africans call 'colored.' Black features but tan skin. Blond hair. Nice-looking fellow, actually."

"Facial hair?"

"I think so. It's been a long time."

"A beard?"

"A mustache, I believe. He didn't like being thought of as black. Didn't like to talk about race. One time Sprentzel brought it up—all that German guilt—and Mellors just walked away. Then Terry showed up with his knife and went into his little fag routine. It was really a boring place."

"Why were Trafficant and Mellors high-status?"

"Denny because he went around telling everyone what a genius Buck was. With Terry it was something else—almost as if Buck looked up to *him*. As if he represented something Buck admired."

"Such as?"

"Who knows?"

"Hatred of women?"

He stared at me. "Hatred of everything, I suppose. The two of them would drink together, get pissed, and take walks in the woods singing filthy songs."

"Did Trafficant ever get into any trouble while up there?"

He ran his fingernails over the ridges of the celery stalk. "Other than playing with that knife and making our lives miserable, I never saw anything. Why?"

"Trying to flesh him out," I said. "I still think it's strange the way he vanished."

"As I said, check the jails. Or the cemeteries. He had a very nasty temper. Anything could set him off. Person like that, the chance of leading a long, peaceful life goes down. That's my business now: risk assessment. Figuring out who'll make it and who won't. Anyway, I must be going. It's been fun, but time to get back to reality."

32

Milo's exhaustion saturated his phone voice.

"Task-force blues?" I said.

"Nothing-accomplished blues. The coroner gave us zero on Nicolette Verdugo. Our copycat's being obsessive-compulsive."

"What about the feccs on the corpse?"

"The *feces*," he said, "are of the canine variety. Another one of those charming details we're withholding from the media."

"Do any of the Bogettes have a dog?"

"They have a goddamn pack of dogs, but try getting hold of a single turd. They're holed up at some dirt ranch out past Pacoima, belongs to one of Shwandt's death penalty lawyers. Mangy mutts and cats and horses behind chain link and barbed wire."

"A commune? At least having them all in one place should make surveillance easier."

"Not really. There's no real cover. Too much open space. Girls come out the front door wearing skimpies and flipping us off. The investigation has not progressed apace, sir. How's Lucy?"

"Haven't seen her today, she's out driving with Ken. And someone else took a drive last night." I repeated what the boys had told me about Doris leaving with Tom Shea.

"They also said she loves to gamble. So if there was some sort of payoff, that could explain why the Sheas live well and she doesn't."

"You said she didn't seem to like the Sheas. Now Tom picks her up?"

"If she's taking a temporary vacation because my questions shook things up, Tom and Gwen could be looking over shoulders, too. They might help her split 'cause it's in their best interests."

"Could be your questions combined with our chat with Mo Barnard. She lives right up the hill from the restaurant. If she dropped in for dinner and let on that Karen's file was being opened . . . wonder if the Sheas'll rabbit, too."

"They already left once. Though now they've got community ties. It's possible they view Doris as a loose cannon and feel once she's gone they can handle the pressure. All *her* ties are out of town: two sons in the army, both master sergeants, one in Germany, one near Seattle. I don't know if they go by Reingold. She could be with either one of them or somewhere in Nevada, playing. She told me she liked it, was thinking of moving there."

"Early retirement, huh? Okay, when I get a chance, I'll look into her. Nothing new on Trafficant, by the way. I can't hit every jail, but so far he hasn't shown up in any of the major ones."

"I learned a little more about him today. Managed to locate one of the Sanctum Fellows, a sculptor named Christopher Graydon-Jones. He's become a biggie at an insurance company in Santa Monica. We had drinks. He remembers Trafficant as a knife-wielding bully and Lowell's pet. Trafficant and Lowell used to get drunk together and take walks in the forest. And the third man in the dream may be a writer named Denton Mellors. Only critic to give Lowell's last book a good review. He had a mustache—though it doesn't match the one Lucy describes in the dreams—and he idolized Lowell. He and Trafficant were a clique at the retreat. So my money's on him as Hairy Lip and Trafficant as the man with his back turned. Graydon-Jones said something else that supports that: Lowell looked up to Trafficant. It wasn't a standard student-teacher thing. Last session I had with Lucy, she described the third man as talking roughly to Lowell. Ordering him to roll the girl into the grave. From what I heard today, Trafficant could've done that and gotten away with it. What do you think?"

"I think," he said, "that you've got threads. Getting closer to a weave. But with all these people gone, so many years passed, it may not happen. Then again, who'm I to criticize? I spent today praying for wisdom in dog shit."

*   *   *

Denton Mellors had been a graduate student at Columbia, but it was too late to call the university. On the chance that he'd returned to New York, I tried Information in all the New York boroughs and New Jersey but found nothing. Then I wondered if he'd stayed in L.A. and gotten a writing job on a newspaper or magazine or in film. Before I could get any further with that, my service called.

"Emergency from Mr. Ken Lowell, doctor. He couldn't stay on the line, sounded pretty upset. Here's the number."

My heart lurched as I copied down the 818 exchange and called it. *Another suicide attempt. Or worse.* Lucy more vulnerable than I'd thought, hypnosis a terrible mistake, weakening her defenses—

"Van Nuys Division."

The police. *Worse.*

"This is Dr. Delaware returning Ken Lowell's call."

"Who's he?"

"Probably a victim's brother."

"Probably?"

"I'm a doctor returning an emergency call to this number."

"What was the person's name?"

"Lowell."

Four unbearable minutes later, Ken said, "Thank God they reached you. We're in real trouble."

"Lucy?"

"No, no, it's Puck. We found him, Lucy and I. It was horrible. She didn't actually see him, I closed the door before she could, but—"

"What happened, Ken?"

"They're saying overdose. He must have gotten hold of some strong stuff or something. He—the needle was still sticking out of his arm." I heard him gag. "Sorry."

"Take your time."

"He was all—but you could see the damned needle." His voice broke, and I heard him choke back sobs. "It wasn't even an arm anymore," he said, gulping. "But you could see the damned needle."

33

The Van Nuys station is part of the municipal complex on Sylvan, just off the boulevard, where thrift shops, pawnbrokers, bail bondsmen, and discount Western-wear barns prevail. Posted just inside the door among the bulletins and wanted posters was a xeroxed flier from a local gang threatening to assassinate officers. Someone had written on it *Come and get it, lowlife.* The front room was noisy and active. Several handcuffed men waited to be booked.

It took a while to get past the desk. Finally, a detective named Almondovar came out and walked me through the squad room to the Robbery-Homicide area. Thirty-five or so, he was compact and stubby, with neat graying hair and curious eyes. His Ultrasuede sportcoat was gray, his slacks a darker gray, and he wore lizard-skin cowboy boots.

"Whose doctor are you?" he said.

"Lucy Lowell's. Was it an accidental OD?"

"Did you know the victim?"

"Just by reputation."

"Big-time addict?"

"Long-term addict."

"From the shape he was in, you couldn't tell much—here we are."

He opened the door of an interrogation room. Lucy and Ken sat next to each other at a folding card table, looking like prisoners of war. Before them were two cups of coffee, untouched.

"Hey, folks," said Almondovar.

Ken's eyes were red and his blond-stubbled face looked

swollen. Lucy didn't move or blink. Her dull gaze went right through me.

Almondovar said, "We already took statements from them, doctor. If there's anything more we need, we'll let you know."

Neither Ken nor Lucy budged.

"What I mean, doctor, is they can go."

"We'll get going soon as possible," I said.

Almondovar whispered in my ear, "We might need the room soon." To Lucy and Ken: "Sorry, folks, we'll do what we can to clear this up."

He walked out.

Ken covered his face and shook his head.

I patted his shoulder. He looked at me, trying to smile, then turned to Lucy. She was staring at the wall. Her eyes were glassy.

I took her hand and gave it a gentle squeeze. She squeezed back. Then she took a very deep breath and stood up.

She seemed unsteady. Ken was out of his chair, grabbing her elbow, but she was okay.

I walked them out through the station. A few cops looked up but most didn't.

We left Ken's Taurus in a city pay lot and I drove them to Rockingham Avenue.

When we got in the house, Lucy said, "I'm tired."

"I'll settle you in," said Ken. The two of them disappeared and I waited in the living room, leafing through a coffee-table book on the great mansions of Newport, Rhode Island. A quarter hour later, Ken came down. He'd removed his jacket and his shirt was wrinkled.

"Can I get you a drink or something?"

"No, thanks. Do you want to sleep, too?"

He made a hard, angry sound that could have been a laugh or a cough. "I guess I should tell you what happened."

"It doesn't have to be now."

"Might as well," he said. "It's not going to get any easier."

We went through the kitchen into the breakfast room and sat down at an oak table.

"We were going to drive out to look at some horse land I'm foreclosing on," said Ken. "First we went out to breakfast this morning. Lucy seemed very uptight. When the food came, she didn't touch it. I asked her what was wrong, and she said she couldn't stop worrying about Puck. Then she started crying."

He gave a pained look. "Sure I can't get you some coffee?"

"I'm fine."

"Okay. . . . Where was I?" Rubbing his chin. "So I said, 'Why don't we go over to his place and see if he left any indication where he went?' She said she didn't know if that was a good idea, in case people were looking for him; she didn't want to tip them off. Didn't want to put me in danger either." He wiped his eyes.

"Drug people?" I said.

"I guess. We never actually talked about his problem. I never even realized he was addicted until later. I mean, when I met him I knew something was wrong. Thin, always coughing, his nose running. I wondered about AIDS. . . . Anyway, we ate for a while—at least I did. Then Lucy said, Maybe we *should* go. We could look around to make sure no one was watching the apartment, and if there wasn't, we could go in—excuse me."

He got up, fixed a cup of instant coffee, and brought it to the table. "Then she said she was sure he was in some kind of danger. Otherwise he would have called her at least once. I asked her what danger. She said she really didn't know, Puck tried to keep his problems to himself, but probably some kind of debt situation. So we went to his place. Lucy had a key." Wiping a tear. "What a rathole. Basically an abandoned building. The store below was vacant. To get to Puck's place you had to climb up some rear stairs near the trash bins."

He ran his hands through his hair and swallowed hard.

"We went in and there was this smell, right away—like stale laundry mixed with badly rotting food—but the place was a mess, open cans, crap all over the carpet, so I didn't think anything of it. It was a surprisingly big place—two bedrooms. But no real furniture. Lucy said the rear bedroom was Puck's, so we went back there. The door was closed but we heard something behind it, like an electric shaver. We looked at each other, scared out of our minds. Then I figured, maybe it's good news, he just got back, he's shaving, cleaning up. So I opened the door. . . ."

He blinked and put the cup down.

"Just a crack, but this *cloud* came out at me. Flies. Hundreds, maybe thousands of them. *That* was the sound. And maggots. The whole bed was covered with them. On the floor, on the drapes, like someone had tossed rice all over. Then I saw—underneath a big mound of them, on the bed—this . . . *thing*. The needle sticking out of it. Shiny and clean. The only *clean* thing in there. He was—under them, on the bed. And on the floor. It was hard to tell what was him and what was—he'd *melted!*"

Milo said, "It's called purge fluid. Stuff leaks out when putrefaction's well under way. It means he'd been there for a while."

We were in the living room of the Brentwood house. He'd just arrived, nearly two hours after I'd brought Ken and Lucy back. Both of them were sleeping.

"How long?" I said.

"Hard to say, there was no air-conditioning in the apartment. Coroner says the most we can expect is an estimate, three- to eight-day range."

"Well, we know it's closer to three, because before that he was in New Mexico. Looks like he came back soon after he called Lowell. But he still didn't call Lucy."

"Came back after scoring," he said. "Van Nuys found a nice little chunk in the toilet tank. Mexican brown, but very strong. Small corner chipped away."

"Sampling the goods and he OD'd," I said. "Too stoned to call Lucy."

He looked around the room. "How long's she been asleep?"

"Hour and a half."

"Ken, too?"

"He went up to see how she was doing a half hour ago and didn't come down."

"Escape to sleep," he said.

"Old Buck tends to nod off when he's under stress, too."

He cracked his knuckles. "Some people just have shitty lives, don't they? And the rest of us live off them. Hey, why don't we blow this joint, go to the circus or something? Did I ever tell you I once busted a clown when I was on patrol? Peeping Tom. Never worked that into his act."

He got up and paced the room. "Nice place the scamsters set up for themselves."

"Crime almost paid."

Ken came down the stairs, holding on to the banister. His

hair was combed but he looked sick. "Guess I dozed off—hi, detective."

They shook hands.

"Is Lucy awake?" I said.

"Just up. She said if you wanted to come up it was okay. She's at the end of the hall."

I went up the stairs. Lucy's room was pale blue with white trim, smallish, with a canted ceiling and a big four-poster with lace-edged covers. She was sitting on the edge, staring out the window.

I sat next to her. She didn't react. Her eyes were dry and her lips were chapped.

"I'm so sorry, Lucy."

"Gone," she said. "Everything."

I patted her hand. Fingers cold as Puck's junkie digits.

"Heard the doorbell," she said.

"That was Milo."

She nodded, then kept the movement going, a faint rocking.

"No surprise," she said. "Guess I always knew, but . . ."

"It's never easy."

"Like being stripped . . . one thing at a time . . . empty world."

I squeezed her fingers.

"He can come up," she said. "Milo."

Almost pleading.

I stepped out to the landing. Milo and Ken were still in the entry. It didn't look as if either of them had moved.

"She'd like to see you."

He bounded the steps two at a time. When we were alone, Ken touched his belly and gave a squeamish look. "Stomach's off, can't hold on to anything. Maybe I'll finally take off some blubber."

I smiled.

"Gained way too much. Fifteen pounds during the last year. My divorce. It hasn't been a friendly one. Kelly—my wife—met another guy. She'd been complaining about being bored, so I suggested she take some classes at the junior college. She met him there, some out-of-work construction guy. I tried to get her to go to counseling, but she wouldn't. When I finally realized we were going to break up, I tried to keep it amicable, for the kids. But she bad-mouthed me to them."

"That doesn't help the kids."

"It's been going on over a year, and we're still in court. Her dad's got lots of money, lawyers on retainer. She says she won't give up until she has everything."

He gave another cough-laugh. "That's why I was motivated to get in touch with Puck and Lucy. Now this."

Milo returned. "She fell asleep again."

"I'd better go lock the door," said Ken.

Milo said, "Why?"

I told him.

"Oh." Turning to Ken: "Call me if you need anything."

"Thanks, detective. Are they treating what happened as an accident?"

"Probably."

"Guess it was," said Ken. "Sometimes it seems like everything is."

Outside at the curb, I asked Milo if Lucy'd said anything.

"She held my hand and took turns smiling and crying. Think she has any chance coming out of this reasonably intact?"

"She's pretty tough, but this . . . she's topping off the stress scale."

"Beautiful day," he said, looking at the sapphire sky. "I had time to make some calls. The surf shop's closed, meaning the Sheas may have split, too. Still nothing on Trafficant, and if your Mr. Mellors is a bad guy, he's been a careful one. Nothing on NCIC. In fact, I can't find any record of him at all."

"What's going on?" I said. "Everyone's just disappearing."

He rubbed his face. "We all do, eventually."

I returned home and tried Columbia University. They'd never heard of Denton Mellors. Either he'd lied about his educational background or was using a false name. Pen name? I got the number for the *Manhattan Book Review* and called the magazine.

The man who answered let out a stuffed-sinus laugh. "Mellors? And who are you, Lord Chatterley?"

"Sometimes I feel like it."

That cut off his laughter. "He's not one of ours. We have no grounds to keep."

"He definitely wrote for you," I said. "Reviewed M. Bayard Lowell's last book."

"That sounds *awfully* like ancient history."

"Twenty-one years ago."

"Well, that's paleo*lithi*c, isn't it?"

"Is there anyone on your staff who was working on the magazine at the time?"

"We're not a magazine," he said, miffed. "We're a review—a state of mind, actually. And we have no permanent staff. Just Mr. Upstone, myself, and a *bevy* of freelance hopefuls."

"What does it take to be a reviewer?"

"One has to recognize the proper criteria for judging books."

"Which are?"

"Style and substance. Now, I fail to see the importance—"

"I work for a law firm out in L.A. Mr. Mellors has come into an inheritance. Nothing big, but he still might want to know about it."

"How nice for him."

"Was Mr. Upstone around when Mr. Mellors's review came out?"

"Mr. Upstone has *always* been around."

"May I speak with him, please?"

"If you're *good*."

"I promise."

He laughed. "California . . . how can you *live* there?"

A few minutes later, a cross-sounding tobacco voice said, "Mason Upstone."

I repeated my request.

Upstone broke in. "I won't tell you a damn thing. Haven't you ever heard of the right to privacy?"

"I'm not—"

"That's right, you're not. Tell your friends at the CIA or the FBI or whoever it is you're with to do something more constructive than spying on creative people."

Slam.

I went out on the deck and tried to relax. The sky out there was even bluer, but I couldn't unwind.

I couldn't stop bad things from happening to Lucy, but I should have been able to deal with a dream. . . .

Lowell, Trafficant, Mellors.

I pulled out the clipping on the Sanctum party and read it one more time.

Lowell holding court.

Trafficant with his own circle of groupies.

Had they tried to outdo one another the night of the party?

Had Karen Best been the victim of that competition?

There had to be some way to connect the pieces.

I ran my eyes down the names of partygoers. The usual Westside showbiz list, no indication any of them had a relationship with Lowell. With one exception: the film producer who'd financed construction of the retreat, Curtis App.

His name had come up before. I shuffled through articles till I found it: A PEN fund-raiser at App's Malibu house had been the site of Lowell's reentry into the public eye.

Fund-raiser for political prisoners.

Had App shared Lowell's sympathy for talented criminals? Or was he just a generous man?

Calculated generosity? Film people's self-esteem often lagged their wealth. Had App tried to buy himself respectability by hitching up with a Great Man?

An "independent producer" had optioned *Command: Shed the Light* for film. App, or some other patron?

Paying to adapt poetry to the screen seemed an absurd business decision. More charity?

Great Man on the skids . . . App buying in cheap?

Sinking money into Sanctum, then watching it all fall apart as Lowell lost interest.

He might very well have a few opinions on Lowell.

No phone listings under his name. No great surprise.

Didn't producers belong to some kind of trade group—the Producers Guild?

I found the address—400 South Beverly Drive in Beverly Hills—and was just about to punch the number when my service clicked in.

"Someone on your line from Mr. Lowell, doctor. She wouldn't give a last name. Sexy voice."

I took the call.

Nova said, "Are you still planning to bring the daughter up?"

"There were no plans."

"I was under the impression there were. He's expecting her —the best time's late afternoon. Five or later. He takes a long nap after lunch, and—"

"There were no plans," I repeated, "and something's come up."

"Oh, really," she said coolly. "And what's that?"

"Mr. Lowell's son Peter was found dead today."

Silence.

"When did this happen?" she said skeptically.

"The body was discovered this morning. He'd been dead for a while."

"How did he die?"

"Heroin overdose."

"Damn," she said. "How am I going to *tell* him?"

"Call the police and let them do it."

"No, no, it's my job. . . . This is *obscene*, the man's been through so much. When he wakes up he'll expect me to tell him about the daughter's visit. You should have her come. Especially now. He deserves it."

"Think so?" I said.

"Why are you being so hostile? I'm just trying to do what's right."

"So am I."

"I'm sorry." Suddenly, a softer tone. "I'm sure you are. This caught me by surprise. I have no experience with this kind of thing. I really don't know what to do."

"There's no easy way to tell him," I said. "Just find the right time and do it."

"What's the right time?" she said, almost timidly.

"When he's not drunk or highly medicated or upset about something else."

"That doesn't leave much . . . but you're right, I'll just have to bite the bullet."

Sounding miserable.

"What's the matter?" I said.

"What if I tell him and he has a fit and—he's in such bad shape. What if he has another stroke? What do I do, all alone with him?"

"He obviously needs a doctor."

"I know, I know, but he hates them."

"Then I don't know what to tell you."

"He likes *you*. Would you come up and be there when I tell him—maybe coach me?"

I laughed. "I think you've got the wrong guy."

"No, no, he does. Said he'd given you both barrels and you'd shot right back. He respects you. It's the first time I've heard him say anything respectful about anyone. I know it's an imposition, but I'll pay you for your time. Please, this freaks me out; I don't do death well. Too much weirdness in this family, this wasn't what I expected when I took the job. But I can't abandon him—too many people have."

"It seems to me he's the one doing the abandoning."

"You're right," she said. "But he doesn't see it that way. He can't help himself—he's too old to change. I'm really worried I'm going to mess this up. Please help me. I'll make it worth your while."

"I won't take your money," I said. "Conflict of interest. But I'll come up. And it has to be now."

The kindly therapist, even as I mapped out a walk through the grounds. Looking for lacy trees.

"You will?" she said. "That's so incredible. If there's anything I can do in return . . ."

Sexy voice.

"Let's just get through this," I said. "I feel sorry for the whole family."

"Yes," she said. "They're a pitiful bunch, aren't they?"

34

She was sitting on the porch and got up to meet me as I pulled up to the hitching posts. She had on a soft black minidress and black sandals. A bra this time, the cups patterned in relief under the cotton. She jogged down the big wooden steps, smiling, and I felt about to be tackled as she came straight at me. Stopping inches away, she took my hand.

Her body was sleek, but this close, with the sunlight bathing her face, I noticed tiny tuck scars where her ears met her jawline.

Face lift. Older than I'd thought?

Her hand held on to mine and I looked down and saw other scars, on her arms. Small, barely discernible, with the exception of one long white line running parallel to the knuckles of her right hand.

"Thank you." She pecked my cheek. "He's still sleeping."

Letting go, she directed me onto the porch with just a touch at the small of my back.

"How long does he usually sleep?" I said.

"He can go anywhere from two to five hours. I try to ease up on the morphine before lunch, so he'll have an appetite, but he generally reacts strongly to it."

"Who prescribes the morphine?"

"A doctor in Pacific Palisades."

"Does this doctor ever actually see him?"

She rubbed her index finger with her thumb, sighed, and smiled. "What can I say?"

I thought of how Lowell had despised Puck for his addiction.

"Come on in." She opened the front door.

"How about a walk?" I said. "I've been cooped up all day."

"Sure," she said, smiling and smoothing back her hair. "Let me get something, first."

She ran up the stairs and came back with a white plastic hand radio with a rubber antenna. The brand sticker said Kid-Stuff.

"It's for babies," she said, clipping it onto her waistband. "But that's what old people are, right? Big babies."

She rotated a dial on the radio and static came on.

"It's got a range of about five hundred feet, so we can't go too far. Sometimes he wakes *up* like a baby—crying out. He wears diapers, too."

She stayed very close to me as we strolled around the house. Directly behind the building was a dry unplanted parcel broken only by an empty laundry line on metal posts.

Beyond that, the beginnings of forest, the brush growing so thick it looked impenetrable. Nova and I crossed the dirt, and I studied the house. No porches or balconies, just rough logs and windows and a single door. Drapes covered three of the windows on the ground floor.

"Is that his bedroom?" I said.

"Uh-huh. It used to be the library but he can't get upstairs anymore."

She started to walk. I kept looking at the house and she stopped.

"Ugly, isn't it?" she said.

"Like a big log cabin."

She nodded and pressed her arm against mine. "Yeah, that old rustic feeling."

"In his shape," I said, "I don't imagine decor means much."

"I doubt it ever did. Money doesn't mean much to him either. Probably 'cause he's always had it. He's cued in to one thing only: himself." Cool appraisal, no malice. Everything about her seemed cool.

"Have you worked for him a long time?"

"Six months."

"What's your background?"

She laughed. "I'm a writer."

"What kind of things do you write?"

"Poetry, mostly. I'm thinking of doing a screenplay. About California—the strange things you see here."

"Are you from the East?"

"No, up north."

"How'd you hook up with him?"

"I wrote him a fan letter and he answered. I wrote back and he sent an even longer letter. We began a correspondence. About writing: style and story structure, things like that. A few months later he offered me a job as a personal assistant. He made it sound as if he was fundamentally healthy and just needed light care. Then I arrived and found out I was going to have to change diapers."

"But you stayed anyway."

"Sure," she said, swinging her arms and picking up her pace. "He's an institution. How could I turn him down?"

Not to mention material for a screenplay.

I said, "My impression was that he's a faded institution."

Her jaw tightened, deepening the tuck scars. "Maybe to fools who follow the best-seller list."

Stopping, she raised the volume on the radio. Nothing but the static. She lowered it again but didn't move.

I said, "I heard this place was once a retreat for artists and writers."

"Long time ago."

"Nice concept."

"What is?"

"Retreating. Getting away from the grind."

"Oh, you never do. You just change gears."

She turned and began circling back toward the front of the house. I stayed with her.

"So you're a fan of his."

"Absolutely."

"Any books in particular?"

"Everything."

"Didn't he write a book of poems that was considered anti-woman?"

She gave me a sharp smile. "You mean, am I being a traitor to my sex by admiring him? Yes, to him women are meat—he grabs my ass at least once a day. But if women were honest, they'd admit men were meat to them, too. Let's face it, big cocks are better than little cocks."

Holding the smile, she swung her arms and brushed my thigh.

"We're all meat," she said, almost singing it. "What else is there? At least Buck's honest about it. I clean his shit, he can't hide anything from me."

"Nor you from him."

"What do you mean?"

"You still have to tell him about Peter."

She made a grumbling sound, nearly masculine. A scarred hand pinched her nose, then scratched the tip.

"Gnats," she said, slapping the air. "They think I'm delicious. Yes, I'll tell him. But just the fact that you're up here makes me feel good—believe it or not." Knowing smile. "You've got a certain aura. You get off on helping people, don't you?" Another thigh brush. "Thanks," she said, touching my chin.

I stepped away from her.

She looked amused. "Any advice for me?"

"What was his relationship with Peter like?"

"Only met the little shit once. Faggodly coward, begging for money. Here's Buck, struggling to live, using dope only as a last resort, and the stupid little snot shoots it voluntarily into his veins. I caught him once trying to rip off some of Buck's ampules. Told him to give them back or I'd tell Daddy. You should have seen the way his mouth dropped. He handed them over. Never came back."

"Maybe he was being honest in *his* own way."

"How?" she demanded, picking up her pace and moving out of touching range. The front porch came into view.

"Maybe being nothing but meat was too much for him to handle."

"Why? What else is there? A house in the suburbs? Look at that." She pointed upward, to a bird skittering among the treetops. "How long will it live? A month? A year? One day it will be flying along, and some predator will come crashing down on it, crushing its bones in its jaws, squeezing the juice out." Her neck muscles were tense. The tuck scars were deep black lines. "But it was *here*. It served its time. We're fools if we think we're any different. Our only meaning is being."

"So what's wrong with cutting it short?"

She stopped. "You advocate suicide? That's a switch for a psychologist, isn't it?"

"I don't advocate it. But I don't judge either."

"I *do*. A writer *always* does, that's the difference. You've devoted your life to learning the rules. I cherish the exceptions."

Good speech, but Lowell's voice seeped through.

She put her hands on her hips. "Get her up here—the daughter. What else does he have left? Isn't he entitled to it?"

"He hasn't been much of a father."

"He's tried."

"Has he?"

"In his own way."

"Which is what?"

"Staying out of their lives so his genius wouldn't overshadow them. Giving them money—who do you think paid for the coward's dope after he ran through his trust fund? Then he tries to pocket those ampules, the little puke."

"Why's Buck so interested in seeing Lucy?"

"Because he's her *father*. A girl should meet her father. If she doesn't, it's her loss. He's one of a kind. There's beauty in that, alone. Don't you see?"

"One of a kind," I said.

"Look," she said, fighting to keep her voice low, "you get off on helping people, but that doesn't mean you know everything. If you were hiking in some strange place and you came across a snake that had never been seen before—maybe it was poisonous, you had no idea—would you run from it? Or would you try to capture it and learn about it?"

"Depends on the danger."

Her nostrils widened and pulsed. She opened and shut her hands several times. "Okay, I tried. You've got your script." A few more steps, then: "He's the *only* thing in her miserable little ground-chuck existence that can make her prime *meat*. But go on, let her continue in the same old way."

Sound came from the radio. Low and anguished, then louder. Wordless moans. Then filthy words, a chain of them.

"Baby's up," she said.

Just past the stairs, she said, "You can wait here."

Alone with the stuffed heads, I walked around the giant room, listening to loud voices from the back of the house.

When she finally pushed his chair out, he was in a dark blue silk robe over white pajamas and his hair was disheveled.

"The Jew!" he said, slapping the wheels with his hands. Trying to go faster but Nova was in control and she steered him right at me. *"Der Yid!"* Spittle flecked his lips and his eyes were crusted. He rubbed one, picked something out, and flung it away.

"And don't tell me your cock hasn't been peeled and your mother goes to Mass. You're a dime-store Freud and that makes you a *Jew*. Thinking you're better than everyone and have a right to nose into everyone's business. Every analyst I knew felt that way; that's why all analysts are kikes."

I stared at a stuffed owl.

He said, "Where's the girl?"

Nova said, "Be nice to him, Buck," in an overly sweet tone. "He came all the way here to tell you something important."

I stared at her. She shrugged and walked over to a window. I said, "Did I?"

She said, "Didn't you? You're the expert."

Then she left.

Lowell watched her. "Those cheeks," he said. "Like sugar-coated sponge rubber. To be between them . . . What's on your mind, Dimestore? The girl still working on her bruised-virgin courage, dispatching you on another reconnaissance mission?"

"It's Puck," I said. "He's dead. Drug overdose."

He nodded. Stopped. Clamped both hands down on his wheels and turned his back on me.

"All right," he said, very quietly. "All right, you've delivered the message. Now fuck you to hell. If I see you again, I'll kill you."

35

He showed up two days later at the funeral, arriving late,
wheeled across the rolling lawn of the cemetery by Nova. Conspicuous in a white suit and shirt and a wide-brimmed straw
hat. He stayed well back from Lucy and Ken as a minister on call
to the mortuary recited a dispirited prayer. Once, Nova's eyes
met mine and tried to hook me into a staring contest. One of
her hands touched a breast. I turned my attention back to the
service.

The cemetery was one of those hundred-acre things yearning
to be a theme park: offices in a colonial mansion, bulldozed hill-
ocks of golf turf, replicas of Michelangelo's statuary cropping up
in odd places. Instead of gravestones, brass plaques were set
flush with the ground. Ken had bought Peter's strip of perpetuity
yesterday, after Milo'd helped speed release of the body.

I'd spent a good part of the past forty-eight hours at the
house on Rockingham. Ken and Lucy had been nearly inert, eating little, resting a lot, barely capable of speech.

I'd experienced some inertia myself, not following up on
Curtis App or doing anything else about Karen Best. Sherrell Best
had phoned once, and I'd had my service call him back to say I'd
get to him in a couple of days. The grief of the moment loomed so
huge, it seemed to have blotted out the dream. I wasn't sure
when—or if—Lucy would ever return to it. Still, as I stood there
among all that barbered green, it chewed at me.

A few feet behind me, two laborers waited under a tree.

The minister said something about the puzzles of life and
God's will. Then he shot a glance at the laborers and they came

over. One of them activated a motor attached to thick cloth straps that supported the gray lacquered coffin. The straps loosened very slowly and descended. As it hit bottom, it made a resonant, almost musical sound, and Lucy let out a high, agonized wail. Ken held her and rocked her as she cried into her hands.

Behind them, Buck said something to Nova.

The laborers began shoveling dirt on the coffin.

Each clump made Lucy cry out. Ken's face looked ready to crumple.

Buck shook his head, and Nova wheeled him away.

The chair bumped its way over the grass, catching a couple of times and forcing Nova to free its wheels. Finally, she got it to the curb of the swooping drive where the hearse sat and worked a long time getting Lowell out of the chair and into the Jeep. Folding the chair and stowing it in back, she sped off.

I dropped Milo off at the West L.A. station and drove back to Malibu. Shooting the Curl was still closed.

Had I flushed the prey too well?

I stopped off at the Malibu civic center and killed an hour locating a business license for the surf shop.

When the original papers had been filed, the Sheas had been living on the land side, up Rambla Pacifica. Three years later, they'd moved to the 20000 block of Pacific Coast Highway.

I drove back south and found the place: a one-story Cape Cod, white board and green shutters, squeezed between two bigger stucco edifices. Probably one of the original beach structures of the twenties and thirties, reminiscent of a quieter, simpler Malibu. Sometimes big storms washed the old places out to sea.

I rang the bell. No answer. The knocker was a bronze sea lion patinaed with salt. I used it to drum the green wooden door a couple of times. Still nothing. Neither Gwen's customized van nor Tom's BMW was in sight. But no mail in the box, not even throwaways.

I went home and called the Producers Guild and learned that Curtis App was president of New Times Productions in Century City.

A call to New Times got me a voice mail system that required an engineering degree to understand. I pushed 6 to speak with Mr. App and got cut off.

It was just after noon.

I drove into the city, heading straight for the university library.

The computer held a dozen references to App, the most recent being five-year-old reviews of a movie he'd produced called *Camp Hatchet II*.

Bomb review. Maybe that was his spiritual link with Lowell. The next seven citations were more of the same. Then I found a thirteen-year-old article in *American Film* entitled APP ON THE DEFENSE: TEEN PIX PRODUCER SAYS HE KEEPS KIDS OUT OF TROUBLE.

The magazine hadn't been microfilmed, but it was in the stacks. The article was an interview in which App acknowledged the dreadful critical notices he'd received on each of the nine soft-sex blood-and-gore flicks he'd produced and admitted that "my pictures aren't Dostoyevsky, they're popcorn for the head. But no pubic hair or nipples. Kids watch them, space out, and have a good time in the drive-in. When they're there, they're off the streets, so think of it as public service programming. As a parent, I'd rather have my kid watch *Janey Makes the Squad* or *Red Moon Over Camp Hatchet* than a lot of the garbage that's on network TV."

The accompanying color photo showed App sitting in the driver's seat of a long-snouted red Ferrari convertible, a satisfied smile on his face, a perfect sky and palm trees in the background.

From the narrowness of his shoulders, a small man. Thin face with ratlike features and an extremely pointed chin.

Gray hair, Caesar cut, white tennis shirt, red sweater that matched the Ferrari. Great tan.

No mention of his ever optioning Lowell's book, so either I'd guessed wrong about that or it was something he wanted to forget.

Scrolling back, I came across nothing on him for the next nine years, then a piece in *The Wall Street Journal* entitled RETAIL FOOD A GROWTH MARKET.

It turned out to be one of those center-of-the-front-page lightweight articles the *Journal* runs in order to amuse nervous businessmen. The full title read *Retail Food a Growth Market If Consumers' Special Needs Are Met: Curtis App Likes Sprouts and Jicama.*

Back in those days—three years before the Sanctum party—App had been a financial analyst for an investors' group specializing in supermarket chains, vending machines, coin-op laundries, and fast-food outlets. In the article he predicted that retailers were going to have to cater to ethnic and special needs to be successful in an increasingly competitive market.

A photoengraving showed the same pointy face with full dark Beatle-length hair.

From groceries to slasher flicks? An association with Lowell must have seemed the next step toward High Art.

I left the library and stopped at an instant-print place in Westwood. No other customers in the store, and it took exactly twenty-three minutes to obtain fifty business cards.

Good paper, ecru shade, classy embossed script.

Sander Del Ware
Freelance Writer

Below that, a phony post office box in Beverly Hills and a phone number I'd used ten years ago while in private practice. Putting three cards in my wallet and the rest in the trunk of the Seville, I headed for Century City.

New Times Productions was located in a twenty-story black tower on Avenue of the Stars. A hit movie a few years ago had featured a building just like it, under siege by terrorists. In the film, a rogue cop had vanquished the bad guys using guile and machismo. Most of the actual occupants of the real-life building were attorneys and film outfits. In real life, the terrorists would have been offered a deal.

The production company took up almost all of the top floor, the exception one office belonging to an outfit named Advent Ventures.

The New Times entry was two huge glass doors. I pushed one of them, and it opened silently on a skylit waiting room. The floor was black granite, the furniture Lucite, white leather, and iron, powder-coated deep blue. *Variety* and *The Hollywood Reporter* were piled up on tables. Big frameless black-and-white paintings hung on gray wool walls.

A girl who looked about eighteen, in a white T-shirt and second-skin jeans tucked into spurred black-and-white cowskin boots, sat behind a deskette. Her long straight hair was buttercup streaked with ebony. A diamond was set into one nostril. Despite bad skin, she had a great face. I stood there awhile before she looked up from her cuticles.

"Uh-huh?"

"I'm here for Mr. App."

"Name."

"Sandy Del Ware."

"Are you the chiropractor? I thought you were tomorrow."

I handed her a card.

She wasn't impressed. The place was silent; no one else seemed to be around.

"Do you—uh—have an appointment?"

"I think Mr. App would like to see me. It's about Sanctum."

Her lips rotated a couple of times, as if spreading lipstick. If there'd been a pencil on her desk, she might have chewed it.

"I've only been here a couple of weeks. . . . He's in a meeting."

"At least ask him," I said. "Sanctum. Buck Lowell, Terry Trafficant, Denton Mellors."

She agonized, then punched two numbers on a see-through Lucite phone.

"It's some producer. About Santa and Dylan—uh—Miller. . . . I'm . . . What? . . . Oh, okay, sorry."

She put the phone down, looked at it, blinked hard.

"He's in a meeting."

"No problem, I can wait."

"I don't think he wants to see you."

"Really?"

"Yeah, he was pretty bent about being interrupted."

"Oh," I said. "Sorry. The meeting must be with somebody important."

"No, he's all by—" She touched her mouth. Frowned. "Yeah, it's important."

"Is a big star in there with him?"

She went back to her cuticles.

To her left was a hall. I strode past her desk and went for it.

"Hey!" she said, but she didn't come after me. Just as I rounded the corner, I heard buttons being punched.

I passed gray wool doors and movie posters depicting gun-toting huge-busted women of the receptionist's age, and leathered, four-day-bearded, male-model types pretending to be bikers and soldiers of fortune. The films had names like *Sacrifice Alley* and *Hot Blood, Hot Pants,* and several had recent release dates.

The drive-in circuit or instant video.

At the end of the hall was a big tooled brass door, wide open. Standing in the doorway was App.

He was around sixty, five-six, maybe a hundred and twenty. His Caesar cut had been reduced to a few white wisps tickling a deep tan forehead. He wore a custard-colored cashmere cardigan over a lemon-yellow knit shirt, knife edge-pressed black slacks, and brown crocodile loafers.

"Get the fuck out of here," he said, in a calm big-man's voice, "or I'll have your fucking ass *thrown* out."

I stopped.

He said, "Turn yourself the fuck *around.*"

"Mr. App—"

He cut the air with both hands, like an umpire calling a runner safe. "I've already called Security, you fucking jerk. Reverse yourself, and you just might avoid getting arrested and your fucking paper sued from here to kingdom come."

"I'm not with any paper," I said. "I'm a freelancer writing a biography of Buck Lowell."

I put a card in his face. He snatched it and held it at arm's length, then gave it back to me.

"So?"

"Your name came up in my research, Mr. App. I'd just like a few minutes of your time."

"You think you can pop in here like some fucking salesman?"

"If I'd called would I have been able to get an appointment?"

"Hell, no. And you're not getting one now." He pointed to the door.

"Okay," I said. "I'll just write it up the way I see it. Your optioning *Command: Shed the Light.* Bankrolling Sanctum only to see it collapse a year later."

"That's business," he said. "Ups and downs."

"Pretty big down," I said. "Especially on Lowell's part. He took your money and funded guys like Terry Trafficant and Denton Mellors."

"Denny Mellors." He laughed without opening his mouth. "She said something about Santa Claus and Dylan Miller. You know who Dylan Miller is?"

I shook my head.

"Grand prize asshole—and that asswipe rag he works for. Every other week we've got droves of assholes just like him, fucking paparazzi creeping around the building like roaches, looking for stars. The other day Julia Roberts was on the twelfth floor for a meeting and they were sweeping the bastards out with brooms. There's no end to it."

"Maybe you need better security," I said.

He stared at me. This time his laughter came with a flash of capped teeth.

Pulling up the left cuff of his cardigan, he peered at a watch so thin it looked like a platinum tattoo.

I heard footsteps behind me. App looked over my shoulder, then leaned against the doorframe.

Turning, I saw a big, heavy Samoan security guard. The name on his tag was long and unpronounceable.

"Some kind of problem, Mr. App?" he said in a tuba voice that made App's sound prepubescent.

App moved his eyes back to me and studied my face the way a casting director would. Smiling, he put a hand on my shoulder. "No, Mr.—Del Rey and I were just having a little chat."

"Delondra called down."

"A misunderstanding. We're going to take a meeting, Clem. Sorry to bother you."

I smiled at the guard. He sucked his teeth and left.

App called out, "Delondra!"

The receptionist came over, taking Geisha steps in her skin-tight jeans.

"What, Mr. App?"

App reached into his pocket and drew out a wad of bills clamped by a sterling silver monkey paw. Peeling off five, he held them out to the girl. Hundreds.

"Thanks, Mr. App, what's this for?"

"Severance pay. You no longer work here."

Her mouth opened. A small smooth hand closed around the bills.

App turned his back on her and said, "Come on in—was it Sandy? Let's hear what's on your mind. Maybe we can conceptualize it for film."

Two walls of his office were windows; the other two, bleached maple burl. The windows showed off L.A. County the way a hawk would see it just before it swooped. The wood showcased a Warhol silkscreen of a smiling Marilyn Monroe and transparent plastic shelves full of bound scripts. Some of the screenplays had titles hand-lettered on their spines, others were blank.

App took a seat behind a blue, triangular marble desk, with nothing on it but a blue marble phone, and offered me the only other chair in the room, an unupholstered, black, straight-backed thing. At his feet was a large marble wastebasket full of more scripts.

"So," he said. "What else have you done besides this book?"

"Journalism." I threw out the names of a few magazines, betting he didn't read much.

"What made you want to write about Buck?"

"Fall from grace. The whole notion of genius gone bad."

"No kidding. Giving him money wasn't one of the brighter things I've done. You can write that."

"What led you to option poetry?"

"Soft heart," he said. "Everything was collapsing around the bastard." He touched his chest. "Got a soft spot for creative types."

"Same reason you financed Sanctum?"

"Yeah. Helping young artists. What could be more fucking important, right?—don't put 'fucking' in—hey, aren't you going to take notes?"

"Didn't bring anything," I said. "I figured I'd have enough trouble getting through the door without a tape recorder and a notepad."

"See?" More capped teeth. "Never know. You caught me on a good day. I'm Mother Fucking Teresa."

There must have been a drawer in the marble desk, because he pulled a piece of paper out of it and waved it at me.

New Times stationery.

"Here," he said, retrieving a bound script from the wastebasket. "Write on this. Do I need to give you a fucking pen, too?"

I pulled out a ballpoint.

"Five minutes," he said. "All you can eat during that time, and then vamoose." Putting his arms behind his head, he sat back.

"So you liked the concept of Sanctum," I said. "What about Lowell's choice of fellows?"

"Terry? Terry was a talented guy, actually. Personal problems, but who doesn't."

"So you never saw him act violent."

"Not to me. He used to put on this Mr. Macho thing, walking around without a shirt, all these tattoos of naked girls. But he had talent."

"Whatever happened to him?"

"Hell if I know. Idiot had all sorts of good stuff coming to him. I coulda had deals for him, and he just split."

"Do you think Lowell knows where he went?"

"I always figured he did, but he never admitted it. That was the final straw between us. After all I did for the bastard, I figured I had some honesty coming. You meet him yet?"

"Just briefly."

"Sick, isn't it? Guy's rolling in money and he lives like a pig."

"If he's rich, how come he needed to come to you for financing?"

He slid his arms from behind his head and placed them on the desk. "Because I was a jackass. Didn't know he was rich, never checked him out. And I used to be a fucking financial analyst, no excuse." Tapping the marble. "Hey, that's showbiz."

Another glance at the platinum watch.

I said, "So you have no idea about what happened to Trafficant?"

"No, but if you find out, let me know. Asshole owes me a script." Shaking his head. "Stupid mudfuck. He coulda made a living. Great ear for dialogue, he knew how to conceptualize in terms of scenes. Now, Denny Mellors was another story— wooden ear, thought he was some fucking Ivy League *literati*-type. And no fucking boy scout, either. He never got the bad PR Terry got, but he was antisocial from day one, nasty temper. Not that I have anything against black people—not that he was even that black. I think his mother was white, or something. He talked like a white. But the guy . . ."

Waving disgustedly, he put his feet up on the desk. The soles of his shoes were shiny black, unmarked.

"What did he do?" I said.

He looked out the window. The San Gabriel Mountains were capped with brown air. "You know, my friend, talking to you is giving me ideas. Any film interest in your book yet?"

"Some."

"You have any experience in film?"

"Not really."

"Then don't jump into anything. People are going to tell you they can do all sorts of things for you; meanwhile they've got a thumb in the Vaseline, ready to yank down your jockeys. I've been in the industry for twenty years, can get things done. And this book of yours is flashing concept lights. Like you said, fall from grace. And did you know the place used to be a nudist colony? How's that for a premise? Writers and artists and *nudists*. They get thrown together and shit happens."

"Violent shit?" I said.

"All kinds of shit. You'd have to change things around, of course. For legal purposes. Maybe make Lowell a musician—a cellist. Yeah, I like that. It's a music retreat—nudists and musicians, rock types and classical types, all thrown together—seductive, right?"

"Interesting. So who's the bad guy, Mellors? That's not too PC."

"So we make him white—he was mostly white anyway. Blond hair, little yellow mustache. Big, strong buck . . . nasty."

"Nasty how?"

"Nasty temper. Talked all the time about hurting things—hurting women. I'm not saying he actually did anything, but you talk like that long enough, who knows?"

"See what you mean," I said. "I've read about the grand opening party for Sanctum. Sounds like a wild affair—a love-in. That might be a good place for the shit to happen."

He looked up at the ceiling. Cheap acoustical tiles. "Maybe, yeah. Like a Felliniesque thing. *Dolce Vita* with acid, pot—kind of a sixties/seventies thing. That's coming back, you know."

"Were you at the party?"

"In the beginning," he said. "Then it got too loud, and my wife made me take her home."

"Did you see Mellors or Trafficant?"

"Nah," he said. "Too many people, noise, mess, all sorts of shit. One of those situations where you see everyone but you don't see anyone, know what I mean?"

"*La Dolce Vita* meets *The Trip*."

"Exactly." He moved his eyes from the ceiling to me. "You know how to conceptualize. Have an agent?"

"Still looking for one."

"You got a book deal without one?"

"Contacts from journalism."

"Who's your editor?"

I made up a name.

He nodded. "Well, get yourself an agent or talk to me directly, and we just might work something out. Let's say an eighteen-month option with first rights to renew."

"What kind of option money are we talking about?"

"Hey," he said, grinning. "Maybe you *don't* need an agent. What kind of money? The usual. Assuming we get a network interested. But I've got to have everything tied up before I go to them. Nowadays, they're more cautious than a virgin on horseback—you weren't thinking big screen, were you?"

"Actually—"

"Forget it, Sammy. TV's the only way to go. They're taking chances the studios won't, and even though syndication's not the honeymoon it used to be, it's still a serious game. Think you can write me up a treatment—one or two pages? Let's say by next Tuesday?"

"Sure," I said, "but I want to discuss some story elements with you first, make sure we're talking the same language."

"Story," he said dismissively. "You're the writer. Give me good and evil, some conflict, resolution—maybe some martial arts. Networks are ripe for martial arts, nothing decent since Kung Fu. Musicians and nudists and evil. 'Course they couldn't be shown nude, but you'll find some way to let everyone know they're buck naked. Like a sly wink, know what I mean? But respectful of the human body. Something women can get behind. Good and evil. The characters arc, but they maintain their basic good-bad nature. The more I think about it, the better I like it."

He rubbed his hands together and stood. "You got thirteen fucking minutes for the price of five, Sam."

"You see Mellors as the evil lead?" I said.

"If you make him white."

"Can you tell me anything more about him that would flesh out the character?"

"Nasty piece of work. Like I said, he hated women, called them manipulative bitches. I took him in, after Sanctum closed. Gave him a job because I felt sorry for him. He was working on a book, couldn't finish it."

"Writer's block?"

"*Money* block. Writer's block was *Lowell's* game. Talk about big talk, no action. Anyway, Denny came to me begging because he knew I was a soft touch. Broke—he'd depended on Lowell. He was writing this novel, gonna be the greatest thing since *Moby Dick* if he could only finish it. Being a liberal do-gooder, I gave him a job with my company in return for first refusal on the manuscript."

"What kind of job?"

"Idiot work. Business Affairs office. Writing memos, filing contracts, xeroxing. The idea was to free him up to write. Then one day he waltzes in, announces no more book, it's a screenplay now. The story *lends* itself to that form. Fine, makes my life that much easier. I wait six months, then six more."

He walked to the bookcase. Eyeing the shelves for a second, he pulled a thin unmarked volume out of the middle, opened it, put it back, and removed another one, even thinner.

"This is what he gives me."

I took the folder. Bound in brown, marbled cardboard. The title page said:

THE BRIDE
A Screenplay by Denton W. Mellors

"Take it home," said App. "I like you, but you're outa here. Got a meeting."

I folded my notes and put them away. App tossed the script I'd used for a writing board back into the trash. We walked to the door.

"I haven't been able to locate Mellors," I said. "Any idea what happened to him?"

"Who the fuck knows? After I told him I couldn't use that

piece of shit you're holding, he cursed me out, threw a chair—broke some pre-Columbian pieces—and left. Last I saw of him, thank God. Scared the shit out of me. First time I hired a body-guard."

We left the office and walked down the postered hall past the empty reception desk. He opened a glass door and held it.

"Nice meeting you, Sammy—what makes you run, ha ha. Let's both of us do some serious thinking about what we want out of this, write something up, and then we can break some bread. Let's say Wednesdayish. Lunch?"

36

I walked over to the Century City shopping mall, found a café with private booths, and sat down to coffee and Denton Mellors's script.

Not a complete script, it soon became clear. Just a five-page triple-spaced summary, what App had called a treatment.

THE BRIDE

We open upon a man watching a woman undressing. From his face we see he is a homicidal maniac, but handsome and muscular. The kind of man women gravitate to.

He holds a boning knife. It is nighttime. The moon hits it and it glints.

The maniac gets up from his crouch and cuts through a sliding glass door. The woman is in the shower, soaping herself up. We see soap on her breasts and her vagina. She is masturbating, enjoying it.

The maniac flings open the shower door. The woman screams as the maniac rapes the woman anally, then fillets her.

The maniac removes his clothing, showers in the woman's shower as the body still lies there. Then he gets dressed and drives home to his marital bed. His bride is young, beautiful, clearly virginal. She loves him madly. He is the love and lust of her life.

The maniac and his bride engage in foreplay and the maniac makes tender love to his innocent young bride: he is capable of great sensitivity when the situation calls for it. As she comes, thunderously, the camera cuts to juxtaposed faces of the bride and the maniac's other savaged women—all of them his chosen.

The bride's prolonged, cataclysmic orgasm alternates with their
anguish. To the maniac, it is all music. . . .

I managed to finish the rest of it, resisting the temptation to
stow it in the garbage.

Instead, I took it home and called Milo the minute I got
through the door. But he wasn't at the station and I had to con-
tent myself with leaving a message at Blue Investigations.

I tried Lucy in Brentwood. Phone off the hook, probably
sleeping again. Checking in with my service got me one message:
Wendy Embrey wanting to talk about billing problems. That irri-
tated me, and I didn't bother to copy down her number.

I got a beer from the fridge and watched a couple of surfers
struggle to master infinity.

Mellors's treatment screamed in my head like a car alarm.

He and Lowell and Trafficant drawn together not by art but
by hatred of women.

Discovering common interests.

Slaking their needs together the night of the party.

Lowell shutting down the retreat less than a year later.

New use for his acreage?

Another type of cemetery?

Robin came home in a great mood and we ended up in bed. I
tried to keep the bad pictures out of my head, wondering if I'd be
able to make love.

When the time came, I did the right things but my mind was
still elsewhere, firing like a strobe light.

She fell asleep quickly, but I found myself itching to get up. I
lay there for a long time, not moving.

"Restless?"

"Maybe I'll get up and take a drive or something."

She started to sit up but I kissed her forehead.

"Rest."

Is everything okay, Alex?"

"Just one of those jumpy nights. You know me."

"Sometimes I wonder," she said. But she closed her eyes and
pursed her lips. I kissed them and touched her eyelids with my
fingers. She gathered the covers around her head and curled up.

*   *   *

I sped past Broad Beach, Zuma, the Colony, Carbon Beach.
La Costa.

One very bright light shone above the Sheas' house. Two
proto-Malibu cars were parked along the highway in front: a
Porsche bathtub roadster and a Corvette. Between them was an
elderly Olds 88 that looked vaguely familiar. I pulled up behind
the Corvette and was walking to the front door just as it opened
and a man backed out, stumbling.

I thought I heard a voice from inside the house, but the combined roars of the highway and the ocean drowned out the
words.

The man approached the house again and I got close enough
to hear a woman's voice.

"Go away! I'll call the police!"

The man shouted, "Just you—"

"*Out!* Get the hell *out!* I'll call the *police!*"

The man stopped and folded his arms across his chest. "Go
ahead, Gwendolyn. Tell them you're a murderer."

Then he charged the door.

The woman screamed again. "You *bastard!*" The man stumbled again, shoved back with force.

Falling into a pool of lamplight.

Sherrell Best, in his dark suit and tie, his hairless dome shiny
as a ball bearing.

I was right in back of him now as the door started to slam
shut. He whipped out his right foot and managed to wedge it
between the door and the jamb. His ankle was trapped. He
shouted in pain.

Threats and curses from Gwen Shea. No backup from Tom,
so she was there alone.

Best tried to pull his ankle free but it was vise-gripped.

Gwen Shea kept screaming through the crack. Putting her
weight against the door, trying to crush the ankle.

I shouted, "Cut it out, he's stuck!"

Her eyes spread with panic as she focused on my face. She
opened the door, kicked at Best's leg as I pulled it free, and
slammed it shut.

Best lay there, groaning. I pulled him up but when he stood
on his right leg, he buckled and I had to support him.

"Let's get out of here," I said, trying to pull him toward the
Olds.

He shook his head. "I'm staying here."

"What if she calls the police?"

"She didn't, did she? Because she knows she's guilty. I can *smell* guilt."

He folded his arms again.

"What if she has a gun?" I said. "This is exactly how bad things happen."

"Then she'll add to her sins."

"That won't solve your problem."

"Will anything else solve my problem?"

"That's not a very religious answer."

He looked away.

"Come on," I said. "Let's talk about this rationally. I've learned some things that may—"

He grabbed my sleeve. "What kinds of things?"

"If you leave and promise not to confront her again, I'll tell you."

He looked back at the house. Shook his right leg and winced. Stared at the speeding cars, then once more at the house. All lights off.

"I take that as a solemn oath," he said.

"Tell me," he said, sitting in the driver's seat and massaging his ankle.

"Do you need to see a doctor for that?"

"No, no, it's fine. Tell me what you've learned."

"I need you to promise you won't act on it."

"I can't promise that!"

"Then I can't tell you."

"You swore!"

"It's for your own safety, Reverend."

"I can take care of myself."

"I see that."

His nostrils widened. For an instant he looked like anything but a man of God.

"All right. I made a fool out of myself. So did Elijah, coming down from the hills, raving at Ahab. So did Moses, talking to a bush, and Jesus, consorting with the low and the needy—"

"Reverend, the last thing I want to do is prolong your suffering. I want to find out the whole truth about Karen also."

"Why?"

"For my patient," I said, keeping it simple.

"That's hard to believe."

"So was walking on water."

He started to touch his sore ankle, then stopped himself and brushed his fingers against the keys dangling from the ignition. "If you really know something, tell me, doctor. Trust me to do the right thing."

"Not unless you promise not to act. Your getting involved the way you did tonight will only slow things down."

"Slow things down? Does that mean there's progress?"

"Some. I'm sorry, I know you've lived with this for a long time, but it's going to have to be a while longer."

"A while," he said, flexing his foot. "Why did you come here tonight?"

"Because you're probably right about the Sheas knowing something. But if you get in the way, we may never find out what. And I won't tell you another word unless I'm sure you'll cooperate."

The pain in his eyes had nothing to do with his leg.

"All right. I promise not to do anything that gets in the way."

"Nothing at all," I said. "No contact with anyone associated with the case until I tell you it's safe."

"Fine, fine. What do you know?"

"I consider *that* a religious oath."

"I won't swear needlessly, but you have my word."

I gave him some of it, leaving out names. The growing possibility that something had happened to Karen at the party and that Felix Barnard had learned about it, tried to profit, and died because of greed.

A tremor of rage took hold of his face. He forced himself placid. An unsettling calm, almost like death.

"I knew there was something about that man," he said. "Polite—too polite. I never completely trusted him. How did he die?"

I told him. "That's why we have to be careful, Reverend. If covering up was worth killing for then, it still is."

"Yes, yes," he said. But there was no fear in him, only a cold, quiet acquiescence. I'd asked a lot of him. Thinking of the picture in his kitchen—*Dinah's Abduction by Shechem*—I wondered if I was putting too much faith in him.

"And them?" he said, looking at the Sheas' house.

"No direct involvement, so far, other than the fact that they may have hired Karen to work at the party. And we still haven't been able to verify that."

"I can't believe that. Their evasiveness. Look what just happened. If she's innocent, why didn't she call the police on me? And their shop's been closed for two days, no sign of *him*. So maybe he knows something's up and has left town. Isn't flight the first sign of guilt?"

"How do you know about the shop, Reverend?"

He didn't answer.

"More surveillance?"

His smile was grim.

"What made you decide to watch them now?"

"Talking to you on the phone the other day. I could tell from your voice that you were on to something. Is your patient ready to meet me yet?"

"My patient's in mourning. Death in the family."

"Oh, no." He put his hands on the steering wheel and sank down. "I'm so sorry. Was he—or she—close to the deceased? Can you at least tell me the sex of the person you've been talking to, so I can pray accordingly?"

"A woman."

"I thought so," he said. "A woman's compassion . . . poor thing. Hopefully the time will come when she'll be able to step away from her grief."

"Hopefully."

"Of course you can't rush her. Those things can't be rushed."

He turned and gripped my hand. "When she *is* able to—whenever it is—call me. Maybe I can help. Maybe we can help each other."

I nodded and got out of the car.

Through the passenger window, he said, "You're a good man. Forgive me for not believing your intentions."

"Nothing to forgive."

"Are you religious, doctor?"

"In my own way."

"What way is that?"

"I don't believe the world's random."

"A major leap of faith," he said. "I try to renew it in my own mind, every day. Some days are easier than others."

37

"Everything's surreal," said Lucy.

It was 9 A.M. and I'd finally reached her at the Brentwood house.

"In what way?"

"One moment I'll be talking to him and it feels so *real*. Then I'll wake up and realize I've been dreaming and the truth hits me. . . . I guess that's normal."

"Very much so."

"I've been doing nothing but sleeping. Can't help it, I feel drugged. Every time I try to get up, I just want to crawl right back. Should I force myself to stay awake?"

"No, let nature take its course."

"God, I *miss* him!"

She started to cry.

"I'm not angry at him, he couldn't help it. Getting hold of such strong stuff, not knowing. . . . When he was hungry for it, he couldn't think about anything else."

More tears.

"Such pain . . . what a waste. My heart feels as if it's really breaking—I don't know if I'll ever feel totally good again."

"Everything takes time, Lucy."

"I can't do hypnosis, can't focus on anything—I'm sorry."

"Nothing to be sorry for."

"Later. We'll do it later. All I can do now is cry and sleep—I don't even want to talk. I'm sorry."

"It's okay, Lucy."

"I'm sorry, I'm sorry," she mocked herself. "Sorry for the

world. For Carrie Fielding and the others. And Puck. And Karen. I haven't forgotten her. I *won't* forget."

Three psychopaths in the forest.

Barnard learning something about it. Dead.

The Sheas, living on the sand.

Doris Reingold, alive and poor. Gambling away her payoff?

Spirited out of town by Tom Shea. Into hiding, or something more final?

I played with it some more. Barnard kept popping up in my thoughts, like one side of a loaded die.

If he'd been murdered because he was a blackmailer, the conspicuous nature of his death made sense: A corpse on a motel bed had plenty of educational value.

Who'd done the shooting? The murder had taken place a full year after Karen's disappearance. By then, Mellors—or whatever his real name was—was working for App, and Trafficant had vanished.

And M. Bayard Lowell was living in splendid isolation in Topanga Canyon.

I didn't see the Great Man risking a meeting at a sleazy motel.

And why that particular dirty-sheets dive?

Because it catered to hookers? Mo Barnard had described Felix as a womanizer. Had he been lured there with the promise of another payoff—the bigger one he'd pressed for? Happy to enjoy a quickie while he waited?

I pictured him, pants down and happily expectant, on a narrow gray bed in a darkened room, porno on video, booze on the nightstand.

A woman in hotpants and spike heels. She smiles and ducks into the bathroom with a wink and a "One minute, honey."

The toilet flushes. Water runs. Barnard concentrates on the movie, oblivious to the door opening.

Someone rushes to the side of the bed and begins squeezing off rounds.

Someone with a key. The clerk paid off? The hooker in on it, too?

But, still, why *that* motel? Three miles east, Hollywood was crammed with mattress palaces.

Maybe because the *killer* knew *that* place well enough to set up an inside job.

The police had never suspected. According to Milo, the motel was a chronic trouble spot, so one more felony—even a homicide—would be no great surprise.

Barnard had led a pathetic life, spending his days prying into other people's secrets, taking money to look into cold cases.

Twenty years later, his own file was stone cold.

An inconsequential man. Had the papers even bothered to write up his death?

This time I stayed closer to home and used the main Santa Monica library on 6th Street. Barnard's name wasn't listed in the computers for that year or any other. But a search under *homicide* struck gold in the newspaper files:

> *Motel, homicide at. Police say the* Adventure Inn *on the Westside is site of numerous crimes, the latest the murder of a retired private investigator.*

The full article was tucked into a bottom corner of the last page of the Metro section.

HOMICIDE PROMPTS IRE ABOUT MOTEL

The early morning shooting death of a retired private investigator in a Westside motel has prompted increased citizen concern about the hostelry. Police confirm a history of criminal activity at the Adventure Inn on 1543 South La Cienega Boulevard, including numerous arrests for prostitution, narcotics, disorderly conduct, and assault. Despite complaints by neighbors, police claim they are legally powerless to close the business down.

The victim, Felix Slayton Barnard, 65, of Venice, was found dead of multiple gunshot wounds in Room 11 by the motel's clerk, Edgely Sylvester, during a morning room check. Sylvester reported hearing and seeing nothing, and by the time police arrived all other residents had vacated the premises. "No surprise," said a bystander, refusing to be named. "They register by the half-hour."

Sylvester denied any personal knowledge of prostitution at the motel. When asked how he could have failed to hear three gunshots, he said, "There's a lot of traffic."

Questioned about why steps couldn't be taken to close the motel, Captain Robert Bannerstock of the LAPD's Westside Division said, "It's a free country. All we can do is go out and investigate occurrences. People need to be careful about where they spend the night."

Ownership of the motel is registered to a Nevada corporation, The Advent Group, and attempts to reach the manager, Darnel Mullins, were unsuccessful.

Darnel Mullins.

Denton Mellors.

Inside job.

Meet me at the Adventure Inn, Felix. There'll be a room reserved for you—have a whore on the house.

I looked up Darnel Mullins in every Southern California phone book the library owned. No Darnels; over a dozen D's spread around various counties. Thirty-five minutes on the pay phone in the entrance eliminated most of them. The rest weren't home.

Roadblocked again.

I sat at a library table, drumming my fingers until I thought of another route.

The clerk. Edgely Sylvester.

Thank God it was an unusual name—and listed in the Central L.A. book on the 1800 block of Arlington.

I took Pico east, toward the center of town. La Cienega was a couple of miles before Arlington, and I veered south and drove to 1543.

Still a motel, now called the Sunshine Lodge and painted turquoise blue. Three arms of cinder block around a dipping, pitted parking lot.

Two pickup trucks in the lot. I pulled in next to one of them. Room 11 was in the northwest corner, catercorner from the office. A DO NOT DISTURB sign hung from the doorknob.

I went into the office. A Korean man sat behind the desk, watching Korean language TV. A wall dispenser sold pocket combs and condoms, and a wire rack on the desk was stuffed with maps to the stars' homes. Robin had shown me one last year, given out by a record company as a party favor. Marilyn

Monroe was still alive and living in Brentwood, and Lon Chaney was haunting Beverly Hills.

The clerk eyed me and said, "Room?"

Not knowing what to say, I left.

Edgely Sylvester's neighborhood was just past the old Sears store near La Brea, not far from the Wilshire Division police station. The house was a two-story brown craftsman bungalow subdivided into apartments. The front lawn had been turned into parking spaces. A rusting Cadillac Fleetwood and a twenty-year-old Buick Riviera shared it.

Two black men in their sixties played dominoes at a card table on the front porch. Both wore short-sleeved white shirts and double-knit trousers, and the heavier of the two wore stretch suspenders. He was bald and had moist mocha skin. A cigar dangled from his lips.

The skinny man was ebony-toned and his features were sharp, still handsome. He had all his hair and it had been pomaded. He could have been Chuck Berry's less talented brother.

They stopped their play as I came up the walkway. The dominoes were bright red and translucent, with sharp white dots. I had no idea who was winning.

"Gentlemen," I said, "does Edgely Sylvester live here?"

"Nope," said the skinny one.

"Know him?"

They shook their heads.

"Okay, thanks."

As I walked away, the heavy one said, "Why do you want to know?" The cigar was between his fingers, wet and cold. He was sweating a lot, but it didn't look like anxiety.

"Reporter," I said. "*L.A. Times.* We're doing a story on old unsolved crimes for the Sunday magazine. Mr. Sylvester worked at a motel where an unsolved murder occurred twenty years ago. The victim was a private detective. My editors thought it would make a great piece."

"Lots of *new* murders all the time," said the skinny one. "City's falling apart, no need to talk about stupid *old* stuff."

"The new stuff scares people. The old stuff's considered romantic—I know, I think it's ridiculous, too. But I just started out, can't buck the boss. Anyway, thanks."

"Is there money in it?" said the skinny one. "For talking to you?"

"Well," I said, "I'm not supposed to pay for stories, but if something's good enough . . ." I shrugged.

They exchanged glances, and the heavy one put down a domino.

I said, "Did Mr. Sylvester tell you something about the unsolved case?"

Another look passed between them.

"How much you paying?" said the heavy one.

How much cash did I have in my wallet? Probably a little over a hundred.

"I really shouldn't pay anything. It would have to be something good."

The heavy one licked the end of his cigar. "What if I could find Mr. Edgely Sylvester for you?"

"Twenty bucks."

He sniffed and chuckled and shook his head.

"Finding him's no big deal," I said. "How do I know he'll talk to me?"

He chuckled some more. "If you pay him, he will, my man. He likes his money." Eyeing my Seville. "What's it, a seventy-eight?"

"Seventy-nine," I said.

"Paper don't pay you enough to get some new wheels?"

"Like I said, I just started." I turned to leave.

He said, "Forty bucks to find the man."

"Thirty."

"Thirty-five." He stretched out a palm. With a pained expression, I took out the money and gave it to him.

Curling his fingers over it, he smiled.

"Okay," I said, "where's Sylvester?"

He gave a deep laugh and pointed across the table. "Say hello, Mr. Sylvester."

The skinny man closed his eyes and laughed, rocking in his chair.

"Hello, hello, hello." He held out his hand. "Hello from the star of the show."

"Prove you're Sylvester," I said.

"A hundred *bucks*'ll prove it."

"Fifty."

"Ninety."

"Sixty."

"Eighty-eight."

"Sixty-five, tops."

He stopped smiling. His skin was as dry as his partner's was moist. His eyes were two bits of charcoal. "Thirty-five for him just for *fingering* me, and I only get thirty more? That's *stupid*, man."

I said, "Seventy, if you're really Sylvester. And that's it, because it cleans me out."

I took all the bills out of my wallet and fanned them.

Frowning, he reached behind and pulled out a mock-alligator billfold. Flipping it open, he showed me a soiled Social Security card made out to Edgely Nat Sylvester.

"Anything with a picture?"

"No need," he said, but he flipped again to a driver's license. It had expired three years ago, but the picture was of him and the name and address were right.

"Okay," I said, giving him a twenty and putting the rest of the money back.

"Hey," he said, rising out of his chair.

"When we're finished."

The heavy man said, "We got ourselves a dude here, Eddy. Street dude, knows what it is."

Sylvester looked at the twenty as if it were tainted. "How do I know you're righteous, man?"

"Because if you complain to the *Times* and my boss finds out I paid you, my ass is grass. I don't want any hassles, okay? Just a story."

"Fair is fair, Eddy," said the heavy man, with glee. "He gotcha."

"Fuck your mama," said Sylvester.

The heavy man laughed and wheezed. "Why should I do that, Eddy, when I already fucked *your* mama and she squeezed *all* the juice outa me?"

Sylvester gave him a long dark stare, and for a second I thought there'd be violence. Then the heavy man flinched and winked and Sylvester laughed, too. Picking up a domino, he slapped it on the table.

"To be continued, Fatboy," he said, standing.

"Where you goin, Eddy?"

"To talk to the man, stupid."

"Talk here. I wanna hear what kind of seventy-dollar story you got."

"Ha," said Sylvester. "Ask my mama about it." To me: "Let's go someplace where the atmosphere ain't stupid."

We walked down the block, past other big subdivided houses. An occasional palm tree skyscraped from the breezeway. Most of the street was open and hot, even as evening approached. The air smelled like exhaust fumes.

When we got near the corner, Sylvester stopped and leaned against a lamppost. A brown-skinned woman in a brown-flowered dress walked past. Several small children trailed her, like goslings, laughing and speaking Spanish.

"They come here," said Sylvester, "taking jobs for crap pay, don't even wanna learn English. Whynchu write about that?"

He patted his empty shirt pocket and studied me. "Smoke?"

I shook my head.

"Figures. Now, what murder is it you wanna hear about?"

"Was there more than one at the Adventure Inn?"

"Could be."

"Could be?"

"That place was no good you know what it really was, don't you?"

"What?"

"Whorehouse. Nasty one—tough girls. I only worked there 'cause I had to. My day job was cleaning gutters on houses and that's irregular—know what I mean? When it rains, you get your clogged gutters and your leaks coming right through the window seams into the house, people start screaming, Help me, help me! No rain, people forget their gutters; real stupid."

"The motel was your night job."

"Yeah."

"Tough place."

"Real bad place. The people who owned it ran it stupid—didn't give a damn."

"The Advent Group."

He gave me a blank look.

"Guys from Nevada," I said. "That's what it said in the original article."

"Yeah, that's right. Reno, Nevada; my check used to come from there. Pain in the *took-ass* because it didn't clear for five days. Stupid."

"The murder I'm talking about is a guy named Felix Barnard. Ex–private eye. The article said you found him."

"Yeah, yeah, I remember that. Old guy, bare-assed, his pecker in his hand." Shaking his head. "Yeah, that was bad, finding that. He got shot up in the face."

He stuck out his tongue.

"What else do you remember about it?" I said.

"That's about it. Finding him was disgusting, I wanted to quit the stupid job after that. I was working too hard anyway. Used to get off at five in the morning, get home, try to sleep for a couple of hours before going off to clean gutters. I had four kids, I was a good daddy to all of them. Bought 'em stuff. The best shoes. My sons wore Florsheim in high school, none of that sneaker stupidity."

"You inspected the rooms at 5 A.M.?"

"I finished by then. Started at a quarter *to*, so I could finish and get the hell out of there by five. If a room was empty, I'd tell the Mexican girl to clean it. If someone was still in it, I'd put a mark in the ledger for the day clerk. Day clerk's job was easy, no one used the damn place during the day."

"You looked in Barnard's room. Does that mean it was supposed to be empty?"

"Supposed to be. He only paid for a short time—couple of hours, I think. He shoulda been out."

"You didn't check the room before?"

"Man," he said, "I didn't do more than I had to, it was a nasty place. Someone else didn't want to use the room, what did I care if some stupid idiot stayed twenty minutes longer? People that owned it didn't give a damn."

"A two-hour rental," I said. "So Barnard wasn't there to sleep."

He laughed. "Right. You must be a college boy."

"What'd you do when you found him?"

"Called the po-lice, what else? You think I'm stupid?"

"What about the manager? Mullins. Darnel Mullins."

He frowned. "Yeah, Darnel."

"You call him, too?"

"Nah, Darnel wasn't there. He was never around except to kick me out of the office."

"Why'd he do that??"

"Thought he was some kind of writer. Showed up every once in a while, looking down his nose at me and kicking me out so he could use the typewriter. Fine with me. I'd go get something to eat—no drinking, don't put in that I drank, 'cause I didn't. Only ale, once in a while. In the privacy of my own home, not on the job."

"Sure," I said. "So Darnel considered himself a writer?"

"Yeah, like you—only he was writing a book." He laughed at the absurdity of that. "Stupid."

"He wasn't a good writer?" I said.

"How would I know? He never showed me nothing."

"Did he ever get anything published?"

"Not that I heard, and he sure woulda told me; he liked to toot his own trombone."

"Well," I said. "I could ask him if I could find him. Been trying to reach him but haven't been able to. Any idea where he is?"

"Nope. And don't waste your time. Even if you find him, he won't help you."

"Why not?"

"He was an uptight dude."

"Uptight how?"

"Uptight and uppity. And mad. Always mad about something, like he was too good for everyone and everything. Looking down his nose. And telling stories. Like he'd went to college, too good for this damned job; he was gonna write his book and get the hell outa here."

He looked at me.

"Like he had somewhere to go and the rest of us didn't."

"Do you remember where he said he went to college?"

"Some place in New York. I never paid attention to any of his stupid stories, all the man did was bitch and brag. His daddy was a doctor; he worked for some movie hotshot, met all these movie stars at parties." He laughed. "Writing a book. Like I'm stupid. Why would a brother who could do all those things be working at a hole like the Adventure? Not that he admitted he was a brother."

"He didn't like being black?"

"He didn't *admit* it. Talking all white. And tell the truth, he was *light* as a white man." Laughing again, he pinched the skin of his forearm. "Too much pale in it. And his hair was yellow—

nappy, but real yellow. Like he'd been dipped in eggs—Mr. French Toast."

"Did he have a mustache?"

"Don't remember, why?"

"Just trying to get a picture."

His eyes brightened. "You gonna put my picture in the paper?"

"Do you want me to?"

"Gonna pay me for it?"

"Can't do that."

"Then forget it—aw, okay, if you want—lot better than Darnel's picture. He was an ugly dude. Big and strong—said he played football in college, too. Wouldn't admit he was black, but his nose was flatter than Fatboy's back there. Yellow hair and these wishy blue eyes—like yours, but even wishier. Yeah, come to think of it, I think he had a mustache. Little one. Fuzz. Weak, yellow fuzz. Stupid."

38

I paid him the rest of the money, and he began walking away from me.

"One more thing," I said. "In the article, you said you didn't hear the shots 'cause of traffic. Was traffic that strong at 4 A.M.?"

He kept walking.

I caught up. "Mr. Sylvester?"

The same dry, angry look he'd shown his friend.

I repeated the question.

"I hear you, I'm not stupid."

"Is there a problem with answering it?" I said.

"No problem. I didn't hear any shots, okay?"

"Okay. Did Barnard check in alone?"

"If that's what it says in your paper."

"It doesn't say. Just that his name was the only one on the register. Was he with anyone?"

"How the hell would I know?" He stopped. "Our business is finished, man. You used up your money a long time ago."

"Were you really there, or was it one of the nights Darnel Mullins asked you to leave?"

He stepped back and touched a trousers pocket. Implying a weapon, but nothing sagged the pocket.

"You calling me a liar?"

"No, just trying to get details."

"You got 'em, now get." Flicking a hand. "And don't send no white boy around a camera to take my picture. White boys with cameras don't do well around here."

*   *   *

My stomach grumbled. I had lunch at a deli near Robertson. Rabbis, cops, and stockbrokers were eating pastrami and discussing their respective philosophies. I asked for matzo-ball soup, and while I waited I tried Milo's home, ready to leave another message. Rick answered with his on-call voice. "Dr. Silverman."

"Hi, it's Alex."

"Alex, how's the new house coming along?"

"Slowly."

"Big hassle, huh?"

"Better since Robin took over."

"Good for her. Looking for El Sleutho? He left early this morning, some kind of surveillance."

"Must be the Bogettes," I said.

"Who?"

"Those girls who worship Jobe Shwandt."

"Probably. He's not pleased having to deal with that again. Not that he's talked about it much. We have a new arrangement: I don't discuss the finer points of cutting and suturing, and he doesn't remind me how rotten the world is."

Back home, I tried Columbia University again. Darnel Mullins had, indeed, graduated from the university and done one year of graduate school before dropping out—shortly after reviewing *Command: Shed the Light*. The alumni office had a home address in Teaneck, New Jersey, and a phone number to go with it, but when I called I got a dress shop called Millie's Couture.

Remembering what Eddy Sylvester had said about Mullins claiming a doctor father, I called New Jersey information and asked for any Mullinses with M.D.'s in Teaneck.

"The only one I have," said the operator, "is a Dr. Winston Mullins, but that's in Englewood."

At that number, a man with an elderly, cultured voice said, "Hello?"

"Dr. Mullins?"

"Yes. Who's this?"

I gave him the biography story.

No reply.

"Dr. Mullins?"

"I'm afraid I can't help you. Darnel's been dead for a long time."

"Oh. I'm sorry."

"Yes," he said. "A little over twenty years. I guess I never called Columbia to notify them."

"Was he ill?"

"No, he was murdered."

"Oh, no!"

"Out where you are, matter of fact. He had an apartment in Hollywood. Surprised a burglar, and the burglar shot him. They never caught the man. I'm sure Darnel would have liked to talk to you. He always wanted to be a writer."

"Yes, I know, I've got one of his articles here with me."

"Really?"

"Something from the *Manhattan Book Review*. He used a pen name. Denton—"

"Mellors," he said. "After a character in a dirty book. He did that because I didn't approve of that paper—too left-wing. After that, he kept using it, maybe to prove something to me, though I don't know what."

He sounded very sad.

"It says here he was working on a novel," I said.

"*The Bride*. He never finished it, I've got the manuscript. I tried to read it. Not my type of thing but not bad at all. Maybe he could have gotten it published . . . sorry I couldn't help you."

"What kind of a book is it?"

"Well," he said, "that's hard to say. There's some romance in it—a young man's book, I guess. Learning the ropes, falling in love. A coming-of-age novel, I suppose you'd call it."

Feeling like dirt, I said, "Would it be possible to send me a copy? Maybe I can quote from it in my book."

"Don't see why not. It's just sitting in a drawer here."

I gave him my address.

"Malibu," he said. "You must be a successful writer. Darnel said that's where the successful people live."

Literary critic to aspiring novelist to motel manager.

Working for some guys from Reno.

The Advent Group. Why was that name familiar?

Even while managing the motel, he'd held on to his ambition.

Kicking Sylvester out of the office to use the typewriter from time to time.

From the way Sylvester had reacted to my questions, I was sure one of those times had been the night of the Barnard hit.

Mullins setting up the hit, maybe even pulling the trigger.

Finished off, himself, a few months later.

A light-skinned black man. Blond, blue eyes.

Light, fuzzy mustache, not the dark scimitar Lucy remembered, but as I'd told Lucy, dreams play fast and loose with reality.

Something else didn't fit. Dr. Mullins's description of *The Bride* bore no similarity to the trash App had given me. Had Mullins used the same title for two disparate works?

Or had App given me the script summary as a diversion? Directing my attention to Mullins because *he* had something to hide?

I remembered my initial scenario of Karen's disappearance: a man in a fancy car picking her up on the road to Topanga. It didn't get much fancier than a red Ferrari.

Still, there was nothing connecting App to Karen, and Mullins wasn't coming across like some innocent shill.

I thought of the way his career had dived after Karen's disappearance.

Lowell distancing himself from co-conspirators?

Eliminating the undependable ones?

Karen, Felix Barnard, Mullins. And where was Trafficant?

But the Sheas still lived on the beach.

I left a note for Robin and hit the highway once more. Gwen's van was parked in front of her house. Cars were lined up all along the beach side. No space for the Seville, but the land side was nearly empty. I pulled over and was about to chance a run across the highway as soon as northbound traffic thinned when I saw the van's headlights go on. It sat there idling, then pulled out.

It took a minute or so to get into the center turn lane, another few to pull off a three-point and head south. I put on as much speed as the traffic could bear and finally saw the van, eight or nine lengths up. It stopped at the light at the bottom of the ramp up to Ocean Front Avenue. By the time it was heading east on Colorado, I was three lengths behind and maintaining that distance.

I followed it to Lincoln Boulevard, where it headed south again, through Santa Monica and Venice, then over to Sepulveda, where it continued at a steady pace, making more lights than it missed.

We crossed into Inglewood, a mixture of Eisenhower-era suburbs and new Asian businesses. Fifteen minutes later, we were approaching Century Boulevard.

The airport.

The van entered the Departure lanes and continued to the parking lot opposite the Bradley International Terminal. It rode around a while, trying to find a ground-floor space, though the upper levels were less crowded. I parked on the third level, took the stairs down, and was waiting behind a hedge when Gwen emerged, ten minutes later, pushing Travis in his wheelchair, her purse over her shoulder.

No baggage.

Jets thundered overhead. Cars sped along the road, which snaked through the airport like a freeway.

Gwen walked to an intersection. A red light stopped her before she could cross the street to the terminal. Travis twisted his head, moved his mouth, and rolled his eyes. Gwen looked around nervously. I hung back and kept my head down.

She wore an expensive-looking white linen dress and white flats. A string of pearls glimmered around her neck. Her short dark hair shone, but even at this distance her eyes were old.

Short hair. Somber look. The grumpy baby-sitter Ken remembered?

Abandoning her post, then returning to discover Lucy gone?

Going to look for her and finding her sleepwalking?

Seeing and hearing what Lucy had would have been grounds for a payoff.

The light turned green and she entered the terminal's big, bright, green-glassed atrium. A dozen airlines flew out of here. She headed for the Aeromexico desk. Waiting in the First Class line, she moved up quickly to the clerk. He smiled at her, then listened to what she had to say. Travis was twisting and turning in the chair. People stared. The terminal was crowded. Phony nuns panhandled. I picked up an abandoned newspaper and pretended to read it, looking, instead, at a TV screen filled with flight information.

Aeromexico 546, leaving in one hour for Mexico City.

The clerk was shaking his head.

Gwen looked at her watch, then turned and pointed at Travis.

The clerk got on the phone, spoke, got off, shook his head again.

Gwen leaned toward him, standing taller, her calf muscles swelling.

The clerk kept shaking his head. Then he called another man over. The second man listened to Gwen, got on the phone. Shook his head. Half a dozen people had lined up behind her. The second clerk pointed to them. Gwen turned around. Her face blazed with anger and her hands were clenched.

No one in the queue said anything or moved, but some of the travelers were staring at Travis.

Gwen took hold of the chair's handlebars and wheeled him away.

I followed as she pushed her way through the crowd to a row of phone booths. All were occupied and she waited, twisting her hair and tapping a handlebar. When a booth opened, she dashed in and stayed on the phone for fifteen minutes, feeding coins and punching numbers. When she emerged, she looked crushed and even jumpier, rubbing her fingers together very fast, biting her lip, eyes darting up and down the terminal.

I stuck with her, back to the parking lot. Running up the three flights and timing my exit from the lot to hers was tricky, but I managed to get two vehicles behind her as she paid at the kiosk. I stayed with her out of the airport and onto the 405 North. She took it to the 10 West, got off at Route 1.

Back to Malibu.

But instead of pulling over at La Costa, she continued on another few miles.

Shopping center across from the pier.

The parking lot was nearly empty. The only business still open was a submarine sandwich store, bright and yellow. I put the Seville in a dark corner and stayed in the car as Gwen got Travis out of the van.

She pushed him up the ramp to the surf shop, then stopped. Opening her purse, she took out her wallet and pulled out a gold credit card. Staring at it blankly, she replaced it and knitted her fingers some more. Travis moved constantly. Gwen took out a key. She was opening the shop's front door when I stepped up and said, "Hi."

She threw up her hands defensively, letting go of the chair. It started to slide back and I held it in place. The boy had to weigh a hundred and twenty pounds.

Gwen's eyes were huge and the hand that held the keys was drawn back, ready to strike.

"Get the hell out of here or I'll scream!"

"Scream away."

Travis had positioned his head at an impossible angle, trying to get a look at me. His smile was innocent and empty.

"I mean it," she said.

"So do I. What was the problem at the airport? Tickets not there as planned?"

Her mouth opened and her arm dropped slowly, the hand settling on her left breast, as if pledging allegiance.

"You're as crazy as your father," she said.

"My father?"

"Don't fool with me, Mr. *Best*." Putting weight on the last word, as if her knowledge would throw me off.

"You think I'm his son?"

"I *know* you are. I saw you with him when he tried to break in. Now you're asking questions all around town, pretending to be someone else."

"Pretending?"

"Pretending to be a customer, buying those Big Dogs. We don't want your business, mister. You get the hell out of here and tell your father he's going to get both of you in big trouble. People know us in Malibu. You get lost, or I'm calling the police."

"Please do," I said, pulling out my wallet. I had an out-of-date card that said I'd once consulted to the police, along with one of Milo's. I hoped the word *Homicide* would impress her. Hoped her panic would stop her from remembering that LAPD had no jurisdiction here.

Confusion clogged her face.

Travis said something incoherent. He was still smiling at me.

"I don't . . ." She inspected the cards again. "You're a *psychologist*?"

"It's complicated, Mrs. Shea. But go ahead and call the police, they'll clear it up for you. Karen Best's death is back under investigation because of new facts, a new witness. I'm involved in helping the police question that witness. They know, now, that something happened to Karen at the Sanctum party and that you and your husband and Doris Reingold got paid off to keep quiet about it."

Throwing out wild cards. The way she fought to stay still told me I had a winning hand.

Her right eye twitched. She said, "Easy, honey," to Travis, even though he looked happy.

"This is absolutely crazy."

"At the very least, we're talking obstruction of justice. Even if the plane tickets had been there, you'd never have been allowed to board. I think it's pretty obvious you were being watched. If I were you, I'd start making arrangements for Travis. Somewhere clean and trustworthy where he can stay while you're tied up in the legal system. 'Bye, have a nice day."

I started to leave. She made a grab for my arm, but I moved away.

"Why are you *doing* this to me?"

"I'm not doing anything. To be honest, I'm not even here, officially. If the police knew I'd followed you, they'd probably be upset. They think I'm a bleeding heart. Maybe I am, but I've treated kids with CP and I know it's not easy under the best of circumstances. What you've got ahead of you is far from the best."

Watching the boy contort and remembering how I'd lied to Dr. Mullins, justice seemed very abstract. Thinking about Karen's buried corpse, Sherrel Best and his grief, brought it a little closer to home.

"What do you *want*?"

"The truth about Karen."

"Why don't the police come themselves?"

"Oh, they will," I said, turning to go again.

"I don't *understand*," she said. "You work with the police, but you're not working with them now?"

"Right now I'm here because Karen's important to me."

"You *knew* her?"

"I'm not going to say more, Mrs. Shea. But I will give you some advice. Some people think you and Tom were involved in her murder. If you were, we have nothing to talk about and I really need to get out of here. If you've done nothing but obstruct,

I might be able to run interference for you. Lying about it won't help, because the evidence is piling up; it's just a matter of time. And if you do make it to Mexico, the police will impound your house and this place."

A group of teenagers went into the sandwich shop. Happy, shouting. Travis's age.

She said, "I don't know about *any* murder, and that's the God's truth."

"Why did you try to leave town tonight?"

"Vacation."

"No luggage? Or was Tom supposed to handle that, too, along with the tickets?"

She remained wooden. I shrugged and walked toward my car.

"What if I don't know anything?" she called after me. "What if I can't help *anyone* with what I know?"

"Then you won't be able to help yourself."

"But I *don't*! That's the truth! Karen—she—"

She broke down and hid her eyes with her fingers. Travis looked at her, then at me.

I smiled at him. His return grin was quick—more of a grimace, his eyes clouded and dull. Most people with cerebral palsy are intellectually normal. The eyes told me he wasn't. Despite the contortions he was almost handsome, and I could see traces of the young man he might have been. A faint, almost holographic image of a golden Malibu kid.

His mother kept her face concealed.

I walked up to the chair. "Hey, pal."

He started to laugh, gulping and whooping. Did it louder and tried to clap his hands.

"*Shut up!*" Gwen screamed.

A crestfallen look wormed its way among the boy's involuntary facial movements. He began stabbing with his arms and kicking his feet. His lips twisted like an out-of-hand garden hose, and a deep, foggy noise issued from his mouth.

"*Aa-nglm!*"

Gwen embraced him. "Oh, I'm so sorry, honey! Oh, honey, honey!"

I felt like surrendering my license.

Gwen said, "He needs *me*. No one knows how to take care of him properly. Have you seen the kind of places they put kids like him?"

"Lots of them," I said.

"But you'll put him in one without thinking twice."

"*I* won't put him anywhere. I have no official power, other than the fact that the police sometimes ask my advice. Sometimes they even listen. I got involved in Karen's case, and I'm going to see it through."

"But I don't *know* about any murder. That's the truth."

"What *do* you know?"

She turned away, facing PCH.

"You know something valuable enough to get paid off for your silence," I said.

"Why do you keep saying I've been paid off?"

I looked at her.

Travis rolled his head out from under her embrace.

She said, "That was twenty years ago."

"Twenty-one this August."

She looked ill. "All I know is she went off with some guys at that party and I never saw her again, okay? Why's that worth anything?"

"You tell me."

She looked at the asphalt.

I said, "Other people were paid off, too. Some of them were murdered. Now that the net's tightening, what makes you think you're safe? Or Tom, for that matter, wherever he is in Mexico?"

A new fear pierced her eyes. She'd been beautiful a long time ago, one of those lithe, laughing beach girls for whom bikinis were invented. Life had glazed her like pottery, and I'd added a few new cracks.

"Oh, God."

A car pulled into the shopping center. As its headlights washed over us, she jumped. The car was going to the sandwich place. An old Chrysler four-door. Two pony-tailed, tank-topped men in their thirties got out. Surfboard clamps were attached to the roof, but no boards.

One of the men cupped his hands and lit a cigarette. Gwen turned her back on them. Not afraid, embarrassed.

"Old customers?" I said.

She stared at me, then at her keys in the lock.

"Inside," she said.

39

Keeping the lights off, she pushed Travis to the back of the store and unlocked a door. Inside was a small neat storeroom: metal shelves filled with merchandise, a desk, and three folding chairs. Positioning Travis in a corner, she pulled a box down and gave it to him. A diving mask. He began turning the package over and over, working hard at holding on to it, studying a photograph of a girl snorkeling as if it were a puzzle.

She started to go behind the desk. I got there first and checked all the drawers. Just papers and pens and staples and clips.

She gave a weak smile. "Yeah, tough old me's gonna shoot you."

"I'm sure you can be plenty tough." I looked at Travis.

She sat down heavily. I took a chair.

"Tell me what happened," I said.

"Promise me they won't put him away."

"I can't promise, but I'll do my best. If you had nothing to do with Karen's murder."

"I keep telling you, I don't *know* about any murder. Just that she disappeared."

"From the Sanctum party."

Nod.

"You hired her to work at the party."

"So what does that make me, a criminal? I hired her as a favor. She needed the money. Her tips weren't that good because she wasn't the greatest waitress, kept getting orders wrong. And that hypocrite father of hers didn't approve of her being an actress, so he never sent her a dime. I helped her, so now people are getting murdered and I'm being treated like a criminal?"

"When's the last time you saw her?"

"How can I remember? It was twenty-one years."

"Try."

Silence.

"In the middle of the party," she said. "I don't know what time it was. We were all working; I wasn't paying attention to her."

"You never told anyone she was there, did you?"

More silence.

"Did the sheriffs ask?"

"They came around the Dollar, a few days after she was gone. They thought she was lost up in the mountains. They had helicopters looking for her."

"And you didn't tell them any different."

"Who says it *was* any different? She could have left the party with someone and gone to the mountains."

"In the middle of work?"

"She wasn't the most reliable person—used to call in sick at the Dollar so she could go to Disneyland. Coming out here was a big vacation for her."

She bit her lip. "Look, I'm not putting her down. She was a nice kid. But not too bright." Tears filled her eyes. "I never wanted to see anything happen to her. I never did anything to hurt her."

She put her hands over her face again. Travis had managed to turn himself around and was looking at her, fascinated. The box slid down his lap and landed on the floor. He reached for it but the leather belt restrained him, and he started to shout.

Gwen uncovered her face and started to get out of her chair.

I retrieved the box and gave it to him, tousling his hair.

"Aa-gaah," he said, grinning. "Aa-gaamnuhuh."

Gwen said, "It wasn't any big intense investigation or anything. A deputy just dropped in and asked if anyone'd seen her; then he sat around and had coffee."

"What about the private eye Karen's family hired? Felix Barnard. What did *he* ask you?"

"He was weird. An oily old guy."

"What did he ask you?"

"Same stuff the police did: When did we last see her?"

"And you told him Friday night, after her shift at the Dollar."

"He was a sleazeball. I didn't want anything to do with him."

"He found out Karen had been at the party. How?"

"I don't know, but it wasn't from me," she said. The way she looked away quickly let me know she was hiding something. I decided not to push, right now. Thinking of the unaccounted-for time between Karen's leaving the Dollar and the party the next day, I said, "Why did Karen go up to Sanctum early?"

"The caterer needed someone to set up chairs and tables before the food got there."

"And you picked Karen even though she wasn't reliable?"

"I felt sorry for her. Like I said, she needed the money." She blinked several times.

"Is that the only reason?"

She took a deep breath and turned to Travis. "You okay, honey?"

Ignoring her, he continued to study the box.

"What's the real reason you chose Karen to go up early, Gwen?"

"Someone called. Wanted us to send the best-looking waitress up early."

"Who?"

Long silence. "Lowell."

"And Karen was the best-looking waitress."

"She was cute."

"Why would looks be important if all he wanted was for her to set up?"

"I don't know. It wasn't like he mentioned that first. More like, As long as you're sending someone, send a good-looking one, and some other stuff—crazy words I don't remember— something about eternal beauty. I don't know why, maybe he had big shots over and wanted to make an impression—it was none of my business. What difference did it make to me who set up? Karen was happy to do it."

"Happy to be with big shots."

"Definitely. She was still a tourist—going over to Hollywood Boulevard, looking for movie stars."

"How'd she get up to Sanctum?"

"Someone picked her up."

"At the Dollar?"

"No, on PCH."

"Where on PCH?"

"PCH and Paradise Cove."

"Right at the turnoff to the Dollar?"

Nod.

"Who picked her up?"

"I don't know." Another look away.

"This isn't very helpful, Gwen." Travis was staring at me. I winked at him. He laughed, and the box slipped from his fingers again. I returned it to him, then stared at Gwen. Making it a hard stare was no effort.

"I saw a car," she said. "We did—Tom and me. Pulling away just as we got there. But that's all. I couldn't see who was in it. I don't even know if that's the one that picked her up. She left twenty minutes before we did. Someone else could have picked her up."

"What kind of car?"

"Tom said a Ferrari."

"Tom said?"

"He's into cars. To me it was just a car and taillights. Tom was all excited."

"What color?"

"It was nighttime—Tom thought it was red. He said most of them are red, it's Ferrari's racing color."

"Convertible or hardtop?"

"Convertible, I think, but the top was up. We couldn't see who was inside."

"Did you ever see the car again?"

She played with her earrings and twisted her fingers, as if wringing them out. "There was one up there."

"Up where?"

"The party. There were all kinds of fancy cars there. Porsches, Rollses. Valets parking them up and down the road, total chaos."

"Who did the Ferrari belong to?"

"I don't know."

I stared at her.

"I don't *know*," she said. "What do you want me to do, make something up?"

"Did it have customized plates?"

"No . . . not that I noticed. I couldn't have cared less, cars don't interest me. My head was into the party, making sure everything went okay."

"Did it?"

"What?"

"Did the party go okay?"

"People seemed to be having fun."

"What about Karen?"

"What *about* her?"

"Was she having fun?"

"She was there to work," she said sharply. "Yeah, she seemed happy."

"All those big shots."

She shrugged.

"Did she sleep at Sanctum on Friday night?"

"I don't know."

"When did you go up?"

"Saturday morning."

"Was she there?"

Nod.

"How early in the morning?"

"Seven-thirty, eight. We drove up early to start getting the food ready. She was already up and running."

"What kind of mood was she in?"

"A good one. She'd set up the tables and chairs and was goofing around."

"How?"

"Playing with some kids."

"Whose kids?"

"Lowell's. At first, I thought they were his grandchildren, 'cause they were so little, but Karen said no, they were his. She was jazzed about that."

"About what?"

"That she was playing with a famous guy's kids. That's the way she was, really starstruck. She started telling me how famous the guy was, won the Nobel Prize or something. Everything was a big deal to her."

"Pretty impressed with Lowell, huh?"

"Yeah."

"What else did she say about him?"

"That's it."

"Did you get the feeling they'd spent the night together?"

"I have no idea."

"Did she mention any other people she'd met?"

Headshake.

"How many of Lowell's kids was she playing with?"

"Two."

"How old were they?"

"Little, three or four, something like that."

"Boys or girls?"

"I don't remember. Why?"

"Boys or girls?" I repeated.

She shrugged. "Probably girls. They both had these long mops of blond hair. Cute kids."

"And Karen was baby-sitting them."

"No, just playing around with them—laughing, chasing them. She *wanted* to baby-sit instead of serving. Said Lowell's regular baby-sitter got sick, some kind of emergency operation. But she was too ditzy, so I said no."

"So who baby-sat the kids?"

"Another girl."

"Name?"

Hesitation. "Another waitress."

Short dark hair. Grumpy.

"Doris Reingold?"

She opened her mouth. Closed it.

"Why Doris?" I said.

"She was older, had two of her own. I figured she'd know what to do."

"Were there any other kids around?"

"Not that I saw."

But I knew of two. Locked in their cabin.

"So what did Karen do then?"

"Worked with the food, like the rest of us. We slaved like dogs. It was a huge party, four hundred people, tons of stuff. The ice ran out and Tom had to make a bunch of trips down to Malibu to get more. The caterer was some little gay guy with a bad temper, brought in some illegals to help out, no one spoke any English. Then all these bands started showing up. Setting up their equipment, doing sound checks, trying to see who could play loudest. Portable fans and lights, a generator, electrical cables all over the place. By the time the people started coming, it was already getting dark. Berserk. Unless you've worked food service, you wouldn't understand."

"Was there a lot of dope and booze?"

"What do you think? But none of the staff messed with it—I had a rule about that. You're behind a buffet table, spooning out coleslaw, you can't be freaking out."

"Was Karen behind the buffet?"

"At first. Then the caterer started screaming for someone to pass around the hors d'oeuvres trays, so I had her do that. That's the last time I saw her: going into the crowd with a tray. Not that I looked for her. I was like a chicken with my head cut off, it was so crazy. I worked till five in the morning. The cleanup was outrageous; the caterer split with all his Mexicans and left it to Tom and me."

"Were you back on shift at the Dollar on Sunday?"

"Sunday evening."

"Was Karen supposed to be on, too?"

"Yes, but like I said, she always took time off, so her not showing up was no big deal."

"When did you first realize she'd disappeared?"

"A couple of days later, I guess. I didn't think much about it. I wasn't her mother."

"When did Lowell call you?"

"Who said he called me?"

"We know he did, Gwen. To arrange the payoff. Our information is that it was three days after the party. Is that true?"

She turned one of her earrings, then reversed the circuit. "More like four or five, I don't know."

"Tell me about his call."

She turned to Travis. "You okay, baby?"

The boy played with the box and giggled.

I said, "He's fine, Gwen."

Another turn of the earring. She cleared her throat, coughed. Picked something out of one nail.

I crossed my legs and smiled at her.

"You're making a mountain out of a molehill. He didn't say anything about any payoff," she said. "He asked for Tom and me to meet him, said he had a bonus for us. For doing such a good job at the party."

"Where'd you meet him, at Sanctum?"

"No, out in the Valley. On Topanga Canyon Boulevard, just before Ventura."

Upper-middle-class residential area. "Where on the boulevard?"

"It was—I guess you'd call it a turnoff. A piece of empty land."

"Right on Topanga?"

"Just *off* new Topanga, actually. Around the corner from Topanga—some side street. I don't remember the name but I could probably show it to you."

"Probably?"

"It's been a long time. It was dark, almost midnight."

"You didn't find his wanting to meet that late strange?"

"I found lots of things strange. *He* was strange, always yakking; most of the time he made no sense. The *party* was strange. He wanted to give us money, I didn't argue."

"Did he come alone?"

Nod. "He was waiting when we got there, sitting in his car."

"What kind of car?"

"A Mercedes, I think. I told you I'm not into cars."

"Just a casual midnight meeting to pick up some money."

"It would have had to be late because Tom and I were working at the restaurant. Some people have to earn a *living*."

"What happened after you got there?"

"He stayed in the car, told us we'd done a great job at the party and he was giving us a bonus."

Twisting her fingers.

"What else?"

"He said there was something else we needed to talk about. He wasn't sure, but he thought one of the girls who'd worked for us had gotten into some kind of fight with a guest and had walked off."

"Did he name Karen?"

"He called her the pretty one."

"Did he say which guest?"

"No."

"You're sure."

"Yes!"

"Did he mean a physical fight?"

"I assumed he meant just an argument—he might have even said 'argument,' I can't remember."

Moisture in her eyes. She stared at me, flaunting the tears.

"What else?"

"Nothing, he just said the girl hadn't behaved properly, had really stepped out of line, but he wouldn't hold it against us or complain because, other than that, we'd done a really good job.

Then he said we also had to promise not to say anything about the fight. Because the press was out to get him, and any scandal would cause a giant hassle for him. Even if the girl disappeared and people came asking for her. Because when she'd cursed out the guest, she'd said something about being disgusted and splitting town."

"Did that sound like Karen? Cursing?"

She shrugged and dried her eyes. "I didn't know her all that well."

"At the Dollar did she ever have problems losing her temper with customers?"

"No, just getting orders wrong. But the party was different— lots of pressure."

"So supposedly she pulled a fit, left the party, and said she was splitting town."

"That's what he said."

"Did you believe him?"

"We didn't think about it one way or the other."

"Then he gave you the money."

"Our bonus."

"How big of a bonus?"

She looked at Travis, then down at the desk. "Five," she said, very softly.

"Five what?"

"Thousand."

"A five-thousand-dollar bonus?"

"The catering bill must have been fifty, sixty thousand. It was like a tip."

"Cash?"

Nod.

"In a suitcase?"

"A paper bag—big one, like from a supermarket."

"Five-thousand-dollar tip in a bag."

"It wasn't all for us. He told us to distribute it to the others."

"What others?"

"The other servers."

"The people from the Sand Dollar?"

"That's right."

"Names."

"A guy named Lenny—"

"Lenny Korcik?"

Nod. "And Doris and two other women, Mary and Sue."

"Mary Andreas and Sue Billings."

"If you know, why are you asking?"

"Korcik's dead and Doris lives in Ventura," I said. "Where are Mary and Sue?"

"I don't know. Both were temps—hippies. I think they hitch-hiked into town together. They stuck around maybe another month or two, then split, no notice."

"Together?"

"I think Sue ran off with a truck driver who came into the restaurant, and a couple days later Mary joined up with some surfers driving up the coast. Or maybe it was down the coast, I don't remember. We weren't close or anything. They were hippies."

"But you split the money with them."

"Sure, they worked."

"Even split?"

Long inhalation. "No, why should we? I contracted the whole thing. And Tom and I ended up doing all the cleanup."

"How much did you give them?"

She mumbled something.

"What's that?"

"Two-fifty."

"Two-fifty for each of them?"

Nod.

"Leaving four thousand for you and Tom."

"They didn't complain. They were happy to get anything."

"Doris, too?"

"Why not?"

"She doesn't seem like a very happy person."

"You'd have to ask her about that."

"We will, once we find her. Where did Tom take her, two nights ago?"

She wrung her hands and let loose a stream of filthy words. Cursing Sherrell Best for spying on her.

"Where?" I said.

"She needed a ride to the airport, so he took her."

"Vacation for her, too?"

She didn't answer.

"Gwen," I said wearily, "if you want to talk, fine. If not, you're on your own."

"Give me a chance," she said. "This is hard, remembering all this stuff. . . . Okay, she decided to split town. She got nervous after you came asking around. She thought you were Best's son—we all did. Raking things up again. She didn't want the hassle."

"Nervous about her role in the cover-up."

"It wasn't like that. Like I said, there was no big plot. We just . . ."

"You just what?"

"Kept our mouths shut. Can't catch any flies that way."

Bitter smile.

"Did Doris see something the rest of you didn't?"

"Maybe—okay, okay, but it's not any big deal. She wasn't even sure herself. It was probably nothing."

Another tug at the bodice.

"What did she see, Gwen?"

"It was—she put the kids to sleep, left to get a drink. When she got back, one of the kids was gone and the door to the outside was open. She went out looking, finally found the kid wandering around in back; there were a lot of trees, paths. And all these other cabins. Like a big summer camp—it used to be a nudist colony. The kid was spaced out. When Doris picked her up, she started babbling. About bad men, monsters, hurting a girl, something like that. Doris figured she was having a bad dream and took her back. But when she put her in bed, the kid started screaming, woke up the other kid, and got that one crying too. Doris said it was a real hassle, they were really making noise. But with all the music from the party, you couldn't hear it. Finally got them both quiet."

"What made her suspect the kid might have really seen something?"

"When Karen didn't show up and I told her the same story I told the others."

"What was that?"

"That she hated her father and he was coming out to bring her back home, so she was going to split town."

"The others believed it, but Doris didn't?"

"She said Karen had told her she liked her father."

"Did Doris tell the others that?"

Headshake. "Lenny was into plants, real stupid; he'd believe anything. Mary and Sue were hippies; they hated their folks."

"So Doris kept her story to herself."

Shrug.

"Why didn't you tell them Lowell's story about the fight?"

"I told you, he didn't want any of that getting out. Nothing that could connect Karen to him. Actually, he made up the other story as a replacement. At first he said to say her father abused her. I didn't make it that strong."

"Why not?"

"It just wasn't right—too much."

Looking at me, as if for praise.

"So the others bought it," I said, "but Doris didn't. And she started to wonder if the little kid had seen something happen to Karen."

"She didn't know anything for sure, but she came to me and told me about finding the kid. Kind of thinking out loud."

"Wanting more than two fifty."

Silence.

"How much did you give her?"

"Seven fifty more."

"One thousand total. How much did she think Lowell gave you?"

Hesitation.

"It's just a matter of time before we find her and ask her, Gwen."

"Two and a half thousand," she said very softly.

"So she thought she was getting more than you. When did she realize you'd held back on her?"

"She didn't."

"Then why are you still paying her off?"

"Who says we are?"

"The police. And Tom was there to pick her up and take her to the airport. There's obviously some relationship there. Do she and Tom have something going?"

She laughed. "No, he hates her."

"Because she's got a hook in you?"

"It's not like that."

"Not like what?"

"Blackmail or anything like that. She just comes to us when she's broke—its like charity. She's got . . . a problem."

"Compulsive gambling."

Her head snapped up. "If you know everything, why do you need *me*?"

"How long have you been financing her addiction?"

"Off and on. Most of the time she's okay, but then she goes off drinking and gambling and wipes herself out. So we help her —it's a sickness."

Remembering the boys on the lawn, I said, "Does she ever win?"

"Play enough, you're bound to. One time she won big. Fifteen thousand at craps in Tahoe—fifteen *thousand*. Next day she blew it all at the same table. We feel sorry for her. She's Tom's first cousin, used to baby-sit him. After she got married, she started drinking and gambling."

"How much have you given her over the years?"

"Never added it up, but plenty. She probably could have bought a house, but she doesn't care about normal things— that's why her husband left her. We help her 'cause she's family."

The room was cool but she was sweating, and her mascara started to run. She grabbed a tissue from a box on the desk and took a long time to wipe her eyes.

I understood Doris's hostility to her and Tom, now. The rage of the charity receiver.

"Okay?" she said. "Is that enough for you?"

"Where did Tom take her?"

"To the airport."

"Where did she fly?"

"I don't know. And that's the truth. She just said she wanted to get out of town for a while. You spooked her. She was worried you'd rake things up."

"Did she feel guilty about never telling anyone what she'd seen?"

"How would I know?"

"Did she start drinking and gambling after the party or before?"

"Before. I told you, it was right after she got married. She was only seventeen, then she had her kids."

"Two boys," I said. "One in Germany, one in Seattle."

She looked away.

"What's the name of the son in Seattle?"

"Kevin."

"Kevin Reingold?"

Nod.

"At what army base is he stationed?"

"I don't know, somewhere up there."

"She's your cousin and you don't know?"

"She's Tom's cousin. They're not a close kind of family."

Glancing at Travis, trying to open the box. But the plastic wrap was tight and his fingers struck at it uselessly.

I peeled some plastic back. He laughed and tossed the box in the air. Again, I retrieved it.

Gwen was staring at the shelves.

"So Tom dropped her off," I said, "then caught a plane to Mexico City."

The box dropped again. This time, Travis rejected it, shaking his head and arching his back. I gave him a can of surf wax and he began rolling it between his palms.

Gwen burst into tears and tried to stop them by pinching her nose.

Travis held up the can and shouted, "Aa-ngul!"

She looked at him, first with anger, then defeat. "This is stupid. You've got me feeling like a criminal and I didn't do anything."

"How much more money did you get from Lowell?"

"Nothing!"

"One-shot deal?"

"Yes!"

"How often have you seen him since?"

"Never."

"He lives in Topanga, you're five miles away in La Costa, and you've never seen him?"

"Never. That's the truth. We never go up there; he never comes down."

"Just one five-thousand-dollar payment and that was it?"

"That's the truth. We didn't want anything more to do with it."

"Because after hearing Doris's story you wondered if Karen had been hurt or worse?"

"We just didn't want anything to do with him—he was weird. The whole scene was weird."

"But didn't you wonder at all about Karen? Five thousand dollars in a paper bag, and then he asks you to keep mum? Gives you a phony story? And she never shows up again?"

"I—it made sense, his not wanting the publicity. He was rich and famous. I figured to him five thousand was nothing—okay, I was naive. Twenty-five years old, working since I was sixteen, what was I supposed to do, give the money back and go to the sheriffs saying something was fishy? Like they would have listened to *me*? *Right.* When that deputy came to the Dollar it was wham-bam-thank-you-ma'am, coffee black and a glazed donut. He wasn't taking it seriously. Told us she'd probably left town with some guy, or maybe she'd gone hiking and was up in the hills. They sent helicopters up looking for her; for all I knew she *was* up there!"

"What about what Doris saw?"

"Doris is weird. She drinks, she blacks out. She blows fifteen thousand dollars in one day. Why should I pay attention to some little kid freaking out?"

"Okay," I said. "Seven fifty to Lenny, Mary, and Sue, another thousand to Doris. That left thirty-two fifty for you and Tom. How'd you parlay that into a business and a beach house?"

"We had more—savings. Five years' worth. We worked hard. Some people do that."

Pulling at the dress some more. The linen had wrinkled. Her face was flushed and moist.

"So who told Felix Barnard about the party?"

"No one."

"Then how'd he find out?"

"I don't know. He probably figured it out. Talking to Marvin —the owner—about Karen's work habits. Marvin told him she was gone a lot; he'd been planning to fire her, he suspected her of cutting work to moonlight."

"Did Marvin tell you this?"

Nod. "As a warning. Barnard came in to the Dollar like he was a customer. He was my table and I served him; then he handed me his card and started asking questions about Karen. I told him I didn't know where she was—which was true. Marvin hated us fraternizing with the customers, so he came over and sent me to another table. Then I saw *him* sit down with Barnard and I thought, Great, he's going to find out about the party. Then Barnard left and Marvin came up to me, asking me if I knew where Karen was. I said no. He said, That idiot thinks something's happened to her, but in my opinion she's off somewhere having fun or working another job. Then he tells me he doesn't approve of the moonlighting we've all been doing. He'll put up with it from me 'cause my work's good, but Karen was an amateur, couldn't even do one job right. So I figure he told Barnard he suspected a catering moonlight and Barnard kept snooping around till he found out which party it was."

No great feat of detection. The Sanctum party had been in the papers.

"Did Barnard ever try to talk to you again?"

"Never."

And he'd never recorded his talk with Marvin D'Amato.

"Did you warn Lowell that Barnard might be snooping around?"

"No! I told you, I had nothing to do with him after he gave me the . . . bag."

"Did Barnard's showing up make you suspect anything about Lowell's story?"

"Why should it? I figured her cheap father had finally decided to spend some money on her."

Her arms were across her chest like bandoliers.

"Five thousand dollars, Gwen. Just to avoid bad publicity?"

She tried not to look at me. I waited her out.

"Okay," she said, "I thought it was possible she'd OD'd or something. What was I supposed to do? Whatever happened to her, she was *gone*. Nothing I did would bring her back."

"Was Karen into drugs?"

"She smoked a little pot."

"What kind of dope was floating around the party?"

"Pot, hash, mushrooms, acid, you name it. People were tripping out, taking off their clothes, going off together into the woods."

Meaning if there'd been a burial it would have had to be far enough away. . . .

"Was Karen the type of girl who'd get into that kind of thing?"

"Who knows? She wasn't wild, but she wasn't any nuclear scientist either. Being at that party was the biggest thrill of her life. There were movie people all over the place."

"But you never saw her go off with anyone specific."

"Nope."

"Not with Lowell?"

"No one. I wasn't looking at who was with who. I was spooning out designer slop and trying to keep it off people's cuffs."

"What about Tom?"

"Working the bar. People were putting it away; he never even stopped for a break."

"Why'd you go to Aspen?"

She frowned, as if thinking. " 'Cause of Best. He was driving us crazy, showing up every day on our doorstep. And we were tired of seeing Marvin's sour puss."

"Why Aspen?"

"Tom had a buddy who spent the winters there, teaching skiing. He'd inherited a house just outside of Starwood. He got Tom a job tending bar at one of the lodges. I found a position at a fur shop. It was good to be away from food."

"I still don't see how you got from there to here."

"Hard work and luck. Tom's buddy needed some cash fast. The house was all he owned. It wasn't much, just a little place—"

"Why'd he need cash fast?"

Tugging. "He got busted."

"For what?"

"Drugs," she said, reluctantly.

"Are drugs what drew you to Aspen?"

"No! *He* was busted, not us! Check the police records there: Greg Fowler. Gregory Duncan Fowler III. He got busted for selling cocaine and needed bail money, so he signed over the house to us."

"For how much?"

"Thirteen thousand. He kicked in two of his own and put down bond on a hundred and fifty thousand bail."

"Lowell's three and ten of your own?"

"That's right."

"Not bad for a house in Aspen."

"The house wasn't as big a deal as it sounds. It was a shack, really. A hunting shack. Tom and I didn't even want it, the plumbing and electric was all shot. But Greg begged us. He said real estate was starting to take off and we'd be doing each other a favor. We lived in it while Tom fixed it up—he's good with his hands. The real estate did go crazy, all these Hollywood types flying in, buying up land.

"Our house was right next to this big parcel owned by a producer—Sy Palmer, he did *Flying Angels*, on TV? He really wanted our land so he could build riding stables, and he paid us seventy-five thousand. We couldn't believe it. Then we found out we needed to buy *another* house or pay lots of taxes, so we used the seventy-five to make a down payment on a bigger place, lived in that, fixed it up, sold *it* for three hundred thousand. We couldn't believe how well we were doing. Then I got pregnant."

Her glance at Travis was full of tenderness and torment. He continued to roll the can.

"The doctors knew something was wrong even before he was born, but at first he didn't seem that different. Then . . . I knew I had to be in a big city, near a hospital with rehab facilities. We thought for sure Best had gone back east. So we moved back, made a down payment on a land-side house on Rambla Pacifica, and opened the store. Tom figured all his old surfing buddies would give us business, and they did. So we sold the land-side house and bought the place in La Costa."

Talking about their financial climb had calmed her.

"That's it. Anyone can go over our tax records with a fine-tooth comb. We never sold dope or chased money. It came to us. When Lowell gave us that bag, we were shocked out of our minds. Kept it in a closet for months, just sitting there. Then I told Tom, What good is this doing, just sitting here? And Greg was already calling us, telling us about the opportunities in Aspen. After we moved there, things just happened."

"Have you maintained contact with Greg Fowler?"

"I haven't."

"What about Tom?"

No answer.

"He lives down in Mexico now, doesn't he, Gwen?"

Silence.

"Near Mexico City?"

Nothing.

"Gwen?"

"No, a small village near the coast. Far from Mexico City. I don't even know the name."

"Still running dope, huh?"

"No!" she said. "*Charter* fishing!"

"Tom's been down there, hasn't he? Brings back a nice catch of corbina or albacore?"

"So?"

"What's the address?"

"I don't know, Greg only told Tom. He's still officially a fugitive. Please don't get him in trouble, he's really a good guy."

"Tom didn't give you the address?"

"No, he was supposed—" Drumming the table.

"He was supposed to what?"

"Meet us. In Mexico City, with a van; then we were going to drive down together. The tickets were supposed to be at the gate. I bought them myself, made sure we had special boarding help, but they said it had all been canceled—that *Tom* canceled them. Why would he do that? *Why?*"

40

I used her desk phone to call Milo's home number and was pleased when the answering machine picked up.

"Detective Sturgis? It's Dr. Delaware. I just had a long talk with Mrs. Shea—no, at her shop. Yes, I know about the airport, that's where . . . I know, but I figured . . . she gave me what I think is useful information, maybe you'll think so, too . . . no, I don't think—do you want to speak to her? When? Okay . . . no, I don't think so. No, he's not . . . already in Mexico . . . some fishing village, she claims she doesn't know where and I'm inclined to believe—what? No. No, I don't think so. Okay, see you then."

Hanging up, I shrugged. "I feel a little stupid saying this, but you're not planning to leave town, are you?"

She hadn't taken her eyes off me since I picked up the phone. "When are they coming to speak to me?"

"Soon. There are other people they're talking to. Your name's on some kind of airport watch list. If you try to leave the country, they'll confiscate your passport."

"Doesn't matter," she said. "I'm staying here, what's my choice."

I gave a last smile to Travis and headed up the coast, thinking about twenty-one years of pretending.

Accepting a payoff and pretending it was a big tip. Feeding Doris Reingold's green-felt habit and convincing themselves it was charity.

Five thousand dollars in a paper bag.

Once they'd been able to reduce it in their minds to a rich man's trifle, the rest had been easy.

Gwen was a mix of callousness and breakability. Waffling, resisting, struggling to paint herself out of any criminal conspiracy. Yet, my instinct was that, over all, she'd been truthful. If she and Tom were killers, they wouldn't have tolerated Doris Reingold's putting the touch on them all this time.

I was driving faster than usual. Before I knew it I passed Latigo Shores and Escondido Beach and came to Paradise Cove, where Karen had been picked up on the highway by someone in a red Ferrari.

Lowell asking for a pretty one to set up the tables and chairs.

App—or a lackey—picking her up.

Private party before the big one.

Lowell and App and Trafficant? Had the producer worn a mustache, back then?

Nothing nasty Friday night; she'd been in a good mood the next morning. But something had gone very bad the next day.

Make it a good-looking one.

Felix Barnard was no Sherlock, but he'd managed to put enough together to merit his own payoff. And a finale at the Adventure Inn.

App, sitting there, talking to me about deals.

Playing with me?

He was *Lowell's* patron. Powerful enough to be ordering Lowell around. . . . I recalled his explosive reaction to my intrusion, then the cold, cruel way he'd fired his receptionist.

Allowing me in when I told him what it was about.

Sounding me out, assessing the threat.

Talking about Mellors/Mullins's violent nature. The script definitely a diversion. Which wasn't to say Mellors hadn't written it.

App, with years of experience weaving and darting in Hollywood.

Had he bought my biography story?

Maybe. He hadn't tried to restrain me or harm me. Hadn't even kept my card.

Waiting for me to get back to him on the deal. . . .

I pressed down on the gas pedal, forging into rural Malibu. This far up, there were no lights on the road. The highway darkened and twisted. I kept picturing Karen, getting into the sleek red car with golden expectations.

Playing with Lucy and Puck the next morning until Gwen had had Doris, the experienced mother, take over.

Doris, putting the kids to bed, then sneaking out to frolic. Returning later to discover Lucy gone.

She runs out to look for her. Finds her sleepwalking, babbling.

Men hurting girl.

Powerful men. Mopping up the evidence of murder . . . in a motel owned by some guys from Reno. The Advent Group. *Now* I knew why the name was familiar.

The other outfit sharing the twentieth floor with App's production company.

Advent Ventures.

App keeping Mellors on a financial leash in order to control him and use him. First, the "idiot job" at the production company, then moving him into the motel job.

Literary critic to brothel manager. Lowell would have appreciated it.

I could imagine App's spiel.

"Think about it, Denny. I know the job is below you, but it's just short-time and all you have to do is look in on the dump once in a while —maybe even pick up some material—how about a series based on a motel? All these crazy characters drifting in and out? We can pitch it to the networks. Don't feel pressure to make a decision right now. Think about it and let me know. Come up to the house, we'll look at the ocean and break some bread."

Everything falling into place, but, still, Gwen had admitted to nothing more than seeing Karen step into the crowd with her hors d'oeuvres tray, and Lowell's payoff *could* be construed as a generous tip.

I heard Milo's voice, superego by way of the LAPD:

No evidence.

41

I tried to call him again that night, and the next morning. No answer at home, and the desk officer at Westside Division was unhelpful.

All this information and nowhere to go. Lucy wasn't focusing on Karen, so that bought some time. But I wasn't sure last night's intimidation would keep Gwen Shea in town and, without her, what did I really have?

I'd keep trying to find Milo. In the meantime, I'd run off the tension.

I was changing into shorts and a T-shirt when my service called with Dr. Wendy Embrey on the line.

Trying to keep the irritation out of my voice, I said, "Hi, Wendy."

"Hi, how's Lucretia doing?"

Off the case, she had no privileges. "She's fine."

"Well, that's good. It was an odd case, I never really felt I had a handle on it."

"In what way?"

"The suicide attempt. She was so adamant about not trying to kill herself, but she seemed so *coherent*. So, no subsequent psychosis or major depression?"

"None."

"Good. Anyway, say hello to her for me. I still think about her."

"Will do, Wendy."

"Actually, I was calling you about something else. This is

awkward and don't feel obligated to answer, but have you had any trouble getting paid for treating her?"

"I'm fine with that."

"Oh. Hmm. I know this is tacky, but I think I told you Wood-bridge is in a major financial bind; the staff's under a lot of pressure not to take on any nonpaying cases. I'm under special pressure since it's my first year there—probationary status. Lucy had no insurance and no clear ability to pay. Strict hospital policy is to take care of the crisis, then transfer them over to County. I didn't do that because I liked her and because her brother told me he'd handle it. But the hospital just notified me that a bill they sent to his company was returned unopened, and he hasn't returned any of their calls. None of mine, either. Have you been in contact with him?"

"He's been tied up," I said. "Their brother Peter OD'd a couple of days ago."

"Oh. God. I'm so . . . sorry for bringing it up. Good-bye."

I ran and had breakfast. On the news, one of the Bogettes, a sunken-cheeked, twentyish harpy named Stasha, was granting an interview to a breathlessly eager reporter. Her hair was cropped to the skin and she wore a goat-hair vest and a necklace of animal fangs. *Jobe Is God* tattoo just above her left eyebrow. Her mouth twisted constantly and her eyes pursued the camera.

The reporter was a blond woman in her late twenties, with conspicuous hair. She said, "So *you're* saying the police have bungled the investigation so badly that Jobe Shwandt deserves a new trial? But surely—"

"Surely Jobe *lives*," said Stasha. "Surely the truth will spawn its own certain *becertitude*." The rest of her speech succumbed to bleeps.

I turned off the set. The phone rang.

"Hey." Milo, finally.

"Just saw one of your girls on the tube."

"Spent all night following those hags around town. El Monte, San Gabriel, South Pasadena, Glendale, Burbank. They drive slowly, use their turn signals, make full stops."

"Where'd they go?"

"Nowhere, just cruising. Pulling over to the curb, waiting, then pulling out again—goddamn game. Final stop was for burgers and fries at an all-night grease palace in San Fernando. One of them comes up to me in the parking lot and offers me a Pepsi. After spitting on it and inviting me to mate with pigs. Then she told me where they'd be going next. 'Want a fucking *road map*, clown?' "

"Fun."

"Join the blue army, see the world. Anyway, that was some message you left me on Ms. Shea. What, you tailed her, then *interrogated* her?"

"It just kind of happened."

"I'll bet," he said, grumbling. "Hopefully she won't sue you. Think she was on the level?"

I told him why I did.

"If App and Lowell are so ready to bump people off," he said, "why'd they let the Sheas live?"

"Several possibilities," I said. "If Gwen was being truthful, she and Tom don't really know much. And each year the Sheas kept the secret and didn't hit on Lowell for extra money would have reassured them. Also, by now the Sheas are as invested in the status quo as Lowell and App. Respectable business people. The fact that they took money to withhold information on a girl who ended up murdered wouldn't do much for their civic image. And if Doris ever found out they held back money from her, she'd blow her stack and probably try to incriminate them. As it is, she resents their success."

"Lovely folks," he said. "The type who pretends not to smell the gas chambers. . . . Okay, so now we know for sure Sanctum was the last place Karen was seen. But—"

"No proof of any crime. I know."

"Not without a body."

"So far Lucy's dream's been panning out, Milo. So the body might very well be right there."

"After all these years? I can see them stashing her there short term, Alex. But why would they be stupid enough to leave her?"

"Arrogance. I'm sure Lowell sees himself as above the law. And when you get down to it, it's a pretty safe place. Who'd think to look for her there? Even if they did, with all that land, who'd know where to look?"

A sick feeling hit me. "Oh, boy."

"What?"

"My meeting with App, yesterday. If he goes checking and finds out my biography story is bogus, he'll start to suspect something. If the body is still up at Lowell's, it could get moved pretty soon."

"Don't scourge yourself, I don't see that it makes any difference. Even if no one touches the body, we can't. Not even *close* to grounds for a warrant. And after all these years, there's probably no body to speak of. Animals get hold of bones, scatter them. If App's smart, he'll sit tight and not attract attention to the place."

"Maybe, but in the past he hasn't sat things out. He and Lowell eliminate people who get in the way."

"So why haven't they bumped off the Sheas and Doris? Answer: They're discriminating. If Gwen's story is even true. Don't forget, all you've got to connect App is the Ferrari. Anyone could have been driving it."

"But Lucy remembers someone ordering Lowell around. App would have been in a position to do that."

"So would Trafficant. And now that you've tossed Mellors into the heap, we've got *four* bad guys. So let's not start thinking of the dream as gospel."

"Okay," I said. "But it's maddening—getting so close and not being able to grab it."

"Join the club. Anyway, let me look into Mr. App."

I gave him the producer's Century City office.

"At the time of the party his home was in Malibu," I said. "On the beach side, no doubt."

I called Lucy. No answer. I got in the Seville and headed south to Topanga Canyon.

Just a quick look to see if any cars other than Lowell's were parked in front of the lodge house, then I'd turn back.

Or maybe, if it seemed right, another visit to the old man. Checking to see how he was coping with his loss. At worst, he'd curse me and kick me out. If he was taking one of his long naps, I'd try to cajole Nova into another walk.

Into the forest.

Lacy trees.

When I came to the intersection at Old Topanga Road, I had to stop for an oncoming truck. As I waited to turn left, I noticed a car parked in the lot of the market across the road.

Blue Colt. A young woman behind the wheel. When the truck passed, I U-turned and pulled over next to it.

Lucy looked out the window, shocked. Then she smiled.

We both got out of our cars. She had on a plaid shirt, jeans, and hiking boots. Her hair was pulled back in a bun.

"Hi," she said.

"Hi."

She looked back at her car, guiltily. On the seat were an empty coffee cup and a donut.

"Not much of a lunch," I said.

"I—you'll probably think it's stupid, but I've decided to go up there and face him."

"Not stupid," I said, "but the timing couldn't be worse. In the last two days I've learned things that indicate Karen Best did disappear at the Sanctum party. And your father paid some people to keep quiet about it. Other men were involved, too. Other people may have died because they knew about it."

The color left her face in patches. "Why haven't you *told* me any of this?"

"I've tried to call you several times."

"Oh . . . I've been out."

"With Ken?"

"No, just driving around by myself. He had to fly up to the home office. He's been good to me, but I've been happy for the peace and quiet. Even though all I do is think about Puck."

Biting her lip, she crossed her arms and hugged herself.

I stepped closer.

She moved back. "The hardest part was the funeral. Seeing them throw the dirt over him. . . . The funeral's what crystallized things for me. The way *he* showed up in that horrid white suit with his bimbo. Making a show of himself, like the whole thing was a big *performance*. Even at a time like that, he couldn't be decent. It brought home to me how he keeps doing rotten things and getting away with them. It's time someone stood up to him. I'm sorry for not consulting you first, but I finally need to do *something* for myself."

"The way I see it, you've always been pretty independent."

"No," she said. "Just alone. And now I'm going up there. Please don't try to stop me, Dr. Delaware. What's the worst he can do? Try to run me down in his wheelchair? Sic his *bimbo* on me?"

"Lucy—"

"And what are *you* doing here?" She smiled. "You were going up yourself, weren't you?"

"Lucy, these people are dangerous—"

"Who *are* they? What are their names?"

"The main guy is probably a film producer named Curtis App." I described the way he'd looked twenty-one years ago.

"That doesn't sound familiar," she said, "so maybe he was the one with his back to me . . . but who was the one with the mustache?"

"There are at least two possibilities. Trafficant or another writer named Denton Mellors. Big light-skinned black man. He had a mustache, though it was skimpy, like Trafficant's, and blond. He was one of those murdered, possibly because he knew what had happened to Karen."

"No," she said. "The man I saw was definitely white. And the mustache was thick and dark."

"Your dream may be accurate in some respects but not in others."

She turned and opened her car door.

I held her wrist. "I met with App yesterday, gave him a phony story about doing a biography of Lowell. He may find out I was lying and get nervous. He or his henchmen could be up there right now."

"No, they're not. No one's gone in or out of the place all day. I've been watching the entry from before daybreak."

"You've been staking the place out?"

"Not intentionally. I was sitting there, building up my courage. I came down here to get some coffee and use the ladies' room. I was just about to head back."

"How can you be sure no one spotted you?"

"No one did, believe me. No one even came close. I was the one doing the watching."

"You sat from daybreak till now?"

"I know you think I'm being stupid, but I need to stand up to him and get him out of my life once and for all."

"I understand that, but this just isn't the time."

"It has to be. I'm sorry. You're a wonderful man. I trust you more than anyone—you and Milo. But this is something that's been building up my whole life. I can't put it off any longer."

"Just a little while longer, Lucy."

"Till when? You've got no evidence on Karen's death. The police will never have a case."

"Till we know it's safe."

"It's safe now. There's no one up there. Besides, my going up there won't look funny to anyone. He wanted to meet with me. What's the big deal about a daughter meeting her father?"

"Lucy, please."

She patted my shoulder. "The patient doing things for herself. That's therapeutic progress, right?"

"My only therapeutic goal, right now, is to keep you safe."

"I'll be *fine*. The prodigal daughter returned. Maybe I can't solve any crimes, but I can try for personal justice."

"What kind of justice?" My voice was sharp.

She stared at me and laughed. "No, no, I'm not going to play Dirty Harriet—search me for weapons if you like. I just need to see him. To show myself I don't need him."

She got into the Colt. "Maybe I'm making a mistake, but at least it'll be mine."

The car started. "I have to do it now," she said. "I may never have the guts again."

She pulled out of the lot.

I waited until she was out of sight. Then I followed her.

42

She drove slowly, and I had to hang back. When I reached the honeysuckle at the mouth of Sanctum's entry road, she was nowhere in sight. I began the upward crawl. A speed-walker could have beaten me to the double gates. Lucy had left them open. The second pair of gates was unlatched, too.

A few more bumps up the shaded path, then the trees parted and I saw the big lodge house, brown as the trunks of the bristlecone pines that nestled it. The Colt was parked nose out, as far as possible from Lowell's Jeep and Mercedes.

No other vehicles in sight.

The front door to the house was shut, and I figured she'd already gone in. But then she appeared from around the back of her car—taking something out of the trunk?

No, nothing in her hands. No pocket bulges.

Her mouth opened as I pulled up.

I said, "Think of it as an extended house call."

Expecting anger, but she stared past me.

Blank and focused at the same time.

Hypnotic.

When she put a hand to her mouth, I thought she'd lost her nerve and I felt relieved, yet sad.

Then she walked quickly to the house, stomping up the wide porch stairs.

I was next to her as she knocked hard on the front door.

No one answered. She tapped her foot and knocked harder. "C'mon, c'mon, c'mon."

I looked through the dusty windows. The big front room was unlit and uninhabited.

Lucy began pounding the door with both hands. When there was still no response, she dashed off the porch and stood in front of the house, taking in its bulk.

Walking toward the right side of the building, her steps were fast and deliberate, scuffing the dust. Another brief pause; then she continued. Toward the back. Toward the high thicket that rose behind the house like some great green tide.

I found her staring at the overgrowth.

"Back there," she whispered.

A voice above us said, "What's going on?"

Nova, framed by a second-story window, her face grayed by a screen.

"Hi," I said, taking Lucy's icy hand. "We knocked but no one answered."

A finger poked the screen. The expression above it was hard to gauge. "So you decided to come."

Lucy's fingers dug into my hand. "Sure," she said. "We were in the neighborhood and decided to pop in. Is there a problem with that?"

Nova tented the screen with her fingertips. "No. Not unless *Daddy's* got one." She gave a strange laugh. "Come around the front."

She was waiting for us, holding a glass of lemonade. The copper in her hair shone like electric wire.

"He wasn't in any great mood when he went to bed, but I'll tell him you're here."

"I'll tell him myself," said Lucy, walking past her into the front room. Taking in the stuffed heads, the shabby furniture, the emptiness.

Staring at the log walls.

Nova seemed amused. Nothing nurturant about her. Why had she chosen to care for a feeble, cruel man?

Kindred souls, just like Trafficant and Mellors?

What was her particular brand of cruelty?

Lucy made her way toward the staircase, moving slowly and cautiously, like a trapper on ice, passing under the steps, then continuing toward the back room.

Nova put her hands on her hips and watched, rubbing one foot against the other.

She wet her lips with her tongue and glanced at me.

Her eyes returned to Lucy and satisfaction filled them.

Lucy's discomfiture turned her *on.*

Lucy looked up at the ceiling, then the floor.

Then back to the walls.

Stopping short. Arms straight at her sides, her face frozen.

She stared at the left-hand door.

Nova said, "That's right, Daddy's back there, dear."

Despite her smile, tension in *her* voice.

Competition—mock sibling rivalry?

Wanting Lucy to come here, certain it would destroy her?

I took Lucy's elbow. She shook her head and moved her arm out of my grasp.

Twenty feet from the room.

I covered the distance with her.

The door was pine, once heavily varnished, the finish cracked, flaking like dandruff.

She sucked in breath and opened it. As we stepped into a big, dark, book-lined room, a sulfurous smell hit us, not unlike the stench of the ER at Woodbridge. A hospital bed was in the center, cranked to a semi-upright position. Lowell's wheelchair was folded in a corner.

Lowell reclined under the covers, his hair greasy and limp, his long arms resting on the blanket, white and blue-veined below frayed gray undershirt sleeves. His chin was coated with white stubble, his eyes unfocused. It was 2 P.M. but he hadn't awakened fully. He turned toward us with obvious effort, then turned away and closed his eyes.

Lucy's hand found its way back into mine, so sweaty it slithered in my grasp. Her shoulders twitched, then began shaking.

I followed her eyes as they reconnoitered, landing on the pine bookshelves that sheathed three of the walls.

A door in the right-hand corner was open, exposing a small bathroom. The other, centered between the windows, led outside. Bolted. Lucy's gaze lingered on it, then moved on.

Books and piles of magazines and newspapers littered the floor. Atop a stack of *New Yorkers* was an aluminum tray laden with dirty dishes: curling bread crusts, congealed eggs, cornflakes swimming in milk that looked bluish in the mean, grainy light. An empty bedpan sat on a stack of old *Paris Reviews*. Packages of adult-size disposable diapers were piled high on a tottering mountain of assorted periodicals. A cardboard box next to the diapers was filled with empty whiskey bottles. A tower of Dixie cups and an old black rotary telephone, the phone's cord snaking into the jumble and vanishing.

The shakes had moved down to Lucy's fingers, and I felt her knuckles slap against mine. Nova was nowhere in sight, but I felt her presence—an icy current.

Lowell moaned and moved his head from side to side. His eyes had closed.

Lucy didn't move. Then she began scanning the room again.

The filthy windows.

The door to the back.

Back to the log walls.

Repeating the circuit. Staying, this time, on the door. Wide-eyed.

This was where she'd slept the night of the party. The room she'd left, sleepwalking.

Her hand was shaking so badly I could barely hold on to it.

Lowell's eyes opened and he flipped his face at us.

Seeing us for the first time.

He let out a deep, pitiful, angry noise and began the long, excruciating process of sitting up. No hoists above the bed. He hadn't availed himself of conveniences—not even an electric wheelchair—and I wondered why.

Cursing, he slid and heaved and finally propped his upper body high enough to rest his back against the pillows. His chest was caved in, his shoulders knobby and narrow. The flair of the white suit and the panama hat seemed a distant joke. The last couple of days had knocked him low.

Grief?

Lucy watched him the way you watch a repulsive but fascinating insect make its way up a wall.

He laughed. She turned away and hugged herself.

"So," he said hoarsely. Several moments of throat clearing. He gave a look of distaste, rotated his lips, and spat a wad of phlegm at the log wall. It missed and landed on the floor. Coughing and grinning, he expelled another wad.

Lucy looked ill, but she didn't move.

Lowell watched her intently.

His fingers scratched the sheets as he continued to pull himself up. Trying to move his head in an upward arc. Pain stopped him.

"So," he said again. His voice had cleared a bit.

"Cute," he said. "Very cute."

"What is?" said Lucy, straining for a light tone.

"You." He chortled, as if she'd set him up for a punch line. He looked her up and down. None of the lasciviousness he'd shown with Nova. Cold, precise, as if taking the measure of a piece of furniture.

"Play tennis?" he said.

She shook her head.

"Those are tennis player's legs. Even through those dungarees I can see them. Play *anything*?"

Another headshake.

"Of course not," he said. "No appetite for games."

He rubbed his eyes and stretched his arms, laughing some more.

"So what can I offer you, Mary–Little Lamb?" he said. "Alcohol? Percodan? Demerol? Morphine? Endorphins? Or is alleged *truth* the dope you're shooting? What kind of stories should I tell you to help you lubricate your mental deadbolt? Is this a monumental *moment* for you?"

Lucy remained silent.

"No stories? What then?"

Lucy looked at the rear door.

Lowell shouted wordlessly and slapped the bedsheet. "Ah, the spectacle! Here to goggle at my groanery, my little serpent's tooth? Barge in with your brain mechanic in tow, so you can listen to the *thrum-thrum* and imagine my torment?"

Grinning. Laughing.

"Yes, I'm in *pain,* girl. Sacramental, sizzling battery-acid synaptic joy. Maybe you'll know it too, one day, and then you'll understand what a fucking *hero* I am to be sitting here, smelling like shit and looking like a Gehenna-leaseholder knowing the only fuck-damn reason you pranced your little tennis butt in here is to drink up my misery so you can say you've had a tall, frosty revenge cocktail at the expense of the best."

Lucy kept staring at the door.

"Ho," said Lowell. "The silent treatment. Just like when you were a baby."

"How would you know?" said Lucy.

Lowell guffawed, very loud. His shrunken body seemed to grow with each expulsion. Laughter energized him, turning him demonic and lively and bringing color to his face.

"The opening movement of The Guilt Sonata! Don't waste

your quarter notes, lass. I've soloed with the best of the Sin Sym-phonies!"

Lucy began circling the room, moving as freely as the clutter would allow.

"Your silence," said Lowell, "is not artillery. It's an empty knapsack—you were a mute baby with skinny legs. No cries, no tears, not a yawp. Dead-mute as an anencephalic accident. Unlike the other one, Peter-Peter morpho-morto poison eater; *he* howled professionally. It was rent a studio down the block or strangle the little snot-rat."

He closed his eyes. "You, on the other hand, kept your lips glued as if your tonsils were treasure." The eyes opened. A bony finger shot out, accompanied by a hoarse laugh.

"You wouldn't *shit*, either, har. Anus on strike, weeks at a time, quite a style, quite a style. Take all, hold in, give nothing. I thought you were abnormal. Your mother assured me you weren't and poured mineral oil down your aphasic little gullet."

Still walking, Lucy mustered a smile of her own. "Is that why you ran? Scared at having an abnormal baby?"

Lowell chuckled, but there was anger in it.

"Run, did I? No, no, no, no, no, I was *invited* to vacate the premises. Menstrually shrill banshee bye-bye from Maw-Maw and a claw at the face."

"Mother kicked you out?" Lucy's turn to laugh. "A big tough guy like you?"

Lowell looked at her, as if in a new light. Sucking in breath, he wiggled his thick eyebrows and stuck his finger in his mouth.

He kept it in there, probing and scraping and breathing roughly.

Pulling it out, he examined a fingernail. *"Mother,"* he said, "was a blindered, bujwhacked, neurally corseted, parlor-bound stumplet with the textbook vision of a suburban storm trooper. Middle-aged at twenty-three, old at twenty-four. Tapioca libido—her sheer *puddingness* turned me into a rebellious adolescent. She wouldn't—*couldn't*—learn how to *be.* She had nothing to live for but rules and rot."

Lucy's hands clenched as she turned. For a moment I thought she'd pounce on him; then she shook her head and put one hand in her pocket. And laughed. Her hips angled forward. A lounging pose as staged as Nova's.

"God," she said, "you're pathetic. Terminally blocked, blah, blah, blah. Hiding behind all that bad Joyce."

Lowell paled. Smiled. Lost the smile. Fished for it and finally found it. But it had lost its cruel luster and his grizzled jaw seemed to weaken.

"Joyce," he said. "Know him well, do you, Mademoiselle Sophomore? I *met* the dwent. Paris, 1939. Clerk face, no lips, woman's hips, lime-suck, lime-suck, lime-suck, bloody gud. That *fucking* Irish lechery for talk with no conclusion . . . but let's get back to lovely *Mother*. She died a virgin and you genuflect to her daily; the truth is, you know as much about her as you do about prostate clog but you defend her because that's your script—well, believe what you will, shutter your limited mind to your heart's contempt."

He wheezed and inflated his voice.

"Whether or not you know it, you've come here to *learn*. If you fail to do so, it's *your* lowered expectation, not mine. The truth, *Constipata: she* invited *me* to leave because she couldn't tolerate a bit of in flagrante *delicious*."

Lucy pretended to remain aloof. But he was talking loudly, and his voice made her flinch.

He rubbed his hands together and looked at me.

"A sad, sick, salacious, *succulent* tale, Braintrust. Perfect for *you*."

Turning quickly to Lucy. "After *you* stretched her womb, she lost whatever feeble interest she'd ever had in the double-backed beast. But like the old song says, her *sister* will—oh, *did* she, little Sister Kate. One of those yawning vaginas the exact color of *bub-blegum*. So who was I to play brakeman to Fate? Her sister *did*, so *I* did her *sister*, oh, yes, oh, yes." Smile. "She bucked and buckled, that one did. Scratched and caromed and screamed like a stuck sow at the moment of truce." Pointing to his groin. "Remembering it almost convinces me something dingled, once upon a spine."

I kept a close watch on Lucy. She was staring in his direction, but not at him. Anger shot through her slender frame like an injection of starch.

"Sisterly *love*," said Lowell. "Maw-Maw found us, sang her ode to virtue, and I creeped off, tail-tucked."

He tried to shrug and managed only a shoulder tic.

"Banished to the horrors of Paris. Reprobate Kate parceled off to California. Then *Mother* caught herself something postnatal and fatal, and suddenly I was called back to be a *father*."

He aimed his thumb at the ground and mock-frowned. "Ill-suited for the care of a mewling snot-jack and a no-tone, anally blocked *normal* infant, I had the wisdom to relinquish parental privilege to ForniKate. By then, she was fucking some pansy Jew journalist."

Gleeful bellowing.

Lucy was standing on the balls of her feet. I could see moisture in her eyes. I was thinking of my dead father.

Lowell said, "Why fight it, girl? You *need* me."

"Do I?"

"Given your insistence upon projecting an air of injured chastity, I'd say so. Really, dear, enough bad theater, let us slash pretense's throat and allow it to bleed out richly into the gutter. The permanent-hymen act won't work with me. I *know* about the summer you spent with your heels in the air, looking into the bile-sooted eyes of Roxbury coons. Quite disappointing, I must say. To rut is nature; to rut for money, commerce. But to rut *niggers* for money and let some boss nigger pocket the *profits*? How sheepheaded, girl. I shall assign a collie to herd you."

Lucy's fists opened and her knees bent. I held her by the arms, whispering, "Let's get out."

She shook her head violently.

"Ah, the self-esteemer plies his craft," said Lowell. "Dispensing turds of wisdom as you try to convince her she's *okay*."

Lucy let her arms fall. She stepped away from me. Right up to the edge of the bed. Stretching her arms as wide as she could, she stared him in the face. *Exposing* herself.

Shock therapy? Or the death of hope?

Lowell turned to me. "She's not okay. She's *planets* from okay." Back to Lucy: "Want to know *how* I learned all about your Moorish mooring? Darling Brother Petey. No interrogation necessary. Lovely, filthy truths emerge when a wretch craves his needle, toof, toof. Ah, yes, yet *another* betrayal, daughter. Not to worry, disillusionment builds character. Stick with me and you'll be *granite*."

"Did you kill him?" said Lucy. "Did you give him that overdose?"

That surprised Lowell, but he rebounded with a snort.

"No-o," he said softly. "He did a fine job of that himself. My error was *kindness*. Giving him cash when I knew what he'd do with it. He'd come up here, in this room. Lie on the floor, rolling around, begging and vomiting—a *craftsman* of cowardice. And evidently you, Stupid Girl, are his apprentice."

"Him," said Lucy. "Me. That's some parental report card."

"Is that what Siggie Fraud, here, told you? That you can blame your shit-life on *me*? That you have some *right* to happiness?"

Shouting and spraying spit, his words pushing him forward.

"You're not meant to be *happy*! There's no grand *plan*. Your happiness doesn't mean two buckets of sour *pus*!"

"Not to you, that's for sure."

"Not to *anyone*! God—whatever *He* is—looks down on you, sees your misery, scratches His balls, cackles, and pisses steaming *buckets* on your head! His condo-mate Satan stops buggering tiny animals just long enough to add to the torrent! The raison d'être isn't *happiness*, you styoopid *nin*. It's *being. Existence. Inherence.* It doesn't *matter what happens, or doesn't, or who else is*! Fuck the *consequences; you occur*!"

I remembered Nova's little speech. Someone had paid attention during class.

He glared at Lucy, breathing hard. Seized by sudden wet, rumbling coughs, he sucked in air, started to tilt back on the bed, and forced himself upright again.

"Didn't know you were religious," said Lucy, nearly breathless herself.

"Get to know me," said Lowell. "You'll learn *lots* of things."

She looked at him, then sat on the bed, hard enough to make him bounce.

Pinching sheet between thumb and forefinger, she rubbed the fabric.

"What kinds of things will I learn, Daddy?" she said in a small voice.

After a second's hesitation, he said, "How to create. How to be a cathedral. How to piss from the heavens."

Lucy smiled and played with the sheets some more. "Be God in six easy lessons?"

"No, it won't be *easy*. You'll change my diapers, wipe my armpits, and powder my thighs. Fetch my papers in your mouth. Get down on your knees and acquire an attention span. Learn what a good book is and how to tell it from crap. Learn how to whore for your *own* good. How to rid yourself of redbugs like that curly-haired leech over there, how to finally stop binge-purging on self-pity."

He shook a finger at her. "I'll teach you more in one day than all the marrow-suck schools full of eighth-wit arsenods taught you in—what are you?—twenty-six years."

He leaned forward and touched her arm. His fingers looked like crab legs on her plaid sleeve. She didn't move.

"You have no choice," said Lowell softly. "As is, you're *nothing.*"

She studied his pale, twisted hand.

Then her eyes moved back to the rear door.

She gazed into his eyes for a long time.

"Nothing?" she said sadly.

"The quintessense of it, Angel-pie."

She hung her head.

"Nothing," she repeated.

He patted her hand.

She sighed and seemed to grow small.

My fear for her rose like floodwater.

Lowell giggled and traced a line from her wrist to her knuckles.

She shuddered but remained still.

Lowell clucked his tongue, cheerfully.

She was breathing deeply.

Eyes closed.

I got ready to pull her away from this place.

Lowell said, "Welcome to reality. We'll do everything to make your stay as interesting as possible."

Lucy looked in his eyes again.

"Nothing," she said.

Lowell nodded, smiled, and stroked her hand.

Lucy smiled back. Peeled his fingers off and stood.

Walking to the rear door, she tried to slide the bolt. It was rusted and stuck, but she freed it.

Lowell's head craned, his body warping as he strained to watch her.

"Fresh air?" he said. "Don't bother. Sweetness is a lie, your senses are despots. Get used to stale."

"I'm going out for a stroll," she said in a flat voice. "Daddy."

"To think? No need to. It's not your strong suit. You finish your homework and then you can play—pay close attention and I'll turn you into something interesting. You'll endure."

"Sounds pretty Faustian. Daddy."

Something new in her voice—punch-line satisfaction.

Lowell heard it right away. His face lost tone, the bones softening, the skin giving way.

"Sit down!"

Lucy stared.

"Sit down!"

Lucy smiled. And waved. " 'Bye, Daddy. It's been educational."

She threw the door open.

Green filled the doorway and sunlight shocked the room.

Lowell squinted as Lucy looked out at the green tide; then he sprang forward, groping for a hold on nothingness. His lower body was leaden, and it anchored him to the bed.

He cursed Lucy, God, the Devil.

"Nice property you've got, Daddy. There's someone I need to look for out there."

A terrible comprehension took hold of Lowell, a preliminary death. He pitched harder, fell forward, flopping face down on the mattress.

Lying there, face pressed against the sheets, he labored to breathe as he watched Lucy disappear.

His eyes met mine.

His were bottomless and terrified.

I glanced at the black phone and considered ripping it out of the wall. But there had to be other extensions in the house—why remind him of the instrument?

As I left, I heard him howling, like a child, for Nova.

43

At first I thought Lucy had slipped into the forest. Then I heard footsteps along the side of the house.

Returning to her car. Good.

When I caught up with her, she didn't acknowledge me. How many sessions would it take to unravel what she'd just been through?

We reached the Colt. But instead of opening the driver's door, she went to the back and opened the trunk.

Personal justice.

Finally pushed too far?

I ran over just as she pulled a shovel out of the trunk and put it over her shoulder.

Brand new, the price tag still looped to the handle. Bearing it like a rifle, she headed back toward the house.

I blocked her.

She passed around me. I blocked her again.

"Come on, Lucy."

She walked away. Once more, I caught up.

I felt like screaming, *This is nuts!*

What I said was, "Don't let him get to you, Lucy."

"*Nothing*. Maybe so, we'll see."

We were hurrying alongside the house now.

"He'll call his friends. They'll come after you."

She ignored me. I took hold of her arm. She shook me off.

"Listen to me, Lucy—"

"He won't do *anything*. He doesn't *do* anything, he just talks —that's his game, talk, talk, talk."

"He's still dangerous."

"He's *nothing*." Furious smile. "Nothing."

We came to the dirt patch behind the building. Women's lingerie flapping on the line. The back door was closed. Nova had heeded Lowell's cries.

Nodding as if in response to a suggestion, Lucy forged forward, into the green.

Low shrubs and tender shoots, shadowed by the tree canopy, gave way quickly to dense ferns, creeping vines, brambles, and broad-leafed things that looked to be some kind of giant lily.

Lucy used her hands to clear the way, and when that didn't work she began hacking with the shovel. The tool proved a poor machete, and soon she was breathing hard and grunting with anger.

"Why don't you give me that?"

"This isn't your problem," she said, chopping. "If you really think there's danger, don't put yourself in it."

"I don't want you in it either."

"I understand what I'm getting into."

She touched my hand briefly, then resumed poking through the brush.

My choices were: Drive back to PCH and try to reach Milo, carry her out bodily, or stick with her and try to get her out as quickly as possible.

Physical coercion would probably destroy our therapeutic relationship, but I could stand that if it meant saving her life. But if she resisted it might prove difficult, even ugly.

Maybe the best thing was to stay with her. Even if she found the gravesite, she'd learn soon that exhumation with one shovel was beyond her physical capabilities. And the thought of her out here, alone, scared the hell out of me.

Maybe I was overestimating the danger. Lowell was a monster, but in his own sick way he'd been reaching out to her. Would he sentence her to death?

She'd gone only a few yards but the vegetation had closed over her like a trapdoor and I could barely make out her plaid shirt. I looked over my shoulder. The house was obscured, too. No visible pathway, but as I followed Lucy's footsteps, a trough-like depression in the earth became evident.

Long-buried trail.

She was moving as surely and quickly as the brush would allow.

Knowing where she was going.

Guided by a dream.

I clawed my way through the vegetation and got right behind her. The plants were taller, the treetops thicker, and soon there was more green than blue in the sky. Things slithered and scampered all around us, but other than a suddenly vibrating leaf or tendril, I saw nothing move. From time to time, I heard the broom-sweep of wings flapping in panic, but the birds stayed out of sight, too.

The growth became jungle-thick. Lucy swung the shovel like an ax, sweat running down her face in sooty streams, her chin set, her eyes hard and clear. I took over and got us through faster.

We came to the first of the small cabins, a fallen-down roofless thing, nearly hidden by emerald clouds. Lucy barely looked at it. Tears were diluting the sweat tracks, and her blouse was sodden. I wanted to say something comforting but she'd just been raped by words.

A second cabin appeared a few minutes later, just a loose pile of logs managing to support a tar roof. Shiny, black, wasplike things buzzed through holes in the tarpaper, swooping in, then jetting out like tiny dive bombers.

Lucy stopped, stared, shook her head.

We kept going.

Our silent trudge took us past three more cabins.

Gnats and chiggers were having fun with our faces. The sudden takeoff of a huge brown bird nearly stopped my heart. I managed to catch a glimpse of the creature as it forged up through the treetops. Big square head and five-foot wingspread. Horned owl. The silence that followed was unsettling.

Lucy didn't seem to notice. Pinpoints of blood pocked her face where the bugs had gotten her, and her palms were raw from wrestling with vines.

"Give your hands a rest."

She said, "No," but she complied.

Getting through wasn't easy even with my pushup-tightened arms. Hers had to be numb. I ripped and sliced, wondering how much grace time we had. Knowing we were leaving an obvious trail for anyone who followed.

"Even if you find her," I said, huffing, "after all this time, she won't look like a person. There may be nothing left at all. Animals carry off bones."

"I know. I learned that at the trial."

The trough deepened and I had to fight for balance. Lucy was looking up at the trees.

Something lacy? Trees of all kinds were everywhere, an untidy colonnade rising through the undergrowth.

It was two-forty. The sun had peaked and was falling behind us, dancing through holes in the overgrowth, a tiny, brilliant mirror.

A new sound: more of the groundwater, a trickle that recalled the one I'd heard driving up.

The kind of moisture that hastens decomposition.

"Even if you find her, what will you do?"

"Take something back with me. They can do tests and prove it's her. That'll be evidence. *Something.*"

I heard something snap behind me and stopped. Lucy had heard it, too, and she peered at the forest behind us.

Silence.

She shrugged and wiped her face with her sleeve. It was hard to gauge how far we were from the lodge house. I tasted my own sweat and felt it sting my eyes.

We started walking again, coming upon a knotted mass of thick, ivylike vines with coils as hard as glass. It refused to yield to the shovel. Lucy threw herself at it, yanking and tearing, her hands wet with blood. I pulled her away and inspected the plant. Despite its monstrous head, its root base was relatively small, petrified, a two-foot clump of burl.

I chopped at the shoot right above the root. Dust and insects flew, and I could hear more animals fleeing in the distance. My biceps were pumped and my shoulders throbbed. Finally, I was able to sever enough tendrils to pull back the clump and let us pass.

On the other side of the vine, things were different, as if we'd entered a new chamber of a great green palace. The air cooler, the trees all the same species.

Coast redwoods, great, repeating roan columns, spaced closely, their top growth a black fringe. Not the three-hundred-foot monsters of the north, but still huge at a third that height. Only a scatter of ferns grew in their shadows. The ground was gray as barbecue dust, mounded with leaves and bark shards. Through the fringe, the sun was a speck of mica.

The fringe.

Lace?

Lucy began weaving through the mammoth trunks.

Heading toward something.

Light.

A patch of day that enlarged as we ran toward it.

She stepped into it and spread her arms, as if gathering the heat and clarity.

We were in an open area, bounded by hillside and the same kind of mesquite I'd seen on the highway. Beyond the hills, higher mountains.

Before us, a field of high, feathery wild grass split by dozens of silver snakes.

Narrow streams. A mesh of them, thin and sinuous as map lines. The water sound diffuse now, delicate. . . .

I followed Lucy as she made her way through grass, stepping in the soft ground between the streams.

Down to a mossy clearing. Centered in it, a pond, brackish, a hundred feet wide, its surface coated by a pea-colored scum of algae, bubbling in spots, skimmed by water boatmen. The globular leaves of hyacinth floated peacefully. Dragonflies took off and landed.

On the near bank was another cabin, identical to the others.

Rotted black, its roof a fuzz of lichen, a decaying door dangling from one hinge.

Something green running nearly the width of the door. I ran over.

Metal. A plaque, probably once bronze. Grooves. Engraving. I rubbed away grime until calligraphic letters showed themselves.

Inspiration

I pushed the door aside and entered. The floor was black, too, ripe as peat, oddly sweet-smelling. Through empty window casements I could see the flat green water of the pond.

These log walls were perforated with disease. Remnants of furniture in one corner: a small metal desk, completely rusted and legless, blotched with green and teeming with grubs and beetles. Something on the desktop. I flicked away insects and humus and revealed the black-lacquer keys of a manual type-writer. A bit more scraping produced a gold-leaf Royal logo.

Next to the desk, a leather chair had been reduced to a few curling scraps of dermis and a handful of hammered nailheads; on the ground, near the desk, three metal loops attached to a rusted spine.

Rings from a looseleaf notebook. Something else, copperish with a green patina.

I kneeled. Something crawled up my leg and I slapped it away.

The patina was moss. Not copper, gold.

A gold bullet-shaped tube with a white-gold clip.

The cap of a fountain pen.

Etched in the head: *MBL.*

I pocketed it and kicked at the loose, fragrant dirt. Nothing else in the cabin.

Lucy hadn't followed me in. Through the window hole, I saw her make her way to the water's edge and stare across the pond.

Two trees on the far bank.

Giant, lush, weeping willows, their surface roots worming into the pond.

Branches of knife-blade, golden-green leaves, looping to the ground, then bending and resuming in a relentless horizontal growth.

Sentries.

Diamonds of light shone through the wispy foliage.

A baby-blue network, ethereal as lace.

I ran out of the cabin.

Lucy's eyes were fixed on a spot between the trees, a bare, sunken area.

She took the shovel from me and began circling the pond clockwise. Awkward, almost hesitant, toeing along the bank, inches from the water's edge.

Her eyes closed and she slipped. Before I could catch her, one leg went into the water, up to the ankle. She pulled it out. Her jeans were soaked. She shook her leg and kept walking. Stopped in the bare spot, tears dripping down her cheeks.

Cradling the shovel like a baby.

Inspiration.

Lowell's private spot.

Burying Karen here . . . for company?

He *needed* company—the adulation of fans and disciples and, when that dried up, the worship of young women.

Send me someone good-looking.

Had other women been buried here?

My initial thought upon hearing the dream was that he'd molested Lucy. There'd been more than a nuance of sexuality in his approach to her just now: comments about her legs and her toilet training. Flaunting his infidelity with her aunt.

Yet I couldn't shake the feeling that with Lucy he was after something different.

Stick with me and I'll show you the world, kid.

Body failing, fame withered, he wanted a family.

He'd stopped coming here a long time ago.

No more inspiration.

Lucy stood up.

Without a word, she began digging.

44

She wouldn't let me help her.

The first foot of soil was forgiving, but after that she hit compressed clay and cried out in frustration. I wrested the shovel from her. Each second weighed on me as I excavated a hole six feet long and three feet deep, getting in the pit and pitching out dirt like a manic paid by the shovelful. My arms felt leaden and detached from my body.

No signs of any bones. The smallest chip and I'd yank her the hell out of here. Even without progress, I'd give it five more minutes.

She got in and said, "My turn," but when I shook my head she didn't argue. Tears had washed her face clean.

The sun was sinking and the pond had grayed. It had been over an hour since we'd come up, but the day seemed timeless.

Each shovelful mixed with the blood rush in my head.

I dug and dug, till my breath grew short and harsh. Then I heard something else.

Another voice—a woman's—from across the pond.

Both of us turned.

Nova was standing near Inspiration. A man had one arm around her waist. His other hand held a pistol to her head.

She looked frightened to death. The man's fingers touched one of her breasts and spidered their way up in a manner that couldn't be accidental.

I pushed Lucy down and ducked. The man's gun arm snapped, as if he was throwing the weapon.

The shot knocked loose a chunk of dirt a yard from my right hand. No marksman, but we had no cover.

Trapped.

I crouched low in the pit, keeping my hand on Lucy's back. Her mouth was open but her breathing was silent.

No sounds. I raised my head for a peek.

The man put the gun back to Nova's head and prodded her with one knee. The two of them slow-danced around the pond till they got within fifteen feet of us.

Her left cheek was scraped raw and her left eye was swelling. I ducked and peeked, ducked and peeked. Finally seeing his face.

His right hand gripped her narrow waist. Manicured nails. The jeans were pressed. His sweatshirt said *Sausalito*. He looked like an executive hanging loose.

Exactly what he was.

Christopher Graydon-Jones.

"You've made some nice progress," he said. "Pity we don't have more spades. Well, get to work. We'll need it a good deal deeper to fit all of you. Go on, will you?"

"She's still his daughter," I said. "When he called you, he didn't expect you to kill her."

"No, I suppose not." He gave a split-second smile that raised one corner of his mouth. "Actually, he had *this* tart call, and look what happened to her. Expectations are so seldom met."

Nova moved, and he kneed her hard in the back.

"True," I said. "*You* wanted to be a sculptor."

His lips drew back and he did something with his free hand that made Nova cry out.

"Though there *is* a continuity," I said. "Molding form, shaping limbs. Big-time power needs—that's what got you into trouble with Karen, isn't it?"

He dug his fingers into Nova's middle. She gasped and shivered and a wet stain spread at her groin.

"Please," she said.

"Start digging or I'll kill this bit of fuzz right now and make you chop up her body with the dull edge of that spade."

I picked up the shovel. He backed out of swinging range.

Nova was nearly limp, straining his grip. Aiming the gun at Lucy, he shoved down on Nova's shoulder, forcing her to her knees, then prone, her face in the dirt. She ate some, gagged, managed to turn her head to the side.

Graydon-Jones put his foot on her spine. Trophy hunter.

But his eyes were jumpy.

"Come, come, faster, faster, or I'll have to finish both these tarts."

I jammed the shovel in the clay. Pulling it out was like towing a barge. My whole upper body felt encased in concrete. The lace pattern through the willows was pewter-colored now. I managed to dig.

He said, "Not that it matters, but I didn't *get* into trouble with *Karen*. *Karen* did it to herself."

"Drugs?" I said, stopping.

"Don't slack off—yes, yes, *drugs*, what else, don't you watch your public-service commercials? I wasn't even the one to give them to her."

"Who was?" The shovel hit the ground again. I pretended to dig deep but got only a few grains of soil on my blade. He was too far away to notice, his gaze leveling off at my elbows. If I stroked rapidly and grunted a lot, that might pass for a while.

"Who gave her the drugs?" I said, faking another hard chop. "App?"

No answer. One of his big hands caressed Nova's rear.

"You were just along for the party?"

I saw Lucy from a corner of my eye. Sitting, knees up. Frozen. Powerless again.

"Yes, a party. There was no *crime*," said Graydon-Jones. "She was the life of it. Coming on to all of us, crawling up in our laps, telling us she was going to be a film star and live in Beverly Hills."

"What kind of drugs did App give her?"

"What's the difference: grass, hash, quaaludes. It was the 'ludes that got to her. No tolerance. Out like a light."

He looked down at Nova, then his gaze shifted to Lucy.

"What are *you* staring at? Make yourself useful. Dig with your *hands*—go on."

Lucy got down on all fours and began scooping up clay.

I said, "Two parties, then. Friday night and Saturday."

He blinked with surprise. Covered it with a laugh.

"The police know, too."

"Is that so? That sounds right out of a telly script. Go on, dig."

I faked some more. "So she came on to you?"

"All saucy talk and meaningful glances, quite a piece. A virgin, though you'd never have known it."

"She didn't stay one Saturday night, did she?" Chop. Grunt.

"*Oh*," he said. "*Are we being politically correct*? Are we saying a saucy little piece who crawls up on your lap and puts her tongue in your ear doesn't *want* it? We treated her like a lady—ill-deserved. She was totally stoned, unbuttoning her blouse, singing Jefferson Airplane songs. Then she *vomited*. All over *me*."

His mouth twitched. "But I cleaned her up anyway. Dressed her and combed her hair. Curt even put makeup on her—are you slacking, Ms. Daughter? Get those hands *working*."

Lucy scooped and tossed dirt. Her eyes were dry and her thoughts were impossible to read. Nova's cheek was squashed against the earth, her swollen eye totally shut, her lip split.

I breathed conspicuously and gave him another few shovel strokes. "So what went wrong?"

"What do you think? She didn't wake up—but how did you find out?"

I didn't answer. He put the gun to Nova's head.

"I remembered it," said Lucy.

"*You?*" Graydon-Jones was amused. "What were you back then, a fetus?"

Lucy started to say something. I shook my head at her.

"The old idiot told you," said Graydon-Jones. "Fucking bloody fool. Well, as usual he's screwed up." Giggles. "You've missed the spot completely." Letting his gaze coast over us, toward the larger of the willows.

Lucy made a soft, catlike sound.

I said, "Who was at the party besides you and App and Lowell?"

"Not Lowell," he said. "Thankfully. He was always such a bore. Friday night, he had her on his lap, sad tales of the writer's lonely life. But Saturday he was too busy for that—Caligula in his toga."

"So why'd he get involved in burying her?"

"Because he's such a kind man." Laughter. "He dropped in to pick up some papers and found me trying to revive her, and panic, panic, panic. All that blood-and-gore verse; turns out he had soft-boiled guts."

"Did he drop in alone or was he with Mellors and Trafficant? How big of a private party was—"

"Shut up. I want you finished well before dark."

I pantomimed more effort. "So the party was right over there?" Glancing across the pond.

He said nothing.

"Far from the madding crowd," I said.

"Far from the meddling *crud*."

Graydon-Jones pushed his foot on Nova. Her eyes had stopped moving and her jaw was being pushed down in an unnatural position, the scars compressing. . . .

I said, "App's got a good thing going. Sits on the beach and you do the dirty work."

"Wrong," he said. "*You* do the dirty work."

Aiming the gun at the center of my nose.

I kept on faking, moving dirt from place to place. Lucy had caught on and was doing the same. Her hair was caked into dreadlocks. The hole was at least five feet deep. I wondered how much longer we'd be able to avoid the next foot.

Graydon-Jones must have been thinking the same thing.

He grabbed Nova by the back of her collar and dragged her closer to the pit. The gun moved back and forth from her head to Lucy and me. Nickel-plated automatic. Plenty of bullets for everyone.

Nova tried to shield her face. Her shut eye was purplish, ballooning, and the gun barrel had made red circles on her temple.

Graydon-Jones stopped six feet from the rim, letting her drop, again, and putting his foot on the back of her neck. It wouldn't take much pressure to snap her cervical vertebrae.

He looked down.

"Bloody *hell*. Playing *games*, are we?"

Training the gun on Lucy, he started to squeeze the trigger.

I dove to push her away but she was up, screaming, throwing a clump of hard dirt at him. Direct hit on his chest. The gun fired somewhere up in the air. Nova seized the moment to arch her back and grab his foot. That diverted his gaze downward as he kicked at her and tried to tighten his grip on the gun.

I drew the shovel back like a javelin and fired it at his legs, blade first, as hard as my sandbag arms could muster.

The tip slammed into his left shin and he yelled in pain and surprise.

Nova managed to break free. Graydon-Jones aimed at her. She ran toward Inspiration as I vaulted out of the hole.

I threw myself on him. As we went down together, I felt the gun pinned between our chests, digging into my sternum. The arm holding it twisted in an unnatural way. I slammed the other down as he tried to bite my nose. He was out of shape but adrenaline had powered him, too, and he pitched and rolled, managing to slide the gun arm out.

Then something came from the left in a brown-white blur, striking him hard in the cheek, quick as a snakebite.

His head whiplashed. Another blow, and his eyes rolled back. He went loose.

I twisted the gun from his fingers.

Lucy's muddy sneaker kicked him again. Unconscious, he started to drool, then vomit. I jumped free of the trickle of filth.

Standing over him, I trained the automatic on his head.

His *Sausalito* sweatshirt a putrid mess.

Breathing but not moving, the left side of his head muddy, starting to balloon.

I was panting. So was Lucy.

She reached down toward Graydon-Jones, then stopped herself.

I put my arm around her. She looked over at the larger willow.

The shovel lay on the ground, not far from Graydon Jones.

"You okay?" I said.

She held her chest and nodded.

Movement across the pond. Nova had made her way into the tall grass and was running toward the forest, the tints in her hair bright as fruit among the green stalks.

"Call the police!" I shouted.

She gave no indication she heard.

45

I needed binding. Thought of something.

I gave the gun to Lucy. The way she took it told me she'd never held one before.

"He probably won't stir, but don't get any closer. Keep it aimed at his head and watch him. I'll be back in a few minutes."

Taking the shovel, I followed Nova's flight into the forest, running hard until I came to the knotted, viney plant that had blocked our way. Bent back now, and trodden—Graydon-Jones following the path we'd laid out for him.

Chopping off several long tendrils, I ran back and trussed him in a loose hogtie. He was breathing fine and his neck pulse was strong and regular. He'd have a badly bruised shin, a monster headache, maybe a concussion, but he'd survive.

We left him there and returned to the lodge.

Lowell's Jeep was still there but the Mercedes was gone. A brown van with a rental sticker sat between Lucy's car and the Seville. The doors were unlocked and I looked inside. Rental form made out to Mr. Hacker. Cash transaction. In back were shovels and a pickax, a hacksaw, a spool of rope, and several boxes of heavy-duty garbage bags. The keys were under the driver's seat and I pocketed them. Fresh tire tracks and oil spots traced the Mercedes' exit.

We went inside the house.

Lowell was in bed, eyes closed.

Breathing very shallowly and slowly.

Ghostly white.

Two halves of an ampule glinted from the floor, just under the bed. I found the hypodermic needle a few feet away, half concealed by the yellowed corners of an old *New York Times Book Review*. A fresh red dot in the crook of his left arm.

Lucy was behind me, at the doorway. I heard her walk away.

I picked up the old black phone and dialed.

Sheriffs and technicians swarmed. Lowell stayed asleep and he seemed to have lost even more color. One of the deputies opined, "He doesn't look too good." Paramedics came a half hour later and carted him away.

Milo was still out of the office, but I asked for Del Hardy, and he arrived right after the first carful of deputies. I hadn't seen him in a while. His hair had turned almost completely gray and he'd gotten heavier. His arrival rescued Lucy and me from the knee-jerk suspicions of cops who didn't know us. As it was, we were stuck answering questions till after midnight.

Del came over. "How you guys doing?"

"Owe you another guitar—oh, yeah, no time. How about dinner?"

"I can always eat."

He asked Lucy if she was okay; then he walked off to drink coffee with a sheriff's homicide investigator. People kept heading back toward the forest.

Lucy'd been back there an hour ago, pinpointing the spot as technicians created a string-and-post perimeter.

Now the two of us were sitting on folding chairs in front of the Seville. Lucy was covered with a blanket. She'd managed to eat half a peanut butter and jelly sandwich.

At 12:45 someone shouted, "Bones!"

Milo showed soon after.

He looked at us and shook his head. "Doctor and patient, perfect match. And I set it up."

He bent and kissed Lucy's cheek. She held his head and kissed him back. When she let go, he shook my hand and squeezed it.

"Del filled me in over the computer. Sorry I missed the cutting of the cake, but I was obstructing a helicopter."

"Whose?"

"App's."

"Leaving town? How'd you know?"

"I didn't. I was watching his office all day, followed him to lunch at Mortons, then over to Bijan to buy a nine-thousand-dollar leather jacket. Then back to his office, but instead of getting off at his floor he continued up to the heliport. Blades whirring, the whole bit. He tried the indignant citizen bit, claimed it was just a back-and-forth to Santa Barbara, tennis with some other shitbag producer. But his stretch limo was packed up with Vuitton luggage, and his chauffeur was carrying paperwork for a private charter to Lisbon out of the Imperial terminal."

He smiled. "Big guy, the chauffeur, but very low pain threshold. Anyway, App's not going anywhere for the time being. Got a suite at County jail."

"What charge?" I said.

He gave a wide, malicious grin. "Traffic tickets. Idiot ran up four thousand bucks' worth last year alone, mostly outside clubs and restaurants and violations of neighborhood permits."

"Traffic warrants won't keep him in very long."

"Hold on, hold on. When I frisked him, I found a nice little chunk of a white powdery substance. Another chunk on the chauffeur. Then I called in a K-9 unit and the dogs went crazy. We're talking half of one of the Vuittons crammed with coke."

"Negotiable currency for an extended vacation," I said. "So even if Graydon-Jones ran into trouble here, *he'd* be long gone."

"Best laid plans. Only vacation he's gonna get for a while is at good old Club Dread." To Lucy: "I hear you're quite a kick boxer."

She shrugged under the blanket and forced a smile. "The things you learn in therapy."

46

Christopher Graydon-Jones, his head bandaged, whispered earnestly to his lawyer.

I sat on the other side of the one-way mirror with Milo, Lucy, and an assistant deputy district attorney named Leah Schwartz. She was a very good-looking woman, tiny, around thirty, with a cloud of blond, kinky hair, gigantic blue eyes, and the sometimes graceless manner of a very bright high school student. She'd been interviewing Lucy and me for most of two days, writing down detailed notes and using a tape recorder. She was writing now, sitting apart from the three of us. The little receiver she'd worn in her ear glimmered in the lap of her black skirt. Milo still wore his.

I said, "Any luck yet with App?"

Headshake.

The cocaine in the producer's luggage had proved to be only a small part of his stash. Twenty times as much had turned up in a vault in his Broad Beach home, sparking the interest of men in suits.

"Another task force." Milo had groaned.

Leah said, "The circus is in town."

She found out, soon after, that the federal government had been looking into App's dealings for a while, believing the Advent Group and its subsidiary businesses—including Enterprise Insurance—to be major conduits for money laundering. Milo'd filled in the details, yesterday, over coffee and crullers, as we waited outside Leah Schwartz's office while she finished a phone conversation with her boss.

"How long have they suspected him?" I said.

"Long time."

"So why didn't they move on him?"

"Hey," he said, "it's the government. They could give a shit about crime control. What they're into is getting precise appraisal of his holdings so they can confiscate everything under the RICO statutes. Better racket than parking meters."

"So what happens now? He weasels out on Karen so they can line their coffers?"

"That assumes there's something to weasel out on, Alex. Thank God for the dope, because Karen's death is still not a homicide."

"What about the bones?"

"No evidence of foul play; all the neck bones we found were intact. And what Graydon-Jones described to you at the pit was an accidental OD."

"He's *credible?*"

"When he told you, he was holding all the cards, no reason to lie. Fact is, attempted murder on you and Lucy's a lot more trouble for him than Karen. But we can't tie *that* in with App."

"It doesn't make sense," I said. "If Karen had died accidentally, they could have left her on the grounds for someone else to discover. Some bad publicity, but by then OD's were no big deal, every week another rock star was collapsing. There would have been nothing to connect the body to them, no need to pay anyone off. I don't buy it, Milo. We're talking nasty guys partying with a naive young woman. Graydon-Jones said she was a virgin Friday night but not Saturday. He and App gave her drugs and it got out of hand."

"Maybe. But with the bone fragments we've managed to pull up, you'll never prove it—it *is* definitely her, by the way. We found enough teeth to match, got confirmation from the odontologist this morning."

"Have you told Sherrell yet?"

"Yeah, I went over in person, early this morning, to his food bank."

"How'd he take it?"

"Like it had just been a matter of time. Then he thanked me and went back to unpacking Rice-A-Roni."

"Poor guy. I called his son this morning. He started sobbing, then hung up."

He ran his hand over his face.

"If it ever goes to trial," I said, "App and Graydon-Jones will make her sound like a whore."

"It probably won't, Alex. With everything else going on, an accidental OD won't prioritize."

"What about two bona fide homicides, Mellors and Felix Barnard?"

He took a bite of cruller and wiped his lips. I could hear Leah Schwartz's voice through her office door, rising in pitch.

"Same problem," said Milo. "Without some sort of evidentiary chain linking Mellors and Barnard to Karen, all we've got are two unrelated shootings. Only link to App is he owned the motel and half of the insurance company that Graydon-Jones runs. So far neither of them are talking."

"Why not make them think you've got more than you do, then try to wedge them apart?" I said. "After a year dealing with Shwandt and his girls, they should be nondairy creamer for you."

Leah Schwartz came out of her office, flushed and hot-eyed. The three of us walked out into the hall.

"Politicians," she said. "They should all be drawn and quartered. We've got a couple of days to turn something up, or the Best girl's case goes to the bottom of the list. Meaning no indictments, and the DEA gets to play Supermarket Sweep."

Milo said, "Couple of days? We talking to the hour?"

"I can probably wangle fifty hours if we get on some kind of track."

"Well." He got up and stretched. "Rome was built in two days, right?"

She laughed. Up to then, I'd never seen her smile.

We were fifteen hours into that edict now.

Graydon-Jones still had his hand cupped over his lawyer's ear. He was in jail blues that nearly matched the hue of the attorney's suit. The lawyer was a lanky, prematurely white-haired handball player named Jeff Stratton. Everyone knew about the handball because each time he showed up at 8 A.M., he announced he'd just gotten off the courts and pulled some kind of injury.

He pushed his chair away from Graydon-Jones and waved a finger. "Ready."

A microphone on our side of the mirror amplified his voice.

Leah Schwartz put the bug back in her ear. She and Milo

went in and sat around the table, facing Stratton and Graydon-Jones. I turned on my hand mike.

Leah Schwartz said, "So, Jeff."

"We'll hear what you have to say," said Stratton, "but we won't respond."

It had taken an hour to get that far.

Leah said, "Detective Sturgis?"

Milo said, "Mr. Graydon-Jones, from your résumé, you seem like an intelligent guy—"

"Hold on," said Stratton amiably. "Is this going to get personal?"

Leah said, "Of course, Jeff, doesn't it always?" She looked at her watch. "Listen, I'm really pressed. If we can't plow through this quickly, let's just forget it and we'll let your client take his chance with not knowing what's going on until pretrial discovery."

"Mellow out, Lee," said Stratton. Every white hair was in place, flowing over his ears. His tie was printed with golf clubs. He wore a wrist bandage. "No need for sarcasm or egregious vituperativeness."

Leah looked at Milo. "Try to watch your vituperativeness, detective. For all our sakes."

Milo frowned at her.

"Go on," she said impatiently.

Stratton smiled. Graydon-Jones maintained a deer-in-the-headlights expression.

"Okay," said Milo, placing both hands on the table. They covered a good part of it. Stratton tried not to stare at them.

"Okay . . . Mr.—um, Graydon-Jones, like I said, you've got an impressive résumé, people in the know say you're a real insurance demon. So we're a little puzzled as to why you keep letting Curtis App call the shots."

Graydon-Jones glanced at Stratton.

Stratton shook his head.

Graydon-Jones said nothing.

Leah looked at her watch.

Graydon-Jones looked up at the ceiling.

I said, "Go for it," into the mike.

Milo said, "He's blaming *everything* on you, friend. Including the drugs. He says *you're* the one got him into dope. *You* were a big user during the seventies. *You* corrupted him. He also says it was your idea to launder dope through Advent and Enterprise and that you *interfaced* with narcotics dealers in England and France and Holland and sold them insurance policies that helped them organize their money laundering—"

"Bloody lies!" said Graydon-Jones. "That was just a contract like any other, I had no idea who they were. *Curt* sent them—"

Stratton touched his hand, and he stopped talking.

Milo said, "I'm just telling you what *App* says. He also claims he had nothing to do with Karen Best's death, that he wasn't even present when she died, and that you and Terry Trafficant and Joachim Spretzel strangled her—"

"Oh, bloody bullshit. Spretzel was a faggot, and Trafficant wasn't even—"

Another touch from Stratton.

"Trafficant wasn't even there?" said Milo.

No answer.

"Okay, let me finish App's story: He and the three of you were partying with Karen, he left to urinate, and when he came back she was dead in your arms and the rest of you confessed to killing her. He says—hold on—" Pulling a piece of paper out of his pocket, he held it out of everyone's view. "Um, um, um—here we go: He says the only reason he got involved in covering up her death was that he was worried someone had seen Karen with him and that you threatened to expose his drug usage to his wife and to tell her he'd been fooling around with Karen and some other young girls. He panicked because he'd been doping and drinking and thought he'd be criminally liable and when M. Bayard Lowell and Denton Mellors came in, shortly after, unexpectedly, and Lowell said Karen should be buried and forgotten about, he went along with it. He's willing to plea-bargain to aiding and abetting and a suspended sentence, in exchange for testifying against you in Karen Best's homicide. He's also willing to trade information on your drug peddling in return for reduction of *his* drug charges."

He put the paper back in his pocket.

Graydon-Jones said, "Bullshit. He never said any of that."

"Call his lawyer," said Milo. To Stratton: "See if he takes your call."

Stratton said, "Maybe I will."

Leah looked at her watch.

"Bloody lies," said Graydon-Jones.

"I have to say App's story makes sense, Mr. Graydon-Jones," said Leah. "You *were* the one who drove up to Sanctum with all those tools and garbage bags. You *were* the one who attempted to murder three people so they wouldn't excavate Karen Best's grave. If you had nothing to hide about Karen Best, why risk all that?"

"Because Curt *told* me—"

Stratton said, "My client has nothing further to say."

I whispered, "Let it ride."

Milo yawned. Leah crossed her legs.

Graydon-Jones shook his head. Suddenly he laughed. "All on me, lovely, lovely. So what now, counselor, do I *defend* myself or keep that low *profile* and allow these arseholes to railroad me?"

Stratton said, "I need to conference with my client."

Leah looked at her watch and clucked. "Last one," she said, collecting her things.

Five minutes later, she and Milo were back in the room.

Stratton nodded at Graydon-Jones. Graydon-Jones was looking at Leah, not him.

Stratton said, "Chris?"

Graydon-Jones said, "First off, it's all bloody lies. I didn't strangle her, no one did."

"We've got bones," said Milo. "Cervical vertebrae that show evidence of—"

"I don't care *what* the fuck you've got, no one *strangled* her! *No* one! She was hit! He *hit* her. In the *jaw*."

Demonstrating an uppercut.

"In the bloody jaw," he said.

"Who hit her?" said Milo.

"Curt, Curt."

"Why?"

"Because she wouldn't put *out*! He wanted her, and she wouldn't, so he slammed her under her jaw and she fell back and hit her head and then he—did her. Then we couldn't wake her up. I was there! You won't find me making up stories and denying that! We were *partying*. The *three* of us."

"Which three?"

"Curt, me, and her. Trafficant was entertaining his own fan club. Mellors was tagging after Lowell, as usual, bloody syco-phant."

"What about Spretzel?"

"I don't know; I told you he was a faggot. Probably chasing boys."

"Ah," said Milo.

"Yes, I was with her, but I never hurt her. I did nothing other than make a little time with her."

"What kind of time?" said Leah.

"Kissy-kissy, grope-grope. She was on *my* lap, the old trousers rubadub. *I* was the one she liked, my mustache—I had one back then—and my accent; she said it reminded her of Mick Jagger. She would have put out for me. It made Curt jealous."

Touching his mouth, he spoke through his fingers.

"He was used to *tarts*, easy lays. 'Slip 'em the 'ludes and you can slip 'em anything else,' he always said. She wasn't easy; she was a virgin, for God's sake." To Leah Schwartz: "Don't look at me like that. You want the truth, I'm giving it to you. That's the way things were back then—free love, no viruses, people doing their own thing."

"I'll take your word for it," said Leah, inspecting her nails.

That inflamed him. "What were *you* doing back then?"

She looked up from her nails and smiled. "Going to school. Fourth grade."

Graydon-Jones shut his mouth.

"Is that it?" said Milo. "That's your story?"

"It's the *truth*. Curt got all *pissed* because she wouldn't climb off my lap into his. When he tried to put his tongue in her mouth, she turned her head and said 'Yuck.' Just like that. 'Yuck.' Like she'd tasted something bad. So he bopped her and she fell back. It all happened in one second. I'll swear to it in court."

"Chris," said Stratton. To Leah: "I want it clear that my client's statement by no means represents a formal offer to testify."

Leah shrugged.

Milo leaned forward. "So that's your story."

"That's what my client just said," said Stratton.

"Then I'll ask your client what I asked Mr. App this morning: If you had nothing to do with killing Karen, why get involved in the cover up?"

Graydon-Jones chewed his lip. His hands played with one another. A full minute passed, then another.

Milo sat back.

Leah looked at her watch and got up. To Milo: "Win some, lose some."

Graydon-Jones said, "I did it because Curt *supported* me."

"Supported you how?" said Leah.

"Emotionally. Financially. The day before that bloody party, he promised to buy six of my sculptures. And to commission a huge atrium piece for his insurance company. I was a bleeding pauper. I hadn't sold anything since arriving from England. If you were an artist, you'd understand. Curt offered to open up a whole new area of opportunity for me—I thought he was a true patron. It wasn't as if he *intended* to kill her. She blew him off and he hit her—one of those *stupid* things. And nothing I did would bring her back. I figured, why should he be ruined because of something stupid like that?"

"You did it for a job?" said Milo.

"Not a job." Graydon-Jones's voice was strangled. "A *career*."

Leah looked at Milo. "I'm sorry, sir. That's a little hard to believe. I'd never go to court with that."

"But it's true!" Dropping his head. "All right, all right, there was one more thing, though it's no big issue."

"What's that?" said Leah.

"The dope. The quaaludes he gave her. They were mine. Prescription for nerves. I was working mad hours at the foundry, my biorhythms were off—"

"Bull," I said into the mike.

"Just for sleep, huh?" said Milo, smiling and shaking his head.

Graydon-Jones flinched. "All right, for sex, too, the chicks loved it—no big crime. As I said, I had a prescription."

"And you shared your prescription drugs with Karen."

"She didn't protest—she *wanted* to try—wanted to try everything . . . *except* doing Curt. *God*, he was pissed. After he hit her, I said, 'What the bloody hell did you do that for?' and he said, 'Don't get all righteous with me,' and started to unzip his trousers. Then he . . . when she didn't wake up, I panicked, tried to leave. He said, 'You've got a problem, Chris. She was in your lap when it happened, you were holding her, she was stoned on your dope.' Telling me if she was found, they'd learn she was on 'ludes and it could be traced to me. He said as far as the law was concerned, I was every bit as guilty as he."

"And you believed that?" said Leah.

"I didn't know American law. I was a fucking starving limey just off the boat!"

"Did you consult an attorney?"

"Right," said Graydon-Jones, "and expose the whole thing— we *buried* her, for God's sake. It was over."

I said to the mike, "Ask him why he stopped sculpting."

Milo said, "How'd you get from art to the business world?"

"Curt offered me a job at Enterprise. Get paid to learn. As Marlon Brando would say, an offer too good to refuse."

"He also offered you sculpting commissions. Why didn't you take them?"

Graydon-Jones looked away.

Stratton said, "I fail to see what—"

"It all goes to the heart of the matter, Jeff," said Leah. "Namely, your client's credibility."

Graydon-Jones said something unintelligible.

"What's that?" said Leah.

"I lost interest."

"In what?"

"Art. All the pretentiousness. The bullshit. Business is the ultimate art."

Talking fast to conceal the real reason: he'd blocked. And App had been ready to exploit it, just as he had with Lowell.

One night of deception rewarded by twenty years of comfort and status. *Success* the ultimate dope. Just as it was for Gwen and Tom Shea.

Uneasy alliances held together by sin and guilt.

It had taken a dream to blow them down.

Graydon-Jones was talking to Leah's stoic face. "Don't you see? Curt *reversed* the entire bloody thing in order to shaft me. All I did was furnish the 'ludes. *He* hit her—take a closer look at those bones, you'll find something on her jaw—believe me, I was there. He's the killer, not me. He's killed other people—"

"Hold on," said Stratton sharply.

"I've got to *prove* myself, Jeff!"

"Just hold on, Chris." To us: "Another conference, please. And make sure there are no open mikes anywhere."

Leah said, "I can't promise I'll be here when you're finished."

She and Milo came out, as Stratton turned his back on the mirror and directed Graydon-Jones to do the same.

"Time for the little girls' room."

She left. Milo chewed two wads of gum and tried to blow bubbles. I counted my fingers several dozen times.

From the other side of the glass, Stratton waved and mouthed, "Come back in."

Milo switched on the mike and entered the room.

"Where's Lee?" said Stratton. "Come on, this isn't some shoplifting case."

Milo shrugged. "Maybe she's powdering her nose, she didn't tell me."

"How professional." Stratton looked at his own watch. "We'll give her a minute."

"Big of him," I said to his ear bug.

Milo smiled.

Leah returned.

I crooked a thumb toward the glass. "Stratton's getting antsy. I'd keep working the time bit."

She grinned at me. "I need your little voice in my ear to tell me how to do my job? No, seriously, it's been useful. We should probably do more in-house shrinking on the big cases. Problem is you'd probably charge too much. And most of the other DA's would feel threatened."

Pressing freshly glossed lips together, she asked Lucy, "Still holding up?"

"Holding up fine. I just hope you crack him."

"Like an egg," said Leah. "Over easy."

She fluffed her hair; then she stepped into the interrogation room.

Stratton said, "Hey, Lee, for a minute I thought you'd given it all up for a life of joyful abandon."

"Okay, let's finish up," she said. "If you have something to say, Mr. Graydon-Jones, out with it. Otherwise we'll just work with what we've got."

Stratton said, "Before we go any further, I'd like some definite quid pro quo."

"Pu-*leeze*."

"You don't care about getting the big fish, Lee?"

"This case, Jeff, they all seem pretty big."

Graydon-Jones cursed under his breath.

"What's that, sir?" said Leah.

Silence.

"You have a comment, Mr. Graydon-Jones, feel free to make it." Glance at her watch.

Stratton said, "My client's willing to offer you information that could clear up two additional homicides. Bona fide homicides, not involuntary manslaughter, which is the most you'll get out of the Best girl, and you know it. You don't want to hear about it, fine." Shrug.

"We'll hear, Jeff. What we won't do is put a price tag on the merchandise until we've had a chance to examine it."

"Believe me," said Stratton, "this is good."

Leah smiled. "I always believe defense attorneys."

Milo said, "My mortgage is assumable, my Porsche is paid for, and the check's in the mail."

Stratton shot him a hard look.

Leah's smile got wider and she put her hand over it. Another peek at her watch. Even though I'd suggested it, I found it an annoying mannerism.

She sighed and got up.

Stratton said, "Fine. Listen and evaluate. I'm sure you're smart enough to see it for what it is."

Leah said, "That's me, Ms. Smart," and clasped her briefcase. She sat down.

Graydon-Jones looked at Stratton the way a baby looks at its mother just after it receives its first shot.

Stratton said, "Give me a commitment that if the information's good you'll go to bat for my client."

"Going to bat for your client's *your* job, Jeff. If Mr. Graydon-Jones's information proves useful, it will be taken very seriously. Even in this day and age, we like to clear bona fide homicides."

"It's more than useful," said Stratton. "Believe me. But I think it's important you realize the scope of what we're talking about. Qualitatively. The information Mr. Graydon-Jones is in possession of, in addition to being revelatory, is four-plus *exculpatory*."

"Of whom?"

"Mr. Graydon-Jones. What he has to tell you goes to the *crux* of the matter and relates to Karen Best, as well. *Motivation*. Two homicides that are the conceptual *fruit* of the Karen Best incident and point a strong finger at original guilt in Karen Best's death. What we're talking about is the fact that someone else, and not Mr. Graydon-Jones, undertook to further these two—"

"Denton Mellors, aka Darnel Mullins, and Felix Barnard," said Milo, in a bored voice.

Graydon-Jones's eyes bugged. Stratton blinked very fast.

"Yeah, we know about those, counselor," said Milo. "Old Curt lays that on you too, Chris."

"Oh, no," said Graydon-Jones, holding out his hands as if scooping air. "Oh, bloody fuck, no, no, *no*, this is—no *bloody* way, *bullshit*! I can *prove* I was out of town the day Denny shot the private eye. Curt paid him thirty thousand dollars to do it. Recorded it as payment for a screenplay Denny never wrote. Thirty grand—he *showed* me the money."

"Mellors showed it to you?" said Milo.

"No, no! *Curt*! He showed it to me and told me what it was for—said Denny was more than happy to do it, Denny was a closet thug, always had been."

"Where did this conversation take place?" said Milo.

"At his house."

"In Malibu?"

"No, no, his other one, Bel Air. He used to have a place on St. Cloud. Now he's in Holmby Hills, on Baroda."

"Was anyone else present during this conversation?"

"Of course not! He invited me for lunch. Out by the pool, his fucking *terriers* pissing all over. Then he pulls out an envelope and shows me the money. Has me *count* it. And tells me about some private eye asking around about Karen, he'd been paying him off for a year, putting him on the books to cover it and giving him odd jobs. Now the bastard has gotten greedy and wants more so he can buy a house somewhere. So now Denny is going to kill him at some motel Curt owns. He owns all sorts of things; he's all over, like an octopus—"

"Why did he tell you this?"

"So I'd be *part* of it! Just as he'd made me part of Karen's murd—death. And to frighten me—it worked, believe me. Scared the shit out of me. I caught the first plane out of the country, back to England. That's how I can prove I wasn't there when it happened—I have my old passport. Look at the date on the bleeding thing and compare it to the date of Barnard's murder!"

"How long did you stay away?" said Milo.

"Two weeks."

"Where'd you go?"

"To my mother's, in Manchester. Curt found me, sent me a newspaper clipping. About Barnard's murder. Then he had *Denny* killed a few months later."

"By whom?"

"I don't know."

"Then how do you know App was behind it?

"Because he sent me *another* clipping. On Denny. Clear

warning. He's a monster, bestowing favors, then yanking them away."

"Sounds like he *kept* bestowing them on you," said Milo. "Career, and all that."

"Yes, but I never knew why, never knew if it would end. I knew I couldn't escape him . . . so I stayed put, kept my mouth shut, did my job—earned every bleeding penny of that salary. But now I see why he really kept me around."

"Why's that?"

"Isn't it obvious? As a scapegoat. If things ever came to light, he'd have someone to dump it all on."

"Scapegoat?" said Milo. "It was you drove up there in that van with a hacksaw and plastic bags."

Graydon-Jones froze. Then his body tilted toward Milo.

Stratton reached out to restrain him. Graydon-Jones waved him off.

"You don't understand," he said. "Twenty-one years I've lived in terror of the man. *That's* why I did the things I did. I was *scared.*"

47

Thirty hours left on the clock. We'd had dim sum at a barn-like place on Hill Street, and it hadn't settled well. I sat alone in that same observation room. No one had cleaned the glass since Graydon-Jones's session, and it was fogged with a distillation of sweat and fear.

Curtis App's counsel was an older man named MacIlhenny, fat and slovenly with the eyes of a sleepy snake and a custom-tailored gray suit that looked cheap on him. He'd managed to get App out of jail clothes. Despite the white cashmere V-neck and the black Swiss cotton shirt, the producer looked weak and insubstantial. Just a few days in jail had wiped out years of Malibu tan.

Leah was inside with them, along with her boss, a grim deputy DA named Stan Bleichert.

MacIlhenny grunted, and App lifted a piece of paper and began to read.

"My name is Curtis Roger App, and I am about to offer into the record a statement prepared by myself, under no duress or coercion, under the guidance of my attorney, Landis J. MacIlhenny, Esquire, of the law firm of MacIlhenny, Bellows, Caville and Shrier. Mr. MacIlhenny is present with me for moral support during these trying times."

He cleared his throat, flirted briefly with the camera. For a moment I thought he'd call for the makeup girl.

He said, "I am *not* nor have I *ever* been a murderer, nor do I condone the act of murder. However, I am in possession of information that came my way, by means of no criminal activity on my part, that if pursued competently could lead to the criminal prosecution of another individual and/or individuals for violation of California State Penal Code 187, first-degree murder. I am willing to offer such information in return for compassionate consideration of my current status including immediate release from prison, under reasonable bail, to my family and loved ones, and in return for reduction of present and pending charges."

Folding the paper.

Looking up.

Bleichert addressed MacIlhenny. "Okay, it's on the record, now let's talk reality."

"Sure," said MacIlhenny. His voice was a bullfrog croak and his eyebrows tangoed when he talked. "Reality is, Mr. App is a prominent member of the business community and there's no rational reason to confine him—"

"He's a flight risk, Land. He was apprehended just about to board a helicopter with a connecting flight to—"

"Tsk, tsk," said MacIlhenny, very gently. "Not apprehended. *Surprised.* At that point in time, Mr. App was aware of no criminal investigation of any sort. Surely, you're not saying that absent such information he wasn't free to travel at will, like any other United States citizen?"

"With his money, he's a flight risk, Land."

MacIlhenny patted his melon paunch. "So you're saying that Mr. App's wealth allows you to discriminate against him."

"I'm saying he's a flight risk, Land." Bleichert's face was round and grim and pinched and he had a five-o'clock shadow. His navy suit really was cheap.

"Well," harumphed MacIlhenny, "we'll pursue that with the appropriate authorities."

"Be my guest."

MacIlhenny turned to Leah. "Hello, young lady. UCLA, class of . . . around five years ago?"

"Six."

"I lectured to your class. Admissibility of evidence. You sat right up in front—wore blue jeans."

Leah smiled.

Bleichert said, "We're all impressed with the Mr. Memory bit, Land. Now, is your client going to poop or get off the pot?"

MacIlhenny put one hand to his mouth in mock horror. The other shielded Leah's eyes.

"Tsk, tsk. My client is willing to read a prepared statement."

"No questioning?"

"Not at this time."

"That's not very forthcoming."

"*That's* reality."

Bleichert looked at Leah. Nothing visible passed between them. He said, "Read at your own risk."

"Release on bail."

"Special holding at Lompoc."

"That's still prison."

"It's a country club."

"No," said MacIlhenny. "My client already belongs to a country club. He knows the difference."

Leah said, "With everything your client's charged with, he's lucky to see fresh air. And why should we bargain with him when he's already lied to us, trying to palm off Karen Best on Trafficant. We know from other sources that Trafficant had no involvement in that."

"Tsk, tsk," said MacIlhenny. "There are sources and there are sources."

Through it all, App sat, looking bored. The inanimate calm of the true psychopath.

Bleichert said, "Transfer to Lompoc and that's it."

"It's quite a story," said MacIlhenny. "First-rate drama."

"Sell it to the movies,"

MacIlhenny smiled and pointed a finger at App.

App smiled and took out another paper.

After clearing his throat, he began.

"I became acquainted with the writer/artist Morris Bayard Lowell, hereafter to be referred to as 'Lowell' or 'Buck,' at a party in New York in the summer of 1969. The party I believe to have been at the Greenwich Village townhouse of Mason Upstone, editor of the *Manhattan Book Review*, though I can't be sure. Lowell and I struck up a conversation, during which I told him I greatly admired his work. Subsequent to that, Lowell and I began a friendly relationship that culminated in my optioning a book of his, a collection of poems entitled *Command: Shed the Light*, for development as a motion picture. In addition to the advance payment for this option, I advanced him money to purchase land in Topanga Canyon to develop a personal residence and to build an artists' and writers' retreat he called Sanctum. I did these things because even though Lowell had experienced a long hiatus in creative output, his previous accomplishments in literature and art led me to believe he would regain his creative powers and resume his place as a major American writer."

Sniff. He touched his nose.

"Unfortunately, this was not to happen. *Command: Shed the Light* received highly excoriative reviews and was a commercial failure."

Rattling the paper.

"As part of my relationship with Lowell, I also became acquainted with various artists and writers. Among these was a British sculptor, Christopher Graydon-Jones, whom I aided in attaining employment in an insurance company in which I am a substantial shareholder, and whom I believed, at the time, to be a major talent and of excellent personal character. Likewise, a writer, Denton Mellors, whose true name I have since learned was Darnel Mullins, an African-American novelist, for whom I found employment in the business affairs office of my motion picture production company and, when he proved to lack skills in that area, as a manager of several motor inns that I own."

Throat clearing. "I might add that I am also a substantial contributor to the United Negro College Fund."

MacIlhenny arched an eyebrow and handed him a glass of water.

He drank and read. "Another individual I met through Lowell was a writer named Terrence Trafficant. Trafficant had spent time in prison and wrote about his experiences in a prison diary entitled *From Hunger to Rage*. Lowell took Trafficant in, as a protégé, helped him get paroled, and aided in getting the diary published. It became a best-seller. At Lowell's urging, I read said book and optioned it for development into a motion picture, advancing money to Terrence Trafficant."

Staring at the camera, as if trying to convince it of something. Sniff.

"I was to find out, subsequently, that I had been defrauded by both Mr. Lowell and Mr. Trafficant, in that *Command: Shed the Light* had been written not by Mr. Lowell but by Mr. Trafficant and passed off by Mr. Lowell to the artistic and literary community, and to the public at large, as an original work. I learned this in conversation with Mr. Trafficant, who showed me his original handwritten notes for the book and gave them to me for safekeeping in exchange for a sum of money. I remain in possession of said notes and am willing to offer them as evidence in the prosecution of Mr. Lowell for the murder of Mr. Trafficant, a crime I have personal knowledge of because Mr. Lowell confessed it to me, several days after the deed, when I confronted him with the evidence of his plagiarism and fraud."

Deep breath.

"That's all I have to say at this time."

MacIlhenny smiled. Bleichert frowned.

Leah said, "So you want to trade Lowell for everything you've done."

App folded the paper.

"All we've got on Lowell," said Leah, "is your word for it."

"And the notes," said MacIlhenny.

"If they're authentic. And even if they are, all *they* prove is fraud. On a dead victim. So big deal."

"A murdered victim."

"I haven't heard any evidence of murder except Mr. App's say-so."

"Would a body help?"

"Depending on whose it is."

"Tsk, tsk, young lady. Let's not be coy."

Bleichert said, "Whose corpus, Land?"

"Speaking theoretically? Let's say Mr. Trafficant's."

"Where is it?"

MacIlhenny smiled and shook his head.

"Withholding information on a homicide case, Land?"

MacIlhenny looked down at his chest rolls. His breasts were as big as a stripper's. "I have no personal information, Stan. All my conversations with Mr. App have remained on a strictly theoretical basis."

"Is this body theoretical, too?" said Leah.

MacIlhenny winked but ignored her. "I'm offering you a gift, Stan. Wrapped and ribboned. This could be your biggest case: internationally acclaimed author, major fraud, plagiarism, bloodshed. We're talking *Time* magazine cover and you write the true crime book."

Leah said, "As opposed to *your* client the piker, with multiple homicides and enough dope to stuff half the noses in Hollywood."

"My client never won the Pulitzer."

"Your client murdered more than one person."

"Tsk, tsk." MacIlhenny laughed softly. "Slander and libel. Where's your proof?"

"I've got eyewitness testimony."

"Tainted witness. Long history of drug abuse, and your own case against him for attempted murder gives him an obvious motive to lie. His word against my client's?"

"Biggest case of the year," said Leah. "Does Mr. App get to buy the film option?"

MacIlhenny gave her a pitying look. "Mr. App will no longer be engaged in the motion picture business. When the dust clears, Mr. App will be retiring."

"When the dust clears?" she said. "I see dust storms on the horizon. Tornadoes."

MacIlhenny turned away from her and back to Bleichert. App remained silent and motionless.

"You're offering squat, Land," said Bleichert.

"On the contrary, I'm offering you fame and fortune and the chance to put an icon on trial in return for dropping all charges on a couple of diddly cases you don't stand a chance of proving."

"If you think we're so weak, why bargain?"

MacIlhenny pulled shirt fabric out of a fold of flesh. "In the interests of justice and efficiency. Mr. App is no youngster. Every day spent away from hearth and home wears on him severely. He recognizes he has certain . . . personal problems due to chemical dependency. He is willing to undergo medical and psychiatric treatment for these problems as well as to offer his considerable talents to the community in exchange for no jail time, beyond what's been served, and no full-court attempt to employ the confiscatory powers of the RICO statutes."

"Betty Ford and community service for multiple murder and dope laundering?" said Leah. "When do you take this act to Vegas?"

Bleichert said nothing. She tried not to look at him, but failed.

MacIlhenny was looking at him, too.

"There has to be some time served," said Bleichert. "But I can conceive of its being at Lompoc or somewhere like that. As far as RICO, you know that's not our bailiwick."

"I've already talked to the DEA, Stan, and they're willing to go along with partial confiscation in return for some valuable information about foreign narcotics commerce currently in my client's possession. The hang-up's these alleged homicides. They don't want to be put in an awkward position."

"Like going easy on a multiple murderer?" said Leah.

Bleichert raised an eyebrow at her. She crossed her legs and looked away. MacIlhenny allowed himself a tiny smile.

Bleichert said, "Some jail time. I mean it, Land."

MacIlhenny glanced at App. "I suppose we can live with that. At a federal facility, protective custody."

"So what happens on Mellors and Barnard?" said Leah, looking at MacIlhenny but adressing Bleichert. "Talk about being in an awkward position. Especially when Lowell's case hits the fan. We'll never be able to keep it quiet. The minute *his* attorney finds out about the deal and squawks, we'll come across softer on crime than the ACLU."

"Tsk, tsk—"

"She's got a point," said Bleichert.

"Come on, Stan," said MacIlhenny. "What kind of crime are we talking about? A scumbag private eye blackmailer and the scumbag motel manager who killed him? Weigh that against the chance to try Lowell."

"*Afro-American* scumbag motel manager," said Leah. "Trading black life for white life? Can't you just see the NAACP having fun with that? And let's not forget, Lowell's victim was no choirboy, either. Is anyone going to care what an old man did twenty years ago?"

"There's a substantial difference, young lady."

"Sure, someone else's client'll be facing the heat."

Bleichert chewed his lip. App looked at him. First interest he'd shown in the proceedings.

Bleichert said, "I hear everything you're saying, Land, but she raises a valid consideration."

Talking about Leah as if she wasn't there.

MacIlhenny thought for a while. "There could be other evidence, Stan. Theoretically."

"Like what?"

"Audiotapes. Terrence Trafficant telling his story."

Leah said, "Theoretical." She looked disgusted.

MacIlhenny shrugged. Pounds of flesh shivered. "It's been a long time. Memories fade. Clean out an attic, no telling what you'll find."

"Malibu attic?" said Leah. "Or the one in Holmby Hills?"

"Here's my offer," said Bleichert, "take it or leave it. Mr. App confesses to his involvement in Karen Best, Felix Barnard, and Denton Mellors. Involuntary manslaughter on Best, conspiracy-second on Barnard because Mellors was the shooter, and straight second degree on Mellors, all sentences to run concur-rently. If we avoid a trial—"

"Stan, Stan."

"Hold on, Land. If we avoid a trial and if Lowell is *convicted* of first degree because of information provided by Mr. App, Mr. App's sentences are suspended."

Leah's huge eyes were hot skillets.

MacIlhenny pretended to deliberate.

"Just one thing, Stan," said Leah. "By all accounts, Barnard was premeditated. We could go for Conspiracy One and by the same token, straight One on—"

Bleichert shushed her with a short, angry hand movement.

MacIlhenny said, "What do you mean by confession?"

"Written, sworn, all the details, no evasion of questions, full acknowledgment of complicity."

"Like in church," said App softly.

MacIlhenny's eyebrows sank. "What about the dope?"

"If you can work it out with the feds, total walk," said Bleichert. "But *only* if he admits guilt in writing and *only* if his information leads *directly* to Lowell's conviction. And no own-recognizance, he stays put. What I said before about Lompoc stands, and I'll grant you the protective custody—hell, I'll put him on a cellblock with ex-senators."

Leah cracked her knuckles.

Bleichert said, "Why don't you go get all the files, Lee? So we know what to ask Mr. App."

She stomped out of the room and walked right past me.

Just as the door to the hall slammed, MacIlhenny said, "Pretty girl."

App and MacIlhenny conferred with the sound off and App started dictating to the lawyer.

During the break, Bleichert returned to his office and Leah Schwartz to hers.

Before she left she said, "Going to wait here?"

"Till Milo gets here."

"Well, be careful. Hang around here too long, you'll need to be disinfected."

She slammed the door and App heard it through the glass and jumped. His fear had always been there, hiding just beneath the cashmere.

MacIlhenny patted his shoulder and App resumed dictating.

Twenty minutes later, Milo still hadn't come back from accompanying Lucy and I wondered why.

A half hour after that, MacIlhenny stopped writing.

Bleichert ran his finger down the center of the page. Speed-reading. Then a slower perusal.

He put it down.

"It says nothing in here about who shot Mr. Mellors."

"A guy named Jeffries," said App, as if it didn't matter. "Leopold Jeffries. He got killed himself, five years ago—check the police files."

"What did you have to do with Mr. Jeffries's death?"

App smiled. "Nothing at all. The police shot him, in the middle of a robbery. Leopold Earl Jeffries—check it out."

Calm again.

Bleichert read the confession again. "This is okay, for a start." Putting it in his pocket. "Now fill me in on Trafficant."

App looked at MacIlhenny. The fat lawyer sucked his cheeks.

"There are tapes," said App. "At my house in Lake Arrowhead. Feel free to get them without a warrant. They're in the basement, behind one of the refrigerators."

"One of them?" said Bleichert, writing.

"I have two basement refrigerators at Arrowhead. For parties. Two Sub-Zeros. Behind the one on the right is a wall safe. The tapes are in there, I'll get you the combination. They've got Terry Trafficant telling me everything. I taped him because I thought one day it might be historically significant. Terry got fed up with Lowell's manipulation and looked to me as someone he could trust. I paid him every penny of his option money. I also paid him for a screenplay he did. Every penny."

"In return for all his future royalties?" said Leah.

"That, too," said App. "He got the better end of the deal. I haven't earned a thing in years."

"What kind of screenplay?" said Bleichert.

"Not really a full script, just a summary of some horror flick —*Friday the Thirteenth* type of thing, women getting chopped up by a maniac."

"Title?"

"*The Bride.*"

The treatment I'd read, Trafficant's. Title stolen from a dead man's novel. For the petty thrill? The allure of crime had never left him.

"I thought," App was saying, "with a few changes—more character arc—it had potential. If Terry hadn't disappeared, I probably would have produced it."

"Hooray for Hollywood," said Bleichert. "So far I don't know much more than when I came in."

App wore a meditative look.

MacIlhenny handed his client water, and App sipped delicately.

Putting the glass down, he said, "The key to all of it is Lowell's creative block. He went into a massive block years ago—thirty years ago. Just couldn't break out of it, maybe because of his drinking or maybe he'd just said all he had to say. But Trafficant didn't know that. He spent most of his youth in prison, found Lowell's old stuff, and read it, had no idea what was going on in the outside world. Then he ended up in some sort of creative writing program the prison was experimenting with and got the idea he could write. So he wrote to Lowell, stroked Lowell's ego, the two of them started a correspondence. Trafficant started writing poems and keeping a diary. He sent it to Lowell. Lowell was impressed and started working for Trafficant's parole."

Pausing.

"That's the part the public knows. The truth is, Lowell and Trafficant cut a deal, back when Trafficant was still in prison. Lowell hatched the whole thing, telling Trafficant poetry was a financial loser in the book business, it was almost impossible to get published. Except for a few famous poets like him. Lowell promised to agitate until Trafficant got early parole; meanwhile he'd also be editing Trafficant's poems, then submit them for publication under his own name. Trafficant would get the money and Lowell would also get the diary published under Trafficant's name."

"And Trafficant went along with this?"

"What did he have to bargain with, a loser behind bars? Lowell was offering him freedom, lots of money, possible fame if the diary hit big. So he wouldn't get credit for the poems; he could live with that. He was a con, used to deals."

"How much money did Lowell get for the poems?"

"A hundred and fifty thousand advance against royalties. Lowell took fifty for himself, Lowell's agent got fifteen. The retreat—Sanctum—was started as a way to transfer the rest of the eighty-five thou to Trafficant."

"Sounds like you were in on it from the beginning," said Bleichert.

"I helped finance the retreat because I believed in Lowell."

"Idealism."

"That's right."

Bleichert said to MacIlhenny, "So far the tone of this is very self-serving."

MacIlhenny said, "Be frank, Curt. This old nose tells me they're operating in good faith."

App hesitated.

MacIlhenny patted him.

"All right," the producer said. "I used the retreat too. To launder money. Nothing big. Some friends of mine—kids, people in the industry—were bringing marijuana up from Mexico. We didn't consider it really a drug, back then. Everyone smoked."

He picked something out of his sweater.

Bleichert moved his head impatiently. "I hope there's more."

"Plenty," said App. "Lowell was hoping the poems he stole from Trafficant would put him back in the spotlight. They did, but in the wrong way. All the critics hated them and the book bombed. Meanwhile, *Trafficant's* book became a fu—a best-seller." He chuckled, wanting everyone else to join in. No one did.

I remembered the enraged letter Trafficant had written to the *Village Voice* in support of Lowell. Mustering the only real passion a psychopath can ever develop: self-defense.

"What made Lowell think Trafficant would keep quiet about the deal?"

"Lowell was desperate. And naive—most arty types are. I've dealt with them for thirty years; take my word for it. And the fact that the book failed *protected* Lowell. Why would Trafficant want to claim authorship of a turkey, especially with his other book doing so well? But Lowell wasn't even thinking in those terms at the beginning. He was *obsessed* with his place in history, freaking out that his reputation was rotting. He used to sit in that cabin on his property all day, trying to produce, but nothing came. He kept drinking and doping to forget, and it only made matters worse."

"How'd the failure of the poetry book affect him?"

"He drank himself unconscious, then came out of it saying it was Terry's work anyway, Terry had no talent, was just a slick criminal who'd taken advantage of him. Meanwhile, Terry's doing interviews with *The New York Times* and selling a thousand books a week. Lowell stopped talking to him, and Terry knew it was only a matter of time before he'd be leaving Sanctum. That's when he transferred his royalties to me for safekeeping. For all his tough talk, he was still a con, had no idea how to cope with the world, so he came to me."

"And you taped him."

"For his protection."

Bleichert grunted.

"Irony," said App. "It's the key to a good story line. Lowell's name on that book of poems was supposed to buy success but it didn't. Trafficant became the darling of the literary set. You could package it as a comedy and sell it to cable."

Bleichert said, "So Trafficant spilled his guts to you because he was worried about making it in the outside world."

"That, and he wanted to talk. Cons always do. No self-control. Never met one yet who could keep a secret."

"Know lots of cons, do you?"

App folded his hands across his sweater. "I meet all sorts of people."

"I still haven't heard any details about murder," said Bleichert.

App smiled. "Lowell killed Terry. Two days after the Best girl's accident. Things finally came to a head, because Lowell was shaken up by what had happened, ready to close down the retreat. And still pissed at Terry. He ordered Terry off the premises. Terry cursed him out and threatened to go public with the whole book scam. When Terry turned his back, Lowell hit him on the head with a whisky bottle, kept hitting him. Then he panicked, called me, blubbering. I went over and we buried Trafficant."

Clapping his hands once.

"And with that," said Bleichert, "you were able to buy Lowell's secrecy on Karen Best forever."

"Keeping quiet about that was in Lowell's interest, too. His reputation was lousy enough without someone dying at his party."

"Where's Trafficant buried?"

"Right underneath Lowell's writing cabin—*Inspiration* he called it. That's where he killed him. The floor was dirt; they just dug down."

"Who's they?"

"Lowell, Denny Mellors, Chris Graydon-Jones."

"Why Mellors?"

"He was a weeny—and I'd say that if he was white. He hated being black, as a matter of fact. Denied it. He thought if he just kept writing and kissing ass, he'd be rich and famous. Anyway, that's where Terry is. I don't know if the cabin's still standing, but I can find the spot—right near the pond."

"Not far from Karen Best," said Bleichert.

App didn't answer.

"Any other bodies we should know about?"

"Not to my knowledge. You'd have to ask Lowell. He's the creative one. Did you know that he published his first book while in college? Everyone told him he was a genius. Fatal error."

"What was?"

"Believing his own reviews. Now can we get the ball rolling on transferring me to a decent place?"

"So you've been collecting Mr. Trafficant's royalties all these years."

"After the first few years it was chicken feed. Nothing's come in for the last five."

"How much chicken feed?"

"I'd have to check. Probably not more than a hundred and fifty thousand, all told."

"And Mr. Trafficant's advance payment for his book?"

"Seven thousand dollars. He blew it all in a crap game the same day he cashed the check. That's why he was so uptight when Lowell threatened to kick him out. Here he was a best-seller, eighty-five g's dropped in his bank account, and he had no idea how to handle it. Now can you get me to a decent place?"

"We'll work on it, Mr. App."

"Meantime, can I have my own food brought in? The crap here is loaded with fat and grease. I have my own chef, he could—"

Bleichert reread the confession and his notes of App's recitation.

The door from the hallway opened, and a stocky black jail deputy came into the observation room.

"DA Bleichert?" he said, scanning my consultant's badge.

I pointed at the glass.

"They in the middle of something?"

"Just finishing up."

He looked through the one-way. Bleichert was still reading. App and MacIlhenny sat in silence.

"Hmm," said the deputy. Then he knocked.

"Yeah?" said Bleichert, annoyed.

The deputy went in. "Sorry to bother you, sir, but I've got an urgent message."

Bleichert was annoyed. "From who? I'm busy."

"A Detective Sturgis."

"What does *he* want?"

"He said to tell you in private, sir."

"Okay, hold on." To MacIlhenny and App: "One sec."

He came out of the room, closed the door, and tapped his foot. "Okay, what's so damned urgent?"

The deputy looked at me.

Bleichert walked to a far corner well away from me. The deputy followed and whispered something in his ear.

As he listened, Bleichert's sour face lightened. "I'll be *damned!*"

"Everything okay with Lucy?" I said.

Bleichert ignored me. To the deputy: "You're sure?"

"That's what the man said."

"How long ago?"

"Hour or so."

"And this is *definitely* confirmed?"

"That's what he said, sir."

"Well, I'll be *damned*—unreal . . . goddammit . . . okay, thanks."

The deputy left and Bleichert stood thinking. Then he returned to the interrogation room.

"So," said App, "can we start the paperwork?"

"Sure," said Bleichert. "We've got *lots* of paperwork." Big smile.

App said, "I eat a high-carbohydrate, low-fat diet."

"Good for you." Hard voice.

MacIlhenny said, "Stan?"

Bleichert opened his jacket and hooked his thumbs in his belt loops. "Bit of a new development, gentlemen. I've just been informed that Mr. Lowell passed away this afternoon: massive stroke. So all deals are null and void and we'll be filing that confession as evidence against Mr. App."

App went white as his sweater.

MacIlhenny shoved his bulk out of the chair, charged forward, waving his hands as if warding off hornets. "Now, see here—"

Bleichert whistled and collected his papers.

"This is *unconscionab*—"

"Not at all, Land. We negotiated in good faith. You yourself said so. No accounting for acts of God. Guess God didn't approve of the deal."

MacIlhenny tottered with rage. "Now you just—"

"No *you* just, Land. All bets are off and *this* stays on the record."

Waving the confession.

"Always put it in writing," said Bleichert, grinning. "I learned that watching *The People's Court*."

48

No funeral.

Cremation took place at the mortician's college across the street from the county morgue. The ashes sat on a shelf until Ken came forward and picked up the urn. He asked Lucy if she wanted to accompany him when he tossed it off the Malibu pier. She said she'd pass.

She *was* experiencing a grief of sorts.

"I guess he didn't have a good life," she said. The ocean was blue and lazy. Yesterday a sea lion had walked out of the surf, ignoring Spike's rage and begging for food before waddling back in. Today, no signs of life on the beach, not even birds.

"No, he didn't," I said.

"I guess I should feel sorry for him—I *wish* I could feel something other than relief."

"Right now, relief makes sense."

"Yes . . . the way he spoke to me. After his words, Graydon-Jones's gun seemed almost silly. That's how I got the courage."

She stared at the water. "I suppose he was a prisoner as much as anyone. Fate, biology, whatever. . . . I'm a part of him —genetically."

"That troubles you?"

"I suppose I'm worried some of him is *in* me. If I ever have kids . . ."

"If you ever have kids, they'll be great."

"How can you be so sure?"

"Because you're a kind, caring person. He elevated selfishness to an art form, Lucy. No one would ever accuse you of being selfish. You almost lost your life because you're not selfish."

"Whatever. . . . So, I guess it's over."

My acquiescent smile was a lie. Her mourning of Puck had been cut short prematurely. I still didn't understand why she'd put her head in the oven. Still didn't know if the Bogettes or anyone else were out to get her. Maybe, with the dream out of her head, we could find the missing pieces.

"So," she said, touching her purse. "Guess I really don't have anything to talk about right now."

"Tired?"

"Very."

"Why don't you go home and catch up on your rest."

"Think I will—only thing is, Ken wants to go places and I don't want to hurt his feelings."

"What kinds of places?"

"Palm Springs, San Diego . . . Driving around. He's a nice guy, but—"

"But you want to be alone," I said.

"I don't want to reject him, but—this is terrible, I know—but sometimes he's *cloying*."

"Wanting too much too fast?"

"What should I do?"

"Explain to him that you need some time alone. He should understand."

"Yes," she said. "He should."

Milo called later that day. "Thought I'd give you some bits and pieces. Lowell's Mercedes was left in the long-term lot at Burbank Airport, so Ms. Nova probably flew the coop."

"Can't blame her."

"We're lifting prints from the house tomorrow, see if we can find out who she is. We can live without her testimony, but it wouldn't hurt to have it so we can add an assault-with-intent-to-kill to Graydon-Jones's trouble. We did locate Doris Reingold at her son's in Tacoma; police up there are watching her till she comes down next week. And Gwen Shea's lawyer called to let us know Tom phoned her from Mexico. Hanging out with his buddy —midlife crisis, casting off responsibilities. Supposedly, he begged Gwen for forgiveness, promised to fly back tomorrow. All three of them are being treated as material witnesses, no charges.

The major good news is that Graydon-Jones is sticking to his guns on App—asshole finally figured out you can't share a sleeping bag with a cobra. App's lawyer is screaming and yelling, trying to void App's confession; the DA says there's a better-than-even chance it'll be ruled admissible. Major good news number two is that the feds are finishing up their bookkeeping on Mr. A, and he's got close to twenty mil in assets that can be snatched. So all in all he's in trouble."

"Still in prison?"

"Languishing."

"No pesto and arugula?"

"Oh, sure. And for dessert, they can move him into general pop. Find him a four-hundred-pound roommate named Bubba, see what cooks up then."

49

The next day I received a package from Englewood, New Jersey. Inside was a blue binder containing two hundred neatly typed photocopied pages. Taped to the front cover was a piece of white stationery with *Winston Mullins, M.D.* on the letterhead.

A handwritten note read:

This is Darnel's book. Hope you like it, W.M.

I read half. Clunky in places, but talent and grace shone through in others. The story line: a young man, half white, half black, makes his way through the academic and literary worlds, trying to define his identity through a series of jobs and sexual dalliances. Expletives, but no violence. The bride in question: art.

I put the binder down and called Lucy. No one home.

She probably hadn't the heart to disappoint Ken.

Or maybe she'd held her resolve and had gone away for some solitude.

Either way, I'd wait. We had our work laid out for us.

That evening, as I was playing guitar and waiting for Robin and Spike to come home, my service called in with an emergency message from Wendy Embrey.

Now what?

"Dr. Delaware?"

"Sure, put her on."

Click.

"Hello?"

"Hello, Wendy."

"How's Lucretia?"

"Fine, but—"

"You've seen her recently?"

"Yesterday."

"This may be nothing, but I just got off the phone with a woman I think you should talk to. I know there are two sides to every story, especially with this kind of thing, but after listening to what she said, I strongly advise you to call her."

"Who's the woman?"

She told me. "I reached her through her father—he's the head of the real estate company. I was trying to collect—not important. Anyway, I gave her your name, said you might call."

"Just in case I can't reach her, give me a summary of what she told you."

She did. "Which might explain a few things."

"Yes," I said, feeling cold. "It might."

I hung up and punched numbers frantically.

Then I scrawled a note to Robin and ran out to the Seville.

Lights shone from the second story of the house on Rockingham Avenue. Ken's Taurus was in the driveway, but no one answered the bell.

I ran around to the side gate. Locked. I climbed over.

He was out on the terrace, slumped in a chair, head down. Half a vodka bottle on the table, along with a glass full of melting ice.

When I got ten feet away, he looked up groggily. Then, as if a button had been pushed, he sat up mechanically.

"Doctor."

"Evening, Ken."

He looked at the bottle and pushed it away. "Little nightcap. *Evening* cap."

His voice wasn't slurred, but the words were coming out too carefully. His hair was mussed, his glen plaid button-down shirt wrinkled.

"To what do I owe the pleasure?"

"Just dropped by to see how Lucy's doing."

"Oh . . . she's not here."

"Where is she?"

"Dunno, out."

"Out driving?"

"Yeah, I guess." He sat up straighter, tried to finger-comb his hair.

"Any idea when she'll be back?"

"Nope, sorry. I'll be sure to tell her you stopped by. Everything okay?"

"Well," I said, sitting. "I'm not sure. That's why I'm here."

He moved his chair back. The wrought iron grated on the flagstone. He looked up at the second story.

"You're sure she's not here, Ken?"

"Of course." His faced changed, turning piggish.

Suddenly, his hand moved toward the bottle. Mine got there first and put it out of reach.

"Listen," he said, "I don't know what this is about, but I'm bushed, doc. All this crap we've been going through, a guy deserves some R and R, right?"

"We? You and Lucy?"

"Exactly. I don't know what your problem is, but maybe you'd better get out of here and come back when you have an appointment."

"Are you making her appointments now, Ken?"

"No, she—listen." He stood and smoothed his pants and smiled. "I know Lucy likes you, but this is my place, and I want some privacy. So . . ." Crooking a finger at the gate.

"Your place?" I said. "Thought it was the company's."

"That's right. Now—"

"I just spoke to your second ex-wife, Kelly. She told me you haven't worked for the company for over a year. She told me the company belongs to her father, and that since the divorce you've been persona non grata there. That's why the company's insurance doesn't cover you. That's why you've got an answering machine instead of a secretary. She also told me you stole computer records and that's how you get addresses of places to crash. Along with lots of other things."

"Oh, boy," he said, backing toward the doors to the house. "It's a divorce case. You believe her, you're as stupid as she is."

"I know," I said. "There are two sides to every story, but Kelly says there are court records that document your drinking and your violence. Not just to her. You beat up your first wife too. And she says it's also public record that you threatened your father-in-law and tried to run him down with your car. That you put your older girl, Jessica, in the hospital with a broken jaw."

"An accident. She—" He shook his head.

"Got in the way? Of what, your fist? Same way Kelly did when you ruptured her spleen? All accidents, Ken?"

"As a matter of fact, yes. They're all accident-prone; runs in the family."

"Ken, where's Lucy? Is she locked in her room because you convinced her she needed to be for her own safety?"

He slumped. Gave me a helpless look. Then he grabbed the glass and threw it at me. I ducked but there was no need, he was way off.

"Get the hell off my property!"

"Or what? You'll call the police? Lucy's up there and I'm going to get her."

He spread his arms and blocked the door. "Don't mess with me, asshole. You have no idea."

"Oh, yes, I do. That's the point, I know exactly what you're capable of. After your father-in-law fired you, you started flying down here. Not to get to know Lucy and Puck but to get rid of them. So you could have total access to the trust fund. Lucy's share of the interest is twelve thousand a year. At a conservative five percent return, that means a principal of almost a quarter million. Times four sibs is a million bucks. You contacted Puck first, learned about his heroin habit, and fed it. Learned from him about Lucy's sleep patterns and her daily routines. The way she came home, ate dinner, and nodded off watching PBS with a glass of apple juice. You started harassing her with hang-up calls. Stole a key to her apartment from Puck, checked it out, fooled with her underwear—that was the fun part."

He cursed.

"A few days later, you let yourself in and put something in the juice—something with short-term effects. She mentioned feeling drugged a couple of times. After she went under, you came back, turned on the oven, and stuck her head in. Then you played hero. Waiting long enough for the sedative to wear off, calling the paramedics and driving her to the hospital. Adding the note and the rat shit a few days later just in case her anxiety level wasn't high enough. The plan was to get her out of there and under your control, and Milo and I played into it perfectly. Though if we hadn't, I imagine you would have found a way to volunteer. Instant family, huh?"

He pressed himself against the doors. Planting his feet. Fists clenching and unclenching, sweating alcohol and his gingery cologne.

"You couldn't kill her outright," I said, "because two young sibs dying that close together, all that money at stake, might have tipped someone off. Like Milo. The key was to get close to Lucy so you could choose the time and make it look like an accident— poor sleepwalking girl takes a tumble down the stairs. Puck made it easy for you with his addiction. He never went to New Mexico. By the time you made that call imitating his voice, he was dead. You didn't even have to be a good mimic. Embrey didn't know what he sounded like. And when you called your father to tell him Lucy had tried to commit suicide, you spoke to his assistant. But Lucy couldn't stop worrying about Puck, so you went with her and discovered the body—Mr. Hero again. Puck never stood you up. He showed for that appointment, though I'll bet it wasn't dinner, it was a dope gift. Unusually strong stuff. He was probably shooting up before you closed the door, dead a few seconds later. How'm I doing so far?"

"Okay," he said, fighting to sound cool. "I think you're a little confused, but come on in, we'll talk about it."

"Two sibs down, one to go? Did Jo really fall off that mountain or was that your maiden voyage in family planning?"

He shook his head as if I were being silly. Then, twisting the handle, he hurled himself through the door and tried to slam it on me. I pushed. His weight worked in his favor but his middle was exposed through the door crack, and I shot my fist forward and knocked the wind out of him. My follow-up didn't land solidly because he'd stumbled and fallen back. Forcing the door open, I dove on top of him, pinning him.

A woman behind me said, "Get up, you idiot, or I'll kill you."

Stunned, I obeyed. Ken came up swinging and I warded off his clumsy drunken blows.

"Turn around."

A slender form, orange-lit by a chandelier dimmed low. Holding an automatic a lot bigger than the one Graydon-Jones had brought to the pit. Looking comfortable with it as she came closer.

"Stand still, asshole," said Nova.

Ken took a blind swing at my head. I pushed his hand away, and he fought to regain his balance.

Nova said, "Cut it out. Don't waste your energy."

He said, "Goddamn asshole."

"Later. Clean yourself up. Look at you, you're a mess."

He wiped his lip.

"Fix your shirt."

He stuffed it into his waistband.

She had clear authority. The kind that imprints early? The scars . . . young for a face lift. But not for patching old injuries?

"Clean yourself up," she said. "Take an upper, then come back and give me a hand."

He complied.

"Big sis?" I said. "Hi, Jo."

Silence. That same smug smile I'd seen at Sanctum.

"One pair against the other," I said. "What are we talking about here? Going for the gold in sibling rivalry?"

She chuckled. "You have no idea."

"Must have been tough," I said. "Daddy leaving *your* mother for *their* mother. Then she got so depressed, she escaped to Europe and left you behind. With *him*, of all people. You and Ken end up locked in a dinky little cabin while the other two get to stay in the big house."

"Free psychoanalysis," she said. "Sit down on that couch—on your hands, keep your butt on your hands."

"Such gratitude. I saved your life."

"Gee, thanks." She laughed. "What have you done for me today?"

Meaning it.

A part of him—genetically. Raising selfishness to an art form.

I thought of the way she'd tended her father. Absorbing his sexual comments. Changing his diapers.

Jocasta. Turning his Oedipal joke against him, secretly.

Lowell so estranged from his own child that he didn't recognize her.

The scars remnants of the fall down the mountain. New face. . . .

Nova. New person.

"Anyone with you when you fell off that cliff?"

No answer.

"Wouldn't have been Ken, would it? He tends to damage women. How can you be sure he didn't push you?"

A toilet flushed. Ken came out of the guest bedroom with his hair slicked like a country kid's on Sunday.

Nova said, "I'll take care of him. You get *her*."

"She's out like a light. I'll have to carry her."

"So?"

He touched his lower back and grimaced.

"*Do* it."

He left and climbed the stairs.

I said, "He's really the walking wounded, isn't he?"

"He's a dear." The gun hadn't moved, and she was just out of reach.

"Dangerous business being a member of *your* family. Then again, that'll work to your advantage. Only two slices of the pie, if you and he don't kill each other first."

She smiled.

I said, "Yeah, you're probably right. You and Kenny will find a nice quiet place, get all cozy, and give in to what you've been wanting to do for such a long time. What you wanted to do to *Daddy*. Changing diapers' a poor substitute for the real thing, isn't it, cutie?"

She was tough and she knew what I was doing, but her eyes wavered for just a fraction of a second. Her grip on the gun must have loosened, too. Because when I chopped down hard at her wrist, she cried out and the weapon fell to the carpet.

She was a strong woman, full of rage, but there are few women who can handle even a small man physically. That's part of rape and battering and a lot of the tension between the sexes.

This time, it worked out for the best.

50

Milo said, "Can't talk long, got a promising suspect on the copycats. Roofer who was working at the courthouse during the trial."

"Does he have a dog?"

"Big surly mutt," he said gleefully. "Aren't you glad you weren't the poor clown who had to give him an enema?"

"How'd you get on to him?"

"One of the bailiffs gave us the lead. Says the guy used to sit in on afternoon sessions, doodle, and write things down; always had a weird feeling about him. Asshole lives in Orange County and has a bunch of DUI's, Peeping Toms, and a five-year-old attempted rape conviction. Santa Ana says their first interview was encouraging. I'm sitting in on the next one in half an hour."

"So it had nothing to do with the Bogettes."

"Not necessarily. Bailiff thinks he saw the asshole talking to some of the girls a couple of times. Shitbag denies any connection to them, but his room was full of their press clippings and a videotape of a TV interview with the head harpy—Stasha. Plus sundry other toys. That and the bailiff's say-so is enough for us to pull those hags in for questioning and sweat them big-time. We're asking for a pretty inclusive warrant before we come knocking. My bet is we find weapons and dope at that ranch, should be able to put 'em away for something."

"Good luck."

"Either way, I like this bastard for Shannon and Nicolette. Santa Ana found a hoop earring that might have been Nicolette's, as well as receipts for three storage lockers in Long Beach. Be interesting to see what the scrote finds worth storing. Forensic's still going over his place with their vacuum cleaners; it'll be awhile before all the fibers are analyzed. Anyway, I wanted you to know."

"Appreciate it. I can always use a little good news."

"Yeah . . . something else. We finally ID'd Ms. Nova's prints. Sorry to shatter your shrink's intuition, but she's not the sister."

"*What?*"

"The real Jocasta Lowell was printed when she was a student at Berkeley. Busted at a demonstration. And again after her body was shipped back from Nepal, so there's no doubt. Ken *was* there with her, by the way, so maybe he did push her off. But *our* nasty girl's a piece of work named Julie Beth Claypool. Nude dancer, druggie, biker babe, bad-check artist. String of arrests back to when she was sixteen. Wrote poetry in stir. Ken met her in Rehab, couple of years ago. Love at first bite."

"She pushes him around," I said, still in shock.

"I wouldn't doubt it. SFPD says she's been known to go for the whips and chains."

"The scars," I said. "God, I missed the boat completely— using the Oedipal wedge to throw her off balance—maybe I wanted her to flinch so badly I *imagined* it."

My heart was hurling itself against my chest wall. I'd broken out in a cold sweat.

"Talk about operating on false premises," I said.

"What'd you tell her, exactly?"

"That she wanted to screw Ken the way she'd wanted to screw Daddy."

"Well," he said, "SFPD says she comes from a real shitty family. Suspected incest—brothers and Dad, back to when she was real little."

"Oh, man. The same old story."

"In this case, lucky for you."

"Yeah . . . maybe I should buy a lottery ticket."

Lucy said, "Are peaches okay? I've already got pears."

The woman next to her said, "Put them in, honey. Those old people, the fruit's good for them."

They were standing at one of a series of long tables piled

high with groceries, along with a dozen other people. Sorting canned goods and boxes of rice and beans and cereal. The Church of the Outstretched Hand's hub was a run-down warehouse.

Men and women of all ages and colors, working side by side, quietly and cheerfully, putting together boxes for delivery and loading them into a couple of old pickups out in back.

There were other places like it, all over the city.

Newspapers, especially those in the cold-weather zones, love to portray L.A. as a Balkanized smog-blinded armed camp with no more substance than a sitcom and no more altruism than a politician. It's not any closer to the truth than a lot of the other stuff in the papers.

Sherrell Best was packing along with his parishioners, distinguishable as the leader only because he had to break to take frequent phone calls.

He came over to us. "This is a wonderful person."

Lucy blushed. "Saint Lucretia."

"The kind of good she's created has to come from a beautiful soul, Dr. Delaware."

"I know."

"*Please*," said Lucy, placing a packet of cookies into the box.

"Wonderful," said Best. "Can I steal the good doctor from you for a second, Lucy?"

"Only if you bring him back."

He took me into a cubbyhole office and closed a particleboard door that didn't cut out much of the noise. On the wall were some of the same type of biblical pictures he'd had in his kitchen.

"I just wanted to thank you for all you've done," he said.

"It was my pleas—"

"It was exceptional, the way you stuck by her. She's blessed to have met you and so am I." He gave me a troubled look.

"What is it, Reverend?"

"You know, for a time I thought if I ever found what happened I'd take the law into my own hands. The Bible exhorts against revenge, but it also permits the Blood Redeemer his due. There were times I thought I'd do something terrible. My faith was lacking."

Tears filled his eyes.

"I could have been a better father. I could have given her money so she didn't need to—"

"Stop," I said, putting a hand on his shoulder. "I'm no Solomon, but I know the difference between a good father and a bad one."

He cried some more, softly, then snapped out of it. Drying his eyes, he took my hand in both of his. "How selfish of me—so much work to be done. Always hunger."

I returned to the packing line.

Lucy's hands moved like a weaver's at a loom. She was trying to smile but her mouth wouldn't cooperate.

"Thanks for coming," she said. "Guess I'll be seeing you at the beach tomorrow."

"Here, too," I said. "I think I'll stick around for a while."

ABOUT THE AUTHOR

JONATHAN KELLERMAN, America's premier author of psychological suspense, turned from a distinguished career in child psychology to writing fiction full-time. His works include eight previous Alex Delaware books—*When the Bough Breaks, Blood Test, Over the Edge, Silent Partner, Time Bomb, Private Eyes, Devil's Waltz,* and *Bad Love*—as well as the thriller *The Butcher's Theater,* two volumes of psychology, and a children's book, *Daddy, Daddy, Can You Touch the Sky?* He and his wife, the novelist Faye Kellerman, have four children.